CW01335768

THE MITUS TOUCH

BOOK ONE OF THE TOUCH SERIES

STONI ALEXANDER

SILVERSTONE PUBLISHING

This book is a work of fiction. All names, characters, locations, brands, media and incidents are either products of the author's imagination, or have been used fictitiously. Any resemblance to actual persons living or dead, locales, or events is entirely coincidental. The author acknowledges the trademarked status and trademark owners of various products referenced in this work of fiction, which have been used without permission. The publication/use of these trademarks is not authorized, associated with, or sponsored by the trademark owners.

Copyright © 2017 Stoni Alexander LLC

Developmental Edits by Johnny Alexander
Copy Edits by Julia Ganis, JuliaEdits.com
Cover Design by Tricia Schmitt, PickyMe.com

All rights reserved.

In accordance with the U.S. Copyright Act of 1976, the scanning, uploading, and electronic sharing of any part of this book without the permission of the publisher is unlawful piracy and theft of the author's intellectual property. Without limiting the rights under copyright reserved above, no part of this publication may be reproduced, stored in or reproduced into a retrieval system, or transmitted, in any form, or by any means (electronic, mechanical, photocopying, recording or otherwise) without the prior written permission of the above copyright owner of this book.

Published in the U.S. by SILVERSTONE PUBLISHING, 2017
ISBN 978-1-946534-00-2 (Print Paperback)
ISBN 978-1-946534-01-9 (Kindle eBook)

To my husband, Johnny.

The best man I have ever known in this lifetime or in any other.

ABOUT THE MITUS TOUCH

She's desperate for the one man she must avoid at all costs...

Wealth manager Brigit Farnay despises Colton Mitus. And with good reason. He ripped away her family's company during the most painful time in her life. Forced to work with him, she can't deny that Colton is gorgeous, brilliant, commanding. *And the enemy.* Her traitorous body craves his touch every moment of every day. And then she finds out about his dark side...

Corporate raider Colton Mitus is success and power personified. He demands control in the boardroom and in the bedroom. So he shouldn't be tempted by the newest member of the Mitus team. *But he is.* Brigit challenges him and frustrates him, but also quiets the demons that haunt him, especially as she agrees to be drawn into his secret, sinful world.

When old enemies return hell-bent on ruining Colton, Brigit is the only person who can save him. But she's been keeping secrets that could destroy *everything...*

1

PROPOSITIONED

BRIGIT FARNAY YANKED OPEN the heavy glass door to the prestigious Porter, Gabriel and Sethfield wealth management firm and beelined toward the corner office. Newbies spun in their chairs, shouting friendly greetings, but Brigit didn't acknowledge them. As she passed the open door to her office, she slowed. *Forget about it.* She shook her head and forged on. *Seth needs to know.*

"He's on the phone," blurted Kaleb, Robert Sethfield's longtime assistant.

She waved him off and barged into her boss's office.

Leaning back in his worn leather chair Seth spouted off about market trends. When he saw Brigit standing there his eyebrows shot up. After holding up two fingers, he pointed to one of his guest seats.

She offered a grateful smile, slung her black handbag onto a chair, and headed to the window. Traffic clogged the maze of D.C. streets while pedestrians skimmed the sidewalks with purpose. The plastic card she'd been clutching had warmed in her grip. *Did I encourage his behavior in any way? Did I lead him on? No, never.*

Her blood had simmered as lunch had drawn to a close, but by the time the taxi dropped her back at work, she'd reached boiling point. Shrugging off her fall coat, she folded it over her arm.

Seth hung up and swiveled toward Brigit. "Did hell freeze over?"

"Sorry I barged in."

"It's okay." Seth furrowed his brow. "But you're not. What's wrong?"

In the five years Brigit had worked there, she'd never stormed into her boss's office. Robert Sethfield expected his wealth managers to do their jobs and let him know when they needed an assist or an intervention.

"A client propositioned me." She tossed the hotel keycard onto his desk and dropped into a guest chair.

"Aw, crap." He stroked his silver goatee. "Who was it?"

She tucked a long blonde strand behind her ear and sucked down a lungful of air. "George Internado."

"Shit."

"We met at a restaurant on the Hill. Today was the first time he didn't tell me a cute story about a grandchild or pontificate about a bill he was trying to get passed. What he did talk about was his wild weekend with his staff assistant that left him so exhausted he'd needed the week to recover."

He shook his head. "Jesus, that's out of line."

"We've met every six months for the past four years. He's always taken an avid interest in his wealth. But not today. He had zero interest in his investments and kept checking his phone. After the waiter cleared our plates he told me there were much more interesting things to discuss besides his money." Brigit shifted in the chair. "I should never have taken the bait. I asked him what could be more important than his financial security."

"Oh, no."

"His exact words were, 'You and me in a hotel room. Fifteen minutes.'" She shuddered, then hugged herself to quell the shaking. "He slid that card toward me and whispered how our afternoon could be as explosive as the Fourth of July."

"What did you tell him?"

"He left before I had a chance. I'm pretty sure my face turned as green as the pesto salad I'd just eaten."

"The good senator has been your client for years. What prompted this?" Seth removed his glasses, rubbed his eyes and slipped the wire frames back on.

She shrugged. "You'd have to ask him. Six months ago, he mentioned having marital issues and how a staffer had offered him a welcome ear. Shortly after that, I heard a rumor his wife left him. Sounds like that assistant offered more than her advice."

"I'd heard those rumors, too."

"I listen to my clients chat about their families, their vacations, their goals, even their fears. I don't care how much he's worth or how this affects my paycheck. I can't work with him anymore."

"That's understandable. I'm sorry this happened, Brigit. You want to take the rest of the day off?"

"No can do. My afternoon is packed, but thanks." She stroked her silver corded bracelet. "He's going to tell you I came on to him."

"Well, did you?"

She hiked her eyebrows. "Seriously? You have to ask me that?"

"Sorry, yes, I do." He leaned back in his chair.

"For the record, I don't do *that*—nor do I give off the vibe of being the least bit interested in doing that—with any of my clients or my coworkers." *I'm not doing that with anyone.*

"I'll handle it. Thanks for telling me."

"Thank you for listening." She exhaled a relieved breath, collected her belongings and headed for the door.

"By the way—" he said. With her hand on the doorknob, she turned. "You've not been yourself lately. Something on your mind?"

Oh, no. Swallowing, she shook her head. "Not a thing. Why?"

"At last week's staff meeting I overheard you tell Kat you were feeling restless. Stop by around four. I might have a new client opportunity that could remedy your situation."

You weren't supposed to hear that. "How's four fifteen?"

3

"That's fine." His phone rang.

"Thanks for your help. I debated whether I should say anything."

"You did the right thing." He gave her a reassuring smile, then snatched the receiver. "Robert Sethfield."

Since Senator Internado's inappropriate behavior was no longer her problem, her spiked heart rate slowed as she set off toward her office. But Seth had heard her off-the-cuff remark and was concerned enough to offer a solution. *Way to go, dummy.*

Brigit was days from becoming the single biggest shareholder of the Francesco Company, with twenty-two percent. But at this rate, it would be years before Francesco was back where it belonged. With family.

Until I'm running Francesco, it's business as usual, don't count your chickens, and stop acting like a six-year-old at a moon bounce party.

She entered her shoebox-sized office, dropped her items on her chair, collected her laptop, and tapped on the office doorframe next to hers. "Ready?"

Phone to ear, Kathryn Langston hunched over the console, dark, wavy hair hiding her pretty face. "Yes, it's my pleasure." Kat flipped her hair away and mouthed *Help me.*

Brigit smiled. She needed this innocuous distraction.

"How 'bout we save the Euro-Asian approach to solar energy for our next conversation?" Silence. "No, thank *you* and I look forward to it, too." Kat married handset to cradle, pushed her black frames against the bridge of her nose, and walked around her desk.

Brigit eyed her friend's bare feet. "You're casual."

Kat tucked her chin. "Oops." Groaning, she squeezed into her heels and the two women headed for the conference room.

Tasked by Seth with familiarizing Matthew Rossmann, the firm's newest agent, with the brokerage's internal systems, the women had concluded within minutes of meeting him that his priorities revolved around *their* internal systems. He'd been trying to poke his nose, or any other body part, into their personal business. Brigit had zero intention of playing dip-the-stick with a coworker.

4

"Hello, ladies," Matthew posed in the doorway, his palms pressing each side of the frame. "Where do you want me?"

Brigit's stomach churned at his cocky smile, puffed chest and slicked-down hair. The overpowering stench of cologne blew into the room. She rubbed her nose, thwarting the urge to sneeze.

"We don't." Kat pointed to the chair between them. "Sit here."

Over an hour later, Brigit's phone buzzed with a text from receptionist, Shaniqua Hall. *OMG. An Adonis walked in. You have got to see this one.*

Fighting a smile, Brigit pursed her lips as she peered through the wall of glass spanning the conference room. Adonis was causing quite the fuss. Several female brokers huddled together like starstruck teens at a rock concert. Brigit's heart had been broken one too many times to let some hunk affect her. Plus, her priorities were focused on getting her company back.

Her phone buzzed with another text from Shaniqua. *He smiled. I melted.*

Seth—*not* his assistant—escorted the man toward his corner office. The stranger glanced into the conference room, then did a double take when his penetrating gaze met hers.

An unexpected frisson ripped through her, shooting her into the stratosphere. A raw, ripe sexual need flooded her body. Her cheeks flushed with heat. She couldn't think, couldn't breathe. She just soaked up his beauty. Tall and broad, with a black wool coat—no, that coat was cashmere—draping his strapping physique. His midnight eyes flashed power and lust. She imagined nibbling his chiseled cheekbones and jutting jawline until her lips brushed his sensual mouth. Her fingers twitched, eager to fist handfuls of his dark chocolate hair resting softly on his cashmere collar.

And then, like a mirage, he was gone.

Oh. My. God.

His face seemed familiar. Was he a client? Unable to make the connection, she shook her head. And then a stinging reality smacked her cheek as if she'd been attacked by a swarm of killer bees. The endorphins stopped firing and she plummeted toward earth with no safety net to break her fall.

No, no, no, no, no! It can't be! It just can't. Jumping out of the chair and away from prying eyes, she Googled a man's name. His image exploded onto her screen. As high as she had been a moment ago, with Cupid's cherubs dancing in her head, she crash-landed with an unceremonious thud.

Oh, dear God, it's Colton Mitus.

2

DROP-DEAD GORGEOUS

NOTHING PISSED OFF COLTON Mitus more than failing. This meeting with Robert Sethfield meant he had, or damn near had. His portfolio resembled a medieval bloodletting, with pools of money draining from his accounts. Something had to be done, so he'd made the call.

But the moment—no the second—he'd laid eyes on that blonde in the conference room, his visit had been worth his swallowed pride. Hot and sexy was easy to find in the nation's capital, but something about her compelled him to take that second look. Her vibrant eyes were laced with innocence and mystery. A deliciously dangerous combination.

But this meeting was strictly professional. He needed to keep his thoughts on his financial affairs, which, last he'd checked, were one hot mess.

"Coffee, water?" Seth's voice jerked him away from much more appealing thoughts. As they entered his office, he tapped a guest chair before easing into his leather seat.

"No, thanks." Colton unbuttoned his coat and sat.

"Hit a round since the Lansdowne tournament in July?" Seth asked.

"A few." Small talk bored him. "You?"

"Same." Seth leaned back. "All right, Colton, what's going on? You said you could use my help."

"I need your best wealth manager."

"You've always used private wealth managers. Planning to steal one away from me?"

"No. My previous wealth manager left the area last year and I've been challenged to find the right fit. I'm considering moving my investments under the Porter, Gabriel and Sethfield umbrella."

Seth grinned like he'd won the fucking lottery.

Colton couldn't help but crack a smile. "We should play poker. I'd make a damn killing."

Chuckling, Seth crossed his legs.

"You know Mitus Mansion is my home and my office." Colton strummed the armrest. "My staff also resides there. My wealth manager needs to be available beyond market hours."

"I see."

"There are overseas calls in the middle of the night, dinner meetings, Sunday strategy sessions for the coming week. I'm always working." Colton raked his hair out of his eyes. "He'd move into the mansion. I'd be his only client. Your firm would make a bundle, as would the appointed advisor. I could sleep at night knowing that I no longer have to play nursemaid to my shrinking portfolio."

"You keep saying *he*. Not considering a woman?" Seth hiked his brows.

"I've interviewed plenty of female wealth advisors over the years. Several had families, which I can't accommodate. The remainder wouldn't have been able to handle my intensity. I can't have a Nervous Nellie managing my portfolio. I'm demanding. That can be intimidating."

"So, you're not opposed to hiring a woman?"

As long as I'm not attracted to her. "No. Why?"

"My best is a woman and she's *no* shrinking violet."

"Tough as nails?"

"She's the best wealth manager I've ever had. Extremely smart, team player, consummate professional. She's got too many clients, she's so damn good. Lately, she seems...I don't know...*restless*. I don't want to lose her, but if I recommend her for associate manager, she'd be relocated to our New Jersey branch. You hire her and everyone wins."

With his elbows propped on the chair's arms, Colton steepled his fingers. He had several female staffers, so onboarding a woman wasn't the issue. But hiring a female wealth manager wasn't going to fly. He liked nothing better than admiring the softer sex, especially when naked and writhing beneath him. If he screwed his money manager and things soured, it would be too easy for her to return the favor and screw him out of millions. "I'll speak with her. Then we'll do it my way."

Seth tapped a button on his phone console. "Kaleb."

"Yes." Kaleb's voice blasted through the speaker.

"Please send Brigit in."

Colton draped his coat over a chair at Seth's corner table and stared out the window. *This had better fucking work.* He'd be losing more in commissions and brokerage fees than most people made annually, but he had to stop the hemorrhaging. Finding the right advisor was crucial to his success. The Francesco Company executives anxiously awaited his loan to begin production of Crockett Boxes. Without capital, the project stalled and any misstep left them vulnerable to the competition. This wireless innovation was two years in the making and the biggest opportunity of his career. His commitment to fully fund the initial rollout meant complete control. *There's no way in hell I'll resort to outside investors.*

Seth's phone buzzed. "Yes."

"Would Mr. Mitus like a beverage?"

"No," Seth barked. "Where is she?"

"I'm having trouble locating her. She's not answering her phone or her texts. Oh, wait, here she is." The line went dead.

Seth's door opened. Colton turned from the window as the

woman sashayed in. Fuck, it was the blonde from the conference room. He wanted to blurt out, *Not her,* but all the blood rushed from his head to his groin.

She was drop-dead gorgeous.

Her sparkling green eyes jolted him to his core and his chest flamed with heat. The thought of burying his hands in her silky blonde hair and kissing those pouty lips made his balls tighten. He'd speak with her to placate Seth, then hire a man from Seth's secondary pool of candidates. Problem solved.

Though Colton towered over her, her sexy figure grabbed his attention. Weights, aerobics, running? Whatever her poison, he'd chase that tight little number anywhere. A primal need shot through him.

Her tailored black suit highlighted her curves and the hint of a white camisole clung to her taut body. She was hot, too damn hot. Someone he'd *want* to interact with daily, nightly and weekends, in all the *best* ways. She smiled at Seth, but the chill in her eyes belied her sweet expression. Most women noticed him right away, but this one wouldn't even glance in his direction.

"Brigit, this is Colton Mitus of Mitus Conglomerate." Seth stood. "Colton, my best wealth manager, Brigit Farnay."

As she pivoted, she raised her piercing gaze, slowly, to meet his. Her eyes grew fiery, then she gave in to a smile. Not the oh-my-God-you're-Colton-Mitus smile he was accustomed to receiving, but a forced one. He liked that she wasn't drooling. Gushing nauseated him.

"My name is—" She paused. "I'm Brigit Farnay." Her sultry voice danced in his ears, but carried with it a touch of defiance that struck a chord all the way down to his toes. She did not want to be there. Again, unexpected.

Two easy strides and he stood in her personal space. She stiffened. Her emerald eyes turned stormy. No batting of her thick black lashes. No pink hue settling over her cheeks. No over-the-top smile. Hell, no smile at all. Full lips he wanted to taste, but her sexy mouth wouldn't crack. A hint of sweet coconut floated in his direction.

When he smiled, her shoulders relaxed. *Much better.*

He extended his hand and she glared at it like it would bite her. As she slid hers into his, energy surged up his arm. She stared into his eyes as if trying to glimpse his soul. Some days he wondered if he still had one. Her cool hand hugged his and he wanted to warm her ivory skin before letting go. Seth was right. She was no shrinking violet.

"Brigit, this is the possible opportunity I intimated earlier," Seth said.

Even though her hand dropped like a brick, her intensity poured into him. Women cowered under his power, but she seemed to draw strength from it.

"Please, let's sit." Seth returned to his worn leather chair.

Colton waited, assuming she'd slip between the two chairs. Instead she kept her distance and hugged the wall. She sat and crossed her legs. Unbuttoning his suit jacket, he eased into the seat. Damn, she was pretty with lustrous blonde hair that trailed down her back. He imagined her plump lips nestled around his cock. *Hire her? No fucking way.*

"Colton, why don't you present your idea to Brigit?"

Could I reject her outright? That would be cold, even for me. "I'm in need of a wealth manager and Seth recommended you."

"Brigit, you indicated you were ready for a change," Seth interjected. "How about we lighten your load? Exchange your dozens of clients for this one. What do you think?"

Brigit leaned back and clasped her hands in front of her, creating a shield. Her full breasts stole his attention, but Colton quickly flipped his gaze back to her eyes.

"I'd interview you to ensure your coming on board would be the right fit, for us both," Colton said.

She'd been staring at Seth like Colton wasn't even in the room. What was it with this woman?

11

Shifting her attention toward him, she arched an eyebrow. "Coming on board?"

An undeniable undercurrent sizzled between them. "Yes, you'd live at Mitus Mansion with me and my staff," Colton said.

Brigit jumped to her feet like her ass was on fire. "It's not something I'll entertain, so please remove my name from your candidate list." She turned to face him and her eyes flashed with determination. "Colton."

"Brigit." The huskiness in his voice sounded more like a growl.

As she walked between the two chairs, the roundness of her tight ass made his dick twitch. He crossed his legs.

She was perfect. Not because she was beautiful and sexy, but because she wasn't interested. Winning was all that mattered. The greater the challenge, the better, and Brigit Farnay was proving to be quite the firecracker.

3

BRIGIT'S SECRET

BRIGIT'S HEART THUNDERED AT a frenetic pace. *Act normal. Just act normal.* She closed Seth's office door and her panicked thoughts spun out of control. *Did he recognize me? Has he found out what I'm up to and he wanted to— Stop! He doesn't have a clue. Relax.*

Try as she might, she could not calm down.

Running out of the office in a panic would draw suspicion, but speaking with a client behind a closed door wouldn't. She hightailed it to her office and kicked the door shut with the heel of her stiletto.

The only thing Brigit wanted to say to that man was a speech rehearsed so many times she knew it in her sleep. *My name is Eve Francesco, of the Francesco Company. The one you ripped away from me shortly after the horrific death of my parents. And now I'm taking it back, you son of a bitch.*

With clammy palms, she grabbed her phone and dialed her attorney. "Melvin Parsons, please. Brigit Farnay."

"Brigit, how are you?" Melvin's familiar booming voice was a godsend.

"Melvin, I have a problem."

"Talk to me."

The words spilled like one long run-on sentence. "Mitus

approached the firm. He's interested in hiring an in-house wealth manager. It appears Seth has recommended me. I had an introductory meeting with him." She placed her fingers over her carotid artery. "It's a wonder I didn't pass out."

"Okay, Brigit, deep breath. What did you tell him?"

"To remove my name from the prospective candidate list."

"Mitus has personal wealth managers. Why the change?"

She inhaled and blew out an hmphhh. "I have no idea."

"Find out."

She cupped the receiver. "What's the chance he learned I've been purchasing Francesco shares and hiding them in the private equity firms we set up?"

"Unlikely. Don't you think he'd confront you? He's more of a take-charge businessman."

"In front of Seth?"

"Hmm, maybe not. Did you say anything to arouse suspicion?"

"I might have muttered eff-you."

"Francesco means something to him. And it would benefit us greatly to know what that is. He's kept his seat on their board of directors and stayed involved in the day-to-day operations, even after he'd taken Francesco public and made millions. And that's the only company he's stayed so closely connected to."

"Lucky me," she mumbled.

Melvin cleared his throat. "Since I have you on the phone, aren't you about ready to purchase more shares?"

"Yes. Waiting on my commission. I'll drop the check by your office next week."

"This will put you at twenty-two percent, won't it?"

"Yes," she said. "The day I finally own fifty-one percent, I'll be too old to care."

"You know my motto."

"Uh-huh. Slow and steady." She dropped into her chair.

"In December, we'll provide Francesco's Board with your revitalization plan and request you be added to their January meeting docket. Twenty-two percent should entitle you to a seat on their board, but nothing is guaranteed. Until then, stealth, Brigit, stealth!"

She hung up and tried to concentrate on work, but a sea of meaningless numbers blurred together on her monitor. As of late she'd been restless, but she always felt that way before purchasing Francesco stock. Meeting Mitus only exacerbated her anxiety. She blinked and clicked on a different screen. *Melvin's right. Stay away from Colton Mitus.*

Fifteen minutes later, her phone rang. *This can't be good.* "Yes, Kaleb."

"Seth wants to speak with you."

"Is he alone?"

"Yes."

She hung up and marched toward his office.

"Go in." Kaleb smirked. "This time he's expecting you."

Seth sat at his conference table, his clasped hands resting on the polished wood. He'd removed his suit jacket and rolled up his sleeves. "You want to explain yourself, please?"

She clutched the back of the chair like a life preserver. "Why did Colton Mitus pay you a visit? Doesn't he use private wealth managers?"

"His portfolio hasn't been managed in months and he's taking colossal hits. He's considering moving his wealth to our firm. You love the challenge of portfolios in distress, so I recommended you. For some unknown reason, you seem to have quite a problem with this."

Maybe my secret is safe. She relaxed her white-knuckled grip on the leather. "Taking him on as a client is out of the question. He's ruthless, cocky, arrogant, self-serving. The list is long. Should I continue?"

As Seth's eyebrows flew up, his light gray eyes grew wide. "I've known him for years and he's none of those things. He's brilliant and one of the most respected businessmen in the metro area, not to mention a great guy. Before you dismiss this outright, consider the advantages."

"From my perspective, there are none."

"You'd learn a hell of a lot and I'm confident he'd make you a lucrative offer. Imagine managing one client's massive portfolio, with a solid opportunity to increase your earnings." He smiled warmly. "Maybe I'll throw my hat into the ring."

She breathed, then pulled out the cushy leather chair and plunked down across from him. "You do know your Jedi mind tricks don't work on me."

He chuckled. "C'mon, Brigit, just have a conversation with him."

"I've heard he's demanding and difficult."

"He's a driven and determined entrepreneur. That's what makes him so successful."

"I'm going to pass, Seth."

"Five years ago, I took a chance on you." Seth removed his glasses. "Every newbie I've ever hired paid their dues elsewhere. Everyone, but you. Yes, you graduated with distinction from Wharton, but you had no wealth management experience. You told me financial peace of mind mattered and you wanted to make a positive difference for your clients. The majority of my team is in it for the paycheck. I believed in you, so I hired you, handed you one of the firm's key accounts and mentored your career."

She eyed him across his desk. "And how'd that work out for you?"

"Dammit, why are you being so stubborn?" His hands flew out, palms up. "I'm asking you to talk to him, for crying out loud, not marry him!"

He's not backing down. "Several excellent brokers on your staff would jump at this opportunity. Why me?"

After slipping his glasses back on, his expression softened. "Mitus came to me for help and I sold him on you. I touted your accomplishments. Bragged about your tenacity, intelligence and professionalism, yet you barely acknowledged his presence. This is a great opportunity."

"It's a strategic move on your part, designed to put a feather in your cap. I can leave and take the lion's share of my clients with me."

"You wouldn't do that to me, though." Leaning back, he clasped his hands behind his head. "You're loyal, like I am."

Seth had this over her and he knew it. His allegiance had been unwavering. He'd given her a chance when she'd needed to start her life over, asked few questions, and had restored her belief that not every man on the planet was a cold-hearted asshole. She owed him.

She ran her fingers along her silver bracelet with the gold lobster claw clasp. "As a favor to you, I'll contact him next week."

He jotted a number on a sticky and handed it to her. "I think you're understandably rattled from Internado's inexcusable behavior. Trust me on this one. I know what I'm doing." A fatherly smile touched his eyes.

"I'm grateful for everything you've done for me, but when I mentioned feeling restless, being at Mitus's beck and call was not what I had in mind."

"I have complete confidence you'll make this work. By the way, he asked for references and is moving forward, full steam ahead."

Not without a fight.

Seth stood. Meeting over. She left his office for the third time in one day, this time with her gut in knots. Glancing at her fingertips, she clenched her jaw at the tacky paper with the oh-so-familiar number. She couldn't disclose her secret, not even to Seth. But she'd never work for Mitus. In a whoosh of unwelcomed memories, her unreturned calls to Mitus Conglomerate came racing back.

"Mr. Mitus, please. This is Eve Francesco again."

"I've given Mr. Mitus all of your messages, Ms. Francesco. He's not interested," said the woman on the phone.

"I know my family's business better than anyone." Eve rubbed her forehead, trying to keep from screaming like a madwoman into the receiver. "I'm confident my ten-year growth plan will benefit him."

"Mr. Mitus isn't interested. Goodbye."

Brigit ripped the sticky off her fingers and smacked it on her desk. For the last six years, she'd shoved her pent-up emotions into an imaginary cellblock, but today the prison door had been blown wide open and they'd escaped.

What a day. First, George Internado. He'd been one of her best clients, until he ruined it. Did he actually think she'd spend the afternoon screwing him? Tasting bitter bile, she crumpled into her chair, then rummaged through her desk for aspirin to silence her throbbing head.

But Internado wasn't enough. Oh, no! Then Colton Mitus had to waltz in. She flung two aspirins into her mouth and swallowed them down. The most devastatingly handsome man she'd ever laid eyes on. And what did he want? Her, to fix his ailing portfolio.

She knew, all too well, that things happened in threes. Goose bumps crawled across her skin and she glanced outside, her thoughts traveling to dark places. *I'm safe. He's behind bars.*

Brigit packed up, said goodbye to Kat, and hoofed it to the gym, a block from her office on 19th Street, NW. She shivered from a chill that had nothing to do with the brisk October evening and tugged her coat around her neck. After scooting inside, she flashed her ID and headed for the locker room.

As beads of sweat rolled down her back, she groaned against the weight of the leg press. She finished the reps and wiped the vinyl seat, but couldn't wipe her scowl. Meeting Colton Mitus had fueled her grit. It had also done something completely unexpected and totally infuriating.

Jolted her libido from a long and lonely slumber.

4

THE POP-IN

T HE COUNTDOWN TO FRIDAY happy hour started after lunch. With the end of the workweek in sight, Brigit could almost taste nirvana. Colton's number, still stuck to her desk, glared at her. She sneered at it. She'd agreed to call him next week and not one day sooner.

Brigit redirected her attention to the power couple sitting across her desk. "So, Frederick, when will our conversations include your retirement plans? You're working more now than you did a decade ago."

Sixty-three-year-old Frederick Mundy, a lobbyist during the Reagan era, had turned into a successful business owner and multimillionaire. His wife, Alyssa, a former marketing exec, now focused her time on philanthropic ventures.

"Fear drives me," Frederick replied. "Greatest motivator in the world."

Alyssa rolled her eyes. "*His* greatest motivator."

"I thought love was the greatest motivator," Brigit said.

"If that's the case, love will guide your life. Doesn't matter how many millions I have, it's never enough." Frederick pushed out of the chair. "And on that note, it's time for me to make some more."

"Thank you for your recommendations." Alyssa stood. "You've been spot-on the past few years."

"Thank you, Alyssa." Brigit rolled back her chair and walked around her desk. "These changes are our first steps toward less volatile investments. Frederick, you've been fighting me on this, but you've taken some recent hits that we need to mitigate going forward. Moving into a more conservative financial arena is key."

She escorted them to reception and almost had a heart attack. Colton Mitus and his attorney, Dez Livingston, were chatting with George Internado. Her business-as-usual day came to a screeching halt.

"Senator!" exclaimed Frederick. "Great to see you!"

After greeting Frederick and Alyssa, George turned his heavyset torso toward Brigit. His smile dropped and his rotund body grew rigid. He stood motionless, refusing to even shake her hand. His comb-over shone beneath the harsh fluorescents.

Brigit's palms grew clammy. "Hello, George."

"You can imagine my surprise when Seth called me this morning." George crossed his chunky arms. "Had to rearrange my packed afternoon. Will you be joining us?"

She swallowed. "No, I won't. Please excuse me." Brigit faced her clients. "Thank you for coming in. Always a pleasure."

"That's Colton Mitus," Alyssa whispered as she hugged her. "Would you like an introduction? Last I heard he's unattached."

She forced a smile. "Thanks. I've met him."

Colton stepped close. "Brigit, I need a moment."

The timbre of his husky voice rumbled through her sex-starved body, setting off a series of mini explosions that warmed her insides. Brigit loved men. But the way her body reacted to *this* man enraged her. "Excuse me a second." She stepped over to reception. "Has Seth been notified the senator is waiting?"

Shaniqua's deep brown eyes twinkled. She glanced at Colton, a smile ghosting over her lips. "Yes. Kaleb is on his way."

Did Colton expect she'd drop everything to speak with him

simply because he'd shown up? Blowing out a muffled huff, she cut her stare to him. The man exuded an abundance of confidence. From the way his tailored charcoal gray suit complemented his sculpted frame to the determination in his dark, powerful eyes, his strong essence was palpable.

And then he smiled. A full-blown, testosterone-laden smile. A blast of heat coursed through her veins.

Whoa.

Her thoughts blurred. Delicious tingles cascaded through her as a collective sigh floated from the bullpen.

But Brigit had more willpower than to fall victim to his charm. Standing tall, her five-foot-five-inch frame was no match for his, but her four-inch stilettos greatly aided her cause. She refused to allow his massive size to make her feel small in any way.

She offered the man standing next to him a cordial smile. "Brigit Farnay."

"Dez Livingston, Colton's legal counsel." They shook hands.

With his impressive bio posted on the Mitus Conglomerate website, the fifty-three-year-old had been Colton's personal attorney for years. A man of few words, Dez was fiercely protective of him and seldom quoted in articles written about the Mitus empire. Also a distinguished dresser, Dez's close-cut Afro, beard and mustache were in sharp contrast to Colton's unruly head of hair framing his clean-shaven face.

"What bring you by t-t-today?" Brigit tried to keep her voice steady, but a tremble caught the last word.

Colton's eyes narrowed. "Unfinished business."

Panic churned in her gut. Was he going to confront her about her shares of Francesco stock? She'd done nothing illegal and had every right to scarf up that stock. "Let's discuss this in my office."

Heads craned from cubicles like prairie dogs poking out of their holes. Colton's gargantuan ego needed no additional stroking. After closing her office door, she shielded herself behind her desk and steeled her spine.

Colton eyed the sticky note affixed to her clutter-free desk. "I see Seth gave you my number."

"Yes, my plan to contact you next week got bumped to now."

Dez reached into his briefcase and pulled out a folder. "We need you to sign a nondisclosure agreement."

"Why?" *What's Colton up to?*

"We're providing you with a list of Mitus Conglomerate's most distressed accounts." Dez set the folder on her desk.

Brigit found her breath and her raging insides settled down. "And if I don't sign it?"

"Your presentation won't be relevant." Dez smiled, his mocha eyes warm and friendly.

"I'm not interviewing for the position, so I don't need to sign anything."

Colton leaned forward and placed his large hand on her desk like he was staking his territory. "Brigit, you *will* interview and you will sign that form." So much power radiated from his dark eyes as his unrelenting gaze drew her in.

Her nipples tightened at the thought of those sexy hands fondling her breasts and caressing her inner thighs.

"Not happening." She crossed her leg and arched a brow. This was *her* tiny office and she was queen of it.

"Let's skip the back and forth and get right to the good stuff," Colton said.

His quiet and commanding voice was hypnotic. *Dammit. Get a grip.*

"You have two weeks to prepare." He removed his hand and leaned back.

His magnetic presence may have worked on others, but his needs meant nothing to her. They held each other's gaze. This time, his intensity fueled her resolve. "Barking orders won't work with me. I'm not your minion, nor do I have any intention of becoming one."

Creases around the edges of Colton's eyes softened and the

corners of his mouth lifted. "Would you prefer I flatter you? Tell you I'm bleeding tens of thousands of dollars daily and that you and only you can save me?"

She perked up at the thought of his groveling. "Yes."

Pursing his lips, Dez slid the one-page nondisclosure across her desk.

Colton crossed his legs. His massive thigh distracted her and before she could stop herself, she checked out his legs, then eyed his crisp white dress shirt hugging his muscular torso. She imagined his black and brown tie dangling around his neck, his dress shirt opened, her palms pressed against his hard chest. Her insides stirred with need and she blinked the fantasy away.

Determined to inflict bodily harm on herself for her feverish thoughts, she fisted her hands beneath the desk and her long fingernails dug into her palms.

Colton's phone rang and he pulled it from his pocket. "Excuse me." He answered. "Mitus." As he listened, he turned pensive.

Brigit swiveled toward her computer and checked email. It was either that or gawk at his face.

"Marjorie, hold on." Colton stood. "Brigit, I need a moment."

"Stepping into the fray won't buy you any privacy," she said. "You're better off in here. I deal with sensitive matters daily. These walls and my lips—" She mimed zipping her lips.

Brigit wouldn't relinquish her office. If he wanted her to leave, he'd have to ask. She would make nothing easy for this man. Nothing.

"Thanks." He eased back into the chair and pressed the cell to his ear. "Marjorie, who from MobiCom contacted Dobb?"

Ohmygod, he's talking to Francesco's Chief Operating Officer, Marjorie McAllister. Heat flamed her cheeks. She had wonderful childhood memories of the larger-than-life Mrs. Mickk. Dobb had to be Bob Dobb, the just-promoted president of the Francesco Company. Brigit turned back to her monitor but beneath her desk she fidgeted with her thick, corded bracelet.

"His timing is coincidental," Colton said. "No one at MobiCom knows about Crockett Boxes. There's too much at stake for anyone to leak the information."

Brigit shot him a hard stare. *What's happening at my company?*

"Dobb knows that. I think you're worrying needlessly." Colton glanced at Brigit. "I'm interviewing a potential wealth manager. I'll call you later." He hung up.

"Sorry for the interruption. Now, where were we?"

Brigit swiveled to face him. "You, about to grovel."

"All right, we'll play this your way, this time." Colton sat tall. "It's my understanding that your specialty is portfolios in distress. Mine hasn't been managed in months and has been neglected for far longer. I trust Seth and his glowing recommendation. I believe you can breathe life back into me." He cleared his throat. "I mean, into my portfolio. Please educate me on your solution, preferably at Mitus Mansion, where I hope you'll move in, in short order."

She could ruin him, or she could save him. Was it payback time, or an opportunity to build trust and gain his confidence so she could find out what had Mrs. Mick so concerned?

5

YES

BRIGIT'S WORLD SHIFTED A little. She wouldn't dismiss Colton as he'd done to her, but she wasn't going to work for him, either. "Until Seth provides you with a list of viable candidates, I'll offer a one-time consultation." Brigit pulled a pen from her center drawer.

Colton's jaw muscles ticked. "You're moving in the right direction."

"Before I sign anything, I'd like to view your list of distressed companies."

On Colton's nod, Dez handed over the summary page. Though the Francesco Company should have been included, it was not. That made no sense. The stock had been lackluster for months, yet he didn't want her reviewing that investment. Unknowingly, he'd cut her a break. She'd no intention of providing him with any counsel on *her* company.

"I sign this and you leave." She placed the tip of her pen on the signature line and shifted her gaze to Colton. His nod left her no choice.

Escorting the men out, Brigit couldn't ignore the stares. Were brokers eyeing Colton because of his wealth or his reputation? Probably both, but neither mattered. The painful irony of her situation was apparent. Had he agreed to a meeting years ago, he might not have been in his current predicament. But the past was just that.

Time to step into her future, which included Colton Mitus sooner than she anticipated, and in a way she never imagined.

Standing in reception, she watched as the two men vanished into the elevator. "There goes a handful."

"Nothing you can't manage," Shaniqua said.

"Taking that man on as a client is *so* not happening."

"I'm not sure even headstrong Brigit Farnay can stop the Colton Mitus locomotive." Shaniqua raised an eyebrow. "And who would want to?"

Brigit tapped the counter twice with her knuckles. "Me, that's who." She took off toward her office, hoping to pack up and leave in the next ten minutes.

Her desk phone buzzed. Kaleb. *Not again.* It had been such a long week. *Here goes.* She lifted the handset. "Hi, Kaleb."

"You might want to leave," Kaleb whispered. "I heard Internado yell, 'How dare you accuse me of *that*?'"

Her stomach churned. "What did Seth say?"

"He yelled back, 'Then why the hell did you give Brigit this hotel key?'"

Brigit's mouth dried up. She had, after all, accused a very powerful senator of a highly inappropriate action. "And?"

"The senator stopped shouting," Kaleb said. "I can't hear anything else. You've spent a lot of time in Seth's office this week. Thought you'd like a heads-up."

"Thanks. Join us at Sullivan's for happy hour." Eager to leave, she hung up and shut down.

Kat popped into her office. "I don't need to ask if you're ready for a glass of wine."

"My sights are set on a bottle." Brigit shrugged on her coat, threw her laptop satchel over her shoulder and grabbed her handbag. "Let's bolt."

In congested D.C. traffic, Kat inched her car toward Sullivan's of Georgetown. Rather than girl-chatter about their day, Kat punched up music on her playlist and belted out the lyrics. Brigit loved how Kat knew she needed chill time.

Brigit stared at the storefronts and office buildings, trying not to dwell on her surprise visitors. The anxiety-inducing events would drift away as soon as she took that first sip. Ever since her parents' deaths, alcohol helped numb her pain.

After Kat parked on a nearby side street, the two women hustled inside the restaurant and claimed their table for six in the bar area. Within minutes, the popular watering hole grew crowded with Washingtonians jump-starting their weekend. The familiar smell of beer on tap, the warm amber lighting and the rich mahogany and leather decor comforted Brigit's restive heart. Rick Sullivan, owner and head bartender, treated Porter, Gabriel and Sethfield's wealth advisors like royalty with discounts on the drinks and eats.

Both women ordered a glass of wine, delivered by their server in record time. "I've had an unusual job offer." As Brigit sipped her pinot noir, the delicious bouquet of berry flavors blossomed on her tongue.

"I had a feeling something was up," Kat said. "You spent most of yesterday in Seth's office."

"Colton Mitus needs a wealth manager."

"Ah, yes, the tall, handsome and intimidating man guilty of causing hysteria amongst the ranks. Everyone is envious, Brig."

"Because of Mitus?" Brigit rolled her eyes. "Puhleeese."

"Newest client?"

"Seth wants me to give up *all* my clients and work only for him."

Kat's eyes widened like saucers. "Does he have enough business to cover your earnings?"

Shrugging, she added, "Doesn't matter. I'm not interested." Brigit tipped more liquid into her mouth.

"Why not? Sounds like a sweet deal."

"I'd have to move into his home."

27

Kat bolted upright. "What!"

"Now you feel my pain. He lives in a mansion in Great Falls, as in crossing the bridge into Virginia. His staff lives with him."

"Sounds extreme." Kat twirled a chunk of her brunette waves.

Just then, a posse of coworkers barreled toward their table. Time to share seats.

"Matthew or me?" Brigit asked.

Kat made room on her chair. "That man makes my skin crawl."

As Brigit started to slide over, Matthew plunked down and wrapped his arm around Brigit's waist, holding her captive. "Evening, ma'am. I appreciate your cozying up with me. A cowboy sure can get lonely on the range."

A shiver flew down her spine and she shot out of her seat. "Well, buckaroo, find yourself a buffalo."

Matthew threw back his head and laughed.

Ew. "Let's sit at the bar," she whispered to Kat. With no stools available, the women squeezed into an open space, flush against the wall. "Matthew's become a pain in the ass," said Brigit.

"He's *been* a pain in the ass," said Kat. "He's going to get an earful if he doesn't back off."

Rick Sullivan laid a napkin in front of each woman. "How are Porter, Gabriel and Sethfield's smartest wealth managers doing this evening?"

Kat smiled. "Growing America's wealth one portfolio at a time."

Rick chuckled. "Mine included, I hope. Brigit, Kat what can I get you?"

"Split a bottle of pinot?" Brigit drained her glass.

Kat nodded.

"A bottle, please," Brigit said to Rick. "The *good* stuff."

Matthew sidled so close his chest brushed Brigit's shoulder. "Rick, put that bottle on my tab."

She jerked away, goose bumps spilling down her arms.

"Not cool." Kat shouldered the wall.

"The lady's not buying whatever you're peddling," a husky voice growled behind them. "Let me clue you in. These women aren't interested."

The women wheeled around. Colton Mitus loomed directly behind Brigit. A lightning bolt shot through her and she gasped. *What's he doing here?*

Kat's jaw dropped. "Okay, well, wow."

"Look, *buddy*, my friend's not interested in you. Get lost." Matthew sounded tough, but looked like he'd pissed his pants.

Colton glared at Matthew, his jaw muscles working overtime. "I'm not your buddy, these women aren't your friends, and you have no idea what Brigit needs." Colton's piercing intensity bore a hole through Matthew.

Brigit pursed her lips. The hovering testosterone needed to go away. Matthew's skirt chasing bordered on harassment and Colton needed to find a wealth manager who *wanted* to manage his wealth.

"I'll be here when you've had enough of this...this *loser*." Red-faced Matthew turned away and guzzled his drink.

Had Colton followed her? Had Seth tipped him off? Slowly his attention shifted from Matthew to her and when their eyes met, his lips split into a charming grin. A zing traveled at Mach *Whoa*. Her body was so not helping. She introduced Kat in an attempt to diffuse the undeniable heat smoldering between them.

"Brigit, I thought I'd pay you a social call." His harsh tone had been replaced with a soothing timbre like rich, creamy chocolate. When his hand jutted onto the bar, separating her from Matthew, a sexual urge flooded her traitorous body.

Pinned by Mitus. And she liked it.

His eyes were the color of Colombian coffee. Deep. Dark. Decadent. She managed a calming breath and caught his scent. Cologne-free, he smelled of cedar soap and lager beer. That particular beer reminded her of her daddy. Her thoughts turned laser-focused in an instant.

Pushing off the bar, she centered her weight like a matador

sizing up the bull. "I agreed to a one-time consult. You agreed to leave my office."

"I did leave." His expression turned playful. Charming even.

As she raised a brow, she crossed her arms. "What are you doing here?"

As if time had stopped, his gaze traveled over her face, pausing briefly on her mouth. "Nailing down the important part. How long do you need?"

Delicious streams of energy shot through her. *One night. I need one night.* "I'm not working for you, Colton."

A scorching intensity deepened his gaze. "Yes, you are, Brigit."

"You don't give up, do you?"

He leaned closer. "Never."

"Well, neither do I."

"Present your proposal, then make your decision."

She pulled out her phone. "I'll let Seth know."

His firm grip on her shoulder sent adrenaline spiking through her. Heat seeped through her clothing, lighting her insides on fire. Desire and need rocketed through her. Trapped by *him*. And she liked it.

Colton leaned closer. "I want the best and you're it." Riveted by his intensity, she trembled. His warm breath puffed against her bone-dry mouth and she slowly moistened her lower lip. "Now, why don't you answer my question? How long will you need to prepare your presentation, *Brigit?*"

It wasn't his striking presence, or his controlling nature, or even his lava-flowing sex appeal. It was the stunning realization that what she'd needed from him all those years ago was available now.

Five and a half years ago, she'd asked for a meeting. He denied her. Robert Sethfield believed in her and placed her in the path of this man. Ahead of schedule and for a different reason, but the opportunity was still there. And all she had to say was *yes*.

She relaxed her stance. By giving Colton Mitus what he needed, she could get what she wanted. "You offered me two weeks. I'll be ready in one."

His beautiful smile could have lit up the night sky. "There now, that wasn't so difficult, was it?" He removed his hand from her shoulder and dropped the other from the bar. A sense of loss, not relief, chilled her bones. His arm separating her from Matthew made her feel safe and his hand gripping her body made her feel alive. *Damn this man.*

Colton pivoted his massive frame toward Matthew. "She's all yours, *buddy,* but neither she nor Kathryn have any interest in you." A sardonic grin spread over his face. Without waiting for a response, he walked away.

Feeling lightheaded, Brigit took a long pull of wine. She needed a moment, so she grabbed their bottle, situated Kat at the team table so Matthew couldn't corner her, and bolted for the restroom.

Once there, she tried calming breaths to quiet her palpitating heart. In a twenty-four-hour period Colton Mitus had become her shadow. He needed her.

Her expertise. *Her* guidance. *Her* counsel. How many times had she wished for this? She let out a nervous chortle and glanced in the mirror, expecting to see frazzled, but a determined woman stared back. *Just because he asked you to present a proposal doesn't mean jack. Put your big-girl panties on. This is Colton Mitus we're talking about.*

Something was brewing at Francesco and this was her golden opportunity to find out what. She smoothed pink gloss across her lips, finger-combed her hair and dreamed of finishing her drink in peace.

Squeezing through the happy hour crowd, she spotted Colton nestled at a table with Dez, a woman with long, raven hair, and a Mr. Muscles type. Colton's eyes were pinned on hers. His intensity seared her from across the room.

Look away. It's like staring into the sun.

Hypnotized by his piercing gaze, she couldn't. His eyes turned stormy, drawing her in with tornado-like force. Everything around her faded away, leaving only her nemesis. A tiny moan erupted from her throat.

Keep walking! But her feet wouldn't budge.

With unwavering attention, he placed the glass to his lower lip, tipping the dark lager into his mouth, his movements so sublime it was like watching a living work of art. The tingling between her legs begged for his caress and she cursed herself for needing him in that way.

He put down the glass, then tossed her a subtle nod which hit her like a bolt of lightning. She imagined his lips molded against hers, his arms enveloping her, his weight on her, his hardness buried deep inside her. She couldn't stop the feelings rushing toward her, over her, through her. As her breasts rose and fell against the satin bra, her nipples pebbled. Her skin flushed from the wildfire burning through her sexually amped body.

Enough!

Breaking their fiery connection, she walked back to the table in a post-Mitus stupor and sank onto the corner of Kat's chair, oblivious to the robust chatter amongst teammates. Kat scooted over, giving Brigit more room.

"Excuse me, Brigit." The woman from Colton's table knelt next to her. Bangs framed her pretty face, her long jet hair pulled into a tight ponytail. "I'm Taylor Hathaway and I work at Mitus Conglomerate."

"That didn't take long."

"Per Colton's instruction, let's schedule your presentation. How's next Friday? And he insists you stay for dinner."

"Friday works, but I'm declining dinner."

"Uh-huh. Let's discuss clothing. Business attire, obviously, for your interview. Dinner will be formal. Colton prefers sophisticated sexy, not slutty. He's hosting a party so the staff can get to know you and vice versa. It's part of his thorough interviewing process. Since it'll end in the wee hours, you'll stay the night and be driven home

Saturday, following breakfast, which is business casual. I'll text you my number."

Brigit caught three little words of Taylor's clothing rant. *Stay. The. Night.* Her eyebrows shot up. "Rewind. Did you invite me for a sleepover? You do know I *rejected* your dinner invitation."

"Colton expects cohesiveness since we all live together." Taylor smiled. "Standard interview protocol. It's no big deal."

No big deal? "I'll drive myself, stay for the interview and leave immediately following."

"Vonn Savage from Colton's security team will pick you up."

Brigit blew out a frustrated sigh. "Taylor, I will not—"

"Awesome! See you next Friday, Brigit."

Taylor scampered back to her seat and whispered to Colton, who lowered his head to listen. His hair shadowed his eyes, giving him a dark, edgy look. Brigit's fingertips tingled, hungry to brush it away. When Taylor finished, he lifted his head and stared at her, his intensity boring into her from across the room.

Seth had thrown her into *his* path. And Colton wasn't backing down. Even his minion had flawlessly executed his orders. The tiniest smile caressed her lips. She had one week to prepare for the most important presentation of her life and she couldn't wait to get started. He wasn't the only one determined to win.

6

MYSTERIOUS PAST

THE WAITRESS POPPED OVER for the umpteenth time, severing Colton's fiery connection with Brigit. *Damn.*

"Need anything else?" She batted her eyelashes and smiled.

"Just the check." Colton turned back to his team. "Mission accomplished. Let's go, before Brigit changes her mind."

"That's my cue." As Chad stood he shoved against the table, sending glasses wobbling. "Cybersecurity, bodyguard, and occasional driver. I do it all."

Taylor grabbed an empty beer bottle before it crashed onto the floor. "And with such humility, I might add."

"Humility? What's that?" Chad flashed a wide grin before plowing through the crowd, clearing a path for Taylor as they headed toward the door.

Colton settled up with the googly-eyed waitress, whose outstanding attentiveness and scribbled phone number went ignored. When an attractive woman made herself available, he'd been known to graciously accept. But Brigit's no-nonsense attitude and chilly demeanor had monopolized his thoughts and actions for the past twenty-four hours, leaving no room for anyone else.

"What do you think?" he asked Dez.

"I like her. She won't back down if she disagrees, so expect to butt heads. Why not interview several?"

"I trust Seth and I have *got* to get someone on board. Francesco needs to start production. Without my loan, the project stalls."

"You'll know how to proceed after her presentation."

As Colton stashed the receipt in his wallet, his phone buzzed with a text from Taylor. "They're pulling out of the garage," Colton said and stood. "I'll say goodbye to Brigit."

Dez headed for the door while Colton set off toward her table. The closer he got, the more heat flamed his chest. After a whisper from Kathryn, Brigit shot him the same disdainful look she'd given him in Seth's office. He was adept at reading women, but not this one. In as much as he didn't want to hire her because he found her so fucking irresistible, he needed the best. Settling for second was never an option.

Pinning her with his gaze, he extended his hand. She rose and stared into his eyes. So pretty, even with the attitude. Instead of shaking his hand, she cocked a brow. Brigit Farnay seemed to enjoy being difficult. Women heaped positive feedback on him—grins, giggles, fluttering eyelashes, pink cheeks—but not this one. *You're one hot handful.*

Just as he started lowering his hand, she slid hers in. The zing from their connection landed smack in his balls and he squeezed her hand tighter. Though she relaxed her glare, she tugged her hand away, leaving his stone cold. Then a hint of a smile played around one side of her sexy mouth. *She doesn't detest me as much as she wants me to believe.*

Time to go. A seemingly harmless conversation could easily undo everything he'd just accomplished. After tossing her a nod, he made his way through the noisy bar. With his hand on the door, he glanced back. Had to see her one more time.

She hadn't moved. Even across the crowded room, he would

have singled her out. With a sly smile, she raised her hand and shot him the middle finger.

She's toying with me. Flashing a smile, he exited Sullivan's and laughed out loud as he slipped into the backseat of his silver Bentley.

Chad eased the vehicle forward in the bumper-to-bumper Friday night traffic. "I could walk faster than this."

"I love Georgetown." Taylor stared out the passenger window. "Wall-to-wall people."

Colton shifted his gaze to the packed sidewalk. Brigit had called him out at her office. Surprising since he rarely encountered pushback. When he did, he'd approach the challenge differently, even more determined to win. His need for control harked back to childhood, where he'd had none. Not only terrified of his abusive father, he was often targeted by school bullies. Whenever possible, his twin brother had protected him. After Cain's death, a timid and desperate Colton had adopted his brother's favorite saying. *You're not the boss of me.* Over the decades, those words had shaped and guided him.

Clenching his teeth, Colton lifted his phone from the inside breast pocket of his suit. He hated thinking about his childhood. "Chad, did you get the results of Brigit's background check?" He loosened his tie and unfastened the top button of his dress shirt.

"I emailed it to you. There's nothing." Chad turned down a side street.

"What do you mean, *nothing?*"

"She has no known relatives and, other than college transcripts, I can't find anything prior to her five years at Porter, Gabriel and Sethfield." Chad looped back around onto M Street, toward Key Bridge. "It's like she didn't exist. No family, no childhood. Nothing."

Taylor turned around, eyeing Colton and Dez in the backseat. "Oooh, a mystery lady."

Colton huffed. "Everyone has a past."

"Not this woman," said Chad.

"What *did* you find?" Colton asked.

"She's won numerous company awards and accolades. The clients I spoke with love her and she's got a shitload of them. Free time is spent volunteering at a D.C. women's shelter. And she's helping fund a college savings plan for a high school senior."

Thumbing through email, Colton opened the attachment. "I've got it. The student is a Monica Hall."

"Shaniqua Hall is Porter, Gabriel and Sethfield's receptionist," said Dez. "Her daughter, perhaps."

He scanned the document for prior arrests, lawsuits, and education. "Brigit graduated summa cum laude from Wharton. That's impressive."

"She's well qualified," Dez said.

"No pets, but she feeds treats to the neighbor's cat before work." Chad headed over Key Bridge into Virginia. "I did my own investigating."

"Do I want to know how you found that out?" Colton asked.

"Speaking as your attorney, no, you don't," Dez said.

"Tell me you're not hacking," Colton said.

"You know I'm thorough." Chad shot him a grin in the rearview mirror. "I staked out her place last night."

"Two years ago, she had a brief relationship with a married man?" asked Colton.

"Scumbag lied," Chad said. "She dumped him when she found out. She rarely dates, lives alone in Georgetown and works out at a gym near her office. And I told you about Friday happy hours at Sullivan's."

"She has Melvin Parsons on retainer," said Colton. "What's his practice?"

"Corporate acquisition," Dez said. "And he's damn good. One of the best."

Colton tapped his finger on his leg. "Hmm. That's notable. Did you find anything?"

"No," said Chad. "She's clean."

"There's a reason she's retained an attorney," Colton said. "Keep digging."

"Oh, sure, now you want me to." Chad picked up speed on the G.W. Parkway.

"How old is she?" Taylor asked.

Colton scanned the report. "Twenty-eight."

"Maybe she married, divorced and changed her name back," Taylor said.

"That would appear on the report," Chad said. "There's literally nothing."

Taylor glanced at Colton over her shoulder. "Past or no past, I like her."

Colton scrolled to his calendar. "Taylor, don't we have some kink lined up for next Friday night?"

"Yes."

"Push it back a week," Colton said.

"Let's cancel it," Taylor said.

In all the years Taylor had worked for him, she'd never once voiced her opinion or disagreed. Her usual fawnlike nervousness endeared her to him. "Not a fan?"

"Nope."

"What would you recommend, then?" Colton closed the attachment.

Taylor spun around. "Host a *normal* party, Colton. Movie night, casino night."

"What's the fun in that?" Colton smiled. "Please move the event to the following Friday."

"Why the kink?" Taylor asked.

"Because it wouldn't be Colton if he wasn't on all thrusters every moment of every day," Dez said.

Chad laughed. "Good one!"

"Time to spice up Ms. Farnay's quiet, predictable life, Mitus style," said Colton. "Taylor, I'm impressed you spoke your mind. A first." His phone rang. "Mitus."

"Sethfield, here. Brigit texted me. I understand she's interviewing next Friday. I'll email you her earnings details. Suggest a trial period. It's less intimidating and gives her a little wiggle room."

He imagined himself balls deep in her while she writhed naked beneath him. "Will do."

"I did my part," Seth said. "From here on out, she's all yours. But you've been warned. She's as strong-willed as she is smart. Handle at your own risk."

Chuckling, Colton hung up. His phone rang again. "Mitus."

"Colton, Wilson Montgomery, MobiCom's V.P. of Mergers and Acquisitions. I hope it's not too late."

Hair on the back of his neck prickled. *Why would someone from Francesco's biggest rival contact me?* "I'm always working."

"MobiCom execs are ready to discuss a merger."

Colton strummed his fingers on his leg. "Mitus Conglomerate isn't a telecom company. I'm a corporate investor."

"Let me clarify. MobiCom is interested in merging with the Francesco Company."

"Why propose this to me?" *And why the fuck now?*

"You hold a seat on Francesco's board and leadership doesn't take a crap without consulting you first."

Colton's stomach roiled. "I'm not—"

"Let's face it," Montgomery interrupted. "That stock has been in a steady decline. Merging would reenergize the organization. I'll email over the proposal."

Assuming prick. "Francesco board members and shareholders aren't interested in your so-called merger."

"They might be when they learn MobiCom is offering eight percent over market for their shares."

Dammit. "Save your proposal. My wealth manager doesn't have time to review it. We're done." Colton hung up and clenched his fist. *Maybe Marjorie was right.* He whipped his gaze to Dez. "The vultures are circling. MobiCom wants Francesco."

"You'd never support a merger and don't have a wealth manager," Dez replied.

"Wilson Montgomery is wasting his damn time pandering to me." Colton's eyes narrowed in the darkened car. "And I sure as hell do have a wealth manager. She just doesn't know it yet."

7

COLTON'S LATE-NIGHT REQUEST

B RIGIT PLACED THE CANDLELIT cupcake bouquet on her dining room table in front of Monica Hall, Shaniqua's daughter. Though Monica's eyes were closed, she had the sweetest smile plastered across her face. This month's Saturday night dinner party was a celebration of Monica's eighteenth birthday.

After moving to D.C., Brigit had started volunteering at a women's homeless shelter. Her parents had taught her the value of charity and she hoped doing something familiar would ease her grief and heartache. Over time, she became friends with Shaniqua Hall and her then twelve-year-old daughter, Monica. Now they were family.

Brigit and Shaniqua exchanged smiles. "Okay, Monica, open your eyes," Brigit said.

Her hazel eyes popped open. "Aw, they're so pretty and so pink!"

"Happy birthday, honey." Brigit ran her fingers down Monica's sleek black hair, then slipped back into her seat. "Make a wish."

The birthday girl heaved in a giant breath and blew out the candles.

"They're almost too perfect to eat," Shaniqua said. "Operative word being *almost*."

Brigit poured coffee and they dug in.

"Colton Mitus and Dez Livingston seemed nice." Shaniqua trickled cream into her mug.

Brigit cringed. She did not want to discuss that man in her home. "Did you tip them off to happy hour yesterday?"

"I preach stranger danger to Monica. Do you think I'd tell a prospective client where you hang out after work on Fridays?" Shaniqua nibbled a pink frosting petal.

"Of course not. My bad."

"If Seth didn't squeal, it must have been Kaleb," said Shaniqua. "That man cannot keep his mouth shut. So, Colton showed at up at Sullivan's? Gotta love a man who goes after what he wants."

"Is he hot?" Monica asked.

Washing down the bite of cupcake with coffee, Brigit shook her head. "No, definitely not—"

"Oh, yeah," Shaniqua said. "And successful, too."

"Enough, you're killing me!" Biting back the smile, Brigit headed into her kitchen.

Shaniqua laughed. "Could those two dress, or what? Did you see the diamond cufflinks on Dez?"

Brigit grabbed an envelope off her counter, her checkbook from her drawer, and returned to the dining room. "How 'bout we talk college? But first, presents!" She placed the envelope in front of the birthday girl and slipped back into her chair.

As Monica opened the card, a check and a gift card slid out.

"That check is for your—"

"I know. Savings." Monica hugged Brigit. "Thank you!" She flashed the Nordstrom gift card. "My favorite store."

Brigit opened her checkbook. "Since you've started applying to colleges, I'll help with application fees."

Shaniqua shook her head. "You're already doing too much by contributing to her college fund."

"Monica kept up her end of our deal. Now it's my turn." Brigit handed Shaniqua the check.

A year before Brigit had met them, Monica's dad, Harlan Hall, a twelve-year veteran of the Arlington County police force, had been killed in the line of duty. Mother and daughter fell on hard times. The once straight-A student lost her way and her failing grades reflected her grief. When Brigit learned of Monica's interest in college, she offered to help fund her education if Monica could refocus her energies into schoolwork. The motivator had worked.

Brigit patted Shaniqua's hand, then said to Monica, "Let's pack your edible bouquet to share with your friends."

"Thanks!" Monica said. "Are you coming to my party tomorrow?"

"Absolutely, but I can't stay too long. I have to prepare for a big presentation."

"For that handsome, intelligent, stylish dresser." Shaniqua winked at her daughter.

After goodbye hugs, Brigit cleaned up, then got busy analyzing Colton's limping portfolio. She had one shot to blow him away and she was damn well going to do just that.

On Mondays, if Brigit arrived at work by nine thirty, her week was off to a rousing start. But this Monday, her ass was firmly rooted in her office chair by seven. An hour later, Seth's smug grin further spurred her moxie.

After work, rather than eating a bowl of cereal or ordering carryout and drinking too much wine, she cooked a healthy meal and made a pot of coffee. She pored over her Mitus presentation until two in the morning, then began her workday again four hours later.

While doing a run-through at home on Thursday evening, she received a text from Taylor Hathaway, Colton's raven-haired assistant. *How much time do you need for tomorrow's presentation?*

Ninety minutes. Doesn't include Q&A, she texted back.

Colton has a late add.

She harrumphed. "Figures. Time to eliminate the middleman." She texted, *Does Colton know how to use a phone?*

Five minutes later, his number lit up her cell phone. Though tempted to hit the red button and give him a taste of his own medicine, she needed to hear him ask for *her* help again, so she tapped the green one. "So, you can use a phone." She spoke softly. "What a relief."

"No, someone had to dial it for me." His quiet, husky voice sent delicious tingles through her. She pressed the phone closer and their conversation turned intimate.

"Why does that not surprise me?" She bent her knee and rested her bare foot on the dining room chair.

"Confirming you need an hour and a half."

Her mind shorted. "Excuse me?"

"Tomorrow's presentation, Brigit." He paused. "What did you think I was talking about?"

As her cheeks heated, she cleared her throat. "Of course. I like to be thorough, ensuring I cover your current holdings, your minimum requirements for growth and my recommendations for maximizing your returns ad infinitum."

His sharp inhale made her insides quiver. "Sounds comprehensive."

"You'll want for nothing more." She allowed an extra beat of silence. "I encourage questions, but please hold them until the end. Are you capable of taking notes?"

"Are you being patronizing?"

"Who? Me?"

"Anything else?"

"You tell me. You're the one who called."

"Vonn Savage will pick you up at one. Does that work?"

"Yes."

"Finally, we have agreement." She could hear a brief smile in his voice. "Brigit, I need a SWOT analysis by tomorrow."

She rolled her eyes. *That'll take hours.*

"Do you know what that is?"

"If I said no, would that eliminate my having to do it?"

"Include strengths, weaknesses, opportunities and threats in your financial report."

"I don't suppose refusing you is going to fly."

"Correct."

"Email me the details, unless you need a minion to do it, because, like cell phones, computers are beyond your technological abilities. See you tomorrow."

Chuckling, he ended the call.

Brigit continued fine-tuning her presentation until the bing of an incoming email snagged her attention. Skimming his request, her temples throbbed. "Oh, no." Colton needed information on MobiCom, Francesco's biggest competitor. Was he severing his longtime association with her company and cozying up with the enemy?

Dammit! I forgot to take Melvin the money for the additional shares of Francesco stock. After scribbling the check, she scooted outside to the corner mailbox. Being investigated for insider trading because she provided a prospective client with a SWOT analysis on the competition seemed far-fetched, but she wasn't taking *any* chances when it came to Francesco. "There's no way I'm failing my parents again." She scurried inside and bolted the door. Her dad's dying wish was that she make Francesco her own.

I'm going to get our company back, Daddy. This time no one will stand in my way.

AT PROMPTLY ONE O'CLOCK on Friday, Brigit's doorbell rang.

"Good day, ma'am. Vonn Savage, Mitus Conglomerate. May I take your bags?"

Sporting a crew cut and bulging muscles that stretched against his black suit, Vonn placed her bags into the trunk of the Bentley.

He held open the back door of the silver luxury vehicle while she slipped inside. *Mr. Fancy Pants is going all out.*

Once settled into the driver's seat, Vonn asked, "Would you like music, Miss Farnay?"

"Please call me Brigit. Frank Sinatra or Michael Bublé would be great."

Within seconds, the timeless crooning of Ol' Blue Eyes surrounded her. She could hear her mom—*Sit tall, Eve*—so she sat upright, leaned against the plush leather seat and smoothed the creases on her winter white suit.

Fiddling with the silver Yurman bracelet clinging to her wrist, bittersweet memories came racing back. The sentimental piece had been the last birthday gift from her parents. A constant reminder of a life she'd loved and lost.

As the car weaved its way out of the city, the hustle and bustle of Georgetown disappeared, replaced by the tranquil drive along the tree-lined G.W. Parkway in Northern Virginia. The ride was less than forty minutes, but felt like an eternity. In the heart of Great Falls, Virginia, and nestled behind a private drive, sat fifty acres of prime real estate. Mitus Mansion, Colton's impenetrable fortress, served as both his residence and his office.

Years earlier, Eve's numerous requests to meet with Colton went ignored, save for one dismissive email. Determined to speak with him, she'd hopped a plane to Dulles. Through the intercom at the compound gates, a woman had informed her that Mr. Mitus was unavailable. Rebuffed again, she left.

Her phone buzzed and she fetched it from her handbag. It was her attorney. "Hello, Melvin."

"Brigit, you didn't drop off your check. You okay?"

She'd stayed up half the night working on a detailed analysis of Francesco's biggest rival and was headed to Mitus Conglomerate to interview for a job she didn't want. Of course she wasn't okay. "The week got away from me, so I mailed the check."

"I have some disturbing news. Do you have a moment?"

"I can't speak freely."

Vonn activated the privacy shield. Though appreciative of his professionalism, she wasn't going to divulge anything.

"MobiCom—Francesco's rival—is headquartered in nearby Reston."

This can't be good. "Yes, I know."

"Their legal team reached out to me."

Heat blasted her body and she cracked open the window. "Why?"

"They expressed interest in retaining my services for an acquisition team they're putting together."

"Oh, no."

"They want Francesco."

Her heart pounded loudly in her ears. "What did you tell them?"

"Full schedule, so I passed. Aside from the fact that I think it's a terrible idea, I'm not dropping you as my client. I'm sorry this is happening."

She rubbed the back of her neck. "Me, too."

"Francesco's sputtering stock isn't helping," Melvin said. "If the companies merge, they could buy you out of your shares and that'll be the end of that."

Her head throbbed as the Bentley pulled up to the Mitus compound. "Thank you for your loyalty, Melvin." She hung up, silenced her phone and shoved it into her handbag. *This cannot be happening.*

The giant gold M in the center of the gate split as the wrought iron swung open. After Vonn drove through, she spun around in time to see the metal clang shut like a prison cell door. Her hands grew clammy. To calm her anxiety, she silently recited her favorite childhood poem. The one she knew word-for-word before she'd learned to read. With Blankie in tow, she'd snuggle in mommy or daddy's lap and ask for Mary Howitt's spider story.

"Will you walk into my parlour?" said the Spider to the Fly,
'Tis the prettiest little parlour that ever you did spy;

> *The way into my parlour is up a winding stair,*
> *And I have many curious things to show you when you are there."*
> *"Oh no, no," said the Fly, "to ask me is in vain;*
> *For who goes up your winding stair can ne'er come down again."*

I'll never *ever* be that fly, she'd proudly proclaim.

The long-awaited invitation into Colton's inner sanctum didn't feel like a milestone and she gobbled down several nervous breaths. Her skills were being used to help the enemy undermine her six-year-old goal. Was she about to derail her chances of ever getting her company back?

8

THE SILK BLANKET

THE BENTLEY ROLLED FORWARD as the lush canopy of autumnal leaves swayed in the cool breeze. Were the giant oak branches waving her in or shooing her away?

The expansive Mitus property and picturesque setting reminded Brigit of the beautiful Virginia horse country with its scenic views and soft, rolling hills. A manicured lawn boasted several exquisite gardens. As the car rounded the bend, she gasped. Tucked at the end of the long, curvy driveway loomed his breathtaking mansion. The horseshoe-shaped brick house had several front-facing windows and two large turrets. *Impressive.*

Vonn parked at the circle, near the bubbling fountain and topiary garden. On cue, the French doors swung open and Taylor, dressed in a chic black pantsuit with a vibrant scarf, emerged.

As soon as Vonn opened Brigit's door, she stepped out. "Th-thank you for the ride, V-Vonn." Her teeth chattered from the chill within. *Get your shit together. You have one shot.*

After taking Brigit's laptop bag from Vonn, Taylor slid her hand into the crook of Brigit's arm and ushered her inside. The warm air mixed with the homey aroma of just-baked chocolate chip cookies reminded her of fun Saturday afternoons spent baking with her mom. But Samantha Francesco was long gone. That thought knocked the nostalgia right out of her.

A life-size sculpture of Michelangelo's "David" stood in the foyer alcove at the foot of the regal, curving staircase. But this David wore an eye patch and a black cloak while a black skirt covered his groin.

"Meet David, our Halloween pirate. We dress him for holidays." Taylor stepped close and whispered, "Even though Colton's not a fan."

Whimsical costume aside, the statue was a stunning replica. The living room mirrored a beautiful layout from *Elegant Homes* magazine. The burning logs in the ornate white marble fireplace crackled and spit embers onto the hearth. In the center of the room, two massive cream sofas flanked a large coffee table with a pair of expensive-looking seventeenth century French vases. Bay windows, facing the front of the property, were draped with handsome burgundy and gold window treatments. *Making millions taking my company public had its advantages.*

"Vonn will take your overnight bag to the guest suite," Taylor said. "Would you like coffee, tea, or sparkling water?"

"Sparkling water, thanks."

"Colton is expecting you." Taylor escorted Brigit down a hallway, past several doors until she reached the intimidating double doors at the end.

Brigit took her computer bag from Taylor and heaved in a lung-filling breath. *Time to rock this.*

Taylor knocked.

"Enter," Colton replied.

Brigit's heart picked up speed.

"Good luck." Taylor pushed opened the door, and with a sweep of her hand motioned Brigit forward.

She walked in and Taylor shut the door behind her.

The large, masculine room with deep brown paneled walls, ceiling and flooring was brightened by a wall of windows with French doors that faced the back of the property. Beyond the shiny mahogany floor lay an immaculate Persian rug. A conference table filled the far corner and a formal sitting area stood in the center, but the reason for her visit loomed larger than life behind his stately antiqued desk.

Colton.

She'd stepped into his world and the magnitude of his power hit her with gale force. This formidable man overshadowed everything in that space. With his eyes locked on hers, he rounded his desk with a confident stride.

Charisma, fortitude, and so much sex appeal oozed from his every pore. The midnight blue tailored suit, stark white dress shirt and navy blue power tie complemented his solid frame, but it was his charming smile and mussed hair that ignited her insides and set her heart aflutter.

"Colton." This time she initiated a strong handshake. His large, warm hand boosted her confidence and settled her butterflies. *I can do this.*

"Brigit." He spoke her name with the gentle fluidity of cool water burbling down a stream. With his unwavering gaze, he continued. "Besides sparkling water, can we get you anything?"

He had been watching her. "Do you spy on everyone or is this special treatment reserved for guests?"

"*Special* guests," he murmured and a shadow fell over his eyes.

Her cheeks warmed. As much as she loathed him, it excited her that he'd been watching. Then she'd been invisible. Now he couldn't look away.

He lifted her computer bag from her shoulder and with a light grip on the back of her arm, guided her to his conference table. A few easy steps and she was ready. After picking up the remote and ensuring Colton had a clear view of the presentation on the screen behind her, she zeroed in on his stormy, mysterious eyes. *This is it. Wish me luck, Mom and Dad.*

She spoke deliberately, but not too slowly. She smiled, but not too big or too frequently. She injected humor, but not too much.

She knew when to pause and when to speed up, based on reading his body language. She was succinct and yet full of knowledge about the businesses to which she was now privy.

Her recommendations were focused on expanding his empire, taking him in new, exciting directions while protecting the vast wealth he'd created. She'd memorized her presentation and her performance was impeccable. Though Colton glanced at the screen, he stayed focused on confident, poised Brigit Farnay, who weaved a lovely silk blanket around him.

An hour and a half later, she was done, for better or for worse. She eased into the chair next to him and poured a glass of sparkling water. Relief washed over her as the bubbly liquid soothed her parched throat.

"In summary, you have a robust and diverse portfolio." She set down the glass. "As I discussed, there are numerous ways to significantly and positively impact your business, thereby increasing your profits. You won't benefit from real financial gain until the losses are managed and your portfolio streamlined. The strategies I outlined are the best, most practical and fastest way to gain solid footing." She closed her laptop. "Thank you for holding your questions. I can address them now."

Colton nodded. Then, he, too, poured a glass of sparkling water. With his gaze cemented on hers, he drank it. Mesmerized by his fluid movement, she wondered if he was aware of his commanding and graceful presence.

"Brigit, your presentation was thorough. I have no questions." Her prideful smile couldn't be contained. *Yes, yes, yes. I nailed it!* "Thank you."

"Should I extend you an offer, I'd double your current earnings." *Whoa. I could buy a ton of Francesco stock.*

"In addition, bonuses would be tied to a percentage of growth realized." Colton set down the glass. "While generous, it's well deserved. Since you can ballpark my worth, offering you less would be an insult, especially since you'll be working round the clock." He raked his hand over his whiskered cheek and the slow, repetitive motion distracted her. All the while, his expression remained unreadable. "It's best to get everything on the table. I have a reservation."

"Just one?" She leaned back and crossed her arms. "I have several."

"You're too strong-willed and too independent."

"How are those *problems*? Don't you want a wealth manager who's as passionate about your success as you are?"

He strummed his fingers on the table. "And I'm confident you'd ignore my orders."

"Wrong again. First, I wouldn't ignore you. That's disrespectful. Second, I don't *take orders* from anyone, but I would hear you out. Doing what you tell me and doing what's best for the health of your wealth might be two completely different things. But since I'm not working for you, this conversation is pointless isn't it?"

He stared at her with the intensity of a lion hunting its prey. At long last Colton Mitus had finally heard her.

9

THE GIFT

COLTON DIDN'T BELIEVE IN luck. He believed in nose to the grindstone, tenacity, and in winning. And then winning again.

Brigit's phenomenal presentation was peppered with charm and humor. Colton despised bullshitters and fast talkers. She was neither. Her intelligence shone though without being showy. And her efforts impressed the hell out of him. Professionally she was quite competent to manage his portfolio and possibly earn a spot in his inner circle of trusted Mitus advisors.

But his initial impression of her hadn't changed. She was independent to a fault and he was confident she wouldn't follow his instructions. Her strong-willed nature could pose a considerable challenge. Bringing a wild card into the fold could hurt his wireless venture and possibly undermine his career. Was Brigit Farnay the right person to manage his flailing portfolio?

Skimming her analysis of MobiCom, he said, "This is well done and concise. You handled my last-minute request well."

"Why was this urgent?"

"The nature of my projects requires immediate turnaround."

"I'll let Seth know. He'll find an advisor who'll meet your unrealistic demands."

Colton flashed her a smile. "He already did."

She swiveled to face him and arched a brow. "Were you testing me?"

Of course I was. Colton held her gaze for a few seconds. "Since you'll be living here, let me show you around."

She stood and squared her shoulders. A chilly demeanor replaced the warmth in her eyes. Her resistance to moving in would be a challenge, but he'd overcome it. He'd keep the tour brief, skipping the underground parking garage along with the additional bedroom suites on the uppermost floor.

The recreation level downstairs had a heated swimming pool, full-sized gym, and state-of-the-art home theater, but he wasn't going to show her those amenities either. The main room was set up for a show. She'd ask questions, none of which he'd answer. She'd see that room *after* his staff had reconfigured it for a party...a G-rated one. Withholding certain things until after she'd moved in might mitigate the likelihood of her moving out.

But Brigit wasn't going to accept the position because of his amenities anyway. *Well, not those amenities.* Inwardly he smiled.

In the library, he showed her his Civil War gun collection passed down through five Mitus generations. She searched his face, paying little attention to the weapons. What was she thinking? A simple smile reached her eyes. He could not read this woman. That drove him crazy. He found it sexy as hell when a woman played hard to get. Although he doubted this woman was playing.

"I could have skipped the guns, right?" he asked.

"Not at all. The weapons are...well...they're part of your family history and...a treasured heirloom." She fiddled with the thick silver bracelet on her delicate right wrist.

As they walked up the staircase to the bedroom suites on the fourth floor his thoughts strayed. How would she feel in his arms, his mouth claiming hers, his hand caressing her curvy ass? How would she taste, *everywhere*? How could he bring her on board and keep his mind, and his body, off her? Well, he'd have to figure out a fucking way or he'd be forced to hire someone else. And after seeing her presentation, he had to have *her*. What he couldn't stop thinking about was all the ways he imagined.

Not one for filler talk, he walked down the hallway in silence. Colton didn't invite women into his private quarters, but he wanted to end the tour in his sitting room, overlooking the scenic view of the back of his property. And he wanted complete privacy, something he could control here.

"After you," he said, pushing open one of the two doors to his spacious suite.

She glanced inside. "Uh, no thanks. I've seen bedrooms. In fact, I have one of my very own."

Squelching his smile, he wanted to tell her to get her ass in there. "I've arranged for wine in my sitting room. Unless you want to scale my home and climb over the balcony, you're going to have to walk through that door."

With an expression he could only surmise was frustration—though it might have been amusement—she stepped over the threshold.

Having Brigit in his bedroom felt right. Until the image of her riding him on his sleigh bed sent a punching jolt through him. But they quickly passed through and into his sitting room, where the late afternoon sun bathed the room in streaming rays of autumnal light.

A fruit and cheese platter along with an open bottle of Chianti awaited their arrival. She popped a cheese square into her mouth.

"Wine?"

Her expression lightened and she nodded.

As he handed her the glass, their fingers brushed. He could warm her soft, chilly skin within minutes if she lay beneath him, then ravage her until she lay boneless and begging for more. *Exercise some damn control.*

"Please, have a seat."

She moseyed over to his built-in bookshelves. "You can read?"

He smiled. He could do so much with her sassy mouth. "Those are for show. They're hollow, like in a movie."

Her burst of laughter surprised him. Finally, she sat, poised on the sofa's edge. Her ruler-straight back and stilted pose made him want to laugh. She could have balanced that cheese platter on her head. Was she skittish in his private quarters? Well, he wasn't going to jump her. Even he had more couth than that. *Not happening. No sex. No sex.*

He wanted her in the absolute worst way.

Settling into his oversized upholstered chair across the cozy room, the welcomed distance allowed him to breathe something other than the coconut lotion he swore she'd slathered over every inch of her sweet body.

"Cheers." He raised his glass. "Best presentation I've ever seen."

Her vibrant green eyes grew dark, like storm clouds masking the sun. "That means more to me than you could know."

"Tell me about your business philosophy." He leaned back and propped one leg on the corner of the ottoman.

As she sipped the wine, her eyes brightened. "Mmm, this is excellent. Just a touch of bitter herbs."

Her sultry whisper floated in the air and he clamped down on his imagination, which was headed nowhere good, fast. "I'm glad you like it. Are you a wine connoisseur?"

"When it comes to wine, I trust my expert taste buds." She cozied into the sofa cushions.

Much better. See, I don't bite. Well, not yet, anyway.

"Now about that business philosophy," she said. "Why don't you tell me about yours?"

She deflected my question. Rather than force the issue, he'd make an exception and play nice. "Winning is the *only* acceptable outcome."

"Yes, it is. So, in light of your reservations, why extend me an offer?" When she crossed her legs, the skirt rode up her thighs. Pausing for a split-second to appreciate her shapely gams, he flipped his gaze back to her eyes, but she'd seen him.

Busted.

She didn't break eye contact nor did she blush or squirm. For several tantalizing seconds, the air grew electric with their energy.

"It would be a calculated business decision that would outweigh the inevitable headaches you're likely to cause me," he said. "I like to win. You like to win. That's good for business. Don't you agree?"

"Of course not." The tiniest hint of a smile brightened her eyes.

Of course not.

Because of her guarded nature, Colton directed the conversation back to wine, which seemed like a safe subject. Nearly an hour later the only thing he'd learned was her impressive knack for deflecting questions. Her specialty might be to drive him insane. The verdict was still out.

The soft rat-a-tat on his bedroom door felt like an intrusion and not an opportunity to escape. He rose, set his goblet on the coffee table and offered his hand. She stiffened, like a mannequin. Taking her wine glass, he placed it next to his, then extended his hand again. This time she accepted.

When they touched, blood whooshed through his veins at a maddening pace. Their eyes locked and her dilating pupils bled black over green. Aching to kiss her plump lips, he pulled her close and hardened. Her breath caught and she stole a glance at his mouth.

A louder knock broke their connection and he released her. *Dammit.*

"Enter."

He couldn't take his eyes off her. *She wanted that kiss.* Given another opportunity, he *would* kiss her.

Taylor appeared in the sitting room doorway and flushed. "Uh... um, you told me to be here, err...now. Bad time?"

That obvious? Throttle back. Slipping his hand into his pocket, he said, "Taylor, Brigit should wear the vintage gown, don't you think?" He'd been fantasizing about her in that number all week.

As Brigit bit out a grunt, she cocked her hand on her hip. "Didn't we just have a conversation about my refusing to take orders from you?"

Fidgeting, Taylor glanced furtively at Brigit while a thick silence hung in the air. The stare down continued. If Brigit wouldn't wear a damn dress, she'd never follow his portfolio instructions.

"More wine before I steal Brigit away?" Taylor asked breaking the silence.

"Yes," they both answered.

Taylor giggled until Colton cut his stare to her. Clearing her throat, she filled their goblets in silence. "Brigit, please come with me." As Taylor removed the platter, she knocked over Colton's glass. Red wine splattered onto the light upholstery of the ottoman, creating a stain resembling a Rorschach test. "Oh, I'm sorry!" Taylor's cheeks turned as red as the spilled liquid.

Colton's nostrils flared. "Taylor, please text Vanessa about the ottoman so housekeeping can work their magic."

Though driven and determined, he maintained an even keel, especially when angered. Seeing the damaged furniture pissed him off, but that was his issue. Taylor made a mistake, and she knew it.

As a result of his father's tirades, fear, humiliation and daily stomachaches had haunted the first ten years of his life. He'd cut off his arm before he'd do that to anyone, especially someone he cared about, like Taylor.

Trying to distance himself from memories of his father, he rose to his full stature, threw back his shoulders and breathed. The man Colton had become wouldn't tolerate cruel behavior. *Never again.*

"Excuse me a moment." Colton retreated into his bedroom. On impulse he'd purchased a piece of jewelry that would complement Brigit's delicate neckline. Returning to the sitting room, he offered her the small, rectangular wrapped box. "A token of my appreciation."

Brigit stepped back. "I...I can't accept this."

Determined she take it, he placed the gift in her palm. "It's part of the onboarding experience."

She cracked a smile. "Thank you."

The two grand he'd spent was worth her adorable expression. He wanted to run his fingers over her pink cheeks until his thumb brushed that pouty lower lip. And then he wanted to replace his thumb with his mouth, for starters.

Taylor ushered her out. Pausing in the doorway, Brigit turned. He'd been appreciating her backside. Her tiny waist, the sway of her ass, those defined calf muscles. She eyed him with such intensity he almost asked her what, or who, she needed. And then, she was gone, her beguiling image charred into his memory.

If he had one night with her, he could get her out of his system. Though he tried convincing himself it was a bad idea, the sweet temptation had taken hold. Against his better judgment and steadfast rule, he had to have her.

And he couldn't wait.

10

KEEPING HIS DISTANCE

BRIGIT ENTERED THE GUEST suite, located midway down the long hallway. When compared with the masculine touches throughout the mansion, this room mimicked an upscale hotel suite. Neutral colors, understated, modern furniture. Surprisingly, she missed Colton's influence. Taupe walls matched the taupe love seat and the taupe throw pillows offset the bright white comforter.

Taylor tapped the remote on the night table and soothing butter yellow and cobalt blue flames soared from the coals in the gas fireplace. As promised, Brigit's overnight bag had been placed on the queen bed.

"The gowns are hanging in the closet," said Taylor. "They're lovely."

Rolling her eyes, Brigit followed. Other than three dresses, the walk-in was bare. Taylor offered each dress like they were sacrificial lambs. First, a conservative black satin with burgundy lace overlay. Next, a sexy eggplant purple halter with train, and third, a classy vintage gold lamé and cream with a center slit. Though she appreciated the exquisite detail and quality of these couture gowns, she'd no intention of bowing to Colton's demands.

"You'd look great in any of these, especially this one." Taylor singled out the vintage gown again.

She's following orders. "Thank you."

Taylor spun the dress on its hanger, displaying the open back.

Brigit laughed. "Why don't you wear that one?"

"Colton wants *you* to wear it." Taylor hung the dress and marched out of the closet.

Like a duckling, Brigit followed.

"Cocktails will be served before dinner. I'll be back in an hour to escort you downstairs. You good?"

"Seriously? I'm in lockdown until tomorrow and I've been given a forced dress choice by the Clothing Czar."

Laughing, Taylor edged toward the door. "Text me if you need anything." She left.

Brigit sat on the love seat and stared at the small wrapped gift. Curious, she unwrapped it and lifted the lid on the David Yurman black box. *How beautiful.* A silver and gold pendant covered with pave diamonds dangled from a thick silver chain. The necklace complemented her Yurman bracelet.

Coincidence, or had he noticed her bracelet? Was Colton attempting to bribe her into coming on board? The cutthroat businessman was being both generous and charming. *He must really need a wealth manager.*

After a hot shower, she swept her hair into a messy updo, applied her makeup and dressed. Standing in front of the beveled mirror in the bedroom, she brushed her fingers over the sparkly pendant resting on her chest. The twinkling diamonds caught the light and winked back. The necklace spruced up her simple black halter dress. The three couture gowns remained in the closet, their price tags still attached. As a courtesy, she'd wear the necklace, but donning a six-thousand-dollar dress was not happening.

Precisely one hour later, there was a knock on her door. Brigit stepped into the hallway.

Taylor's mouth dropped. "Oh, no, you're wearing *your* gown. I'll wait. You change."

"No."

Nibbling a fingernail, Taylor murmured, "Oh boy, this should be interesting."

A small army mingled in the opulent living room. Disappearing briefly, Taylor returned with two crystal glasses of red wine. Light-bodied and fruity with a hint of oak and chocolate, the Cab rolled down Brigit's throat. And her expert taste buds rejoiced. The verdict was in. Colton Mitus drank the good stuff.

Brigit met several guests who turned out to be Mitus staff. His organization included a business team, a housekeeping staff, a groundskeeper, a culinary duo, and personal shoppers. Colton had surrounded himself with dutiful subjects. The Clothing Czar was also King of the Castle. *No wonder he expects me to fall in line. Everyone else does.*

A leggy, chestnut-haired woman joined her and Taylor. "I'm Simone Redding, Colton's business manager. Call me Red." She shook Brigit's hand. "I heard your presentation went well. When are you onboarding? I need help, like yesterday, with my dwindling investments."

News travels fast. "So, the previous wealth manager advised the staff?"

"In theory, but Colton kept Todd crazy busy," Red said. "I keep saying I'm going to find an investment manager, but…no time." She shrugged. "I live and breathe my job."

"How long have you worked at Mitus?" Brigit asked.

"Three years," said Red.

"Over four," said Taylor.

"Do you like working here?" Brigit instantly regretted asking the question. It sounded like she was contemplating a career move. She was not.

Suddenly, her body warmed. An ache, deep inside, burned for release. Glancing around, she found her answer.

Colton.

Her heart skipped a beat. She'd sensed his strong presence before she'd even seen him.

With one hand in his pocket and the other holding a glass of whiskey, he chatted with Dez, the Mr. Muscles guy from Sullivan's, and a lanky fellow. Colton hadn't shaved. The dark whiskers gave him a rough, edgy appearance. That shadow would leave red marks if he dragged his mouth over her face, down her neck, her breasts, her stomach, and between her legs. She would feel the raw burn, a sweet, painful reminder, long after he'd ravaged her.

She trembled at the thought. Though the room temperature was comfortable, she wished she'd worn a wrap. Bare shoulders made her feel vulnerable.

Aside from the obvious quality and expense, there was nothing special about his duds. A brown suit paired with a white dress shirt, and a vibrant tie bursting with reds, oranges and yellows. Yet on Colton the material lay against his steel frame as if it was an extension of him. A suit of armor designed to enhance, not distract. He had the ability to demand attention simply by existing.

Their eyes met in a fiery exchange of lust and need, but something unexplainable flowed between them. As he strolled toward her, heat bubbled off him with the ferocity of a lava-spewing volcano.

His hard body, angled face and those shadowed eyes, the windows to his mysterious soul, had her body thrumming in all the right places. The closer he got the faster her heart galloped. Had someone turned up the thermostat?

"Ladies." Colton pecked Taylor and Red on their cheeks.

Her body tensed in anticipation. But he didn't take her hand or kiss her cheek. Instead he slid his free hand back into his pocket. Had he done that on purpose? Maybe he was getting the message or trying to provoke a reaction. Well, he wasn't getting one. His hair was one hot mess and she bit the insides of her cheeks to keep from smiling. The man lived with a house full of females. Could no one tame his unruly mop?

His eyes grew cold and a shudder ran through her. "Brigit, your dress is festive."

Ohmygod, he thinks I look like a Christmas tree.

An attractive woman with short blonde hair sidled next to him. Her canary yellow gown left little to the imagination. Brigit recognized the sturdy employee from the Mitus website where leadership posted their bios.

"Vanessa, have you met Brigit?" Colton asked.

Ignoring Brigit, Vanessa kept her attention glued to Colton. "Handsome as always." Wrapping her hand around his arm, she leaned close, forcing his obligatory kiss on her cheek. The warmth drained from her face when she addressed Brigit. "I'm Colton's staff manager, Vanessa Ellison."

"Vanessa's a wealth of knowledge about all things Mitus Conglomerate," he said. "She's put up with me longer than anyone else."

Vanessa's shrill cackle pierced Brigit's eardrums and she hid her grimace behind her wine glass.

"I understand you're interested in the accountant position," Vanessa said when she'd gotten her shrieks under control.

Accountant? "Not exactly," Brigit replied. "One of my firm's partners volunteered me."

Vanessa glanced at Colton, but his attention was diverted when a young man appeared with a glass of red wine balanced on a small silver platter.

Colton placed his empty lowball glass on the tray but didn't take the goblet. "Shane, I'll have wine with dinner."

"Would you like another whiskey?" the attendant asked.

"No, thanks." Colton shifted his attention to Brigit. "Shane is a recent culinary school graduate who's been spoiling the staff with his sinful chocolate pastries."

Shane beamed, his bright blue eyes standing out against his

flushed face. Although his hair appeared combed, the wavy ends jutted every which way, giving him a disheveled appearance. He puffed his chest. "Thank you, Colton. Dinner is ready."

Colton extended his arm, offering Brigit an escort. Rather than placing her hand in the crook of his elbow, she wrapped her fingers around the muscular curve of his bicep.

Big and hard. Her insides melted a little. It had been too long since she'd laid hands on a man. And she'd never touched one who felt like this. Tightening her grip, she peeked at him through her lashes. Although he didn't look at her, his eyes turned stormy and sexy as hell.

The dining room's focal point was an impressive cherry table that spanned the length of the room, with twenty upholstered chairs outlined in a rich cherry border. Another stately room made cozy with a wood ceiling, and burnt cinnamon walls accented by dark wood wainscoting. In contrast, the white china, with its thick gold border, was simple yet tasteful.

Another sensational room in Colton's castle.

As he escorted her past the grand china cabinet, she stopped. "These tea sets are exquisite. What an unusual collection."

"Passed down from my grandmother. Each boasts a unique design. Which is your favorite?"

As she examined the sets, she tried ignoring his intense gaze boring into her. After a pregnant pause, she removed her hand from his bicep and pointed. "That one."

"Why?"

"At first glance, it's a simple white cup. But a town bursting with color has been painted in magnificent detail on the inside. With each sip of tea, the magic is slowly revealed. Everything happens beneath the surface." Refusing to get pulled into the rip current of his penetrating stare, she fixed her attention on the china. Then, his hand glided across her bare back between her shoulders, leaving an eruption of fireworks in its wake.

For years, all she'd wanted to do was scream at him for what he'd taken. As he caressed her skin, the only thing she could think of screaming was *more*. Her body tingled, tantalized by the sensual way he touched her. His hand trailed down her back, separated from her heated skin by the thin layer of black cloth.

Hypersensitive nipples strained against the silky material, hungry to feel his hands, his mouth. A sexual need sent blood racing to her core. Had he touched her *there*, she would have shattered. Her heart pounded too fast and too loud.

Breathe. Nice and easy.

She didn't want him to know the effect he was having on her, but she might as well have been holding a sign flashing *orgasm-ready*. His hand came to rest on the small of her back, above the curve of her ass. Another tectonic shift. Her core throbbed. His heat seeped through the clingy material, setting her skin on fire.

Though wrong, she wanted him in the absolute worst way.

"I will never look at that teacup set the same," he murmured, stepping close.

Shifting her gaze from the cabinet to the man, she found her breath and her voice. "Having an open mind makes life exciting." She spoke softly. "It keeps the magic alive." As soon as their eyes met, her senses took over. She inhaled his musky scent. Her fingertips itched to stroke his sexy, unshaved scruff. And then she heard it. A low growl shot out from the back of his throat. Her panties grew damp. Damn him. Damn her for reacting this way.

He held her gaze for several seconds while the air crackled between them. Then, he leaned close and whispered. "You will not defy me."

With her free hand, she gripped her hip. "Oh, is that so? I'll assume you're referring to my wardrobe selection."

"My employees do as I tell them."

"I wore the necklace. Consider it a compromise."

"That's not a win."

"I disagree. Everyone wins with compromise."

With a guiding hand on her back, he escorted her to the far end of the long table and pulled out the chair.

She turned to face him. "Don't assume I'm naïve Little Red Riding Hood skipping through the forest to Grandmother's house. You, however, are—"

"The big, bad wolf." He gave her a devilish smile.

Her blood pressure spiked. *Yes, you are.*

He seated her, then left to dine at the complete opposite end. Gazing at her across the lengthy table, he raised his wine glass in a silent toast. Was he keeping his distance on purpose or making a point by placing her in the opposing power position?

To be cordial, she raised her glass, though her middle finger itched to salute him. Without question, he was the most infuriating man she'd *ever* met. By standing her ground, she was proving a point *and* tormenting him.

Who knew payback could be so much fun?

11

THE BIG BAD WOLF

B RIGIT HAD NO WAY of knowing whether the staff always ate like royalty, but the sumptuous five-course dinner gave her pause for thought. *C'mon, it was only food. No, I eat food. That was culinary perfection.*

Immediately following after-dinner liqueurs and specialty coffees, Taylor whisked Brigit into an elevator with several other staffers, but no Colton. As the doors opened to a large room in the lower level, they were greeted with the twang of a country singer determined to win back his long-lost love. Mr. Muscles sat behind the DJ console, spinning tunes with Zoe, Colton's personal shopper.

Unlike the elaborate style upstairs, the only furnishings were two sofas and a smattering of chairs in the far corner. A wooden dance floor took up most of the space and a rotating disco ball dangled from the ceiling.

What held her attention were two stunning seventeenth century French tapestries clinging to adjacent walls. On closer examination, the artwork featured nudes in various sexual positions. Brigit dropped her gaze, not because the scenes were graphic, but because she hadn't had sex in a long time. Staring in envy didn't seem like polite party etiquette.

Shane offered a tray of crystal flutes filled with champagne. Though she loved her bubbly, Brigit declined. Time to sober up. While Red and Ryan Catalano—the lanky fellow from earlier—bantered about the pros and cons of protein supplement shakes, Taylor and Dez weighed in.

Brigit's first impressions of the staff had been positive. Most everyone made her feel welcome and encouraged her to take the position, but she assumed their controlling boss had something to do with that. And Seth had been right. The magnificent home was one of a kind. If she didn't have her own agenda, she would have given serious consideration to accepting the position, even with Colton's demanding personality.

Just then, Colton walked in and Brigit's heart did that annoying little flippy-thing. Beyond his dashing looks and magnetic presence, she was drawn to him in a way she couldn't explain.

Within seconds, Vanessa tugged him onto the dance floor.

Though the group conversation had moved beyond protein shakes, the chatter couldn't hold Brigit's attention. While Colton tried dancing at a respectable distance, Vanessa kept cozying up. By the end of the third song, her octopus arms encircled his neck. But he wasn't holding her snugly. Instead, he'd grasped his own wrist with one hand, while his other hand fisted against the small of her back. Even with his arms draped around her, he wasn't actually touching her. *Interesting choice.*

The song ended. After detangling himself, Colton raised his hands in surrender. Not even Vanessa's exaggerated pout could deter him. He folded his suit jacket over the back of a chair and spoke briefly with Mr. Muscles and Zoe, busy at the music controls.

When finished, Colton glanced around the room.

Brigit couldn't look away fast enough. Their eyes met. His raw gaze made her heart beat faster. With each step sexual energy billowed off him, his magnetic pull undeniable.

"Dance with me, Brigit." Her insides quivered from his melodic timbre.

"And if I won't?" The loud music drowned her quiet voice.

He leaned closer and a chunk of hair shadowed his brow. Her fingers twitched. Though dying to finger-comb his hair out of his eyes, she didn't.

"I'll make it impossible for you to refuse me." His warm breath caressed her cheek.

Their unblinking connection remained unbroken. He collected her hands, and bolts of coiled passion traveled up her arms, over her neck and down her chest. She tried tugging her hands away, but he tightened his grip.

"You know you want to dance with me." His playful smile wasn't helping.

She raised her brows. "You know nothing about what I want."

His warm lips brushed against her sensitive ear. "I love a good challenge, just like you."

Oh God, yes. Her throbbing core made thought impossible. Though she shouldn't take that next step with *this* man, she couldn't deny herself what she so desperately needed.

Him.

As if on cue, a love song bathed Brigit's lonely soul in romantic lyrics and a soothing melody. With their hands still entwined, Colton stepped backward. She stood her ground. Their fingers separated, but he slid his arm around her waist and pulled her close. Pinned against his granite chest, she quietly moaned. *Mmm, hard and strong.*

"We'll dance here." He wrapped his arms around her, pressed his massive palms against her back and swayed to the music.

She pushed up on her tiptoes and pressed her mouth to his ear. "Take me," she whispered. His breath caught and another low growl echoed in her ear. Her panties grew moist. "Onto the dance floor."

With a possessive hold around her waist, he slow-danced their way onto the wooden flooring, so they could sway beneath the silvery moon. But they still weren't close enough. He twirled her halfway around, encircled her chest with his muscular arms and continued moving to the erotic beat. His long, thick erection pressed against her backside. Closing her eyes, she floated in his arms.

"I've got you exactly where I want you." His breath heated the back of her neck. "In my arms and in my control." Her eyes flew open and she pulled away. But he gripped her tighter. "You can't escape me."

A tiny whimper shot from the back of her throat as muscles deep inside ached. His strong grasp turned her insides into liquid heat. Feeling alive and safe, she needed to surrender herself to him. *I've lost my mind.*

One dance turned into many. Colton loosened his tie, unfastened the top button of his dress shirt and rolled up his sleeves. Watching him slowly bare his skin confirmed what she had to do.

She had to have him.

Tomorrow would be too late. The light of day would give way to rational thought. Consumed by an unrelenting need, she imagined his mouth on hers while his large hands forged trails across her sensitive skin. How could she want this man so desperately? *This* man? He captivated her like no one she'd ever met.

For one night she'd let go. Not think about her painful past or her uncertain future. She'd free her lonely soul. Like the black widow, she'd wrap him in her web and take him.

For. One. Night.

As the song ended, Vanessa appeared. "Can I steal him?" she asked Brigit.

"He's all yours." Brigit stepped away, but the distance left her feeling cold. And lonely.

"We've already had our fun tonight, Vanessa." Colton threaded his arm around Brigit's waist.

And just like at Sullivan's, his anchoring grip exhilarated her. Her senses magnified everything around her. *Everything Colton, that is.*

Though Vanessa smiled, the warmth didn't reach her eyes. "A rain check," she said and left the dance floor.

A tender love ballad broke the awkwardness. Without hesitating, Colton snaked both arms around Brigit's waist. Though she wanted to run her hands along his shoulders, she left her arms dangling by her side.

"It's easier and a lot more fun if you actually touch me." The thickness in his voice landed at the apex between her legs.

I want him. So badly.

His smoldering stare sent a jolt of electricity pounding through her. "Here, let me help." He draped her arm over his shoulder. "Your turn."

Pursing her lips to hide the smile, she placed her other hand on his shoulder. Her body heated, but not from the warmth of his skin seeping through his cotton shirt and onto her fingers. Laying her hands on his strong, hard body cemented her decision.

Tonight, she would sleep with the enemy.

His stare never left hers. Could he feel her unrelenting need? The song ended and the lights brightened. Some staff continued drinking and talking, while others headed upstairs.

The connection hummed between them and her heart kicked up speed. Time to make her move. "Thank you for the opportunity to interview and meet your staff."

"Calling it a night?"

With a sly smile, she nodded.

"Are you tired?"

"No. You?"

As he shook his head, his gaze wandered from her eyes to her mouth, then back to her eyes. "Thirsty?"

Slowly, she nodded. "I'll text Taylor for sparking water."

His lips curved just enough to let her know he was amused. "Putting me through the paces, aren't you?" He offered his arm and she gripped his bicep. Rather than heading upstairs, he led her out back, onto the cobblestone walkway.

The blast of frigid air against her overheated skin felt invigorating. The full moon shone through the swaying tree branches illuminating their way like dancing fireflies as they headed toward the light in the guesthouse cottage.

Halfway there, he stopped. Slowly, he pivoted toward her. His deep, dark pools confirmed she wanted this—she wanted *him*— more than her next chilly breath. She squeezed his arm, set her sights on the house and continued forward in silence. He pressed a code on the keyless entry pad and the door clicked open. He pushed it wide and waited.

"No water in the main house?" She crossed the threshold.

"None." He closed the door behind them. "Fortunately, I've stashed some bottles here. You know, for emergencies."

"What a godsend! I can't imagine having to drink tap water."

On a chuckle, he held her hand and led her through the small foyer. Sizzling energy skirted up her arm. Her hand felt tiny nestled in his large one, but as soon as they entered the kitchen, she tugged her hand away.

"Shane whipped up a surprise dessert. Shall we be naughty and have a bite?"

He planned this. "Perhaps a nibble."

Opening the refrigerator, he pulled out a tiramisu cake. "This is going to be a sweet, creamy delight." He dragged his tongue over his lower lip.

Oh, God. Her insides quivered. They held eye contact for an extra second before he set the dessert on the table. While he sliced two pieces and placed them on dessert plates, she opened cupboards.

"Let me help." As he stepped behind her, he opened an adjacent cupboard then pressed against her backside. The weight of his body stirred her insides. Though he set the glasses on the counter, he didn't move away. Gulping down a breath, she turned around and peered into his eyes.

So close. So handsome. So wrong.

His rapid breathing blew wisps of her hair. Though desperate to kiss him, she would make him work for everything. "My, what a deep voice you have," she said.

Up went his eyebrows. "Thank you, I think." She waited for him to step back. He didn't.

Closer still, and so deliciously tempting.

"Your eyes are filled with tiny yellow flecks, like glittering stars," he murmured.

Her insides pulsed from the vibration of his hushed voice.

"They're beautiful." His lips parted.

Glancing at his mouth, she dragged air into her lungs and placed her hands on his shoulders. "My, what big eyes you have."

He chortled as she nudged him back. With glasses in hand, she sauntered to the refrigerator. Her hips swished left, right, left, right.

"I should have known you weren't complimenting me," he said.

"You'll catch on."

Awareness lit up his midnight eyes. "All the better to see you with." He set forks on the table.

She opened the refrigerator door and pulled out a bottle of sparkling water. Feeling his eyes on her, she placed the items on the table and sat, then lifted her gaze to face him. Sitting catty-corner, he scooped tiramisu onto the fork and offered it to her. She placed her hands over his and guided the utensil into her mouth. When the sugary dessert flooded her taste buds, she closed her eyes and moaned.

"You are beyond beautiful."

On a flutter, she opened them and held his piercing gaze. "My, my, what big hands you have." Her voice dropped an octave, her breath coming fast. She ran her fingers over his hands. *Big, strong, and sexy.* She imagined him fondling her breasts, caressing her ass, stroking her back, their lustful bodies locked in a rhythmic dance.

"All the better to touch you with." He scooted his chair closer. Only inches away.

Every fiber, each nerve sizzled with anticipation. Scarcely breathing, she broke eye contact, refusing to make this easy for him.

Women fell at his feet, but she would not. She scooped a heaping piece of tiramisu onto her fork. "Open."

He hesitated.

"Don't you want a taste?"

With a gleam in his eyes, he opened his mouth.

She slipped the fork inside, depositing the yummy treat. "My, what big teeth you have." His raw stare sent torturous jolts of sexual energy crashing through her. And she hadn't even kissed him yet.

"I don't know if you're smarter than you are beautiful or vice versa." His throaty whisper was filled with raw desire.

With a racing heart, she waited. The wall clock thundered in her ears. *Tick tock tick tock.* "Don't you want to finish the bedtime story?" Her voice quivered. She could barely contain herself.

"More than you know."

"Then say it."

"Why should I?"

"By your own admission, you're the big, bad wolf."

He gave her a toothy grin. "Indeed I am."

She leaned close. "Say it, Colton."

"All the better to eat you with, my dear."

12

TAKE ME

BRIGIT WHIMPERED AS COLTON cradled her face and kissed her. Instead of deepening the kiss, he pulled away, leaving her aching for more. Drawing in a jagged breath, she opened her eyes to find him gazing into them, his hands still cupping her cheek.

"Your lips were made for kissing." Releasing her face, he murmured, "I need to show you something."

She sucked down a sharp breath. That tender kiss had been nothing like she'd anticipated. But the enemy had stepped into her web and she had no intention of releasing him anytime soon. "I'll bet you do." Brigit cleared the table. Walking away seemed ludicrous, but she was having too much fun toying with him.

Clasping her hand, he led her into the living room. Was he trying to throw her off balance with his charm? Well, it was working. Unlike the mansion, this furniture was simple, like a cozy country cabin. He clicked a remote and the gas fireplace roared with life.

"You brought me in here to show me your fireplace remote," she said. "Golly day, you *can* use technology."

Smirking, he shook his head. "You're a handful. Just sit down. I want you to review a document."

Her mouth dried up. Had he learned she was about to become

the majority shareholder of the Francesco Company? Did he bring her here to interrogate her? Thumbing her bracelet, she blurted, "Isn't it a little late to be working?"

"It's not work, it's personal."

Ohmygod, he knows. "Let me grab my drink. Would you like yours?" Before he had a chance to answer, she was in the kitchen chugging her water. Not even slow, deep breaths could calm her palpitating heart. Unprepared for what to expect, she returned to the living room.

Looking relaxed and so damn sexy, he'd removed his shoes. She fought a smile. Somehow seeing his socked feet made him human, almost. "Getting comfy, are we?" She eased next to him on the espresso brown couch and braced for the worst.

In silence, he fiddled with his phone, then handed it to her. With a furrowed brow, she navigated around the document. It appeared to be his medical report dated that week. She breathed. "Was that the kiss of death?"

"Read it."

Colton Mitus was a healthy, cootie-free thirty-three-year-old, weighing a little over two hundred pounds on a six-foot two-inch frame. *Good God, he's perfect.*

"Is this also part of the interview process?" She handed him his phone and their fingers brushed, the sparks running rampant through her. Though hungry to pull him into an embrace and ravage him, she dropped her hands in her lap and threaded her fingers.

His chest rose and fell as he studied her face. "I wanted you to… never mind." His cheeks turned light pink. "I'll take you back to the main house."

Colton Mitus with rosy cheeks was her green light. She imagined his flushed face while he thrust again and again, his hardness rooted deep inside her. "Okay. Thank you for the tiramisu and for the treat following. They were both yummy."

She rose and sashayed toward the front door. Before she'd fully realized what had happened, he'd pulled her into his arms and kissed her. Long. Ardent. Strong.

Oh, God. Yes, yes, yes. Her panties dampened.

He slowed the kiss until it came to an end. They opened their eyes, but neither moved. Colton anchored one arm around her waist while the other caressed her back. Slow, hypnotic strokes, up and down. All she could hear was his breathing, hard and strong in her ears.

Trapped again. And she loved it.

With her palms pressed against his solid chest, she slid her hands up his broad, muscular shoulders. Her nipples hardened and her insides burned with unrelenting desire. On a muffled moan, she leaned up and kissed him. The sensation of his soft lips sent blood whooshing through her veins. And then he deepened the kiss. His tongue tangled with hers, back and forth, around and around. His erection jutted against her belly. Her primed body grew wet with need.

The kiss continued. Time became meaningless. Gasping for breath, she pulled away and stared into his eyes.

Then, he cradled her in his arms and carried her into the kitchen, set her down on the center island and pulled a remote from a drawer.

"I don't know if I'm more aroused from that kiss or from the fact that you've been holding out on me," she said. "You've used two pieces of electronics in the last two minutes."

"What are you doing to me?" He grabbed her shoulders and kissed her again, his tongue pushing past her lips. Fast, tempestuous strokes that showed no mercy. She released a series of muffled, throaty whimpers.

He kissed her harder still, then abruptly stopped, his chest rising and falling as he dragged air into his lungs. "I showed you my medical report because I needed you to know I'm clean." His eyes turned dark, and he clenched his teeth, his jaw muscles tightening.

Power and lust poured from him. "You *will* work for me, Brigit. And tonight, you'll stay here with me."

One guilt-free night with the enemy.

"I'm not working for you. But staying here?" A smile flitted across her face. "Now that has potential."

A quick tap on the remote and jazz floated all around them. Lifting her as if she weighed no more than a feather, he carried her down the hallway to the master bedroom. The soft light of the table lamp illuminated the four-poster bed, its linens turned back and the pillows plumped.

"Hmm, that's a shame," she murmured.

"What's wrong?"

"No fancy chocolates on the pillows."

A smile ghosted across his lips. "Candy isn't what you need."

"You are quite presumptuous. Trust me on this one. You have no idea what I need."

"Then educate me."

His husky voice and possessive gaze stilled her. Still cradling her in his arms, he kicked the door closed with his heel, then set her down. Standing behind her, he pressed his hands on her tummy and nuzzled close. Everything above and below begged for his touch. *Everything.*

When he nibbled her earlobe, she grew dizzy with need. She closed her eyes and leaned back against his granite chest. As he left a trail of smoldering kisses down her exposed neck, he whispered, "You're so delicious I could devour you whole."

Ohmygod, yes.

She stood on rubber legs. His raw words confirmed the all-consuming desire that had turned her sexually amped body into a fiery ball of need. She sucked in a harsh breath and his virile scent filled her lungs. And then she felt his straining erection pressing against her buttocks.

Turning to face him, she peered into his eyes. This was it and she was ready.

He kissed her again and she couldn't hold back. Opening her mouth, she pushed her tongue past his lips and connected with his. Powerful kisses that were soft and worshipful one minute and impassioned and fervent the next. She needed their clothing gone so she could touch every inch of him and feel his hands stroking her tingling skin.

While still kissing her, he reached behind to unzip her gown, but halfway down, the zipper stuck. He stopped the kiss and her eyes popped open. Ruthless, cocky Colton Mitus had the cutest look on his face. "I've exceeded my skill level."

"Oh, well. We tried." After a pregnant pause, she gave him a playful smile, then turned around so he could unzip her.

The gown fell away, leaving her dressed in black lace panties and stilettos. "Fortunately for you, I don't give up," he whispered then kissed her shoulder.

She whirled to face him. "Fortunately for *me?*"

He was smiling. *The enemy has a sense of humor.*

"I'm the lucky one," he murmured.

Rather than ravage her, he stepped back. His gaze floated over her bare breasts and plumped nipples, her abdomen, her tiny black panties, and her legs. As if he had all the time in the world, he retraced his steps until their eyes met. Her throbbing clit ached for his touch, her core slick with desire.

"I could stare at your beauty all day."

Maybe that was a line and the man didn't have an ounce of decency in him. But this night was all about her needs, so she shot him an appreciative little smile. She untied his colorful tie and left it dangling. With her eyes locked on his, she slowly unbuttoned his shirt. Something she'd been fantasizing about for days.

His gaze darted to her breasts.

"Are you waiting for an invitation?"

"Yes."

Was he a gentleman or on his best behavior because he wanted her to work for him? That was irrelevant. *Move forward. No regrets.*

Trembling with anticipation, she picked up his hand and traced the outline of her pink areola with his index finger. Her nipple pebbled in his wake. When he moaned, she closed her eyes and pressed his palm over her breast so he could cup her womanly flesh. She wanted him to take her nib into his mouth and suck.

Arching into his hand, she murmured, "That feels good."

Without prompting, he repeated the action on her other breast. Now, the need between her legs was the only thing she could think about. Opening her eyes, she slowly pulled his shirt off his shoulders. He unclasped his cufflinks and the shirt slipped off.

He's gorgeous.

Colton Mitus was masculine perfection. With a delicate touch, she trailed her fingers over his broad, hard shoulders, bulging biceps and defined triceps. Pressing her hands flush against his hard, sculpted pecs, she dragged her fingers through his sprinkling of chest hair. His torso was a glorious slab of granite that nipped in at the hips.

On a breathy moan, she tongued his pink nipples, one at a time, while loosening his pants. They dropped and she slipped her hands inside his black cotton boxers. As she knelt, she pulled them over his erection and down his legs.

His massive cock stood proud and ready. With one hand, she cradled his balls and wrapped her fingers around his thick, hard shaft.

"You feel good," he said. "I like how you touch me." His eagerness trickled out and she ran her fingertip over his smooth pink head so that it glistened. His smoldering gaze turned her insides to liquid. He slid his hands into her hair, grabbing fistfuls. "Taste me."

It had been years since she'd taken a man into her mouth. She eased his head inside and ran her tongue over the smooth skin.

He bit out a low, deep groan. "Oh, Brigit."

Hearing him say her name triggered a maelstrom of passion. Moaning, she pushed his shaft deeper and sucked. Evil tasted good. It would be easy to unleash her pent-up inhibitions until he exploded in her mouth. But this man didn't deserve *that*, so she slowed to a stop and pulled off.

A far-away drunken look lit up his handsome face. She started to wipe her glistening mouth, but he grasped her hand, pulled her to him, and devoured her in a hungry kiss. His wet shaft pressed against her belly. She couldn't wait to take him inside her.

He knelt in front of her and stared into her eyes. Though captivated by his essence, she liked seeing him on his knees at her feet. With a delicate touch, she fingered the hair from his eyes. As she pulled her hand away, he kissed it. Evil was definitely a charmer.

His penetrating gaze floated over her breasts. With his warm breath caressing her tummy, he blazed a path of sensual kisses down to her panties. No other man had *ever* made her feel so unhinged and she quivered from his tender touch.

Moving at a snail's pace, he covered her bottom with his large hands and kissed her sweet spot through the lace. As the anticipation consumed her, she kept reminding herself to breathe. Peering into her eyes, his dilated pupils were half hidden behind heavy lids. "My turn."

Oh. Yes.

One quick tug and her panties landed on the floor. He ran his fingers down her thighs, pressed his face to her pubic hair and kissed the hood of her clitoris. She was a mass of explosive nerves and he'd barely touched her. Like a coiled cat, she was ready to pounce.

Nudging her legs apart, he stroked her with his tongue. Long deep licks, light quick flicks. She moaned and tugged his hair.

"Mmm." He pinned her with a searing gaze. "Your pearl is perfect."

Ohmygod. Her knees wobbled. She thrust her hips toward him and fisted chunks of hair. As he ran his tongue along her opening and over her clit, she started losing control. Chugging in air, she rested her knees against his chest for support.

He slid two fingers inside her, thrusting in and out while his tongue circled over her tender mound. She groaned, loudly, and gyrated against his face. Tiny yellow stars floated into view, then disappeared when she remembered to breathe.

"You're dripping wet and taste so good."

At the sound of his hypnotic voice, she opened her eyes. Her juices slicked his mouth. Never having seen anything so sexy, her knees buckled. He grabbed her hips to steady her, then tongued her with fast, hard strokes. Moaning, he thrust his fingers back inside.

His guttural sounds crashed through her ears. Then everything blurred into a blinding frenzy, the orgasm ripping through her. Crying out, she convulsed wildly against him, surrendering to the pounding waves of ecstasy.

Slowly, she floated back and opened her eyes. When her gaze found his, he stood and wrapped his arms around her, devouring her in a kiss that went on and on. Boneless, she relaxed into him, unable to support her weight.

As if she were his, he carefully removed her stilettos, scooped her up, and laid her on the bed. Crawling over her, he smiled. "Nothing snarky?"

Fighting a grin, she replied, "Not at the moment, but it's temporary, I assure you."

He gave her a lingering kiss, then lay sideways, facing her. "There it is."

"There's what?"

"A glimpse of your beautiful smile. Well worth my efforts."

Though she tried smothering her expression, she couldn't. As soon as she rolled toward him, he stroked her cheek with the back of his fingers, caressed her shoulder and breasts, then thumbed her engorged nipples. Adrenaline streaked through her. She wanted his mouth locked on her nipples and his hard shaft inside her. And she wanted all of him all night long.

As his fingers trailed her heated skin, she soaked up his beauty, hoping that, like a camel drinking his fill of water, she would quench her insatiable thirst for him. When their lustful night ended and she was left with only a memory, she could call upon her overflowing reserves.

With a light hand on her chin, he tilted her face toward his and kissed her. Their tender exchange soon turned ravenous. Panting, he reached into his night table drawer. With the condom packet in hand, he asked, "Do we need this?"

Medical reasons kept her on the pill, but sheathing him was necessary. A thin layer of latex shielded her from feeling *him* inside her. Refusing to permit that level of intimacy, she murmured, "Yes."

Lying on his back, he rolled it on. She straddled him. Letting the anticipation build, they stared into each other's eyes for what seemed like an eternity.

Then she rose up and took him in hand, positioned him at her opening and in one gloriously fluid movement took him inside her. He moaned. She cried out. Her body flooded with wetness and she closed her eyes, the pleasure overwhelming her. At long last, he was deep inside her and she had never felt more alive. Never.

She opened her eyes to find him admiring her body. Slowly, so she could appreciate his long, thick shaft, she glided on his hardened length. Somewhere in the back of her mind, this felt like more than a casual one-night hookup.

"You feel fucking phenomenal." His voice jolted her back. *One night. That's all.*

As she traced his lips with her index finger, her insides clamped around his straining cock. In and out, again and again, until their bodies found their rhythm and moved as one. He cupped her breasts and pinched her nipples. She pushed her breasts into his hands, begging for more, harder, faster.

So. Much. Pleasure. *Everywhere.*

And then the mounting ecstasy overtook her. She threw her head back and cried out, "Ah, I'm coming."

He grabbed her hips and thrust, hard, released a long, guttural moan, and came.

Shattered, she collapsed on him. He tipped her face toward his and kissed her. The more she kissed him, the more she wanted to kiss him. She couldn't stop.

With his hardness still buried deep inside her, he wrapped her back like a warm, cozy blanket. She'd had sex with the enemy and she liked it.

She liked it a lot.

13

INSATIABLE

COLTON COULDN'T GET BACK in bed fast enough. The Brigit Farnay with the guarded, chilly demeanor was nothing like the sensual, erotic one waiting for him in his bed. This Brigit was insatiable. The more he gave her, the more she wanted. He exited the bathroom and slid under the covers.

Within minutes of caressing her silky skin, he hardened. This time, she rolled on the condom and he wasted no time doing something useful with his boner. He'd pinned her beneath him, his shaft burrowed inside her core. Captive, she'd raised her arms over her head and he gripped them at the wrists with one hand. The more she struggled to break free, the tighter he squeezed.

"Let me go." She gazed into his eyes.

"No." He withdrew and tunneled inside her.

"Ahhh. Yes." She bucked her hips. "You shouldn't be doing this to me."

"I should and I am." With his free hand, he stroked the side of her naked body, letting his hand linger over the swell of her breast.

"You're holding me against my will." She struggled to free her arms.

"Am I hurting you?" He stopped moving.

"What?"

"I need to know you're okay."

With half-closed eyelids, she cracked a lazy smile. "This is me, way better than okay. I like our game of control."

"And here I thought *control* would be our bone of contention."

"Oh, it definitely is, but for now, the only bone that matters is yours, inside me, which is exactly where it should be."

A relieved smile spread over his face. He felt drunk from the excessive firing of endorphins. The sex high bordered on addictive. *She feels that good.* He could do this with her all night, and from the looks of things, they would be. For someone who battled for control, she seemed eager for his in bed. He kissed her, hard, then resumed his slow, deep thrusting. She released a long, low moan, and flung her legs around his back.

"I'm the one trapped now," he said.

Hot, gorgeous Brigit Farnay was all his, all night long. Picking up speed, he thrust harder. She gasped, and then everything intensified. Her grunts and panting echoed in his ears. Her body writhed and squirmed beneath him. She was about to come again. And so was he.

Breathing fast, he tugged on her nipple with his teeth. Then, hard, fast flicks with his tongue that matched his intense thrusts.

"Oh, my God," she cried, shuddering beneath him.

Thrusting to her end, he plunged his tongue into her mouth and slipped his arm beneath her back. Her insides squeezed his cock and waves of ecstasy tore through him. Groaning, he came with more intensity than he had the first time. Being with her felt fucking fantastic.

"I can't get enough of you," he said between breaths. He relaxed his taut muscles and the full weight of his frame pressed on her petite body. A coo escaped her lips. Without withdrawing he repositioned himself, then raised his head and smiled. And again, she returned his smile with no additional prompting. Her flushed face, her sparkling eyes, and that cute grin were as much of a reward as the sex.

He released her wrists and she dropped her legs from around his torso. He kissed her and then kissed her again, until they were breathless once more. He pulled out. Hated doing that. He could have stayed nestled inside her, but he had something fun in store and wanted to get right to it.

"Don't move a muscle. I'll be right back." He retreated into the bathroom.

Since Brigit wasn't his wealth manager yet, he'd not broken his rule. But after tonight he'd never have sex with her again. With that in mind, he was damn well going to make the most of their time together. He exited the bathroom and slipped beneath the covers. Her back was to him, so he spooned close, covered her thigh with his hand and kissed her shoulder. "You're so damn sexy."

She didn't reply, but her back muscles relaxed against his chest. Knowing she was comfortable in his bed and in his arms said plenty. They lay quietly for a few moments until she rolled onto her stomach. Her mussed hair fell freely around her face and she peeked at him through her long eyelashes. *So pretty.* He liked her playful. Sweeping her hair from her shoulder, he rested his lips on her heated skin.

"Game over?" she asked.

"No." He pulled a handful of ties from his bedside drawer and tossed them on the bed. "I'm going to tie you up and eat you. Pick your poison."

A flash of something dark replaced the spark in her eyes. Fear? No, more like the frostiness she'd displayed when he met her. *Fuck.* The last thing he wanted to do was ruin the moment. "The ties are optional." He waggled his eyebrows. "Think about it. I'll be right back."

He padded into the kitchen. If Colton knew about anything, it was raw, meaningless fucking. Hedonistic pleasure with no strings attached was more his style. This night with Brigit was nothing like that. But even so, the sex stopped after tonight.

He pressed a small bowl against the icemaker and the crescent cubes tumbled out. Returning to the bedroom, he sat next to her on the edge of the bed, planted a long, luscious kiss on her lips, then gazed into her eyes. With a mischievous grin she selected four ties.

"Good choice." He tied her wrists and ankles to each of the bedposts.

"I can wriggle out of these."

"I know. But I want you relaxed. You and I both know that once I get started, you won't want to go *anywhere*." He cocked an eyebrow.

"Look at me." She flipped him off with both hands.

He grinned. "I can't wait."

The sparkle returned to her eyes. *Much better.*

She was spread-eagle, his for the taking, and he paused to admire her feminine form. Soft, kissable shoulders. Beautiful, full breasts with pert nipples that begged to be sucked. Though she lay on her back, his balls tightened just thinking about her curvy ass. He loved a woman with muscular legs and hers were the perfect proportion to the rest of her frame. Fit and fantastic. He started to harden.

Planked over her, he kissed her neck, letting his lips linger on her tender skin. And she rolled her head back, giving him complete access to the vulnerable spot over her pulse. Every several seconds a moan escaped from the back of her throat. Her sexy sounds drove him wild. But his needs would wait.

He liked teasing her until she melted with pleasure. There was something different about being with Brigit. But he wasn't about to analyze the situation. He was having too much fucking fun.

"Mmm." Her raspy sounds hit him where it mattered. His throbbing dick.

He fondled her breast and pinched her nipple between his

thumb and index finger until she gasped. Leaning down, he covered her erect nipple with his mouth, flicking his tongue across it.

"Oh, you feel good," she murmured. "I like the way you kiss me there."

He loved how she responded to his touch, how open she was to him and how eager she was for more. After planting a smoldering kiss on her lips, he said, "Tell me what you want."

"Fuck me with your mouth and make me come again."

Her unexpected dirty talk made his balls ache. He wanted to drive himself inside her and fuck her into next week. "With pleasure."

Taking his time, he kissed, licked and caressed her body, familiarizing himself with her curves and dips, her soft skin and sweet fragrance. Her flushed cheeks and sexy moans sent zings of adrenaline to his scrotum. With his gaze pinned on her, he leaned down and licked her pink, tender folds. Damn, she tasted good.

Another throaty moan leapt from her. He buried his tongue inside her until she squirmed and tugged on the restraints. While sucking and licking, he slid two fingers inside.

"Ohhhhh, yeah," she cried.

"Ahh, so wet and so soft," he whispered.

On a loud groan, she clenched around his fingers.

"Mmm, you want me inside you, don't you?"

"So badly." He was taking her, licking her, penetrating her with his tongue and lapping her clitoris. "Ohhhhh, fuck, Colton, you feel—"

He slipped a crescent-shaped ice cube inside her and the freezing shock sent her over the edge. Shuddering and yanking on the ties, she cried out, the orgasm shattering her. Her breathy erotic sounds made him want to take her again and again until her essence seeped into his dreams.

"I. Need. You. Inside. Me," she blurted between breaths.

As he started to untie her ankles, she panted, "No, leave them."

"Are you sure?"

"Yes," she said. *"Now."*

Colton couldn't roll on a condom fast enough. There was nothing he liked more than a gorgeous, smart, sassy woman commanding him to fuck her.

14

SLIPPERY WHEN WET

B RIGIT STRUGGLED TO STAY awake. She had to draw the line *somewhere*. The music had ended hours ago and the silence, along with Colton's slow, rhythmic breathing, lulled her to dreamland. Having sex with Colton was bad enough, but snuggling?

Saturday's first light streamed through the windows. *We pulled an all-nighter. Crazy marathon sex with the one man I shouldn't even be speaking with.* After extracting herself from his embrace, she turned around. He looked peaceful, angelic even, his disheveled hair framing his handsome face. She raised her hand to caress his stubbly cheek.

No! She recoiled.

Trying not to make a sound, she slipped out of bed and quietly closed the bathroom door. The white marble double vanity with its shiny, gold faucets provided ample room for two. The glass-enclosed shower housed two heads and a marble bench built into the stall.

While the water heated, she unclipped what hair was still piled on her head. *I look like I've just had best sex of my life.* Wild hair, flushed cheeks and chest, and a brightness to her eyes that defied getting zero sleep. *Figures.*

If Sleeping Beauty had been *any* other man besides Colton Mitus, she'd trip over herself to crawl back into bed for more. But her fairy tale evening was over, so she stepped into the stall and stood beneath the spraying water. The more she thought about what she'd done, the angrier she became. By sleeping with Colton, she'd complicated an already dicey situation. If he offered her the position, would Seth hold her job over her head if she refused to work for him? And how awkward would it be if she were forced to work at Mitus after their wild night together? *Well, I'm not working here, so stop worrying.*

If she left Porter, Gabriel and Sethfield, not every client would follow. It could take years to rebuild her business. The more money she made, the more Francesco stock she could purchase. Her stomach roiled at the reality of her situation. *What the hell have I done?*

"Brigit?"

Her eyes flew open.

"May I join you?" Colton asked.

Yes! No! She had to push him away, ensuring he wouldn't offer her the job. A stabbing pain pummeled her chest, but things had to end. Here and now. She pointed. "Over there."

He stood under the opposing faucet, the water sluicing his hard body. Everything dry became slippery wet. *Everything* included the condom that covered his straining erection. *Oh, this was a bad, bad idea.*

He tilted his head back and raked his hands through his hair. Wet, dry, vertical, supine. Any position, *all* positions suited him. He looked fine. Damn fine. But she'd had her fun. Time to shut this down. "We made a mistake. Got carried away. Let's forget this ever happened." *I'll never forget this.* "It would be best if we didn't—"

Before she could finish her sentence, he'd cradled the back of her neck in one hand while he snaked his arm around her waist and pressed into the small of her back with the other. His erection pressed against her abdomen. Their slippery bodies sandwiched together were a recipe for *disaster*.

He kissed her. His mouth lingered. A powerful kiss laid on her lips with the gentleness of a lamb and the sensuality of a man consumed with overwhelming passion. The kiss ended but he didn't relinquish his hold. As if her hands were moving independently of her brain, she placed them midway on his chest between his shoulders and pecs. The best spot to push him away. Only she didn't.

For the first time, his unruly hair wasn't masking his eyes and she longed to trace the curve of his cheekbones and jutting jawline. How could one man evoke so much raw emotion?

"You choose, then." He broke the silence. "A career at Mitus, or a weekend in Paris."

"Forced choices don't work on me, Colton. I agreed to meet with you as a favor to Seth. Favor delivered, and then some, but you and me—we're done."

"You haven't pushed me away because you want this as much as I do."

The simmering fire between them burst into a blaze of white-hot heat. In a flash, his lips pressed against hers while the water pounded their hungry bodies. Before she could stop herself, she wrapped her arms around his neck, pushed her tongue into his mouth and deepened the kiss. Moaning into him, she raked her fingernails down his broad, muscular back.

Breathing hard, he pulled away, his eyes brimming with lust. "Turn around and spread your legs."

Refusing to budge, she stood beneath the pounding water jets.

He spun her around and nudged her legs apart with his knee. "Put your hands on the wall."

His bossiness didn't work in the real world, but here, she secretly craved it. Leaning forward, she pressed her hands against the marble. Steadying her, he grabbed her hip with one hand and plunged inside her hot, wet core.

"Ahhhh." A strangled cry left her lips.

With an aggressiveness that made her moan with delight, he fondled her breasts and squeezed her nipples. The sharp sting of pain heightened her arousal and she started gyrating. He bit her shoulder and growled, his grunts making her clit throb. The build was intense, fast, and powerful. And then he reached around and rubbed her.

"Oh, God." She gasped for breath, the sexual haze making thought impossible. "So. Good. Everywhere."

Her knees buckled as euphoria exploded through her shaking body. Unable to hold herself up, her hands slipped on the wall. He wrapped his arm around her waist, thrust hard and groaned through his orgasm. She quivered from the sounds he made as he came inside her.

"I can't get enough of you," he whispered in her ear.

When he withdrew, she turned to face him. His ravenous need bore into her. Terrified, she slammed her eyes shut. She wasn't terrified of *him*, she was terrified of their passion, their intensity, and their blazing hot connection.

"Look at me," he said.

She opened her eyes and wiped the water from her lashes.

"Did you like that?"

Don't answer him.

"Brigit, please."

Don't do it.

He cajoled her with a smile. A breathtaking, just-got-fucked-again smile.

Damn him. "I loved it," she whispered.

He wrapped his arms around her and kissed her.

Sheltered in their cocoon, she felt safe. Something she hadn't felt in a long, long time. "But we can never, ever do that again."

"Agreed," he said.

15

BAIT AND SWITCH

A SUNNY GLOW BRIGHTENED the horizon. Though Brigit was both an enticement and a challenge, Colton needed to refocus his attention. Francesco Company executives were making noise. Time to free up thirty million so production of Crockett Boxes could begin. Knowing which of his investments to keep and which to sell wasn't his forte. That was Ms. Farnay's specialty, amongst other things. *Going forward, she's off-limits.*

The faster he could onboard Brigit, the sooner Crockett Boxes would revitalize Francesco and revolutionize the wireless industry. Now with MobiCom breathing down his neck, the need for urgency skyrocketed.

In silence, they pulled on their fancy duds from the previous evening. The lack of chatter brought no awkwardness on his part. Brigit, on the other hand, seemed mired in thought. That woman was impossible to read. "Brigit, how about I make us French toast?" he asked.

She blinked, then shifted her attention in his direction. "Uh, no."

"Then I'll take you out to breakfast." He dropped his cufflinks into his pants pocket and rolled up his sleeves to just below his elbows.

With one shoe on, she'd stopped to watch him. Something held her attention, but he had no idea what. "There's a great hole-in-the-wall in Arlington that serves a mean eggs Benedict."

She slipped her bare foot into her stiletto. "Sounds quaint. I'll pass."

"Why don't I scramble eggs at your place, then?"

She laughed. "My place? That is *so* not happening."

Although he was miffed at how she took pleasure in her steady stream of rejections, her spunkiness fueled his drive to win.

He tied his dress shoes and straightened, then raked his damp hair from his eyes. Already dressed, she sauntered toward him. With each step he envisioned her mouth on his, her body draped around his, while their slow, erotic connection climbed to a frenetic pace. She stopped inches away, her almond eyes filled with frisky energy. She turned. The dress needed zipping. *Damn.*

Unable to resist, he ran his fingers down the length of her back, appreciating her silky skin. Her breath caught. It would be all too easy to pull her into an embrace and begin again.

No. We're done.

He slid the zipper, cloaking her slinky body. Losing her in this way left him with an unexpected emptiness. He shook his head. Sleep deprivation had muddled his brain.

He touched her shoulder. A simple courtesy to let her know he was finished, and then he stepped away. Seeking the best for his business wasn't new, but hiring a strong-willed person was. While his loyal staff was comprised of intelligent, hardworking individuals, they did as he instructed. No balking, no pushback. How much could this change of strategy cost him? He was about to find out. "Brigit, the wealth manager position is yours. When can you start?"

She pivoted, the playful spark gone. "I'm declining your offer, Colton. Nothing has changed."

He clenched his jaw. She was being so damn stubborn. While he needed her expertise, this would be a great career move for her, as well.

She glided past him and into the living room. Suppressing the urge to roll his eyes, he followed, but sank into the recliner, prepared to stall her. She paced in front of the sofa.

Here comes serious.

Cocking her fist on her hip, she stopped in front of him. Her eyes narrowed and the feisty woman he'd met in Seth's office returned. "It's my understanding that you've had six wealth advisors in the past decade. Most resigned because you're impossible and incorrigible. Their words, not mine."

He relaxed against the crinkled leather and remained silent. Best to let her regurgitate her issues, so he'd know what challenges to overcome.

"From what I've learned, you rarely agreed to their proposals and made financial decisions based on what *you* thought best. When you made poor choices and lost money from bad investments, you blamed them, even if they'd advised against your suggestions. Those business tactics make my head hurt. I've worked too hard and come too far to work with a hot-headed tyrant like you."

He tapped the armrest, but said nothing. She was nowhere near done.

Brigit pinned him with a hard stare. "It's one thing to *let* you boss me around in bed, or in the shower, but I'm the expert when it comes to wealth management. You are not. My recommendations are the culmination of a well-thought-out strategy with only your best interest in mind. If you won't allow me to do my job, which by your own admission I'm the best at, why on earth would I work with you?"

Fuck, she had a point.

"It's my understanding that your staff's investments haven't been managed because you monopolized Todd's time. I'll tell Seth. Expectations with potential wealth managers must be set. You employ a staff of twenty, therefore time must be set aside quarterly to meet with everyone."

"Todd managed." He strummed his fingers over the worn arm of the chair.

"No, Colton, he did not. News flash. The world doesn't revolve around you."

Although frustrated she'd declined his offer, he was pleased to hear her champion his staff. "You're negotiating with me *already*? I don't see how you're in a position to do that."

She cocked an eyebrow. "Negotiations began the moment you laid eyes on me in the conference room. Others may cut you slack, but I will not."

And then he knew. She wanted control, respect, and autonomy. If he wanted her, he'd have to play by her rules. This was definitely a first. His heart thundered in his ears. Handing over control, no matter how seemingly small, made his blood boil. There was no such thing as insignificant power.

Colton had to tread with caution. Brigit Farnay was quite the contender. If he gave her an inch, she'd want more. A smile ghosted across his lips. Time to roll out his plan. "Your presentation was spot-on and your analysis of MobiCom was exactly what I needed."

Gripping her hips, the hint of a smile danced on her lips. *Nice.* Even tough-as-nails Brigit Farnay wasn't impervious to a compliment.

"And therein lies the problem," she said. "I followed your orders. How are you going to manage when you give me another unreasonable request with zero turnaround time or I disagree with your investment strategies?"

As he paused, he studied her face. She was so damn sexy all fired up. "Brigit, let's trial this for ninety days."

"You really know how to entice a girl." On a *harrumph*, she crossed her arms. "Try this on for size. Trust my judgment and give me control over your wealth."

Control over my wealth. Colton gritted his teeth. From a young age, he'd learned that control and power went hand in hand. The room closed in. He needed air.

"Colton. *Colton.*" Her voice snapped him out of his thoughts. "I'll call a taxi."

"No, Chad will drive you home after breakfast." Rising to full stature, Colton raked his hair out of his face. "Negotiations aren't over."

When they stepped outside the chilly October dawn air wicked away the thin line of perspiration on his brow. His head pounded. Needing help displayed weakness. But what alternative did he have? Brigit's professional expertise was key to ensuring Francesco's success.

Shivering, she hugged herself. He wanted to warm her body with his, but hiring her meant hands off. Instead, he draped his suit jacket over her shoulders. The oversized clothing hung like a boxy dress. *Adorable.*

Though she whispered her appreciation, she refused to make eye contact.

Under a dark cloud of unresolved conflict, they continued up the porch stairs and into the quiet kitchen. He owed no one an explanation, but in this particular situation, it was better they not be seen together in last night's duds. He glanced at the time on the wall clock. Just after seven.

"Taylor will escort you to breakfast at eight thirty."

In a thickening silence, they walked upstairs and down the hall to the guest suite. Brigit opened the door, crossed into the room, and turned to face him. Her shamrock green eyes were no indication she'd gotten no sleep. "Last night was—"

"Yes, it was," he said.

"Seth can assign a temporary broker to handle any trades you might make, based on my recommendations." She handed him his suit jacket and started to close the bedroom door. "Goodbye, Colton."

He jammed his foot against it. "Why do you defy me at every opportunity?"

Holding his gaze, she whispered, "Because you love it."

Her pouty lips were inches away. On impulse he leaned in to kiss her, but she shut the door in his face.

16

THE MORNING AFTER

BRIGIT LEANED AGAINST THE back of the closed bedroom door
and slowly inhaled. Once her lungs had filled, she let the air
seep out with a sigh. The sex high she'd only read about had her
head in the clouds, courtesy of the man she'd done nothing but
despise for five long years. Though Colton's offer was financially
tempting, working with him would only further his needs while
putting a hard stop to her own. *And who in their right mind teams up
with the enemy?*

She tugged on charcoal leggings and slipped into a camisole and
long gray sweater. Blow-drying her damp hair, she strategized next
steps. A quick getaway, then a text to Seth, letting him know the
arrangement wouldn't work. By noon she'd have her life back on
track.

After setting her phone alarm, she flopped onto the guest bed.
An hour and a half later, she woke and brushed her teeth.

At eight thirty, Taylor escorted her to breakfast. "Did you have
fun last night?"

Sex-crazed fun. "Yes, thanks." Brigit waited for a snide comment,
a sideways glance or a snicker, but Taylor said nothing more.

A tall and fit man covered in chef's whites whirred around the spacious kitchen. He wore a small pierced hoop in his left earlobe, and his salt and pepper hair peeked out from the sides of his toque.

"Our chef, Elliott Towne," Taylor said. "Elliott, meet Brigit Farnay."

"Welcome to my little slice of heaven!" Elliott exclaimed. "Any food allergies, my dear?"

"Good to meet you, Elliott. No, none."

"I don't cook for the staff on weekends, but a little birdie told me we had a *special* guest. I whipped up a few quiches along with some other goodies."

"Smells delicious." His big hazel eyes reminded her of her mom. "My mom made a killer quiche." Brigit's cheeks heated and she pursed her lips. *Where did that come from?* She never spoke of her parents.

"Well, I hope mine measures up." He smiled warmly. "Tell me you're starting soon. Not that I don't love working here, but I'd like to retire *before* I'm dead."

Brigit laughed. "Gotta love a man with hardy goals."

"Once you've started and have settled Colton down—" Elliott chortled. "Rewind. Once you've settled Colton's *finances* down, please review my retirement fund first. That account has dwindled to chump change."

Smiling sweetly, she followed Taylor to the coffee cart next to the dark granite counter. "Coffee or tea?" Taylor asked.

"Coffee." Brigit pulled a white mug and Taylor filled it.

"Sugar and cream?" Taylor pointed.

"No, thanks." The hearty aroma wafted in Brigit's direction and she took a sip. Hot and strong. *This'll clear the cobwebs.*

Brigit stopped using cream and sugar when her parents died. If her parents could drink their java black, so could she. She wanted to preserve their memory. Even the little things helped keep her connected.

Taylor plopped on a cushy chair at the long walnut table and Brigit eased in beside her. The sweet sting between her legs reminded her of Colton. Was there no escaping that man? As Elliott and Shane whisked and stirred, baked and flipped, she questioned whether she'd fit in. *No, no I wouldn't. Stop thinking.*

Six hickory leather chairs lined the center island. Eye-catching ruby and peach glass lights hung from the ceiling, casting a soft glow on the shiny granite surface while winking copper pots dangled from an overhead rack. Even the professional-grade stainless steel appliances and a restaurant-size refrigerator didn't detract from the charm and homey feel of the room. But the harsh light of day brought the realization that she was enjoying another fantastic meal with Colton's staff. The situation seemed a little too cozy for her liking.

A group of seven trickled in and Taylor reintroduced Brigit. The second Elliott announced breakfast was ready they swarmed the center island like starving children. If the spread was designed to impress, it was a rousing success. Spinach quiches, hash browns, blueberry pancakes, chicken and apple sausage links and oven-fresh cinnamon muffins lined the island.

"Ryan, dude, Elliott made this for *Brigit*." Red tapped his shoulder. "You need to step aside for our guest."

"It's fine." Brigit waited to fill her plate, then slipped back into her seat.

"So, Brigit, did Colton make you an offer?" Vanessa asked, seated across the table.

"He did." Brigit buttered her muffin.

"Are you giving two weeks or starting Monday?" Red asked.

"I declined," Brigit replied.

"Shit," Red mumbled.

"Stop eating my food." Elliott winked.

Brigit smiled at him.

"I commend Brigit," Vanessa said. "If it's not the right fit, why throw her life into turmoil? Colton's a handful. No one knows that better than me."

"Save it," Red mumbled.

Brigit braced for another cackle, but silence prevailed. Vanessa's smug expression soured her stomach. Why would Vanessa care who Colton hired?

Loud laughter interrupted her thoughts. Colton and Mr. Muscles entered the kitchen play fighting like two little boys. She couldn't help but crack a smile.

Colton wore a long-sleeved white running shirt and black running pants. Snug material designed to wick away perspiration. And there wasn't a drop of sweat on that man, anywhere. His windblown hair and reddened cheeks made her heart patter wildly. That man was a whole lotta yummy.

Her gaze roamed over his sculpted arms and down his rock-solid torso. By the time she feasted on his thick thighs, she was plain old gawking. Thoughts of those strong legs beneath her as she straddled his steely length had her fidgeting in her seat. *Stop.*

To distract herself, she turned her attention to the other man. Football-player big with the face of a surfer, he wore basketball shorts and a cut-off T-shirt. But it was his bedhead blond hair and dimples that stood out, even over that hard body. *Those two are serious eye candy.*

Colton scanned the faces at the table until he found who he was looking for.

Brigit.

His expression turned from carefree to fiery. A ripple of excitement burst through her and she crossed her legs. The soreness made her flinch. "Brigit," Colton said, "this is Chad Wright, my—"

"Human cyborg creation," Chad said, and they started laughing all over again.

If things had been different, Colton might have captured her heart with his playful nature. But they weren't and he hadn't. He was still the man who'd snatched her family's business, treated her with total disrespect, and guarded her company as if his life depended on it.

Chad got his laughter under control and extended his hand.

"Good to finally meet you, Brigit. I handle security for Mitus. I hope you start soon because this guy"—he punched Colton's shoulder—"hasn't stopped talk—"

"Brigit," Colton interrupted. "Did you have a restful sleep?"

"I slept on a slab of granite, but Elliott and Shane's delicious breakfast made up for my restless night." Though her face warmed, she held Colton's gaze.

His mouth quirked up, but he cleared his throat and the smile vanished. "Once again, we disagree. A firm mattress provides a more restful sleep. Studies show hardness ranks high."

Chad chuckled, his dimples front and center. "When did you become a sleep expert?"

"In fact, the Mitus mattress might be the reason you change your mind and agree to come on board." Colton kept his fiery gaze pinned on Brigit.

"I think I'd like a new mattress," Elliott chimed in.

When Colton glanced at the food spread on the island, Brigit guzzled her ice water hoping to cool her internal thermostat.

"I'll have breakfast in my sitting room," Colton said.

"It's Saturday," Chad said. "Your scepter wields no power."

"I'll bring you something." Vanessa set down her fork. "Be up shortly."

"Thank you, Vanessa," said Colton. "Someone cares about me."

"Always." Jumping, Vanessa filled a plate.

Colton excused himself. Like a dutiful servant Vanessa followed, a plate of food and a mug of coffee balanced on a tray. Chad wolfed down a piece of quiche while standing at the island, then bolted.

After breakfast, Taylor escorted Brigit upstairs and waited while she packed. In addition to leaving the couture gowns in the closet, she left the stunning diamond pendant on the bureau. She needed no reminders of that man or their torrid night.

Taylor picked up the necklace. "Colton bought this for you. You should take it."

107

Chad knocked as he poked his head inside the open door. "I'm driving you home. You ready?"

"All set."

Wearing khakis, a polo shirt and lightweight jacket, Chad collected her computer and roller bags. Slinging her handbag over her shoulder, she followed into the hallway. Just then, Colton's bedroom door opened and Vanessa emerged with the tray. Brigit's heart dipped.

"Bye bye, Brigit," Vanessa called, sounding a little too happy.

As they headed toward the grand staircase, Brigit waved. In the foyer, Taylor opened the front door and Brigit turned to admire the home one last time. Seth had been right. The house and its furnishings were exquisite. While Chad secured Brigit's bags in the trunk of the Bentley, Taylor walked her to the car.

"It would be great if you worked here," Taylor said. "You got the message loud and clear. Your wealth management expertise is definitely needed. Work aside, I like you, Brigit. You have an invincible energy." She leaned close. "That's what Colton needs."

Brigit knew *exactly* what that man needed. Taylor hugged her, then opened the back door. After sliding into the backseat, Brigit said, "Oh, no. Not you again."

17

THE SEXY RIDE HOME

B RIGIT'S HEART LODGED IN her throat. Colton's sly grin sent a sexual jolt pinging through her. The familiar scent of his just-washed hair wafted in her direction and her insides came alive. Damn traitorous body.

He grinned. "I knew you'd be pleased to see me."

"Thrilled," she deadpanned. "What are you doing here?"

"After we take you home, we're golfing at my club." His khaki pants and navy blue jersey outlined his solid frame. She fought the urge to run her fingers over his scruffy cheeks, pull him close and kiss him. *Enough.*

"I hope you packed the necklace." Colton pushed a button and the privacy divider rose.

"Oh, sure," Chad said. "Shut me out of the conversation, like I'm not even—"

Brigit flipped her gaze back to Colton. "No, I left it."

"Rejecting my gift. Rejecting my job offer. I'm going to have to work harder at getting you to say *yes*."

"I agreed to plenty, if memory serves me."

"What do you want, Brigit?"

Spinning her bracelet so the gold lobster clasp was visible, she shifted her gaze past him and out the window as trees and large brick estates blurred by. What did she want?

She wanted to go back in time and right a terrible wrong. She should have listened to her parents and worked at Francesco right after college, like they'd planned. If she had, they'd still be alive and Francesco wouldn't be...

When he caressed her cheek with the back of his fingers, she blinked away the regretful thoughts. Though she wanted to let his titillating touch erase her loneliness, she removed his hand.

"You're driven, determined and need a challenge," he said. "Working at Mitus is the perfect fit."

"Yesterday you told me I was too strong-willed and too independent."

"A lot has transpired since yesterday."

Before she could process what was happening, he kissed her. And she didn't fight him. Nope, not at all. Relishing his tenderness, she closed her eyes. Instead of deepening the kiss, he pulled away. Leaving her wanting.

"I've made my intentions known." He paused while the energy vibrated around them. "I don't want anyone else Seth is going to recommend. I want you. And only you."

"I thought we agreed. No more kissing or touching or—"

"And we'll stop, as soon as you agree to manage my wealth."

"So, we're back to forced choices, again? If you think I've any interest in—"

This time he unbuckled and slid into the center. His large frame dwarfed the too-small space and his legs spilled onto either side. With his gaze cemented on her, he reached over and unsnapped her belt, gathered her in his arms and placed her on his lap.

The most she could utter was a whimper. With a gentle touch, he cupped her cheek and turned her face toward him. Raw intensity paired with his deep, dark eyes sent a wildfire raging through her. She knew the ecstasy he could bring her. And that made him a dangerous temptation.

Moving at a snail's pace, he ran his hand up her thigh, then back down. And then he repeated the motion. Up and down so very slowly. Every nerve ending came alive, tingling with anticipation of what he would do next. Unwilling to stop herself, she placed her hands on either side of his face and leaned close, but she didn't make contact with his lips. His whiskers prickled her palms and his minty breath stung her eyes.

He threaded his other hand through her hair, cupped the back of her neck and gave her a gentle nudge. Lip-to-lip contact was her tipping point. Brigit could have pushed him away, scrambled off his lap, broken the connection any number of ways, but she didn't. Closing her eyes only magnified his breath, roaring hard and fast in her ears.

The kiss turned ravenous. Her mind shorted. All she could do was absorb the erotic sensations. *More, I need more.* Straddling him, she placed her hands on the sides of his face and devoured him with another ferocious kiss. He slipped a hand beneath her sweater and cupped her braless breast.

"Oh, Brigit," he said between kisses.

Moaning, she ground against his erection. Her panties grew wet. Colton's powerful touch, his sexy smell, his delicious taste, and the way he made her feel magnified each breath, all sensation, the tiniest movement, every intention.

It would be easy to let go, to unravel. But she had to stick with the plan. Time to sever all ties. Sucking in a steadying breath, she grew still and ended the kiss. With a quick squeeze on her waist, he removed his hand from beneath her clothing.

"I can't control myself around you," he whispered. "What the hell is wrong with me?"

A smug smile spread over her face. "Ah, now that's a question I *can* answer." Why did he have to be so damn addictive? She tugged down her sweater and clambered off him, shielding herself with the seat belt.

"I can't hire you." He slid away, leaving her cold.

"Finally, we agree." But the relief quickly subsided, replaced by the unexpected sting of rejection.

"I can't hire you because I'm crazy attracted to you. That's not the kind of relationship I'll permit with my wealth manager."

"Then you'll have to work with someone else. Problem solved."

Chad tapped on the separation shield. They were parked in her driveway. That was the fastest forty minutes of her life. Opening the door, she turned back and stared into his eyes one final time. "I'll let Seth know."

She scooted up her walkway as Chad pulled her bags from the trunk. Her heart felt heavy, like this goodbye shouldn't be happening. *How ludicrous.* With a flick of her mane, she tossed the thought and slipped her key into the deadbolt. "Thank you for the ride, Chad. I can take it from here." Brigit turned and startled.

Colton held her bags. "I'll carry these inside for you."

Was there no escaping this man? As she stepped into her townhouse, she cried out, "Oh, my God!"

18

HOME INVASION

UNABLE TO FULLY COMPREHEND the devastation, Brigit stared in disbelief. Colton dropped her bags in her small foyer and pushed past. "What the hell happened?" he asked.

It looked like a tornado had ripped through her living room.

Chad burst in, his weapon drawn. "What the fucking fuck?" He quickly cleared the powder room, off the foyer.

"You can't clear her home alone," Colton said to Chad.

"Like hell I can't. Stay here." Chad flipped his gaze to Brigit. "Three-level townhome?"

"What? Uh-huh." With a trembling hand, she pointed. "Basement door is around the corner. Second set of stairs is off the living room."

Chad took off, leaving Brigit and Colton amid the debris. The furniture had been tossed, sofa cushions ripped to shreds, their innards scattered all over the floor like piles of snow. Books in the built-in had been pulled, pages ripped and strewn everywhere. Though the baby grand had been spared the wrath of the violent intruder, the piano bench cushion had been sliced several times and its legs broken off.

"This can't be real," she said, white-knuckling the piano.

A few moments later, Chad returned. "The house is clear," he said catching his breath.

In stark contrast to the living room, the dining room was undisturbed. Her table, chairs and china cabinet were untouched. She zombie-walked back into her living room, the sight impossible to absorb. This had to be a nightmare.

"Brigit, we've got to get you out of here." Colton pulled out his phone and dialed.

Moving at a snail's pace, she headed toward the kitchen, but Colton stepped in front to block her. "No, stay with me. This call will take a second."

"Who are you calling?"

"My cousin."

"My house is in shambles. Can you chat with your family later?" She stormed into the kitchen. "God, no."

Chad followed close on her heels.

"Tucker, I need your help," Colton said. "Seven twenty-four Zander Place, Georgetown. End unit townhome. Bentley's in the driveway." He waited. "How long?" He listened then ended the call.

"How's the rest of the house?" Colton asked.

"Basement is untouched. Upstairs was ransacked," Chad said.

"Brigit, do you own a gun?" Colton asked.

"No."

"Where are your knives?" Chad asked.

"They used to be on the counter in a knife wedge," she said. "They're probably in that huge pile on the floor, where my kitchen table used to be." The rush of emotion overtook her. Tears stung her eyes. Spinning away, she sucked in several stilted breaths. She would not cry. No way would she allow Colton to see her weak.

Gently pulling her into his arms, he stroked her back while she buried her face in his chest and fought the urge to sob. "I'm sorry this happened, Brigit. I'll do whatever's necessary to make this right for you."

Tearing herself from the security of his arms, she said, "Thank you, but you don't have to. I mean, we hardly know each other and —" She straightened up and swiped the lone tear.

"Let's find a knife and do a walk-through," Chad said.

"I thought you cleared my home," Brigit said.

"I don't like surprises," Colton said.

Brigit stared at the pile of broken dishes, shattered pieces of glassware, pots, pans, and silverware. *What a disastrous mess.* She handed a large knife to Colton.

After confirming the basement door lock had been picked, but nothing had been stolen, they headed upstairs. The guest room was destroyed. Mattress thrown against the window, shredded bed linens, scattered down feathers. Bureau drawers had been emptied and tossed. There was so much destruction they couldn't even enter.

"Oh, no," she whispered from the doorway. "This is unbelievable."

When they entered her bedroom, she gasped, then covered her mouth with her hand. Her bra and panty sets had been placed on her comforter in two neat rows.

"Did you do this?" Colton stared at her bed.

"No." Brigit's face warmed. Though humiliated that these men were staring at her intimate apparel, she was sickened that the intruder had gone through her things, then arranged them neatly on her bed. Grabbing the undergarments, she stuffed them into her drawer. She'd never wear them again, but she couldn't leave them on display.

"This is one effed-up dude." Chad stood in Brigit's bathroom.

"What is it?" As she bolted toward the doorway, adrenaline shot through her.

There was a note scribbled on the mirror with bar soap. *Sorry I missed you.*

Fear surged from her gut and gripped her around the throat as her insides twisted into a series of painful knots. Though scarcely able to breathe, she grabbed a towel and tried rubbing out the message. The harder she rubbed, the faster panic pumped through her bloodstream.

Vinny Ray.

Chad gently stopped her mid-stroke. "Easy. You're eliminating evidence."

She tugged away her hand, flipped on the faucet and drenched the end of the cloth. Now, frantically scrubbing, she blurred the words into a soapy froth. This was no random break-in. She'd been targeted. *No way. He's in prison.*

She'd confirmed that fact four months earlier through the D.A.'s office. Was it possible he'd escaped? And how had he found her after all these years? She dried the mirror and stared at her terrified reflection. Colton and Chad stood behind her, their eyes laced with concern.

Her nerves of steel had been reduced to rubble. She wasn't safe in her home. She wasn't safe *anywhere*. A chill skirted down her spine and she started shaking. Had she been at home, she'd be dead, but not before being raped and tortured.

Panicked, she had to get out of there. She pushed past both men and stood in her bedroom trying to think. *Where can I go?*

"Can we check your jewelry box?" Chad pointed to her bureau.

Feeling like a caged animal, Brigit nodded.

Using a tissue, Chad opened the lid.

"Anything missing?" Colton asked.

Brigit examined the contents. "I don't have much, but it's all there."

"Do you have someone you can stay with until your home is back in order and a security system has been installed?" Colton asked.

Think. Think! Where can I go? Could I stay with Kat or Shaniqua? No, I can't put them in danger.

Trembling, she rubbed her arms. "No, no one."

"Let's get you packed. You're moving into the mansion." Colton opened her closet door. "Suitcase in here?"

"What? No, you and Chad need to get going. You have plans, and a tee time, and a life." Her shoulders sagged.

"Leave?" He shook his head. "Not without you."

Brigit waved her hand around, like what had happened was no big deal. "I got burglarized. Happens all the time." *I could start over, in a new city.* Her chest tightened. She didn't want to run again.

"I'm not budging, Brigit. You can pack or I'll damn well do it for you." Colton retreated into her closet and emerged with a suitcase.

I can't move into Mitus Mansion. But what other choice did she have? At least she'd be safe behind the massive iron gates, and able to lie low until she had answers.

Before she could rationalize the many reasons why moving into Colton's home was a bad idea, she blurted, "If the wealth manager position is still on the table, I accept."

19

GET HER OUT

COLTON'S TEMPLES THROBBED. HE couldn't change his past, but he could damn well help Brigit today. He'd have her packed and out of there within an hour. "You've made the right decision, Brigit."

She'd agreed, albeit under horrific circumstances, to manage his wealth. With so much at stake regarding Francesco, he needed her head in the game. Would she be up to the challenge?

The devastation reminded him of the hell he'd spent years fighting to forget. Even two decades later the horrific images still seeped into his dreams. Demolished rooms in his parents' home and so much property taken. But in the end, what forever changed him and ultimately defined him was the lifeless body of his twin brother. A sharp pain pounded through his chest, but he pushed past. "Let's get you packed."

Brigit couldn't hide the utter fear in her eyes, but the scribbled message had given her away. Her past, already shrouded in mystery, had taken a dark turn. By insisting she move into his home, was he risking his staff's safety?

"Colt?" Tucker called.

"My cousin's here. Let's go talk to him." With a gentle touch, he guided her downstairs. Her body had gone rigid. More than likely, she was in shock.

"Hey, man, thanks for getting here so quickly." Colton hugged his older cousin.

"You betcha," Tucker said, then shook Chad's hand. "Good to see you. Premises cleared?"

"Twice," Chad said.

"Tuck, this is Brigit Farnay," said Colton. "She's agreed to be my new wealth manager. Brigit, this is Tucker Henninger of Henninger Investigations and Security."

Tall and sturdy, with a rugged appearance, Tucker's short, dirty blond hair and tanned skin were a stark contrast to his long-haired, fair-skinned cousin.

"Sorry we're meeting under these circumstances," Tucker said. "You wanna tell me what happened?"

"I...I walked in and found this." Brigit gestured with a sweep of her hand.

Her fingers trembled and Colton wanted to pull her into his arms and comfort her. Under the circumstances, she was keeping herself together damn well.

"Have you checked with neighbors?" Tucker asked.

She shook her head.

"Anything taken?"

"Nothing obvious like jewelry, but some of the rooms are—" She glanced into her living room. "I don't know."

"Called the police?"

Stepping back, Brigit hugged herself. "No."

"I'll call." Tucker dug out his phone from his jeans pocket.

"I'm not required to file a report," she said.

Tucker shifted his gaze to Colton.

Let it go, Tuck. With a subtle shake of his head, Colton hoped his by-the-book cousin would drop it. "We're taking Brigit back to the house as soon as she packs."

With his gaze fixed on Brigit, Tucker nodded. Colton could see him thinking, strategizing, sizing up Brigit and the situation. "Okay, no police," Tucker said. "How about we install grade-A locks and a security system?"

"Thank you." Brigit relaxed her stance.

Tucker glanced over his shoulder into the kitchen. "We'll salvage what we can."

She cleared her throat and squared her shoulders. "I've been through worse. I'll get through this."

Colton whipped his gaze to her. *Worse than this? Chad needs to keep digging.*

She handed Tucker her credit card. "I'll give you my phone number. Anything ruined can go. Only the piano has sentimental value."

Tucker took the card, but Colton plucked it from his cousin's hand. "You were on Mitus Conglomerate time. I'll take care of this."

"No," she said. "You aren't paying for my mistake...I mean, for *this.*"

She blames herself? What the hell is going on?

Tucker threw his hands into the air. "While you two kids work out the payment plan, I'm going to make some calls."

"Tuck, discretion please," said Colton.

"You got it." Tucker smiled reassuringly. "No worries, Brigit."

"Brigit, Chad and I will help you pack." Colton handed Tucker his credit card as the three retreated upstairs.

At the top of the flight, she paused. "You're going to a lot of trouble for me." She mustered a feeble smile. "You must really need a wealth manager."

I do, but I'm not abandoning you, either.

Back in her bedroom, Brigit pulled a storage container from beneath her bed, lifted the lid and sighed. The box was filled with photo albums and childhood keepsakes. A smile ghosted across her lips when she held the Barbie tucked in its original packaging.

"My sisters must have each had ten Barbies," Chad said. "Was she your favorite?"

Brigit looked up at the two men flanking her. "I was only allowed one. But she did have a kick-ass dream house and a fabulous wardrobe."

One Barbie? What was that all about? His sister had once owned a slew of dolls.

"I'll carry that for you," Chad said.

"No, thanks. I've got this one."

Under her instruction, Colton and Chad carried suits and several shoe boxes to the Bentley. "What is it with women and shoes?" Colton asked Chad as they loaded the vehicle.

"My sister told me that shoes complete the outfit." Chad stacked the boxes. "I told her a beer completes mine."

Back in Brigit's bedroom, Colton pulled her aside. "Since you're leaving your lingerie. I'll have Zoe get you whatever you need. She's my personal shopper. Did you meet her?"

"I did, but I'll purchase my own undergarments. Thanks, though."

"Should I guess your sizes or do you want to tell me?"

"Are all our conversations going to be this contentious?"

"Only if you disagree with me."

"Better buckle up, then." She gave him a little smile. "It's going to be a bumpy ride."

BRIGIT BACKED HER BLACK Escalade out of her garage. Sweaty palms and racing heartbeat aside, she hated leaving her home in shambles, but staying wasn't an option. As she followed Chad through Georgetown and over Key Bridge into Virginia, she kept glancing in the rearview mirror. The sheer volume of traffic made it impossible to know if she was being followed. Had Vinny Ray escaped prison? And how had he tracked her down?

Six years ago, the abrupt and violent deaths of her parents launched Eve Francesco into a downward spiral. She was confident

Vinny Ray would be found guilty, but he got off on a technicality. His manslaughter acquittal gutted her. Drowning in grief, she'd returned to Philadelphia, desperate for comfort from her longtime boyfriend. But when she found him in bed with another woman, his betrayal crushed her. While she was at Ray's trial, a hotshot investor named Colton Mitus snatched up her family's business, then refused to even discuss her future at the Francesco Company. That broke her.

When the need to avenge her parents wouldn't subside, a straight-laced Eve had dropped off the grid and reemerged in Ray's hometown an hour outside Philly. While her disguise was extreme, her plan was even more so. She hid her cropped mouse-brown hair beneath a long black wig, threw on glasses, and dressed in provocative clothing that left little to the imagination.

She found the neighborhood watering hole and watched from the safety of her rental car. When Vinny Ray showed up, she followed him inside. He bragged about getting away with murder and acted like a hometown hero. As he celebrated with a round of drinks, she snapped. There was no turning back.

Later that evening, a sloshed Ray invited her to his place. Before leaving the bar, he popped pills and offered her a ride. She'd wanted to kill him on the spot. Instead, she followed, stashed baggies of cocaine in his toilet tank, then tried to make a quick escape. But he demanded sex. In the ensuing struggle, he pulled off her wig and recognized her from the trial.

"I don't know what you're up to, but you won't get away with it." Ray stumbled and fell. "I'll hunt you down and when I find you, I'll slit your fucking throat."

Police received an anonymous drug tip that resulted in a ten-year prison term for Vinny Ray.

Eve Francesco never returned home to Ohio or to graduate school in Pennsylvania. She just vanished, resurfacing several months later in Washington, D.C. as Brigit Farnay. Her new identity sported new looks and the promise of a new beginning. But somehow, she'd slipped up. Vinny Ray had found her.

Brigit felt sick to her stomach by the time she pulled up to the Mitus compound. A car sped by and she whipped around to see a mom in a minivan. Could someone be watching from behind a bush? *Stop, I'm being paranoid.*

After they drove through, the wrought iron clanged shut. She was hiding from one enemy by moving in with the other. *I'm safe, for now.*

She parked next to the Bentley at the fountain, got out and opened the hatch. Several staffers trotted out to carry Brigit's clothing to the guest room. Yesterday, being at the compound reminded her of a prison cell. Today she couldn't scurry inside fast enough.

"Brigit, do you golf?" Colton asked.

Vonn transferred Colton's golf clubs into the trunk of his Mercedes-Maybach as Chad hoisted his from the Bentley.

"On occasion my club makes contact with the ball, but I'm not sure that counts as golf," Brigit said.

Colton smiled. "Why don't you join Chad and me? We're heading out."

"I've already impinged on your day. You two enjoy."

Taylor returned from taking an armful of Brigit's clothing upstairs and walked over. "Once you've unpacked, I can show you around the mansion and help you get settled in this weekend."

"Thank you, Taylor," Colton said.

Taylor smiled sweetly. "Of course. I'm happy Brigit changed her mind."

Brigit's heart swelled and her churning guts subsided. "Thank you both."

He placed his hand on Brigit's shoulder. "Welcome to your new home."

Surprisingly, his touch further settled her nerves. Though her fear could easily overwhelm her, she needed to control herself until she was alone. Going forward, she was Mitus Conglomerate's wealth manager. Just because she'd taken the position under duress didn't mean she'd slack off. No, she'd roll up her sleeves and dive in.

To Colton's finances, that is.

Colton removed his hand. "I do have one question. Do you think your new closet is big enough to hold all those shoes?"

Brigit cracked a smile. Maybe her self-imposed prison wasn't going to be as bad as she thought.

20

NOTTAMBULO

C OLTON'S PHONE BUZZED AS Crockett slid out of the booth in the crowded McLean restaurant. "Order me a coffee and a slab of that chocolate cake if the waiter returns before I do." Crockett headed toward the restrooms.

Colton's longtime friend and former Harvard roommate Crockett Wilde was mired in work. Heavy bags hung under his eyes and his short brown hair looked unkempt. Not only was his wireless invention going to turn Francesco into a powerhouse, it was going to make Colton tens of millions. Colton knew to tread lightly. Crockett's inability to balance work and play was nothing new.

After the server took Colton's dessert order, he read Taylor's text. *Brigit settled in. Seems okay. A little quiet. Chad, Ryan, Red and I are with her.*

Though he'd considered changing his Saturday night plans, he didn't want to send Brigit mixed messages. His newest employee would receive the same respect and space he gave everyone at Mitus. Problem was, she wasn't like anyone he'd ever hired. Even so, he had to back off.

Crockett slid into the booth. "What's wrong?"

"Nothing." Colton slipped his phone into his inside sport coat pocket.

"Bullshit."

"My new wealth manager starts Monday."

"Why don't you look relieved? Did you hire the woman Sethfield recommended?"

"Yeah. She's smart. And so damn strong-willed."

The server delivered two coffees, a piece of chocolate cake, and the check. Colton handed his credit card to the server.

"But you don't like when your financial advisors actually advise you. Will you listen to this one?" Crockett forked cake into his mouth.

Colton smiled. Crockett knew him too well. "Possibly. You know I don't like giving up control, especially regarding my wealth." Colton sipped his coffee. "Being around her is energizing and kind of addictive."

With a smirk, Crockett shook his head. "Ah, shit, you're attracted to her."

Maintaining a poker face, Colton took another sip.

"Well, that shouldn't matter," Crockett said. "You have that rule about not screwing your wealth manager. Come to think of it, you have a lot of effing rules."

"She's gorgeous. I mean really beautiful."

"Just keep your hands off her." Crockett pulled out his wallet and tossed his credit card on the table.

"Too late on both accounts."

Crockett raised his brows. "What does that mean?"

"The first is self-explanatory and the second is because I already paid."

"You slept with her? *Already?*"

"It wasn't like that. It was different. When you meet her, you can tell me if you wouldn't have done the same thing. Now I have to make damn sure I don't do it again."

"Someone needs to put you on a tight leash, Colt."

Colton laughed. "Maybe so."

The two men went quiet while Crockett dug into his dessert.

"You sleeping? Getting out at all?" Colton asked. "You look like hell."

"What are you, my mother?"

"You work too much. What happened to balance?" Colton signed the receipt.

"No balance until I find Sophia." Crockett sipped his coffee.

Colton's gut churned for his friend. "Whatever you need. Just say the word."

"I know, thanks." Crockett eyed Colton's clothing. "You headed to a kink party?"

"That obvious?"

"Only to me, Darth Vader." The two men laughed. "Black sport coat, black sweater, black pants. Are your cloak and mask in the car?"

Pushing down a smile, Colton asked, "You dating?"

"No time."

"I'll get you a membership to an exclusive sex play club I belonged to before joining the private group. Incognito is a great place to learn about the lifestyle. You deserve a break. Even if it's just for an hour or two."

"That's not my thing, bro."

"Just check it out. No pressure."

"All righty. Thanks."

"Did I tell you Alexandra might be moving back from California?" Colton finished his coffee.

Crockett's expression brightened. "How is our Goth Girl?"

"It *has* been a while. Goth Girl is long gone."

"Give her my best and thanks for dinner." Crockett tossed his napkin on the table.

The two men left the restaurant. "I'll talk to you next week," Colton said in the parking lot.

"Stay out of trouble." Crockett man-hugged Colton and walked toward his car.

Twenty minutes later, Colton parked in the upscale Potomac neighborhood, lifted his black devil masquerade mask from the passenger seat and covered his face. He walked to the front door and buzzed. Within seconds, it opened.

"*Nottambulo*," Colton said. The door opened wide enough for Colton to step inside, then shut behind him.

"Hello, Spencer." Morticia's face was hidden behind an ornate feathered mask. "You look scrumptious. We should get together."

"You know I don't mess around with married women."

She laughed. "Half the women here are married."

"Ignorance is bliss." He tossed her a playful salute and headed toward the lower level.

Trotting downstairs, he wondered how Brigit was doing. But his thoughts were interrupted by the sheer volume of chatter coming from the other side of the closed door.

He stepped into the plush art deco room with its elaborate hand-painted ceiling of Paris nudes in the roaring twenties. Two red velvet lounge chairs were strategically placed in each corner, but the room was too crowded to see the chairs on the far side. The number of guests appeared to have doubled since the last time he was there. *What the hell?*

Squeezing through the crowd of decked-out, masked partygoers, he headed to the black lacquered bar along the far wall to grab a drink before the show.

With his scotch in hand, he turned and almost bumped into a familiar redhead, her face partially concealed behind her red and white jeweled mask. All he could see was her mouth slicked in a thick coat of bright red lipstick. *That's unappealing.* "Hello, Darby."

Darby was a reliable good time. Her breasts spilled from her low-cut crimson dress and her skin sparkled under a light layer of golden flakes. As much as Colton appreciated the opposite sex he preferred them clothed, so he could undress them himself. But here he didn't care how the women presented themselves. The end result was always the same.

"Hello, you sexy devil." Darby smiled. Her front teeth were smeared in red lipstick. "Interested in a threesome?"

"Not my thing."

"Spencer! Welcome!" Masked as a silver gladiator, Burke shook Colton's hand. The host's wavy black hair tumbled onto his shoulders and his open-collared white shirt revealed a tuft of dark chest hair.

"Good to see you, Burke," Colton said. "What's with the crowd?"

"Morticia's idea. She thought our group of sixty-something had gotten too cozy, which I *thought* was the whole point of these parties." He rolled his eyes. "Everyone's verified clean."

"Anything special tonight?" Colton asked.

"Audience participation." Burke waggled his eyebrows. "Morticia's restless. You should hook up with her."

Colton's stomach churned. "She's your wife. Even I have to draw the line somewhere."

"Wife, shmife." Burke slapped his back. "Enjoy and thanks for coming." Burke winked, then launched into the crowd.

Darby squeezed his butt cheek. "Let's grab two chairs."

Normally aroused by her touch, Colton felt nothing. "You go ahead."

The lights dimmed. As guests made their way toward the rows of theater-style seating, the black velvet curtain rose. The king bed was covered in a black sheet with several orange pillows. Colton sunk into the aisle seat, back row.

Burke, still masked, strode on stage and waited for the chatty crowd to quiet down. "Welcome to Burke's Playroom and our special Halloween celebration. Releasing your inner demons is expected and *comes* guilt free." He beamed like a proud papa while the audience applauded. "For new members, the Playroom is always at the ready for you to have your own fun. And you don't have to wait for the show to end, either." He pointed to the door in the back. "Now put your hands together and help me welcome the Devil's Lair."

As Burke exited the stage, the lights dimmed. Red spotlights shone on the bed while eerie Halloween music played in the background.

Colton sipped his scotch.

From the shadows, a man and a woman stepped on stage. She wore a full-length angel costume and he dressed as the devil with a red cape, black pants and a stiff red tail attached to the back of the pants. She hid her face behind a white mask and he behind a red one.

Devil asked for a female volunteer. Several eager hands shot up. He selected Darby and escorted her center stage. With a quick unzip, her dress fell away. Devil took her hand and slowly spun her around so the audience could see her from all sides. She had large, enhanced breasts and a well-cushioned ass. As soon as Darby faced front again, Angel began kissing and caressing her naked body.

Body type meant little to Colton when he donned a mask. In fact, the more variety, the better. Everything about Burke's parties fed his need, but tonight he couldn't engage. His throbbing dick was normally a constant reminder of his pent-up energy. But tonight his penis hadn't stirred.

After Devil helped Angel remove her dress, she turned toward the audience and rubbed her breasts until her nipples plumped. One hand dipped between her legs and she caressed her clean-shaven pussy. As she continued with her self-pleasuring, Devil guided Darby to the bed. She lay on her back and waited, her chest quickly rising and falling.

He picked up a long feather, a black sash, and a vibrator from the side table and set them on the bed next to Darby. After removing his pants, he climbed on the bed, tied the sash over Darby's eyes and kissed her. When he whispered in her ear, she bent her legs at the knees and spread them wide.

He rolled on a condom and plunged inside her. Darby cried out, then bucked against his thrusts. Not wanting to be excluded, Angel climbed on the bed and sucked Darby's engorged nipples. As Devil's thrusts gained speed, he reached out to stroke, then slap Angel's ass. A few couples scurried toward the back of the room while the performers' shrieks and grunts filled his ears.

Surprisingly, Colton had had enough. He pushed out of his chair, set his unfinished scotch on the tray next to the bar, and walked toward the back of the room. Normally aroused by the erotic shows, he felt restless.

Maybe he needed to have his own fun. He opened the Playroom door and stepped inside, his eyes quickly adjusting to the candlelight. The large room of sofas and beds wouldn't fill up until after the show, but there were already a handful of masked couples. Most were fucking, but on the nearest sofa, a woman with an elaborate gold mask that covered all but her mouth was sucking a man in a Day of the Dead Venetian masquerade mask. Colton watched, expecting he'd get aroused. Again, nothing.

A naked woman sauntered over, her face partially hidden behind a plumed masquerade mask. She'd clamped a metal handcuff around her wrist, the other cuff dangled from the chain. She grasped his hand. "Fuck me."

Tugging it away he said, "I can't stay."

In frustration, he left the Playroom. He'd never rejected anyone at Burke's before tonight. *What the hell is wrong with me?*

As he walked past the living room, unexpected groans and cries pierced the silence. Morticia was screwing a masked pirate on her sofa. Any other time Colton would have stopped to watch, but tonight he didn't look twice.

The chilly night air was a welcomed contrast to the stuffy party room. Feeling more aggravated than when he'd arrived, he slipped into his vehicle and drove away. Only after turning the corner did he remove his devil mask and place it on the passenger seat. In the red glow of the traffic light, the evil disguise revealed his self-loathing image.

For the first time in his messed-up life, he wasn't aroused by the live sex show and he had no desire to fuck a masked stranger, either. And he knew damn well why. What he didn't know was what the hell he was going to do about it.

21

WELCOME ABOARD

EARLY MONDAY LIGHT BRIGHTENED Colton's man-cave office. He was eager to put Brigit to work. Well, that wasn't totally true. He was ready to put her to work and eager to take her to bed. The first scenario was about to happen. The second never would.

His phone rang. He punched the speakerphone button on his desk console. "Mitus."

"Sethfield, here. How'd Friday go?"

"Brigit did a phenomenal job."

"As I expected. Did you extend her an offer?"

"She's due in my office any minute."

"To accept it?"

"No, she moved in Saturday and she starts today."

"Well, that's fantastic. I'm surprised I didn't hear from her."

"She got caught up in the move. You know women and their shoes."

Seth laughed. "Ask her to check in with me or email her key accounts that require white glove treatment."

"Will do. I'm going to keep her tied up all morning, though."

Thoughts of Brigit anchored to his guesthouse bed shot a jolt of heat straight to his groin. What he would give to make *that* happen again.

"Congratulations, Colton. Mitus Conglomerate is going to benefit from her smarts and tenacity. Thanks for your business. Next round of golf is on me."

Colton chuffed out a laugh. "I bring your firm a boatload of business and you thank me with a round of golf?"

"You've got Brigit. She's worth her weight in gold." The call ended.

There was a light tap on his office door. So light, he wasn't sure it was a knock. "Enter."

Brigit walked in and his heart pumped faster. Her tailored brown suit fit snugly over her sexy curves, but her naked form had been branded into his mind. She'd pinned up her hair and he imagined kissing her exposed neck. *She's the best way to start my day.*

Colton pushed out of his leather chair and extended his hand. "Welcome to Mitus Conglomerate." He shook her hand as he would any new employee, but the energy that soared up his arm was anything but normal. *Damn, she feels good.*

"Good morning," she said. "I'm ready to dive in."

So am I. His desk phone rang. Crockett Wilde's name flashed on the console. "Have a seat."

He hit the speaker button. "Tell me good news."

"Beta testing rocked. The string of Crockett Boxes along the I-95 corridor from south of Baltimore to Fredericksburg outperformed even my stringent expectations. The success rate is off the charts. We're ready to go live. Has Francesco solidified which wireless carriers are rolling this out first?"

Still standing, Brigit inched closer to his desk.

"The industry leader is ready to go. The second is negotiating production expectations with Francesco. I expect the final two will be moving forward as well. My new wealth manager, Brigit Farnay, is with me."

"Hey, Brigit. Welcome. Colt, take me off speaker."

"Brigit, meet Crockett Wilde," Colton said.

"Am I off speaker?" Crockett asked.

He cradled the phone to his ear. "What's wrong with you?"

"What happened to keeping this under wraps?" Crockett asked. "Marjorie is itching for that loan."

"And that's why Brigit's here. Congrats. I'll call you later." He hung up.

Brigit looked keenly interested. *That's a good sign. She's jumping right in.* He gestured to the chair across from his desk. "You're welcome to sit. I need to make one quick call, then we'll get started." Colton hit the speed dial on his desk console. After several rings, the caller answered.

"Good timing," Marjorie said. "I'm headed outside to grab a quick smoke. Hang with me a second." Her gravelly voice sounded like she had a perpetual frog in her throat. "So, is that crack wealth manager on board yet?" Marjorie liked small talk even less than he did.

Colton flipped his gaze to Brigit. A whisper of a smile softened her expression. "Yes, she's with me and you're on speaker."

"Did she sign an NDA?"

"Of course," Colton said.

"I just got out of an exec meeting and we have a serious problem." Marjorie clicked a lighter, inhaled slowly and blew out sharply. "Bob Dobb was contacted, *again*, by MobiCom's V.P. of Acquisitions, Wilson Montgomery." She inhaled. "He put Dobb on notice. MobiCom is giving serious consideration to a merger. Merger, my ass. They're going to make an acquisition play. Everyone in that conference room looked like they'd soiled their pants." She inhaled, coughed, then started hacking.

This is the worst fucking news. "Marjorie, put out that damn cigarette before you hock up a lung."

"Leave me alone, Colton. It's my one vice. If it hasn't killed me by now, it's not going to. Now, where was I?"

"MobiCom," Colton said as he flicked his gaze to Brigit, who stared at the console like it was the bogeyman.

"Right." Marjorie cleared her throat. "Bob said he and Montgomery had an exhilarating discussion about the next generation of wireless until the conversation turned contentious and he told Montgomery to back off. Do you know this Wilson Montgomery?"

"No, I don't."

"Isn't MobiCom spitting distance from your mausoleum?"

"Yes, twenty minutes away, in Reston," Brigit interjected.

"Thank you, dear," Marjorie said. "MobiCom is putting together an investment banking team. They're talking with acquisition attorneys, one of them being Melvin Parsons. And thank the gods he wasn't available because if he were, we'd be screwed! He's fantastic." Marjorie inhaled a sharp breath.

"Someone leaked the information and MobiCom wants in," Colton said. "Who on Francesco's executive team would do that?"

"I haven't a clue. I'm sucking down antacids over here," Marjorie said. "Do you think someone on Crockett's team contacted MobiCom?"

"No," Colton replied. "Speaking of Crockett, he's ready for phase one rollout."

"Then stop gabbing with me and get to work. We're waiting on your loan," Marjorie said. "I swear to God, if Sammy Francesco were alive, she'd find the mole in less than a week and hang him by his toes. Lord, I miss her! Keep me posted." On another nicotine inhale the line went dead.

All the color had drained from Brigit's face as she sank into the leather chair across from Colton's desk.

"Dammit!" He pounded his fist on his desk and she jumped. "Someone at Francesco is a damn traitor." Colton punched a number on the console.

"G'morning," Chad replied through the speaker.

"Get me everything on a Wilson Montgomery of MobiCom and

his association with anyone on Francesco's executive team and board of directors."

"Got it." Chad hung up.

Colton cut his gaze to Brigit. For reasons he couldn't explain, having her there assuaged his agitation. "Let's get started. Seth needs a list of your key accounts. You'll have time later to get that to him."

Colton pushed out of his chair. MobiCom's interest was real and the timing couldn't be worse. Brigit needed to free up the monies as soon as possible.

"Chad will connect you to the network so you can review my complete portfolio," Colton said. "Today, we'll use my computer." He opened a closed door at the far end of the room. "Your office."

"I'm working in your closet?" She hopped up and walked past him and into her workspace. Her swaying hips distracted him for a split second. Even that was too long. *Dammit, stop.*

Brigit's office was a smaller version of his, but instead of dark paneled walls, these walls were painted pale green. The color of money. He'd not replaced the dark oak desk or leather chair. Once she got settled, Ryan would assist with any changes. She could also choose new furniture for her cozy sitting area. Though he assumed the small conference table and four chairs would remain, she could redecorate the entire room to her liking. Floor-to-ceiling windows lined the back wall and French doors opened to a small patio overlooking the backyard.

"This is nice, but—"

"Ryan will work with you on furniture selection," Colton interjected.

"Furniture works. It's just that my office is an offshoot of yours. I'll be in and out constantly—I didn't mean that. It came out...uh, never mind." She pursed her lips.

He cracked a grin. "Is all that *in and out* going to be a problem for you?"

"It's...well—" Her cheeks turned pink and she blew out a notable sigh. "It's fine."

"Intrusive or controlling?"

Her mouth quirked up, but she shook her head from side to side and the smile fell away.

Controlling. "We'll be working closely together," he continued. "At some point, you'll know the intimate details of all my business transactions."

The air sizzled between them as they held each other's gaze. He wanted to caress her soft shoulder or run the back of his finger down her sweet, pink cheek. When she moistened her lower lip, his dick moved. Hell, at this rate, he'd never get anything accomplished. Though her sweet coconut scent drew him in, she was off-limits. He shoved his hand into his pocket and tossed his thoughts in the gutter.

She swallowed, hard. "You've confided that you're financially bleeding to death. I'm ready to get started. Will I be working with Red?"

"No, with me." Colton pointed to three boutique shopping bags on the tawny-colored loveseat. "Those are for you."

Brigit peeked inside one of the bags. "Bras and panties?"

"I understand you took the weekend to settle in and didn't get to the mall. Knowing you don't have any lingerie is a torturous distraction."

Her lips curved into a Mona Lisa smile. "Thank you. How much do I owe you?"

"Do your job well and we'll call it even." He started walking toward his office.

"First I'll stop the losses," she said as she fell in line with him. "Next, I'll pinpoint investments we should sell in order to free up the cash you need." She sat in the chair across from his desk. "How much money are we talking about?"

Colton eased into his swivel leather chair, propped his knee over his other thigh and leaned back. "Thirty million."

"Time frame?"

He held her gaze. "Yesterday."

"I'm a wealth manager, Colton, not a magician."

With the exception of Shane delivering lunch and Red dropping off a revised weekly itinerary, along with an update of what urgent issues she'd handled, they worked uninterrupted until after five o'clock. "I'll expect the thirty million transferred to my cash account tomorrow," Colton said.

She stared at him for several seconds. "We only reviewed a portion of your investments. Once I analyze each position, I'll make my recommendations."

"Do you need an extra day?"

"At least. I have to study industry trends to determine where you have the most to lose or gain by selling. My recommendations will focus on two key areas. First, investments that depleted your bottom line. Second, yielding lucrative results by redirecting those monies elsewhere. Since you need a sizeable amount of cash, that'll take priority. I'll have my findings summary and detailed report completed by close of business *Friday*. Are there any investments you're committed to keeping?"

"The Francesco Company and all real estate, both commercial and residential. I need your report by *Wednesday*, close of business." He checked his watch and clicked on a screen.

"I'll have my analysis to you by noon, *Thursday*."

"You do like to negotiate."

She shook her head. "I'm setting reasonable turnaround expectations."

There was a knock on his door. "Enter."

Chad barreled in. "Is now a good time?" He glanced at Brigit.

"Did you find anything on Montgomery?" Colton asked.

"It's going to take several days for the reports, but here's what I've got. People hop from one wireless company to another, even at the executive level. At first glance, he's crossed professional paths with several on Francesco's board and leadership team. I suspect he's got more than one source feeding him information."

Fuck.

22

NEW GIRL

E YEING COLTON, BRIGIT ROSE. He'd morphed into a fire-breathing dragon, with flared nostrils and lips drawn into a thin line. He might not need a break, but she did. It was almost five thirty. *Where'd the day go?* "Excuse me. I should check in with Seth. Chad, am I connected to the network?"

"We have to set your passwords," Chad said.

"Let's do that after dinner. I need to get started on an urgent project."

Chad smirked. "All of Colton's projects have a short fuse."

On the way into her office, she read her texts. *Couldn't resist the challenge, could you? Miss you, but happy for you,* texted Shaniqua. Brigit texted back, *Temporary assignment. Miss you.*

Don't forget about me, here in the real world, Kat texted. *Back before you know it,* Brigit texted back.

Her phone buzzed with a text from Taylor. *Gym before dinner?* Brigit didn't want to leave the compound. *Where?* she texted back.

Lower level. I'll swing by your bedroom 5:45.

Surprised and relieved to learn Mitus Mansion had a gym, she opened her French doors leading to the patio and stepped out back.

The chilly breeze caressed her heated cheeks and she inhaled a Zen-like breath.

As vibrant streaks of sienna and fuchsia infused a lapis sky, the fiery yellow ball hung low on the horizon. From the lack of humidity, it must've been a crisp fall day, but the last ten hours had been consumed by everything Mitus.

She'd learned a lot her first day, the worst being that MobiCom, the wireless and mobile products behemoth down the road, was making a play for Francesco. *This is bad.* Grunting her frustration, she dialed Seth's number.

He answered on the first ring. "Brigit, congratulations! I'm thrilled you took the position."

She thought of her trashed home, the disturbing placement of her lingerie on her bed, and the terrifying message on her mirror. "Under the circumstances, it made the most sense."

"I had a feeling you wouldn't be able to resist Colton's charm or his beautiful home." She could hear the smile in his voice. "How was day one?"

"Charm? The man's a workhorse. I'll email you my list of clients requiring kid gloves, but you do know this situation is temporary, right?"

"Thank you, Brigit. This is a great win for the firm. Let me know if you—"

"Need anything." A rueful smile touched her lips. "Just don't give away my office."

She hung up and did a three-sixty, ensuring the grounds were quiet. Confirming she was alone, she dialed the district attorney's number. Though her pulse pounded in her temples, she needed to know Vinny Ray's whereabouts.

"Good afternoon, Jim Sausalito's office," said the young woman.

Brigit followed the cobblestone path toward the guesthouse. "This is Eve Francesco. Is Jim available?"

"I'm sorry, Ms. Francesco, but Mr. Sausalito had a family emergency. He's on personal leave. Can I take a message?"

"Is Peggy there?"

"His assistant is on maternity leave. Can I get your number?"

Brigit didn't like leaving messages as Eve, but in this case, she had no choice. After providing her contact information and request for inmate status, she retreated inside and collected the shopping bags. Since she'd no intention of leaving the compound for bras and panties, she was grateful for Colton's thoughtful gesture.

As she headed out of her office, she abruptly stopped. She had two choices. Either trek through the backyard, up the porch stairs, into the kitchen, down the hallway and upstairs to her bedroom, or pass through his office. *Don't be ridiculous. Just go in.*

She stopped in the doorway. Colton sat at his desk with his back to her.

Hours ago, he'd removed his jacket and rolled up his sleeves. She'd tried not to notice how his white dress shirt clung to his sinewy chest. And she tried not to imagine removing that pink tie, unbuttoning his shirt and running her fingers down his sexy, muscular torso. But she'd failed, and her cheeks had heated from the erotic thoughts. Hopefully he hadn't noticed.

Colton's hair rested on his collar and she wanted to finger his unruly waves. Her body stirred with thoughts that had nothing to do with business. *Stop.* Shaking her head, she tapped on the doorframe.

He swiveled around. "You don't have to knock."

"Day one, you know." With shopping bags in hand, she paused near his desk. "I haven't found the Mitus Conglomerate instruction manual and I'm flying without a net."

His gaze floated over her face. "I'll catch you." His voice dropped, the husky timbre making her forget why she was standing there in the first place.

She cleared her throat. "I'm not going to fall."

"Thanks for your efforts today, Brigit. I'm glad you're on my team."

His kind words made her chest tighten. "I was counting on you being a first-class jerk. Please stop proving me wrong."

He smiled, but the spark quickly faded and his expression grew stern. "Just don't ever deceive me."

A chill careened down her spine. She couldn't leave his office fast enough.

After lifting and spinning in the lower level gym, Taylor and Brigit headed upstairs to shower. "What rules does the Clothing Czar impose for dinner?" Brigit asked.

Taylor snickered. "Casual is fine, but no jeans, sweats or yoga pants."

So many rules. Brigit showered and dressed in leggings and a sweater. Taylor escorted her into the already crowded dining room and parked her at the opposite end of the table.

"Who did I oust to sit in this coveted spot?" Brigit asked.

"Doesn't matter. It's yours now." Taylor scampered off to her own seat in the middle of the table.

As Brigit sat, she stole a glance at Colton, seated at the far end. While listening to Dez, he swirled his Cab, then, as if he'd felt her watching, flipped his gaze down the lengthy table, pinning her with his intensity. She could stare at that man all day long. A sliver of a smile crossed his lips before he turned back to Dez.

Brigit treated herself to a glass of Cab and then another, but that was nothing compared to what Vanessa tossed back. Even Chad, seated across from Vanessa, told her to ease up.

"Vanessa, how about we review your portfolio sometime soon?" Brigit asked.

"I'm good," said Vanessa.

After dinner, Colton tapped his water goblet. "Can I have your attention, please? I'd like to welcome our newest Mitus Conglomerate employee, Brigit Farnay."

The cadre stared in her direction. *Nothing like being the center of unwanted attention.* She gave a little wave to the group.

"Please make Brigit feel welcome," Colton said. "Living with coworkers is new. Keep in mind your own challenges when you moved in." He glanced in Ryan's direction. "Ryan, I still don't know how Taylor survived with you as her mentor, but fortunately for us all, she did."

A beaming Taylor raised her glass. "Here's to Brigit."

A glassy-eyed Vanessa toasted Brigit. "That's the best seat at the table," she whispered. "And it used to be mine. If I were you, little Brigit, I wouldn't get too comfortable in that chair. Permanence at Mitus Conglomerate is a fucking illusion."

23

VANESSA'S WARNING

ORKAHOLIC BRIGIT FARNAY HAD spent the first few days
hunkered down in her office. By ten thirty Wednesday
evening the numbers on her computer screen blurred together.
Enough. She pushed out of her desk chair and tugged open the
French doors in her office. *Ah, fresh air.*

As she stepped outside, she triggered the automatic patio light. A
sudden wind gust blew her hair as the leaves rustled in the tall oaks
bordering the property. She glanced into the darkened backyard
and a shiver ran through her. Could someone be lurking nearby,
watching?

Ever since the vengeful intruder had tornadoed through her
home, she'd been overly jumpy. Only one person harbored that
much wrath. Up until Saturday, she'd assumed Vinny Ray was
behind bars. The Pennsylvania D.A.'s office hadn't returned her call
and she was *not* calling the prison directly.

"Hey, there," said a voice behind her.

Squealing, Brigit whirled around as the hair on the back of her
neck prickled.

"Easy there." Vanessa loomed in her doorway, wine bottle in one hand, crystal glass in the other. "You've been nose to the grindstone since you got here. Can I tempt you?"

Even though Brigit's mouth watered, she didn't want to encourage Vanessa to stay. "No thanks. I'm headed upstairs."

That evening Colton had been absent at dinner. Had he tasked Vanessa with babysitting the newbie? Brigit walked past her, bolted the French door and retreated to her desk to shut down.

Rather than leaving, Vanessa meandered over. Seemingly preoccupied, she dragged her manicured finger along the border of Brigit's desk, then shifted her attention to Brigit. "How are you settling in?"

"Pretty well."

Vanessa filled the glass and slid it over to Brigit. "I'm here to help. You know, put things in perspective."

Not interested. "I'm good."

"I've known Colton for a long time. He needs *variety* to quench his sexual thirst and he does what he pleases, in all things." Vanessa gaveled the wine bottle on Brigit's desk. "I hope you don't think your intimacy meant anything to him. It didn't, and that can be a hard pill to swallow."

Holy hell.

How did Vanessa know she'd had sex with Colton? Muscles traversing her shoulders turned to stone. "I don't think—"

"It's okay." Vanessa made herself comfortable in the chair across from Brigit's desk. "Colton is a complicated man with unusual needs."

What does that mean?

Leaning back, Vanessa crossed her legs.

That is one short skirt and two powerful thighs. "I'm not comfortable talking about him, but thanks for the heads-up." Brigit walked around her desk hoping Vanessa would take the hint and leave.

"He'll discard you when he grows restless, and I can assure you, he will. Take tonight, for example. He's doing something so kinky you'd blush at the thought, if you didn't need someone to explain it to you first." Laughing, Vanessa threw back her head. Brigit cringed. "If I didn't know him as intimately as I do, I'd say he was a scoundrel. But I know better." Vanessa shrugged. "Colton's just being *Colton*."

Did her super sexy client have a dark side? Though curious, Brigit would stay clear of office politics and gossip, especially where it involved Colton. "My only concern is his wealth. Perhaps he's at a business function."

Vanessa rose and, looking down her nose, pinned Brigit with a cold stare. "It's hump night, you fool."

Out of the corner of her eye, Brigit detected movement. Colton filled her doorway, clad in his black cashmere coat. Her heart skipped a beat. But tonight, his brooding expression and mussed hair overshadowed his striking looks. Even still, her fingers ached to tame his locks. *Are you windblown or did someone unleash her hands in all those waves?*

As he strolled into her office, his dark expression lifted. "Vanessa, thanks for going the extra mile to ensure Brigit feels the Mitus welcome."

Oh, I felt it all right.

"Anything for the team." Vanessa's condescending tone had been replaced with a submissive purr. "You, of all people, know that."

The scent of expensive perfume wafted from his direction, the flowery fragrance reminding her of Vanessa's comment. *He's doing something so kinky you'd blush at the thought.*

"You two having a little nightcap?" he asked.

"No, Brigit's drinking alone," Vanessa said. "Loved our girl talk, Brig. Keep it in mind and remember, I'm happy to help anytime." She walked toward the door and called over her shoulder, "Night, Colton."

Brigit was too stunned to speak.

As Colton shrugged off his coat, he couldn't take his eyes off Brigit. Her beauty left him breathless. He hungered to take her into his arms and into his bed. *Too damn bad, Mitus. A deal is a deal.*

He'd had one of the worst fucking evenings of his life. After dinner with his mom, which he did most Wednesdays, she'd confided that she'd not been well. A recent imaging scan had revealed a brain tumor. With surgery scheduled, Kimberly Mitus had already arranged for post-surgery nursing care. Colton's brain had short-circuited. She sounded like she was rattling off the amenities of a luxury home, but this was not a real estate transaction and he was not her client. He'd insisted on being by her side every step of the way. She would not endure this horrific ordeal alone.

Raking his hands through his hair, Colton shoved away the pain and anger. "I'm flying out of town tomorrow morning to do damage control."

"I'll push to complete my financial analysis and recommendations and email my report over," Brigit said. "You can review on your return flight."

Colton stepped close. "You'll be joining me."

She gripped her hips. "No can do."

He couldn't help but smile. He detested resistance, but for some inexplicable reason, Brigit's pushback amused him. "We have an eight o'clock flight. Be downstairs, ready to go, by five forty-five."

Her big green eyes popped. "You can't boss me around like that."

His cock moved. She was so damned hot when she got feisty. *Watch me.* "I can and I am. We'll prep on the way to the airport."

As if she'd gotten an unexpected chill, she hugged herself, then rubbed her arms. "Fine. Where are we going?"

He lifted the wine glass and took a hearty sip. "The Francesco Company."

24

HELLO, MRS. MICK

B RIGIT TOSSED AND TURNED all night. Not since the death of her parents had she set foot in the building that had once been her second home. And she was about to waltz through the doors of the Francesco Company with the very man who'd taken it from her. Not as his adversary, but as his ally.

Though she'd racked her brain for an excuse to keep her from flying to Ohio, she'd come up with nothing ironclad. Grunting her frustration, she sat up. Oh-dark-thirty. Brigit dragged herself out of bed.

As the hot shower pounded her awake, she ruminated on Vanessa's warning. *Colton is a complicated man with unusual needs.* And what was it about *that* man that made statements like those so intriguing? She dressed in her favorite black suit and black heels, then returned to the bathroom to make up.

Brigit had been close to Marjorie McAllister, Francesco's COO. Had she changed enough to fool Mrs. Mick or would she see right through her mask of deceit? Trembling, she smeared mascara across her brow. *Dammit! Get it together.* After wiping the smudge, she plumped her lashes with the black wand.

Ready early, she headed downstairs to find the sleepy-eyed

group drinking coffee. Red and Dez sat at the kitchen table while Colton thumbed his phone at the center island.

"Good morning," Brigit said. "I hope you weren't waiting for me."

"No, you're fine," Dez replied.

"Ugh." Red sipped her coffee. "I'm going to need a three o'clock caffeine hit, big time."

"Morning, Brigit," Colton said.

Even at this godforsaken hour, Colton looked phenomenal. Dark olive suit paired with a burgundy tie and white dress shirt. And he'd styled his hair out of his eyes, giving her a clear line of sight to his handsome face.

"Colton, I discovered several Mitus investments that haven't been managed in years." She stood near him at the island and inhaled his delicious scent. "There's a sizable amount of money wrapped up in those positions. I'll stay behind and work on that today."

"No. You can slide your deliverable to Friday."

Damn. There was no escaping Francesco.

Colton's phone buzzed. "Chad's out front."

In silence, they trudged outside to the waiting Bentley. Dez rode shotgun, while Red slunk into the back, behind Chad.

"After you," Colton said.

"Why don't you sit in the middle?" Brigit slid inside and scooted over.

"In that tiny space?" He got in and slammed the door.

That seat worked just fine the last time we were in this car. She glanced in his direction and he waggled his brows. Pursing her lips to keep from smiling, she buckled in.

As the giant gates swung open, Brigit sucked down a nervous breath. Leaving the compound made her very, very uneasy. In the pre-dawn hour, the eerie quiet sent a shiver down her spine. Chad waited for a few cars to pass, then pulled onto the road. If someone was lurking in the shadows, she didn't see him. Brigit glanced out the rearview window. The Bentley traveled alone on the darkened road. *Deep breath. No one even knows I'm in this car.*

"Yesterday, MobiCom's entourage toured Francesco," Colton said. "Bob Dobb, Francesco's CEO, claimed they showed up unannounced."

"Yeah, right," Dez said. "A pop-in from Northern Virginia to Columbus, Ohio."

"Did they visit the factory?" Brigit asked.

"Yes." Colton shifted in the seat and his leg pressed against hers.

His massive thigh stimulated her in the most scrumptious of ways. Even though she desperately craved his touch, she had to fight those feelings. *Move away.* While she *should* have repositioned herself so they weren't touching, she didn't. As casually as possible, she peeked at him. Dark eyes full of lust and power stared back. If his intensity could have devoured her, she'd have been eaten alive, right then and there. She couldn't look away.

"Sounds like they're taking stock. Positioning to make an offer," Dez said. "This is classic acquisition."

"And deceptive," Red said. "What are your expectations today?"

Silence.

"Colton?" Red asked.

Colton blinked, then refocused on Red. "What did you say?"

"Goals? Expectations?" Red asked.

"Get through the day unscathed," Brigit murmured under her breath.

"Sounds good to me." Red shifted her attention out the window. "I need a double shot of espresso."

Colton shifted his attention back to Brigit. No, more like he feasted on her with his eyes, digesting every pore, every fine line, every imperfection. If staring at that man could be classified as a drug, she was a full-blown junkie. His face was perfect in every way.

"We need to determine if leadership and board members are for or against the acquisition," Colton said. "No snitch would fess up, but someone might slip. Francesco is anxiously awaiting my no-interest loan. Based on Brigit's projections, they'll have the funds next week."

After Chad pulled up to valet parking at Dulles International Airport, the five piled into a waiting van.

"Where are we going?" Brigit asked.

"Charter flights," Red replied.

The driver parked in front of a small building at the far end of the airport. They got out and waited while Colton and Chad spoke with the clerk. She smiled too big and batted her eyelashes too many times. Brigit wanted to laugh. Did the men even notice?

"The craft is ready," Chad said.

"Where's the pilot?" Brigit asked as they walked toward the Beech King Air 350 turboprop.

"You're looking at him," Colton said.

"*You?*"

"He's good," Dez said. "It's his maverick copilot I worry about."

Spinning around, Chad grinned.

"This isn't your first flight, is it?" Brigit asked climbing up the short flight into the belly of the plane.

"Nah, it's my second." Chad winked.

Brigit sank into the plush leather seat across from Dez and Red while Colton and Chad readied the plane for departure. After belting herself, she leaned over to observe them in the cockpit.

With his headset on, Colton said, "Dulles ground, Beech King Bravo five-three-zero Bravo Whiskey requesting to taxi to the active runway for a departure to the north."

After a pregnant pause, he continued. "Dulles ground, Beech King zero Bravo Whiskey taxiing to runway one-niner."

As the aircraft taxied to the runway, Brigit gripped the armrests. After six long years, she was finally going home.

"Dulles tower, Beech King Bravo five-three-zero Bravo Whiskey holding short of runway one-niner, ready for takeoff," Colton said.

Chad got busy fine-tuning knobs.

"Dulles tower, Beech King zero Bravo Whiskey cleared for takeoff, runway one-niner," Colton said.

The aircraft rolled forward and as they gained speed, Brigit watched out the window.

"Wheels up, baby!" Chad said as they went airborne.

Dez chuckled. "Peter Pan is flying."

Brigit spent much of the flight in the airplane lavatory. Shattered nerves had jumbled her insides. Returning to her beloved company was affecting her more than she'd expected. They landed and disembarked. Brigit ushered them through John Glenn Columbus International Airport and into the waiting sedan.

"You have a great sense of direction," Red said. "Airports overwhelm me, but you walked through that place like you owned it."

Brigit shrugged. "Stocks, bonds and airport navigation."

Mrs. Mick had sent a driver. When he turned down the familiar street, Brigit's chest tightened. The three-story building with THE FRANCESCO COMPANY emblazoned across the facade turned her insides to jelly. *I will not cry. I will not cry.*

As they tumbled out of the vehicle, a lump formed in her throat. Her life had changed so much since she was last there. Panic crept in. What if Marjorie recognized her and blamed her for not fighting to keep the company? Under the horrific circumstances, she'd done the best she could.

Colton opened the front door and waited while Red and Dez shuffled through.

Tears filled Brigit's eyes, but the blustery day whisked away the emotion as she approached the building entrance. With a racing heart, she silently recited the familiar poem, hoping to settle her nerves. *Will you walk into my parlour? said the Spider to the Fly. 'Tis the prettiest little parlour that ever you did spy.*

"Thank you." She walked past Colton and into the lobby.

He stopped her. "You okay?"

"I'm fine." Her gaze skirted across the familiar space. They were on her home turf, yet she was a stranger to everything she held most dear.

Hooking a gentle finger beneath her chin, he tilted her face toward his. "I need you or I wouldn't have asked you to join me."

She stared into his eyes. "I won't let you down, and if I recall, there was no *asking* involved."

"Colton," called a familiar voice.

Marjorie McAllister ambled toward them, a cigarette tucked behind her ear. She'd not aged much since Brigit had last seen her. Maybe she'd gained a few more pounds and her short hair sported more grays. With a pounding heartbeat, Brigit cleared her throat and stood tall. *This has got to work.*

Marjorie hugged Colton, then patted his back. "You look good, old man."

Colton laughed. "Glad to see your sense of humor is still intact."

"I wasn't trying to be funny," Marjorie said. "You've aged a damn decade since I last saw you."

Colton reintroduced Dez, Red and Chad.

As Marjorie pivoted, Brigit's heart lurched into her throat. "So, is this your hotshot money lady?" Mrs. Mick thrust out her hand. "Marjorie McAllister. I expect nothing less than a miracle from you, young lady."

Bracing for the recognition, she shook her hand. "Brigit Farnay. I'll put in a special order, just for you."

Marjorie laughed, the gravelly sound reminding Brigit of the many lectures her mother had had with her about the dangers of smoking. She wished her mom were there now to pluck the cigarette from behind Marjorie's ear and throw it away. A scene Brigit had witnessed hundreds of times. Marjorie removed the cigarette and tapped it on her palm, but her gaze remained fixed on Brigit.

Does she recognize me?

As Marjorie fiddled with the cigarette, she studied Brigit's face. "You're a soccer fan. Am I right?"

She knows. Swallowing hard, she shot Colton a furtive glance. "I keep my sport obsession under wraps. What gave it away?"

Marjorie's expression softened and a whisper of a smile kissed her lips. "You have soccer fan eyes."

Hello, Mrs. Mick.

"I definitely missed something," Red said.

"Yeah, I'm right there with you," Dez said. "I've no idea what they're talking about."

"I like football." Chad puffed his chest. "Can you tell?"

Giving Chad the once-over, Marjorie said, "D-1 linebacker. Where'd you play?"

Chad grinned. "Damn, you're good. Virginia Tech."

"Okay, if we're done with the sports chitchat, let's get started," Colton said.

Marjorie stuffed the cigarette behind her ear and took off toward the elevator bank. A quick ride to the top floor, then Marjorie led them down the hall to the executive conference room. After walking in, Brigit gasped.

"Nice view, isn't it?" Marjorie winked.

It wasn't the familiar park-like setting or the duck pond that had her fighting the surge of emotion. Two beautiful oil portraits of Samantha and Nicholas Francesco adorned the far wall. Their likeness so real she wanted to throw her arms around them. But the paintings were also a harsh reminder that her parents were gone because of the selfish choice she'd made. Grief and guilt lodged in her throat and she turned away.

"Who are the portraits of?" Red plunked down at the lacquered mahogany conference table.

"Our company founders, Nicolas and Samantha Francesco." Marjorie sat at the head. The rest of the Mitus team joined her.

"Did they retire?" Chad asked.

"They were killed in a drunk driving accident," Marjorie said. "It was the single most tragic event in my life. I could talk about my dear friends for hours, but we'll save the nostalgia for another day. Today is all about saving Francesco." Marjorie glanced at Brigit.

Spurred by the determination in Mrs. Mick's eyes, Brigit felt empowered. Fierce loyalty to Francesco flowed through their veins. And even though Brigit wasn't privy to the wireless secrets or details surrounding the merger proposition, Colton believed she'd add value or he wouldn't have insisted she go. For the first time since he'd told her she'd be joining him, her queasy stomach settled down.

"I'm sorry for your loss," Chad said.

"Thank you." Marjorie flipped open her notebook. "Let's get started, shall we? Yesterday Wilson Montgomery, MobiCom's V.P. of Mergers and Acquisitions, sailed in here with an obnoxious take-charge attitude. The worst part is that Bob Dobb—our president—failed to mention the meeting. I saw them gallivanting around during the tour."

"When do you anticipate an offer?" Dez asked.

"By Thanksgiving," Marjorie said. "Dobb acted like a proud papa introducing the MobiCom team. All that was missing was a handful of cigars, which I'd have gladly shoved up his ass!"

Brigit snorted. Mrs. Mick hadn't changed a bit.

"Sounds like you suspect Dobb of being more than a gracious host," Red said as a second door at the far end of the room swung open and a squirrely man entered.

"Just because you can't see his horns doesn't mean they aren't there," Marjorie muttered under her breath.

Brash, bold and no holds barred Mrs. Mick.

After introductions, faux smiles, and a heavy dose of bullshit from Bob Dobb about how thrilled he was to see the Mitus team, he slipped into a seat next to Red. Everything about Dobb screamed *average*. But a mediocre leader wasn't good enough for the Francesco Company.

"Bob, I'm in your seat." But Marjorie didn't move.

"We don't stand on formalities," Bob crooned. "Please stay where you are. Sitting here works." He turned to Red and drew back his lips.

His leering smile made Brigit shiver. *Creepy.*

Bob shifted his gaze across the table to Colton. "Were you in the neighborhood, like MobiCom?"

"No, Bob, we weren't." Colton's cold tone caught Brigit's immediate attention. "Speaking of MobiCom, what prompted their visit? Sounds like your position has changed since we last spoke."

Bob leaned back in the cushioned chair and rested his ankle over his opposing thigh, then clasped his hands behind his head. More relaxed he could not have looked. "Colton, I appreciate your directness. MobiCom floated a merger proposition. There's no harm in listening, is there?" His disingenuous smile turned Brigit's stomach as she spun the cold silver bracelet adorning her wrist. The president of the Francesco Company was terrible at talking out of both sides of his mouth.

Pinning him with a cold stare, Colton stayed quiet, save for the strumming of his fingers on the polished wood.

"But rest assured, *listening* is all I'm doing." Bob continued. "I have no intention of championing a merger."

Colton squared his shoulders. "What do they know about Crockett Boxes?"

Bob bolted upright. "Nothing! MobiCom's offer is unrelated, though the timing couldn't be better."

"Better?" Marjorie's eyebrows jutted up to her forehead. "We're not announcing our deals with the wireless carriers until *after* they place their initial orders. The timing couldn't be *worse!*"

"I disagree," Bob said, shifting in his chair. "Seeing Francesco trending would be great publicity."

"Yes, it would." Colton glanced at Marjorie. "Thanks for stopping by, Bob."

"We've made some improvements at the factory." Bob turned toward Red. "How 'bout I *personally* give you a tour?"

Refusing to acknowledge Dobb, Red locked eyes with Brigit across the conference table.

Weasel.

"Another time, Bob." Colton rolled back his chair.

Marjorie stood. Meeting over. Brigit eyed the portraits one last time. After a brief and somewhat frosty goodbye to Dobb, the Mitus team followed Marjorie down the hall and into her spacious corner office. "Back in two minutes. I need a smoke or I'll die." Marjorie snatched the lighter from her desk and left.

Though Colton had his back to the team as he stared out Marjorie's window, anger billowed off him. Not wanting to further aggravate him, Brigit remained quiet.

Nothing had changed in Marjorie's office. The familiar tobacco smell hung like an invisible cloud, the cluttered desk had stacks of folders piled high, and the beautiful view of the duck pond brought back many special memories.

Turning to sit at the conference table, her mouth fell open. The back wall was covered with pictures she'd drawn or painted for Mrs. Mick. *She saved everything.* Brigit swallowed the plum-sized lump in her throat.

Red lifted a framed photo from Marjorie's desk and turned it around. "Her daughter?"

It was a photo of a beaming six-year-old Eve Francesco, dressed as a warrior princess. Plastic shield in her outstretched hand, while her other hand clasped Marjorie's. Marjorie had accompanied her mom and dad to the school Halloween parade. *Oh no.*

"Cute kid." Colton stared at the photo for several seconds. "Hmm, that's odd."

"What?" Brigit stopped breathing.

"I've seen that child somewhere. Her eyes are so familiar."

25

SINFUL PLEASURES

COLTON PIVOTED IN BRIGIT'S direction, then eyed the photo again. There was something special about that little girl. Brigit spun away and dropped into a chair at Marjorie's conference table, then grabbed her water bottle and drained it.

"Gotta love a warrior princess!" As Chad sat next to Brigit he glanced at the busy wall. "Hello, that's a lotta artwork."

A squawking flock of geese landed on the pond and Colton turned back to stare out the window. Dobb was guilty as hell, but of what, he wasn't sure. While Dobb was kowtowing to Montgomery, that didn't mean he'd bared his soul and divulged company secrets. Or did it? With any luck, their string of afternoon meetings would yield answers. *No one has more skin in the game than I do and no one will stop me from seeing his project through to fruition.*

"Colton—" Brigit cleared her throat. "What's our strategy to ensure the executive team votes down the merger?

"Great question," Marjorie said as she shut the door. "I've scheduled in-person meetings or video conferences with each executive and board member. Let's find that damn traitor."

Marjorie had lunch delivered and immediately following they met with Francesco leadership, one at a time. Five hours later, the last person filed out. "That was exhausting." Marjorie shut her office door.

Colton closed his laptop and leaned back. "They could be telling us what we want to hear while quietly campaigning for this merger."

"A few seemed uncomfortable, but that didn't mean they were lying," Chad said.

"Colton, you alone can be intimidating," Dez said. "The sheer number of us might have made some folks nervous."

"Not if they've nothing to hide," Colton said.

"That's what worries me." Marjorie pulled a cigarette from her desk drawer and tucked it behind her ear. "I don't know who to trust at this point."

Colton was beat, but not beaten down. "Marjorie, you did a great job pulling this together."

"This baby means everything to me and I'll defend her to my death." Marjorie walked toward her door.

"Speaking of babies." Red lifted the photo. "Is she yours?"

"No. That little girl is Eve Francesco, the only child of Nick and Sammy, but I loved her like she was my own. We spent Fridays after school together. I promised her mom I'd talk shop." Marjorie snickered. "What child wants to learn about the day-to-day operations of a wireless and mobile products company? Don't get me wrong. They adored their daughter, but they were obsessed about indoctrinating her into the business when she was a wee little thing. So I'd steal her away for creative time." She gestured to the artwork.

Dez reviewed the list of meeting attendees. "Why didn't we meet with her today?"

"She disappeared after their deaths and I couldn't find her," Marjorie said. "Losing her devastated me."

"There was a lot going on when I bought Francesco, but I don't recall meeting the owners' daughter," Colton said.

"You didn't," Brigit blurted.

The room quieted. Everyone looked at her.

Way to go, dummy. "Er, um, I..." Brigit's cheeks heated.

"Chop, chop! Everybody out!" Marjorie threw open her door. "Time to catch a plane!" She shooed them into the hallway and bustled toward the elevators.

Thank you, Mrs. Mick.

The driver, waiting at the curb, exited the vehicle and popped the trunk. Marjorie lit up and inhaled. "God, I needed that."

After they said their goodbyes, the five headed toward the waiting sedan.

"Oh, Brigit," Marjorie called. "Can I borrow you for a quick second?"

Colton checked his watch. "We've got time."

Brigit returned to Marjorie and the two huddled close.

Watching, Colton rested his arm on the roof of the car. "Those two seem cozy."

"Brigit's easy to like." Dez opened the front passenger door and got in.

After a quick hug, Brigit ran-walked to the waiting vehicle. She slid inside and Colton followed.

"You two looked like old friends," Red said.

Clearing her throat, Brigit said, "Nah, she's in need of a new wealth management firm. I told her I'd connect her with Seth."

Colton stole a glance as she swiped a tear from the corner of her eye.

"Whew, it's windy here in Columbus," Brigit murmured as the driver left the parking lot.

In silence, they rode to the airport. Their afternoon of intense meetings had changed Colton's position on Dobb. He no longer bought Dobb's bullshit story and wanted to wring his neck. From the get-go Dobb had been a staunch supporter of Crockett Boxes and advised Marjorie to keep things under wraps for as long as possible. And now, with product weeks from rollout, MobiCom had wormed their way into the picture. Coincidence? No fucking way.

Colton ground his teeth. He could lose Francesco. *I need to let off some steam.* After texting Vonn to bring the Mercedes to Dulles, he stared out the window as the blurred stream of blinding white lights whizzed past.

The flight home was as uneventful as the one to Ohio, something Colton never took for granted when he taxied the bird to a stop. While the quiet group waited for the valet to bring the Bentley around, Vonn pulled up.

"Thank you all for your efforts today," Colton said. "I think we should prepare for a tough fight. Vonn will drive you home."

"Later dude," Chad said to Colton.

As Colton opened the Mercedes door, he glanced at his crew. Brigit stood on the sidewalk watching him. Even during the intense afternoon meetings at Francesco, the chemistry between them had been palpable. He sought her opinion and found himself looking at her even when she didn't have the floor. He was attracted to her in more ways than he'd imagined.

He needed to pull her into his arms, take her into his bed, blanket her with his body and let her intoxicating essence soothe his troubled soul. But he couldn't, which only made him want her that much more. Driving away he punched up his playlist and headed east onto I-66, toward D.C. His mind was cluttered. Time to clear his thoughts and relieve his stress.

Forty minutes later, he parked in the familiar lot and strode across the street to the unmarked door on Waterway Street in Georgetown. Three taps and the door opened.

"Hey, Big D, Spencer Lockhart," Colton said.

The door opened and Colton stepped inside.

"How ya doin', Mr. Lockhart?" Big D asked.

"Ready to unwind." Colton set off down the short hallway. It dead-ended and he turned left into the large, low-lit room with several dining tables and a bar running the length of the mirrored wall, chock-full with top quality liquors. Background music was loud enough to make conversation an intimate experience, but he wasn't interested in talking. He was there for one reason and one reason only.

Thursday night always brought a full house, but it was early. There were two small groups of women, a large group of men, and several couples. He sat at the end of the bar, ordered a Glenlivet, and loosened his noose of a tie. After undoing the top button to his dress shirt, he rubbed his aching neck. Tight didn't even begin to describe his muscles.

Tossing back the whiskey, he ordered a second. With glass in hand, he headed toward the closed door in the back. As his eyes adjusted in the darkened hallway, he ducked into the second entryway on the left. A throaty growl escaped from the back of his throat. *This is exactly what I need.*

26

UNINHIBITED

BRIGIT WOULD HAVE PILED into the Bentley and returned to the mansion if that lone taxi hadn't been idling nearby. Where was Colton headed after such a long and stressful day? *He's doing something so kinky you'd blush at the thought.* She had to know. Before Chad could object to her lame excuse about running a quick errand, or join her, she'd slammed the door shut.

"If you can stay on that black Mercedes-Maybach without letting the driver know, I'll tip you a Ben Franklin," she said to the taxi driver.

As the taxi raced down I-66, Brigit's thoughts drifted to her private conversation with Marjorie.

"And just like that you return," Marjorie said. "No explanation or advanced warning? I almost passed out when I saw you standing in the lobby." She smiled. "I've thought about you every day since you vanished."

"I've missed you too." Brigit stepped a little closer. "I had to start my life over."

Marjorie hugged her. "I'm afraid if I let go, you'll disappear again."

Brigit pulled back. "No, I won't, Mrs. Mick."

Marjorie heaved in a big breath. "We have to save Francesco. Can I count on you?"

"Absolutely. Please keep my identity a secret."

Marjorie nodded. "Best get back to Colton. He doesn't miss a thing."

The taxi turned onto K Street in Northwest D.C. tailing behind Colton's vehicle by two cars. By the time Brigit realized what a boneheaded move she'd made, they were already in Georgetown. Alone and vulnerable, she was an easy target. But Vinny Ray would have had to have followed her to Columbus and followed her home. Possible, but farfetched.

"Okay, lady, now what?" asked the taxi driver.

"Pull in front of that unmarked entrance and wait for me. I'll probably need a ride home."

Colton had quickly slipped inside when it opened. Had she looked away, she would have sworn the man had vanished into thin air. But she'd not lost him as he'd raced down I-66 and she wasn't about to lose him now.

"Take your time." The driver stopped out front. "Meter's running."

Brigit handed the driver one hundred dollars, exited the taxi and banged on the metal door. It opened and a burly man stepped outside. "Can I help you?"

"I'm a guest of Mr. Mitus."

"No Mr. Mitus here." The man, clad in a T-shirt and Dockers, crossed his thick bare arms over his wide chest.

"Okay, then, I'm here to see Colton."

"Look, ma'am, I got no idea who that is." The man stepped back inside and started to close the door.

"Wait! I'm a friend of the tall man who just arrived. He was wearing a dark olive suit and has wavy hair to here." She rested her hand on her suit collar.

The burly man shot her a cool smile. "I'll see if he's available." He shut the door and left her standing on the dark street.

A few moments later the door flew open and Colton stepped outside, frustration rolling off him. He wore no smile. "What the hell are you doing here?"

"Surely you can do better than that." She gripped her hips.

"You followed me."

"There's no fooling you. Are you going to buy me a drink?"

Colton glared at her. "In there? Absolutely not."

Muttering under her breath, she started toward the taxi. But before she reached the vehicle, Colton grabbed her and swung her around. His heated intensity excited her. She glanced at his mouth. God, she desperately wanted to kiss him.

"This club isn't what you think it is." When he pulled her close, his whiskey breath warmed her face and heated her insides.

She held his heated gaze as the intensity swirled around them. "Oh, it's a strip club. Well, girls shaking their titties and hanging from a pole do not intimidate me. Maybe I'll get some pointers."

"*You* need no pointers," he murmured.

He paid the taxi and reclaimed his hold on her arm. "I use the name Spencer Lockhart. Do *not* call me by my real name. Can you manage that?"

She arched a brow. "Only if you don't call me by mine."

Colton rapped on the door and the super-sized man opened it. "All set?"

Colton tossed him a nod.

"Should I reserve a room for you this evening?" the man asked.

"No," Colton bit out.

The man stepped aside. "Welcome to Uninhibited."

For a Thursday night in Georgetown, the swanky lounge wasn't that busy. There were no naked women and no poles. Brigit scanned the room for high-powered clients, but there were none of those, either. Black linens covered the candlelit tables and the servers wore pristine white shirts, black vests and black pants. With a vise grip on her arm, Colton guided her to the bar and gestured for her to sit. She slid onto the cushioned stool.

"Your Glenlivet, Mr. Lockhart." The bartender set the glass on a napkin. "What can we get you, ma'am?"

Brigit kept her gaze firmly on Colton. "Spencer knows what I like."

"A glass of your best pinot noir, Scotty." Rather than sitting, Colton stood with his hand on the back of her barstool, as if shielding her from view. She tilted her face to peek at him from beneath her lashes. "Playing coy won't work." His tone was still frigid.

"Where are the dancing nudies?"

The bartender placed a wine goblet on the napkin in front of her and showed Colton the bottle's label.

"Your expert taste buds will like this one," he said to Brigit before tossing Scotty a nod. The bartender uncorked the bottle and poured the dark liquid into her glass.

"Here's to a productive day." She lifted the glass, toasted his, then tipped the wine into her mouth. Berry and caramel flavors burst onto her tongue. She closed her eyes. *I needed that.* The day had been grueling, stressful and a game changer in so many ways. On a sigh, she opened her eyes. He'd sat and was staring into his drink, his hair obscuring his face. Before she could check herself, she brushed it away.

He grabbed her hand and swiveled on the barstool. "I've never met anyone so unequivocally—"

"Charming, beautiful, intelligent, headstrong?" She gave him a playful smile.

"I was going to say *annoying.*" Colton tossed back the remains of his drink.

Brigit snickered. "Even better."

"I want to kiss you," he murmured and released her hand. "So fucking badly."

Not as much as I want to kiss you. Brigit shook her head. "Not happening. We agreed. Plus, you're my client and I'm not even attracted to you." *Yeah, right.*

She cradled her glass to keep from wrapping her fingers around his bicep and eating him alive in a kiss that went on and on and on. As she gazed into his fiery eyes, an explosive need shot straight to her core. *Oh, God, I want him.*

"I don't believe you," he whispered.

She hated that he was right. Erotic thoughts drew her toward him and she ran her tongue over her tingling mouth. The tip of his index finger glided over her lower lip. As if under a hypnotic spell, her mouth parted. She wanted to take his finger into her mouth and suck, but she wouldn't. She couldn't.

"Can I get you a another Glenlivet, Mr. Lockhart?" the bartender asked.

Interrupted, his hand fell to the bar and he severed eye contact. "No thanks, Scotty." Colton's phone chirped and he fished it from his breast pocket.

Brigit tossed back a mouthful of wine and leaned against the back of the barstool. What on earth was she thinking, following Colton to his club? She'd never looked twice at any other client, yet she couldn't stay away from this one. And this one was the enemy, no less. She took another full sip, relishing the robust bouquet, then realized she had to use the restroom.

With Colton busy texting, she walked to the back of the club and tugged open the door. Wall lamps hung over each of the arched doorways, but there were no restroom signs. Hoping she'd get lucky, she entered the closest room on the right.

About twenty people stood huddled in a semi-circle with their backs to her. *Welcome to Antarctica* was painted across the back wall. Brigit edged forward. *Is this a co-ed bathroom line?* She walked to the far end and stopped short. This was no line to anywhere.

No, no way. Her mouth fell open. She'd found the dancing nudies, but they were doing a hell of a lot more than dancing. Two young women, both naked and sprawled in a graphic position on the couch, were going at it like their lives depended on it.

"Whoa," she whispered as her hand flew to her mouth.

The women's moans and cries escalated to squeals of quivering delight. The audience clapped as they tumbled into an embrace. As the crowd thinned, they hopped off and draped themselves in full-length fur coats, which had been piled in a heap on the floor.

Brigit hadn't moved. *Colton is a complicated man with unusual needs.*

"Good show, don't you think?" asked a man standing next to her. "You interested in using the couch next?"

27

COLTON'S DIRTY LITTLE SECRET

"OH, SHIT," COLTON BIT out.

Brigit was gone. *Dammit. I shouldn't have taken my eyes off her.* Colton left a Benjamin on the bar, then strode to the back of the room and opened the door. Ten rooms, five on each side, lined the hallway. And that was just this floor. The private rooms were upstairs. *She could be anywhere.* He strode into the first room on the left. A small group watched two women and a man having sex on a man-made beach. No Brigit.

He walked across the hall and exhaled a relieved breath. Brigit was firmly rooted in place near the sofa with some guy standing too damn close. Two seconds later, Colton laid a possessive hand over her shoulder and pulled her to him. *You must have gotten an eyeful and one hell of an invitation.*

"She's not available," Colton said.

"If she were mine, I wouldn't leave her alone for a New York minute." The stranger threw his hands up in surrender. "But hey, no problem." He moseyed out of the room.

"What the hell are you doing?" Colton growled.

Brigit darted to her tiptoes, brushed aside his hair and whispered, "I need to pee."

He almost laughed. He'd come here to unwind and forget about the mountain of trouble facing him with MobiCom. How had the opposite happened?

Brigit.

He gripped her hand and tugged her out of the room and down the hallway, quickly passing the open doorways. "You'll get whiplash if you keep jerking your head like that."

"You're walking so fast, I can't see inside the rooms."

"That's the idea." He stopped in front of the ladies' room. "I'll wait here."

"You might want to check to make sure there's no naked women on sofas in here. If there are, I might be a while." With a smirk, she walked in.

Pressing the sole of his shoe against the wall, he slipped his hands into his pockets. *She's one hot handful.* Since the age of ten, Colton's need for control had turned into an obsession. But controlling Brigit was impossible. As soon as Big D had told him a hot chick who wouldn't take no for an answer was waiting outside, he had to see her. Anyone else would have gotten the boot, but there was something exhilarating about feeling a little out of control whenever she was by his side. Brigit's unpredictability aroused the hell out of him.

From his vantage point, she'd done him a favor by forcing him to expose his fetish sooner than planned. Based on her shocked expression, she'd seen plenty. Now that she'd glimpsed his fucked-up world, she'd stay clear of him and *that* would solve his nagging need to have her by his side every damn moment. Brigit Farnay was his newest employee—his wealth manager, no less. His life needed no additional complications. *Keep your distance, Mitus.*

She opened the bathroom door and stepped so close he could see the bright golden flecks in her eyes. "Much better, even without the wild sofa girls. Are you going to show me around your sex club?"

Desire surged through him and he started to harden. It would be too damn easy to take her face in his hands and kiss those luscious lips. Instead, he kept his hand in his pockets. He'd come here *alone* to be *alone*. He sure as hell wasn't going to invite Brigit to watch alongside him. "You've seen plenty."

She rose on her tiptoes. "I've never seen a show like that."

"I would imagine not." Women walked in and out of the restroom, making it impossible to have an intimate conversation. "It's late and we've had a long day."

Rejection flashed across her face.

Dammit. He didn't want to hurt her. "I'm trying to do the right thing here," he murmured. With a light hand on her back, he guided her toward the front door.

"Leaving so soon?" asked Big D.

Colton pressed a folded hundred into his palm. "Thanks for tonight, Big D."

Big D pushed open the door. "You betcha, Mr. Lockhart."

Colton and Brigit stepped into the chilly night. He removed his suit jacket and covered her shoulders. "I'm parked across the street."

She furrowed her brow, but didn't move. "Why do you belong to a club like this?"

"It's complicated."

"I dated this guy who needed porn to get aroused," she said as she searched his face. "But that's not you."

"You arouse me, every time you're near," he murmured. A smile ghosted across her lips as Thursday night foot traffic tromped by. *She liked that.*

"So, is that why there are so many cameras in your home?" Shivering, she pulled his jacket closed.

His guts churned. *She thinks I'm a predator.* "Chad recommended the surveillance system to ensure our safety. There are no cameras in the bedroom suites, but even if there were, I would never spy on my employees. My interests involve *willing* participants."

"I'm sorry." Brigit broke eye contact. "I didn't think you were spying."

"It's okay. The club wasn't what you were expecting."

Pinning him with a sultry gaze, she scooted closer and her coconut scent wafted in his direction. "And what do you do with these *willing* participants?" she whispered.

Debating, he stared into her eyes for a long moment while the electricity swirled around them. "I like watching strangers fuck." Colton clenched his jaw muscles and waited. Would she resign on the spot? Would she lose all respect for him? Of one thing he was certain. Brigit Farnay wouldn't hold back.

She slicked her tongue across her lower lip. "That's so erotic."

Mother of fuck, what was this woman doing to him? Her raspy voice made his balls ache. He hardened and sparks burned a heated trail through him. God, he wanted her. Desperate to kiss her, he pulled her into his arms. *Do the right thing.* Pressing his lips to her forehead, he closed his eyes and breathed her sweet scent. Then he released his hold. That about killed him.

Slowly, she opened her eyes. They were black with desire.

She's making it impossible to stay away. They walked in silence to his car. She'd barged into his world and yet here she was, by his side. Was there nothing he could say to keep her at a safe, respectable distance? He opened the passenger door.

Instead of getting in, she stared into his eyes. "If I thought you were a monster, it wouldn't be because of this." After handing him his jacket, she dipped into the vehicle.

He draped his jacket on the backseat, then slid into the driver's seat. "Buckle up."

She belted herself. "Did you start with magazines and porn?"

Heading toward Virginia, he remained quiet. He should change the subject. Discuss work. Turn the tables and barrage *her* with a stream of questions. Hell, he'd hired her *no questions asked* even though her mysterious past had violently landed in her living room.

At the red light, their eyes met in the darkened car. "No magazines, no movies." Though he'd guarded the origin of his secret from the world, he wanted her to know. "My childhood was complicated and challenging."

"Mine was a little weird, too. I doubt we could find a person who could stake a claim on normal."

"Tell me about your childhood."

"I was an only child. My parents obsessed over me and encouraged me to excel."

That's it? A quick glance over, then he accelerated when the light changed. "That doesn't sound so bad."

"When I was three, I was reading at the first-grade level, and I'm no brainchild. Spreadsheets by five, and I probably could have managed a sales division by fourteen." She looked at him. "It was intense. Like living in a pressure cooker, every moment of every day."

"You turned out okay. Better than okay, actually."

"Thanks." She touched his shoulder and raw desire pulsed through him. He wanted her so fucking badly. "How about some quid pro quo?"

Don't do it. "When I was nine I saw my dad having sex." Refusing to look at her, he took the ramp onto the parkway.

"Your parents must have freaked out."

"My dad wasn't having sex with my mom. He was screwing someone else."

"Oh, wow," she whispered. "That's messed up."

"My mom had gone back to work when my sister was in first grade. She'd gotten her Realtor's license and worked weekends. My dad claimed to be working from home, so my mom arranged for my siblings and me to be at friends' houses for playdates. I got home early one afternoon and spied him screwing some woman. There was a different woman each weekend. And once there were two at the same time. He was fucked up. I think he knew I was spying and he liked it."

What was it about *this* woman that made him want to spill his guts? Colton glanced at her. "I've said too much."

"Do you think you're the first client who's ever confided in their wealth manager? All our discussions are confidential."

Again, she reached out and touched him, this time caressing his arm.

Her tender touch helped quiet the storm raging within. "My confiding in you has nothing to do with the fact that you manage my money."

"No child should have to suffer through that," she murmured as she removed her hand.

"Watching became my dirty little obsession. I was angry, confused, and conflicted over whether I should tell my mom. Yet I had this hard-on and a fucked-up solution of what to do with it."

"That's a lot for a little boy. Plus, a ruined relationship with your dad."

Colton tightened his grip on the steering wheel. "There was no relationship. My dad was the meanest son of a bitch I'd ever met. Watching him screw all those women was the nail in the coffin."

"I'm sorry that happened to you," she whispered. "Thank you for trusting me. I'll never betray that confidence, Colton."

He'd shared a twenty-three-year-old secret and she'd thrown him a lifeline. "Thank you."

"Did you ever talk with anyone? You know, to help you work through it?"

"No one." He glanced in her direction. "Until you."

28

FORNICATION NATION

THE TREADMILL WAS ON the last leg of the preprogrammed workout and Brigit felt the burn. But no matter how fast she jogged she couldn't outrun her thoughts. It was late afternoon on Friday and she'd somehow made it through her first workweek at Mitus Conglomerate. Even with the stress of returning home to Francesco, the unknown whereabouts of Vinny Ray, and MobiCom's acquisition play, she couldn't stop thinking about Colton's painful childhood and the abuse inflicted by his dad.

Earlier that afternoon, she'd forwarded Colton her summary report of his wealth overview. She'd have no problem freeing up thirty million. Her challenge? She disagreed with his current investments. The lack of direction was reflected in his meager earnings. Her immediate and five-year plans would revitalize his lackluster portfolio. Based on his need for control, she did not look forward to *that* meeting.

The machine completed the cooldown lap and slowed to a stop. Taylor—spinning nowhere fast—shouted, "I'll come get you."

With a thumbs up, Brigit headed upstairs to shower and dress. Tonight, Colton was throwing a Halloween party in the lower level Tapestry room. Though she loved dressing in costume, the Clothing

Czar mandated formal wear and masquerade masks, neither of which she had.

She walked upstairs and down the hallway toward her bedroom. Propped against her closed door was a medium-sized box gift-wrapped with a black velvet ribbon. She brought it into her room and shut the door.

An elegant, hand-painted masquerade mask rested on a fluffy pillow of black tissue paper. *How sexy.* Rich, robust shades of red, gold and black popped against a bright white papier-mâché background. This gift included a handwritten note.

> *Dear Brigit,*
> *I thought of you when I saw this beautiful mask.*
> *Please wear it to the party tonight.*
> *Colton*

She smiled. The Clothing Czar could be quite charming.

After showering, Brigit dressed in the black satin couture gown with the burgundy lace overlay, still hanging in her closet. Since she'd brought no gowns, she had little choice. But as soon as she slipped it on, she felt like a princess.

While smoothing pink gloss over her lips, her phone buzzed.

Ready? Taylor texted.

Yes.

Two minutes later, there was a knock on her door. Brigit stepped into the shadowy hallway and startled at Taylor's black cat masquerade mask covered in sparkly silver gems.

"Do you need to borrow a mask?"

Brigit's eyebrows shot up. "You have more than one?" Before Taylor answered, Brigit retrieved hers and returned to the hallway. "Please tie the ribbons."

Stepping out of the elevator in the Tapestry room, Brigit assumed the party would be teeming with Beltway big shots, but the milling guests didn't extend beyond the staff. Even as she scanned the masked partygoers, she sensed Colton's absence. Her libido was fast asleep. No Colton and no silver disco ball dangling from the ceiling. And the dance floor had been removed. Instead, four rows of cushioned folding chairs had been placed in front of a black velvet curtain. *What is this? Movie night?*

Red moseyed over, her face partially hidden behind an ornate gold mask. Her rich umber gown accentuated her leggy figure.

"When do the guests arrive?" Brigit asked.

Red gave her a cryptic smile. "Just us."

Masked employees dressed in their best duds tossed back champagne and feasted on fancy hors d'oeuvres. Why would Colton host a party and not invite anyone besides his staff? And where was the masked crusader?

Shane, wearing a Batman mask, appeared with another platter of hors d'oeuvres and more champagne. The bubbly was chilled, crisp and delicious. Over an hour later, as she finished her second glass, the lights flickered. Staff gravitated toward the chairs. Still no Colton. *What is going on?*

"Good evening, ladies and gentlemen." Vanessa's voice punched through the sound system. "It's time for our senses to be aroused, our bodies to be titillated and our minds to be blown. Please be seated and help me welcome Mandy and Tony to Fornication Nation."

What did she say?

The staff took their seats as the curtain rose to reveal a stage bathed in soft red spotlights. The only item on it was a king bed covered in a fitted crimson sheet with four pillows.

Oh, boy. Taylor tried to guide Brigit forward, but Brigit dug her stilettos into the carpet. She could see plenty standing four feet behind the last row.

"Colton wants you up front," Taylor whispered.

"Bully for Colton." That expensive champagne sloshing around in her stomach had suddenly lost its appeal.

Taylor sat in the last row and motioned for Brigit to join her. Holding her ground, Brigit shook her head.

A man dressed in a full-length, dark, smoking jacket and black mask escorted a woman onto the stage. She wore a red gown and matching stilettos, her face partially concealed behind a red sequined mask. As she faced the audience, the man unzipped her gown and pulled the straps off her shoulders. The dress tumbled to the floor. Clad in only her mask and stilettos, she waited.

Brigit lowered her head, her heart thundering loudly in her ears. It was one thing to go to a club, but Colton brought his fetish home.

Was this his idea of fun on a Friday night? Though she could only see the backs of Mitus's minions, no one fidgeted in their seats. Did they like this erotic entertainment or were they forced to endure because their controlling boss demanded it?

And then she knew. Colton hadn't expected her to follow him to his club. She'd stumbled into his erotic world of her own volition. But tonight? Tonight was premeditated. Was this his way of letting her know what to expect? Or was he testing her, watching her reaction from the shadows? Whatever his reasons, she would meet this challenge head-on. Lifting her head, she eyed the nude performer.

Mandy was fair skinned with large breasts and silver-dollar-sized areolas. She had a contoured midriff, meaty hips, ample buttocks and full legs. One beat at a time, Brigit's heart rate returned to normal. She could do this. Yes, she could.

Tony collected the discarded dress, sauntered into the shadows and returned with a bottle of body oil. Drizzling the liquid into his palm, he fondled her breasts until her nipples hardened. His sensual rubdown continued until her entire body glistened under the red lights. Then, he untied his sash and dropped the robe, revealing dark skin and a hairless, well-defined chest. As she stared at his firm abs, massive erection, and body-builder thighs, her pulse quickened. Mandy's turn to coat him in oil until his toned skin glistened beneath the lights.

And then, Colton appeared next to her. The heat radiating off him warmed her body. *Don't look at him. Do. Not. Look.* As she peeked through a coating of thick lashes, a jolt of adrenaline ripped through her. Framed by the black masquerade mask, his feral eyes glowed wildly.

Shrouded in mystery, he looked dangerous and sexy as hell. Her skin tingled and her cheeks flushed with a primal need.

His magnetic pull, commanding power and restrained lust poured from him. She couldn't think beyond grabbing his broad shoulders, pressing her mouth to his and losing herself in him. For hours. And hours.

With his gaze fixed on the performers, he closed the small gap between them. When their arms touched, a surge of electricity flew through her. She imagined *all* of him pressed against *all* of her. Sucking in a sharp breath, his shoulders rose and his chest expanded.

Move away.

She couldn't. But she had to stop staring, so she turned back to the show. The pair had moved to the bed. As she watched Mandy taking Tony's long, thick shaft into her mouth, she wanted—no, she needed—to do that to Colton.

She craved him in a way that scared her.

Brigit's breasts felt heavy, her tender nipples straining against the soft fabric. She closed her eyes, trying to suffocate her unrelenting desire, but on hearing Mandy's long, throaty moan, they sprung open. Tony was fervorously sucking her oversized nipple.

Ohmygod.

With his steel rod sheathed and ready, he tunneled inside her. Their roaring cries slickened Brigit's core. Gliding hard and fast, Tony's grunts and groans reminded her of the sounds Colton made when he was inside her. If she ran her fingers over the curve of Colton's bicep, she wouldn't be able to stop. Her need for him so strong she couldn't breathe.

Colton placed his hand on the small of her back and a moan shot from her throat. Her body burned; the ache between her legs throbbed. No longer able to resist, she gazed up at him. And he was waiting. His eyes shone with a dark desire.

A hungry, desperate need shorted her mind. Once hadn't been enough. She had to have him again. *Oh, God, no. Stop, stop, stop.* Drawing in a long breath, she tore her gaze away.

Tony rolled them over. Mandy sat up and glided on his rooted shaft. As he tugged her nipples, she threw back her head and moaned. "You fuck me good, baby," he growled.

Brigit was losing control. Her breathing quickened. Her hypersensitive body, primed for a release, was a few strokes from shattering onto the floor. Suddenly, the avalanche surged toward her. She couldn't move out of the way fast enough to avoid being buried under the weight of her pent-up passion. And there was only one way out.

Colton.

She had to get out of there. *Go, now.*

Spinning around, she took off toward the back of the room and hightailed it up the stairs. She burst through the door and stepped into the deserted hallway near the kitchen. After pausing to get her bearings, she took a few steps forward.

Before she could fully process what was happening, Colton whisked her into his arms.

29

TELL ME NO

COLTON CONTINUED WALKING IN one direction. His bedroom. Where he could deposit her curvy body on his bed and bury himself inside her heat. Heading down the hallway toward the foyer, he rounded the corner. And then he stopped at the foot of his grand staircase.

He waited for her to slap his face or scream at him, but all he heard was her strained breathing thundering in his ears. Though he ached for her, he'd never approach her again if she said no. He needed her for more reasons than he cared to admit. If she quit, he'd be screwed. If she said no, he wouldn't be screwed. *Dammit, stop thinking.*

"Tell me no and I'll put you down," he rasped.

Silence.

And then he looked at her.

Though her beautiful face was shrouded in mystery behind the mask, her bright green eyes were pinned on his. A low, rumbly moan cut through the silence and her pouty lips parted. He waited for her bossy command or snarky comeback. But she said nothing as her breasts rose and fell against his chest.

Placing one foot in front of the other, he started to climb.

Why in the hell isn't she stopping me?

He paused at the top of his expansive staircase and stared into her fiery emerald eyes. "Brigit, tell me to stop. If you don't, there's no turning back."

Her silence spurred him forward, but halfway down the long hallway, he stopped. His breathing was labored, but not from the climb. From her. Hell, it was all from her. His need for her could bring him to his knees.

"Dammit," he growled. "End this."

"I can't." Her husky voice filled his ears with her unbridled anticipation.

A sense of urgency hastened his steps. He had somewhere to be and someone to be with. And not just anyone. The *only* one he wanted in his bed.

Brigit.

All damn night long.

A twist of the doorknob and they were inside his private sanctuary. He kicked the door closed and set her down. Free from his grasp, she could storm out.

But she didn't move.

He threaded his arms around her waist and waited, making absolutely sure she wanted this.

Tenderly, she placed her hands on his masked cheeks. Even though he couldn't feel her warm fingers caressing his skin, muscles running along his shoulders relaxed while his dick grew firm. Her touch soothed and stirred him in the best of ways.

From behind her mask, she gazed intently into his eyes, pulled him close and kissed him.

Provocative. Irresistible. Perfect. The aroma of sex hung in the air, but they'd not even laid hands on each other. She kissed him again and when he opened his eyes, her fluttering lashes loomed into full view.

The need to drive himself into her, the same one that plagued him each night this week, vanished. He wanted to make love to her, over and over again. He wanted to fuss over her, spoil her with doting kisses and tease her with a lick or a stroke. He needed to make her writhe with pleasure beneath him.

"We agreed we wouldn't repeat last weekend," she murmured, but her sultry voice defied her words.

"Then we won't. We'll do different things. You can tie *me* up."

The lyrical sound of her sweet laugh seeped into his hardened soul. He stepped back to admire her in one of the gowns he'd personally selected. A goddess stood before him.

The lacy material flowed over her curvy hips, her petite waist and jutted over her mounds of womanly flesh. He moistened his lips, hungry to taste every inch of her creamy skin. Finally, his journey stopped when his eyes met hers. "You're stunning, Brigit."

As she modeled the gown, he appreciated her form. The material clung to her ass, making his stiff dick ache.

"I think this elegant dress would look good on anyone," she said.

"It's the dress. Definitely the dress."

Stepping close, he picked up her hand and dropped light kisses along each knuckle. "No, it's you. Definitely you." Her beauty reminded him of why he'd carried her away. Stolen her from the world. Captured her for his bed. For him.

He pulled his phone from his pocket, thumbing through until he found what he needed. Within seconds the hypnotic sounds of Enigma floated all around them from built-in speakers, creating an illusion they were one with the music.

"Please, dance with me." He held out his hand and watched her struggle with his request.

He waited and would wait for as long as it took for her to come willingly to him. What they were about to start couldn't be reversed. No rewind. No regrets. This was it and she needed to *want* to take this forbidden step with him.

She lifted her gaze from his outstretched hand to his face. Searching, searching. What did she hope to find? Goodness? Safety? Security? Agony? Despair? Misery?

When she placed her hand into his, the lightness of her soul brightened his dark one. He weaved his arm around her waist. Vibrating on a powerful wavelength, they'd let their bodies convey what they wouldn't say. As they slowly swayed, the sensual rhythm spun a protective cocoon around them.

The world fell away and she became his entire universe.

Pulling him closer, she tightened her grip. And then she whispered, "Yes."

The only answer he ever really expected.

Cupping her face, he kissed her. She snaked her fingers into his hair and tugged fistfuls. As she deepened the kiss, her guttural groan filled him with passion. He stopped thinking. Started feeling. Everything was pleasure. He wanted her to let go and give in. And he would take everything she had to give him. Like the treasure she was, he would relish her.

The kiss ended. She loosened his mocha tie and left it dangling. One by one, she unbuttoned his dress shirt and pulled the cloth away. As she pressed her hands on his heated skin, her moan sent another shock wave through him. Though hungry to take control, the anticipation of what she would do next kept him firmly rooted in place.

She pressed her supple lips to his chest and slowly dotted a line of kisses down to his nipple. Her throaty moan pumped adrenaline through him while she flicked his sensitive nipple with her tongue.

"Your touch makes me feel so fucking alive," he murmured.

Working quickly, she unbuckled his belt, then unfastened and unzipped his pants. They dropped like lead. After toeing off his shoes, he stepped out of the pants. His throbbing erection tented his boxer briefs.

Her eyes glowed and his cock ached from pure need spiraling through him. She gripped his thick shaft and squeezed. "So big and all mine."

Fuck, yes. His penis strained against the confines of his underwear.

When she released him, she murmured, "Undress me, Colton." After sweeping her hair over one shoulder so it hung like a cat's tail, she turned.

First, he untied the ribbon and set her mask on the cushioned bench at the foot of his bed, then removed his own. Though he wanted her masked, he wouldn't bring her into his world. He was already breaking his most sacred rule by having sex with his wealth manager. That was enough.

While pressing his lips to her delicate neck, he slowly unzipped her gown. His soft, worshipful kisses blazed a trail to her shoulder and she released a long, breathy groan. The dress fell away and tumbled to the floor. With her back to him, she collected the gown and draped it across the arm of the bench. Then she shot him a sultry glance over her shoulder.

Her beautiful, naked backside stilled him. The reality of Brigit standing there in only stilettos exceeded the stream of fantasies that had gotten him through the week. Her toned back, the hourglass curve of her waist, her rounded ass. He removed his jacket and shirt. His dick banged against the cotton briefs and he shed them, eager to free himself.

She was so fucking irresistible.

In one stride his hard shaft pushed against her ass. He folded her in his arms, wrapping one across her chest while the other curled around her taut tummy. Now captive in his embrace, she was his. His need for control almost complete.

With a soft touch, he skimmed her toned torso up to her breasts. Simultaneous groans. He rubbed his fingers across her erect nipple and fondled her breast.

She rolled her head against his chest and arched her back, forcing her breast into his palm. He squeezed her engorged nib. She whimpered. He pinched and she rewarded him with a moan. With his other hand, he followed the contours of her waist and hips then slipped his hand between her legs and cupped her sex.

"Mmm, I need your touch," she murmured. "So badly."

"You're mine. All night long," he whispered into her ear. "And I won't stop until we both have nothing left to give."

He slipped two fingers between her folds and into her dripping core and slowly pulled them back out. On a long whimper, she raised her arms over her head and sank her fingers into his hair. Now, with her completely open to him, he glided freely over her feminine form.

Suddenly she spun and jumped into his arms, clawing his back with her fingernails. Their lips met in an explosive embrace. He eased her onto his bed and covered her body with his as her lusty sounds filled his ears.

He could wait no longer. Sliding open the night table, he froze. He wasn't in the guesthouse where he kept his condoms. *Fuck!* He rolled onto his back, his throbbing dick protruding like his own personal monument. Her heavy breathing made his balls ache.

"What's wrong?" She rolled onto her side, facing him.

He tucked a loose tendril behind her ear. "I have no condoms here."

"What?" Her brow furrowed. "You ran out?"

"I've never invited a woman into my bedroom."

Reeling back, her eyes grew wide. "What? *Never?*"

"Until now. How the hell did I fuck this up?"

"Sprint to the guesthouse. I'll hold your spot." She waggled her eyebrows.

Smiling, he rolled out of bed.

"I was joking, sort of."

He trotted into his closet. Returning, he held up the new box of condoms and grinned. "Forgot I bought these."

Propped on her elbow, beneath his linens, she looked like she belonged in his bed. He opened the box, pulled out a string of condoms, and lay next to her.

"That should hold us." She straddled him, ripped a packet at the perforation and tore it open with her teeth.

Colton never relinquished control, but Brigit's take-charge attitude in bed was sexy as hell.

Without a moment's hesitation, she rolled it over him, rose up, and slowly worked him in and out of her hot, wet core. As pleasure spiraled through him, her beauty stole his breath.

Slowly, she glided back and forth.

So. Fucking. Good.

He fondled her breasts and gazed into her heavy-lidded eyes. On a moan, she threw her head back and glided faster. Watching her unravel around him was too much.

"Lie on me." He ran his hands down her arms and gently tugged.

A simple course correction so he could last a little longer. Her feminine curves molded against his body and he palmed her ass. Between kisses, she bit his lip, his earlobe and his shoulder. Brief, painful stings only heightened his euphoria.

He had to take back control, so he rolled them over and stilled, his hardness nestled deep inside her. "We need to slow down."

"Slow down? We're just getting started." With her hands firmly on his ass, she pulled him close, further rooting him inside her.

"Are you trying to make me come?"

"Who? Me? That's crazy! Why would I want to do something like that?"

He laughed. Having a beautiful, sexy woman beneath him was great, but add feisty and playful into the mix and, well, that was the damn tipping point. He widened his grin, coaxing her to give him what he really needed. She pursed her lips.

"Brigit, why are you holding back?"

She bucked her hips.

Fuck, that felt good.

"I'm not," she said.

"You know what I want."

"No."

He withdrew.

She whimpered. "You *are* the big bad wolf."

STONI ALEXANDER

With his shaft in hand, he rubbed it across her opening and over her clit. His arm burned from supporting his weight. But when compared to how badly his balls ached, it was nothing. He'd wait. For as long as it took until she gave him what he really needed.

"Mmm, you feel soooo good," she murmured.

And then he abruptly stopped. "I mean it, Brigit."

Tenderly she fingered a chunk of his hair from his brow. Slowly, a dazzling, deliciously wicked and just-for-him smile spread across her pink-cheeked face. *That* was what he needed. There was something about seeing Brigit happy that did it for him.

"Now, why don't you show me how *naughty* a wolf you can be?" She raised her ass off the mattress.

Positioning his head at her opening, he tunneled inside her.

"Oh, yes," she cried out.

That space was meant for him. And only him. A million pleasure points. "You feel incredible and I can't wait to watch you come while I'm inside you."

Groaning loudly, she dragged her fingernails across his shoulders. Again and again, he thrust. Slow and deep. When he kissed her, she moaned into his mouth. He licked her nipple, then sucked, but always returned to her mouth. She was beautiful and sexy and his. All night long.

For reasons he didn't want to understand, being with Brigit was different. He wanted to bring her pleasure. Feel her unravel around him. Watch the ecstasy explode across her face. Hold her sated body in the afterglow. And then do it all over again.

Undulating beneath him, she convulsed and groaned as she came. Her sex contracted around his rod and he released an explosive orgasm that rocked him dry.

In those seconds of nirvana, he called out her name. That should never have happened. Sex for Colton was never personal. But, in that instant, everything changed.

And that scared the living hell out of him.

190

30

THE MASKS

PANTING, BRIGIT ROLLED OFF him. Beads of sweat glistened between her breasts. It was near dawn and they could not stop. She'd never had so much sex in her life and she couldn't satiate her need when she was with him. More wasn't enough. And each time she felt like she was selling out to the enemy, but the switch to stop had jammed. So, she kept going with yes, yes, and yes again. If pheromones were real, she'd been marked—or marred—by this man, for all eternity.

"Colton, we have *got* to stop."

He wouldn't wipe that damn grin off his sex-flushed face. "I said that forty-five minutes ago and you climbed on me."

"Sure, blame me, but that *thing* keeps finding its way inside my body." She pointed to his penis.

He rolled toward her. "You've cast some kind of spell on me."

With a triumphant smile, she said, "I'm glad to hear my magic charms have worked on you." Then her jubilant expression fell away. "I should sneak down to my room before someone sees me."

Holding her gaze for several seconds, he kissed her. "Don't leave. I'm making us breakfast."

"Stop bossing me around."

"I didn't hear you complain once in the past seven hours." He got out of bed, flashed her a smile and vanished into the bathroom.

A few minutes later, he emerged in his black robe. "You're welcome to take a shower. Fresh towels in the linen closet." He closed his bedroom door behind him.

Hot, jetting water pounded Brigit awake. She refused to ruin her sex high by chastising herself for sleeping with him again. *Best sex ever. Just don't get used to it.* After drying off, she checked the bathroom closet for a spare robe. Not finding one, she emerged naked. Colton hadn't returned, so she padded across the sandstone floor in search of one from his closet.

Of all the rooms in Colton's home, his bedroom was Brigit's favorite. Besides his elegant taste and unlimited funds, the stately armoire, bureau and night tables were perfectly placed in the suite. But the room's focal point, the king sleigh bed with its dark gold comforter, luxurious bed linens and fluffy pillows, was the right balance of posh and inviting. The floor-to-ceiling umber curtains created a cave-like atmosphere made even cozier with the floor lamp softly illuminating the comfy-looking chaise tucked in the corner. Was the soothing ambiance the reason why she felt so safe and protected in there?

From the elaborate box ceiling with its rich merlot border and sparkling chandelier, to the marbled gas fireplace, the bedroom lacked nothing, except a clue as to what he did in there. There was no television, no stacks of unread books, not even a phone or a photo. Did he just sleep? And was she really his first guest? *Why me?*

She opened his walk-in closet, flipped on the light and startled. Amidst the rows of neatly lined clothing, eight masquerade masks hung on the far wall. Though unsettled, she stepped closer to examine them. The first hook had no mask. Perhaps that was for the one he'd used last night. Two ornate eye masks, one silver and one gold, dangled from their black ribbons. The fourth mask was a black devil.

Hanging on the row beneath were five full facial masks. These were downright ominous. Elaborate in design with jutting chins or noses. The last mask was macabre. Outlined in gold scroll with a long white nose, gold spectacles, black eyes, and a large black hat. A shiver flew down her spine. Had she discovered Colton's dark side?

"What are you doing in here?"

She jumped from the harshness in his voice. Colton's lips were drawn into thin lines and the coldness in his eyes made the hair on the back of her neck prickle. "I need a robe." Feeling vulnerable, she crossed her arms over her bare breasts. "I...I should go."

"Why don't you wear this?" he said pulling a white dress shirt off its hanger. As he helped shrug the shirt over her shoulders, his lips curved, the smile touching his eyes. "You look sexy."

To avoid eye contact, she got busy buttoning the shirt. When she finished, he took her hand. "Time to eat."

As he led her from the closet, she threw a furtive glance over her shoulder at the masks. *That last one is terrifying.*

He brought her into his sitting room where the early morning light burst in with unfiltered exuberance. The furnishings matched those in his bedroom, though this splendid space boasted the sunshine and that delightful wall of bookshelves filled to the brim.

Covered dishes, a carafe, a small pitcher of orange juice, and two place settings filled the rolling cart. Famished, Brigit lifted lids. Scrambled eggs with chives, bacon strips, English muffins with butter and jelly on the side.

"Can I serve you?" He lifted one of the plates.

"Please." She poured their juice and sat on the sofa.

He filled her plate, handed it to her, then filled his own.

"I hope you didn't wake Elliott." She buttered the muffins.

He sat next to her. "I did this."

"You cooked all this?"

"Was that a compliment?"

"I slipped. My bad." She bit into the muffin.

Pouring their coffee, he smiled. "My business is worth tens of millions, I run a thriving enterprise and you're impressed because I scrambled eggs?"

"You cooked *me* an egg." She sipped the hot java.

"You've worked nonstop all week. It's the least I could do." Colton drank his orange juice.

"Some of your masks are frightening." She shifted toward him.

"Yes, they are," he said, then forked egg into his mouth.

"Do you wear them at your home parties?"

"Just the silver or gold ones."

"So you wear the others, too?"

"I do."

"I didn't see any masks at your club."

"No masks at Uninhibited."

She finished her juice and took a few bites of egg. He said nothing further. The less she knew, the better. But she could imagine plenty. Their relationship had already crossed so many lines and boundaries. She'd be smart to collect her runaway hormones and stop interacting with him outside normal working hours in positions other than vertical. "I should get out of here," she said. "I'm meeting with several staff today about their investments."

With his eyes locked on hers, he gripped her shoulder. "This shouldn't have happened."

Her face heated. *He's going to tell me it was a mistake and blame it on the booze or the wild sex show.* Unable to look at him, she stared at her plate of half-eaten food. *Dammit. I knew better.*

"But it did," he said. "Last weekend and last night. And I—"

A loud *rat-a-tat* on Colton's bedroom door made Brigit jump. Before Colton could respond, Chad burst into the sitting room.

"Oh, shit, I'm sorry." As Chad flipped his gaze from Colton to Brigit, a large grin exploded on his face. "You two crazy kids."

Brigit's chest flushed with heat. The staff would know within hours. "I don't want to be seen here like this."

"You're fine," Colton said. "Chad will be discreet." Chad nodded.

"I didn't realize our relationship had progressed to an open-door policy."

"I thought we were going running, plus I need to discuss something urgent with you."

When Colton glanced at Brigit, she said, "That's my cue. I'm outta here." She set her plate on the coffee table and rose.

"No, not you," Colton said. "I was trying to give Chad a subtle hint that *he* should leave."

"Okay, but you're going to want to hear what I have to say sooner than later," Chad said.

"Tell me," Colton said.

Chad snatched a bacon strip and popped off a hearty bite. "A tender offer was filed with the Securities and Exchange Commission. MobiCom is charging full steam ahead and their target is the Francesco Company."

God, no. Her hand flew to her neck to stave off the feelings of suffocation.

"Dammit to hell." Colton pursed his lips and shook his head. "That son of a bitch Montgomery is driving this and he's got his flunky Dobb eating dog kibble out of his hand."

Brigit sprang a look at Colton. Anger clouded his normally bright eyes. "This setback involves my future, my career, and a company I will *not* give up," Colton said. "Brigit, I need you now more than ever."

Brigit went tight everywhere. Jaws and hands clenched. Neck and back stiffened. Losing Francesco had become very real. She started shaking and as the room began to spin, she grabbed the sofa arm.

Chad eased her onto the cushion. "You okay?"

"Yeah, just light-headed." She took a long pull of juice.

"Finish your food," Colton said. "You've hardly eaten."

"I can't," Brigit protested.

"Sorry to have barged in," Chad said.

"Relax. Both of you." Colton handed Brigit her half-eaten plate of food. "Brigit, eat something. Chad, what do you know?"

Brigit placed a forkful of cold scrambled eggs into her mouth and almost gagged. Appetite lost, replaced by nausea.

"MobiCom has been discreetly buying stock," Chad said. "Not so much that they can do serious damage, but enough to show their intention is real."

"How do you know this?" Colton asked. "Never mind. Don't answer that."

"I have a friend at the SEC," Chad said.

"One of *those* kinds of friends?" Colton asked.

"What does that mean?" Brigit asked.

"I'm a hacker," Chad said. "No, Colt, this was legit."

"Fuck. This cannot be happening, not when everything is at stake. MobiCom is definitely building their position. Brigit, I need that cash."

She leapt up and the plate tumbled off her lap. "Oh, what a mess!" She grabbed the remnants of her scrambled eggs and lobbed them onto the plate. "I have to get ready."

"We haven't finished our private conversation," Colton said.

"You've said plenty." She quickly collected her things and bolted from the room.

Scurrying down the hall, she gritted her teeth. If she had any chance of saving her beloved Francesco from being absorbed by MobiCom, she'd have to join forces with the one man who'd taken it from her. The same man who took her breath away and made her blood boil. Losing her company and failing her parents all over again seemed inevitable.

31

THE SAUNA

BRIGIT CLOSED HER BEDROOM door and bit back tears of frustration. *I'm so stupid.* Going forward, she would act like the consummate professional. Colton's comment—*this shouldn't have happened*—infuriated her. But she knew better. Having sex with any client was taboo, but twice with the same man? Never mind how phenomenal a lover he was, or how she felt while in his arms, Colton Mitus was not to be touched.

Her focus would remain fixed on the urgent business at hand—protect Francesco from MobiCom's merger play.

Saturday afternoon she texted Colton. *Can you meet Sunday to review my investment strategies?* He replied, *Sunday morning, ten thirty.* If he spent the day at home, she'd not seen him. Relieved, she worked with several staff on their investments.

At ten twenty Sunday morning, she sipped strong java while staring out her office window at the spacious grounds. Her phone buzzed and she read the incoming text from Colton. *Can't meet until Monday. Sorry for the last-minute change.*

What could be more pressing than losing Francesco? *His kinky sexual needs,* she thought.

Though grateful for the additional time to let the tension cool, she caught herself daydreaming about their fiery romp more than once. *Never again.* While working in her office Monday afternoon, Colton's deep voice broke her concentration.

"Any calls?" he asked.

"Several," Red said. "Only Marjorie McAllister's was urgent. I handled the others and sent you a summary email. The invitation you requested is in your center drawer. I hope your emergency was resolved."

Emergency?

"Thank you, Red. Please close my door on your way out." Colton pressed the speaker on his desk console and a number auto-dialed.

Should I close my door and give him privacy? Instead, Brigit sat ever so still, like a spider in its web.

"Hello, Colton," Marjorie rasped through the speaker. Her voice sounded froggier than usual. "MobiCom extended an acquisition offer. It's official."

"What's Dobb's position?"

"Bait and switch."

"Not surprising. What's his spin?"

"He thinks the merger will benefit Francesco in the long run. What a load of crap. The deal he's made with the devil will benefit *him*. We've called an emergency meeting for executives and board members this Friday."

"They'll reject the offer and MobiCom will move on."

"How's your crack wealth manager doing?"

"I'm about to find out."

"The sooner we secure that loan, the faster we can start production. Good luck, Colton."

The line went dead.

Not wanting to get caught eavesdropping, Brigit grabbed her report and pretended to read it.

"There she is." Colton's sexy timbre sent a flurry of energy skittering over her.

She lowered the analysis and their eyes met. Zing! *Nope, not going there. Fly right.* His massive frame filled the doorway. Wearing khakis, a blue button-down open at the collar and a navy sport coat, his relaxed swagger couldn't hide his troubled expression. The knot between his brows was more pronounced than usual. While his emergency wasn't her concern, his whereabouts niggled her like an annoying little Eeyore cloud.

"For you." He offered her a cream envelope with her name handwritten in calligraphy.

Ms. Brigit Farnay

She read the beautiful gold engraved invitation. A black-tie event this Saturday evening hosted by Colton Mitus and Crockett Wilde. All gala proceeds would benefit a Maryland-based nonprofit war veterans' organization. The cost? Fifteen thousand, or twenty-five thousand per couple.

"Is this my golden ticket?"

"Red booked me a room. I asked her to reserve one for you. You'll be joining me."

She arched an eyebrow. "Date back out?"

"I was going alone."

"Perhaps I'm busy." Her stomach roiled. She didn't want to leave the compound and his invitation baffled her.

"You've been working nonstop since moving in," Colton said.

"Tell me that's not a complaint."

As he held her gaze, he ran his fingers over his scruffy cheeks. "Let's try this tactic. My wealth manager must attend this important business function."

She set the invitation on her desk. "Fine. Okay. Whatever. I'll go. It's a worthy cause. Who can I pay for my ticket?"

"Not necessary."

She stood. "Let's get started."

He started rolling a chair around her desk.

"Not here. Let's spread out on the conference table." *No, no spreading of anything.* She grabbed reports, laptop and bottle of water.

His quiet moan landed in the apex between her legs. Going forward, she'd ignore her damn physical reactions. So what if he was the sexiest, most handsome man on the planet? He pulled out a chair at the conference table and gestured for her to sit, then sat next to her. She crossed her legs. He eyed them. His delicious cedar scent reminded her of their bodies curled around each other's like vines crawling up a tree.

Stop.

She handed him a copy, set meeting expectations, then launched into her summary. While listening, he furrowed his brow again. Something—besides the MobiCom merger and his ailing portfolio —was eating away at him. She wanted to run her finger down his forehead and erase the knot.

"You're concise and organized," he said.

"Are you okay?" she blurted before she could stop herself.

He stared into her eyes for several seconds as if contemplating a response. "I'm good."

What is wrong with me? Brigit Farnay didn't sleep with her clients and she certainly didn't pause during a meeting to inquire about their emotional status. But she felt his pain, and for reasons she couldn't explain, she wanted to help him through it. "Why isn't Francesco using multiple investors or borrowing from a financial institution?"

"No outside investors." He strummed his fingers on the polished wood. "I need complete control over this project."

Stroking her bracelet, she stared into his eyes. "Control is fickle and fleeting." She pulled up his portfolio and highlighted her recommendations.

At one point, he placed his hand over hers to direct the mouse. The heat from his hand skirted up her arm while arousing tingles flowed through her. She'd craved his touch all day. Time to douse her internal fire. She wiggled her hand out from beneath his and picked up her water bottle. As soon as her lips curved the rim, he stopped talking, midsentence, to watch. The cool liquid should have drowned the smoldering embers, but their eyes met and the sparks burst into flames. She set the bottle down, but couldn't look away. The longer she held his gaze, the stronger his pull. He glanced at her mouth and started to lean toward her.

No!

She whipped her face toward the laptop, severing their explosive connection.

He had so many questions. Why liquidate these mutual funds? Why dump those international stocks? Why purchase those positions? Why unload his junk bonds? Why invest in that biotech company over this one? Why purchase those particular shopping centers? He fired question after question. Like ripping a Band-Aid, she was candid and succinct.

He disagreed with each of her recommendations and his own suggestions were a clear indication of why he needed her to manage his wealth. His flaring nostrils and exasperated tone proved he wasn't adjusting to their agreement. She stayed calm, the voice of reason, patiently explaining why her decisions were necessary to grow his business to the next level.

In the end, he acquiesced. She'd execute the trades in the morning and he'd have his thirty million as soon as they sold. Although he wasn't pleased, this new financial direction would lead to a more lucrative future.

Ten o'clock. Shane had delivered dinner hours ago and they'd eaten while they worked. Even so, she'd still lost track of time.

He cracked his knuckles. "Losing is a new concept."

She shook her head. "No, Colton. You didn't lose. You just didn't get your way. *Big* difference."

"This damn well better work." He pushed out of the chair and stretched. He'd long since removed his sport coat and the blue shirt clung to his hard body. "Let's swim. I need to blow off some steam."

She shifted her gaze from his broad-shouldered torso to his eyes, then she cleared her throat. "No, thank you." Seeing him bare chested would not help.

"No one swims alone here. You'll have to join me. Plus, you've been sitting for too many hours."

"You're so bossy." She closed her laptop.

"I find that ironic coming from the woman who spent the last several hours dictating the direction of *my* financial future."

"Why don't you work through your frustration at your club?"

His eyes turned stormy and he moved dangerously close. "Seeing you in a bathing suit will help me far more than anything at Uninhibited."

Her insides quivered low in her belly. Fighting the urge to smile, she stood. Though she wasn't impervious to a compliment, she'd swim because she needed the exercise.

Once behind her closed bedroom door, she slipped into her black bikini. The halter-top hugged her breasts and she repositioned them beneath the spandex. After throwing on a long tee, she left her bedroom and almost bumped into Colton. Like a posted sentry, he stood outside her door, clad in brown swim trunks.

That man was nothing but broad shoulders and strong, well-defined traps and lats. Mouth-watering hot. And then she glanced at his firm ass. *Oh, God, help me.* Why swimming? Why not ping pong in really baggy sweats?

He didn't say a word, nor did he hide his frustration. She was his wealth manager, not his therapist, and under no obligation to help him work through his angst. So, she too remained silent as they headed downstairs. She fully expected Colton would be headstrong and he'd proven her right. Her recommendations were sound, made with the best of intentions, and would yield handsome profits. *I need complete control over this project.* Those words echoed in her mind. Why was he so protective of her company?

The Olympic-sized heated swimming pool was painted

Bermuda blue. White chaise lounge chairs were positioned around the perimeter with a folded white beach towel atop each. The sauna was nearby and the hot tub bubbled at the far end. *This is heaven.*

They were alone. She pulled her T-shirt over her head.

His eyes grew dark as he perused her body. "Laps," he grumbled. "Join me."

She dove in. The heated water soothed her aching muscles. Together they swam back and forth, but she kept her distance.

Swimming seemed to calm him. The tightness around his eyes and mouth disappeared. With their laps completed, he pretended to be a shark and her squeals of mock fear made him laugh so hard he stopped chasing her to catch his breath. Their play continued until he trapped her in his strong embrace. Before the message of *no physical contact* had been delivered to her limbs, she'd wrapped her arms and legs around his torso. Chest to chest. His erection pressed against her.

"No, Colton. I'm not your fuck buddy. You told me and I quote, 'this shouldn't have happened.' Rest assured, it won't again."

She dropped her legs, but in one fluid movement, he reached under the water and strapped her legs around him, then with his hands on her bottom, held her close. "I also said, 'but it did,'" he murmured. "Chad burst in and I never finished."

"We can't do this."

"Brigit, this shouldn't have happened, but it did." With a furrowed brow he clenched his jaw muscles. "I can't turn back. I have to have you. I don't regret one second we've spent together, nor am I going to apologize for what I want now. If you don't want the same thing, tell me and I will back off, for good."

She wanted him in every way imaginable, so she tightened her hold and remained quiet. Was she trapping him in her web or clinging to his? Her eyes stung, but not from the chlorine. They burned from staring so intensely into his.

Delicious, erotic feelings came online as her senses took over. His hard body pressed against hers, but she wanted him even closer.

She needed him inside her to complete their connection. His achingly handsome face made looking away impossible. And his moist lips beckoned to be kissed. Every part of her wanted more of him. Now.

He kissed her, hard. No mercy. No easing into the moment. A rush of adrenaline left her breathless. He claimed her, devoured her and when he pulled away they gasped for breath, and for the unspoken expectation. Standing in water up to his chest, the warm liquid flowed between them but, when he tightened his grip, not even air separated them. She buried her face in the crook of his neck and deposited lingering kisses on his glistening skin.

His breathy, husky moan vibrated against her mouth.

Muscles deep inside clenched in anticipation. She pulled away and gazed into his eyes. His frustration from earlier had been replaced with a fiery desire. He caressed the sides of her body, pausing to appreciate the swell of her breasts. He kissed her again. This one was slow, sensual, and intoxicating.

And, a third kiss, but something was different about this one. She whimpered from the gentle way his mouth pressed against hers. His breathing had quickened, but he didn't deepen the kiss. It was filled with so much passion there was no need. Kissing this man in this moment felt right.

Her lips curved into the subtlest of smiles. *Shit, shit, shit, maybe he can't tell.*

"Having fun, are we?" A smile danced in his eyes.

Yes.

"The big, bad wolf wants you to enjoy yourself before he eats you."

"Oh, God, yes." Her nipples hardened. Wetness pooled in her suit. She needed to get out of the water. Now. *Right now.*

Colton closed the door as hot, dry sauna air surrounded them. She picked up a plush white towel from the pile and opened it across the length of the extra-wide wooden bench. With her eyes on his, she unclasped her bikini top and slowly removed it.

His gaze floated over her breasts and down her torso. "You're a gorgeous woman, Brigit."

A smile breezed across her lips. What was it about *his* compliments that affected her so deeply? With her gaze fixed on his, she wiggled out of her bikini bottoms, lay on the towel, and after draping her wet hair over the teak bench behind her, gripped the wood. She placed one foot on the floor to balance herself and lifted her gaze to his. "Come here." Her sultry command dripped with need.

He removed his suit springing his erection free. After kneeling next to her, he kissed her breast, then covered her nipple with his mouth. Pleasure spiraled through her. "Harder," she murmured. Burrowing her fingers into his wet hair, she fisted a handful when the sting of his teeth tugged her nipple.

Pleasure and pain.

In an instant he was on her, thrusting his tongue into her mouth. As her hands slid down his wet back, her core ached for him. Covering her hot skin with his passionate kisses, he blazed a scorching path toward her belly button. "Tell me what you want," he murmured.

"I don't *want*. I *need* your mouth, your tongue, your—"

"My what?" Lifting his head, he stared into her eyes.

"Penis."

"Boys have penises. Call it what it is."

"Light saber," she snorted.

"I'm about to wipe that snark right off your hot little lips." He sat up and grabbed his shaft. "This is a cock."

"I need that *cock* inside me."

So much fire radiated from his eyes. "Yes, you do." With his gaze cemented on hers, he placed his face between her legs.

Reaching over her head, she gripped the bench. The eroticism tore through her. Her world spun away. Surrounded by suffocating heat, she sucked down breath after breath as she writhed from the unrelenting pleasure. He licked her folds, thrust his tongue inside and moaned. His guttural sounds shot right to the deepest, darkest part of her. "Oh, God, I like how you do that." Her sultry voice ripped through the silence.

The pleasure skyrocketed when he thrust thick fingers inside her slickened core. Her eyes flew open and she lifted her head. His face—*his* face—buried between her legs was too much. He stopped, his thumb poised over her clitoris, and gazed into her eyes. "Do you like what I'm doing to you?"

She loved it. "Yes. Don't stop."

"I want you to come for me." His commanding voice hurtled her toward a crescendo.

Then, he buried his face between her legs. Her orgasm started low in her belly and she cried out, waves of ecstasy pounding through her. Shattered, she slowly drifted back to earth. How could being with the wrong man feel so right?

He rewarded her with a smoldering kiss. In one graceful movement he added water to the rocks. "No snarky remark?" He laid another charged kiss on her lips, then straddled the bench.

"Me? Snarky?" she rasped. Feeling sated, she sat up and straddled the bench, facing him. As she pressed her mouth to his shoulder, his salty skin piqued her taste buds. He cupped her face and kissed her.

"My turn." She knelt on a folded towel.

Lust poured from his heavy-lidded eyes and she couldn't wait to taste him. She placed her mouth around the smooth head of his cock and twirled her tongue over his sensitive skin. On a long, slow moan, she eased him inside.

The more she pleasured him, the louder he moaned. And the more ravenous her need became. When his juices seeped into her mouth, her insides quivered. Though she desperately wanted to finish what she'd started, she needed to prove a point, so she slowed to a stop and pulled him out. He'd tilted his face to watch her, his chocolate-brown eyes black with desire.

He gave her a crooked smile. "Wow, that felt great."

Checking his swimsuit pockets for a condom, she found one. "You're a naughty boy, you know that?"

With an expression of complete confidence, he nodded, slowly. Straddling the bench, she ripped the packet and sheathed him.

"I'm all yours." His gravelly voice made her wetter still.

She wanted to bury him inside her and ride him hard. Instead, she lifted off the bench, positioned him at her opening and with his shaft in hand, rubbed him over her sensitive folds. Back and forth she teased, placing his head inside, then pulling him out. Her thighs burned from holding up her weight, but she wouldn't give in to the pain.

As soon as she pressed her lips to his, euphoria spread through her like wildfire. With each stroke of her tongue, she picked up speed, building to a ravenous pace.

Panting, Colton squeezed her waist. "Take me inside you."

"No." Her breath came in short, fast bursts.

Raking his hands down her back, his cock grew firmer. She tightened her grip around his shaft, positioned his head at her opening and, at last, took him inside.

"Oh, Brigit," he growled. "You feel so fucking good."

With him deep inside, she stilled. As he cracked open his eyes, a faraway look lit up his handsome face. Then, gyrating slowly, she rocked forward and up, taking him, again and again. Gasping for air between kisses, she rode him so hard she thought she'd pass out from the pleasure.

"You're making me come," he bit out. The orgasm tore through him and he tightened his embrace, his body rocking with ecstasy. When he stopped, he clasped both arms around her back and rested his forehead against her chest. Holding him securely in her arms felt good and she caressed his back while they caught their breath.

Once quieted, he raised his head and gazed into her eyes. "You're amazing and that was—that was, *wow*," he murmured. "I needed control, but you wouldn't give it to me."

She smoothed his hair out of his face. Speaking softly, she said,

"Even though I took control, you still benefited greatly from the outcome, didn't you?"

Searching her face, he stayed silent for a long moment. "Point well taken."

Neither made any move to separate, and stayed entwined until he slipped out. In a satisfied and peaceful silence, they dressed. Exiting the sauna, Brigit caught a glimpse of someone, shrouded in black, rushing out the door. Bile rose and she swallowed, hard.

Was someone watching us?

32

ALEXANDRA REED

B RIGIT SPENT THE REMAINDER of the week in a frenzy of activity. After executing the trades in Colton's portfolio, she kept an eagle eye on their performance while hunting for new opportunities. Friday's arrival allowed her to take a breath.

"Payday," Red said from Brigit's doorway.

From behind her desk, Brigit blinked. "C'mon in."

"Your first Mitus paycheck." Red handed her a sealed envelope. "And now, it's officially happy hour. I'm going to plant my ass on a kitchen stool with a bottle of wine."

"You're not working out tonight?"

"Let me demonstrate my workout." Red lifted her hand to her mouth, brought it down and repeated the motion a few times. "Filling the glass adds weight resistance."

Brigit laughed. "Is the team going to Colton's benefit tomorrow night?"

"No, just you two. My work ends when yours begins. Taylor and I have immersed ourselves in that fundraiser for months. My reward is one long weekend sleep." Red took a few backward steps, then spun toward the door. "I'll save you a barstool."

Tearing open the envelope, Brigit gaped at her paycheck. *This would buy a lot of Francesco stock.* Even though she didn't know what the top secret Crockett Boxes did, or what Francesco would be doing with Colton's thirty million, ignorance would be a hard thing to prove if charged with insider trading. For now, she'd put Francesco stock buys on hold.

Her cell phone rang. The Pennsylvania District Attorney's number flashed on her screen. Brigit jumped up and bolted outside.

"Hello," Brigit said as she closed the patio door behind her.

"Ms. Francesco?"

"Yes, it is."

"This is Tanya from Jim Sausalito's office. You called regarding an inmate status check."

Brigit's pulse soared. "That's correct."

"The prisoner is still incarcerated. Can you hold a second? I'm alone in the office and the phones are going crazy."

Before she could reply, Brigit was placed on hold. As she paced on the cobblestone path, she questioned whether she'd heard correctly. *Vinny Ray behind bars?* She raked her fingers through her hair. If Ray was still in prison, he must have hired someone to trash her home.

"Thanks for holding," Tanya said. "Did you have any further questions?"

"Please confirm the name of the prisoner is Vincent Ray."

"Uh-huh. Can you hold again?"

"No. Thanks for calling me back." Brigit hung up, rubbed the knot in her stomach and continued pacing.

If Ray wasn't responsible for the devastation in her home, had his accomplice moved on? Was she free of Ray's wrathful revenge or was someone watching her every move? As the chilly November breeze rustled the crisp leaves that clung to the giant oaks, she trembled. Dusk blanketed the remaining rays of light in early evening shadows and the tree-lined property looked ominous.

She hurried inside to find Colton's cousin, Tucker Henninger, sitting on her love seat, sporting jeans, work boots, and a red and black plaid flannel shirt.

Oh, crap.

"Do you usually take your calls outside, darlin'?"

Just the secret ones. She forced a friendly smile. "I like your lumberjack look, Tucker. Headed into the forest to chop down trees?"

He chuckled. "If I wasn't up to my eyeballs in work, I would play hooky. But I'm more of a nature lover. I'm here to update you on the break-in."

The hairs on her arm stiffened. "Great." She sat in the chair across from him and clutched her bracelet.

"Good news first. We put your home back together the best we could."

"Much appreciated." She swallowed. "There's bad news?"

"We couldn't lift any prints. Not a damn one, which surprised me since there was so much destruction." His cell phone rang and he silenced it.

Her thundering heartbeat calmed. *I've bought myself a little more time.* "Thanks for everything, Tucker." She popped up.

Leaning back, he crossed his legs. "Now sugar, burglars don't stop to scribble messages in soap or drape intimate apparel on a bed. They grab what they can and they're outta there. Since nothing was taken, and no other homes in your neighborhood were hit, I'm lookin' to you to help me, darlin'."

"Nope, sorry, Tucker. Wish I could."

He pushed off the cushion. "Slow down there. You went out of your way to eliminate evidence. Sometimes we anger someone without realizin' it. Old boyfriend with a grudge?"

A chill careened down her spine. "No one comes to mind."

He rested a hand on his hip. "What about a client who lost money on an investment that went belly-up, and blamed you?"

Or a killer who got prison time for a crime he didn't commit. "I'll give it some thought and let you know." With his eyes pinned on hers, he remained quiet. "Thanks, Tucker. Really, I'll let you know." Taking sideways steps, she meandered toward her door.

Rubbing the back of his neck, he followed. "How are things goin' here?"

"You ask a lot of questions." Out of the corner of her eye, Colton appeared in her doorway.

"Yeah, second nature, but my last question was me makin' small talk, darlin'."

"Uh-huh. Your cousin keeps me busy."

"I do." Colton strolled in and stood so close their arms touched. "You two make any headway?"

Even more than his arm pressed against hers, Colton's inner strength and confidence bolstered her spirits. When she looked into his eyes, she calmed down a little. Maybe things would be okay if she stayed near him.

"Brigit's going to holler if she thinks of anyone she coulda ticked off," Tucker said. "Angry client, ex-boyfriend, that kinda thing."

Chad came charging into Brigit's office. "Hey, Tucker, sorry I couldn't talk when I buzzed you in. Stay for happy hour and catch me up on the latest in surveillance."

"Sure thing," Tucker said.

Chad turned toward Colton. "I've got the information you've been waiting for."

Tucker's phone rang and he glanced at the screen. "Gotta take this. Somethin' smells damn good. I'm followin' my nose." Moseying out, he answered. "Hey, Mac, whad'ya find out?"

"I have confirmation Bob Dobb is Francesco's snitch," Chad said. "He and Montgomery worked together at MobiCom. Shortly after you took Francesco public, Dobb jumped ship. He went from an underperforming sales manager at MobiCom to a superstar at Francesco. Dobb won several key accounts away from MobiCom. It would appear MobiCom handed over the business to make Dobb look good."

A low growl rumbled from Colton's throat, the air electric with his anger. "That son of a bitch has been feeding Montgomery information about the innovation from the get-go." He pulled his cell phone from his pants pocket and dialed. "Marjorie needs to be warned." Phone to ear, he waited. "No, I didn't hear the news. I'm calling you with information."

As he listened, Brigit studied his chiseled features. Even with his jaw set in a hard line, and his eyes jet black with anger, he remained in command and in complete control.

"Brigit and Chad are with me." He pressed his speaker button. "Tell them."

"Francesco's board voted against the merger!" Marjorie cleared her raspy throat.

"Great news," Brigit said.

"Enjoy the moment because it's going to be short-lived," Colton said. "In light of what Chad confirmed, we've not heard the last of Montgomery."

"What did Sherlock Holmes dig up?" Marjorie asked.

Colton briefed her.

"Hmm. Three years ago, you took Francesco public," Marjorie said. "Same time Montgomery sent over a mole. Since no one knew what Crockett had been working on, he couldn't have planted Dobb for that reason. Was Montgomery interested in the competition or in you, Colton?"

"Sherlock Holmes, here," Chad said. "I'll keep digging."

"Did our crack wealth manager whip your finances into shape?" Marjorie asked.

When Colton looked at Brigit, his gaze turned smoldering hot. "Yeah, I've been whipped and then some. Dez contacted your legal team to solidify the loan details. Losing Francesco is not an option."

Marjorie huffed. "No, it's damn not."

Colton hung up.

"Sorry for the bad news," Chad said, then barreled out.

"Crockett's innovation must be a big deal," Brigit pivoted toward Colton. Maybe with the heightened stakes, he'd tell her.

"Everything we've been working on has been compromised." Colton raked his hand through his hair. "I'm so furious I could—"

"Head to your club?" She sauntered close. "Toss on a mask?"

His heated gaze floated down her body, then slowly back up until their eyes met. "Take me with you," she whispered.

"Colton? Where are you?" called a woman from his office. A statuesque beauty sashayed through Brigit's doorway. Her side-swept carob brown hair was pulled into a ponytail. The young woman had a movie star smile sitting behind dark lipstick on full lips. Her finely tailored cream suit screamed couture.

Colton looked surprised. "What are you doing here?"

The woman glided into the room. "What kind of a greeting is that?"

"Brigit Farnay, Alexandra Reed," said Colton.

"Colton speaks highly of you." Alexandra's voice was lyrical, the words rolling from her supple lips.

"Alexandra and I have known each other—"

"Forever," Alexandra said, and the two smiled at each other.

They're finishing each other's sentences.

"Colt, I need you. It's important." Alexandra looked at Brigit. "Sorry." Without waiting for a response, she grabbed Colton's arm and tugged him out of her office.

Good thing I don't care about him because I don't stand a chance against that woman. Brigit plunked into her desk chair, closed her eyes and rubbed her throbbing temples. *Tucker saw right through my bullshit and this Montgomery guy is getting on my nerves.*

Unable to distract herself with an online investment article, she left her office. *I need a drink.* Before she'd realized what she'd done, she'd barged into a very private conversation. Colton and Alexandra sat huddled on the sofa. He caressed her back while she gazed at him with teary eyes. His whisper-quiet voice and tender touch confirmed the intimacy of their relationship.

Her chest tightened as she walked toward the kitchen. Clearly, Alexandra Reed was special. *Girlfriend? Kink partner?* Rounding the corner, she bumped into Vanessa waiting for the elevator. "Hey, you'll mow someone over if you're not careful," Vanessa blurted. "What's the rush?"

"I didn't see you," Brigit mumbled.

"Oh, I know." A sly smile spread over Vanessa's face. "You've met the apple of Colton's eye. Those two have a longstanding and *cozy* relationship." Vanessa stepped into the elevator and spun toward Brigit. "Seeing Alexandra is proof positive, isn't it? Can't say I didn't warn you, honey." The elevator doors closed and Vanessa descended to the basement.

"Down to hell you go," Brigit mumbled under her breath. But Vanessa's words stung.

33

THE GALA

EVEN THOUGH BRIGIT HAD been wrangled into attending the Mitus Conglomerate benefit, she couldn't help but admire her dashing client as he drove through heavy afternoon traffic into D.C. Looking damn sexy in his fancy tuxedo, Colton's dark facial stubble and styled hair confirmed her undeniable attraction. *My God, he cleans up well.*

Hoping to sound nonchalant, she asked, "Why didn't you bring someone from your security team?"

He shot her a quick glance. "The hotel arranged amped up security for the event. You want to tell me why you're worried?"

Nice try. "I'm fine."

He hitched a brow but said nothing.

Though she'd taken a risk leaving the compound, the chance Ray's accomplice would attack her in a crowded ballroom, surrounded by security, seemed unlikely. Telling herself that didn't mitigate her fear. Anxiety hounded her all the way into the district.

When Colton pulled up to the D.C. Marriott Hotel entrance, one of two valets whisked open Brigit's door and she stepped out. "Welcome, ma'am."

"Welcome to Wardman Park, Mr. Mitus," said the second valet.

"Your bags will be taken to the Presidential Suite, tenth floor. Registration has your room keys."

Colton handed his car key and a folded twenty to the valet, then offered Brigit his arm. "You look gorgeous."

Her heart fluttered. Holding his gaze, she slid her hand through the crook of his elbow and whispered, "I'm glad you like."

His confident smile was both breathtaking and empowering. "Showtime, Mitus style. Ready?"

With a confident nod, she set her sights on the entryway and they breezed into the building.

In the center of the hotel's spacious and pristine lobby stood a lighted obelisk surrounded by a squared bench with maroon cushions. The dusk-colored, dome-shaped ceiling resembled a planetarium. As a child, she and her dad would visit the museum every Father's Day. Staring up at the magical light show, they'd pretend to be astronauts journeying through space. Severing the bittersweet father-daughter memories, she set her sights toward registration.

"Good afternoon," said the clerk. "Checking in?"

"Yes. Colton Mitus."

The clerk clicked the keyboard. "Yes, sir, we have you in two Presidential Suites, located in Center Tower. Elevators are through the lobby, down the hallway, on your left. The Grand Ballroom is right around that corner." Like a flight attendant, he pointed with both hands, then placed their keycards on the counter. "Enjoy your stay."

Colton's phone buzzed and he lifted it from his tuxedo breast pocket. "Crockett's here."

Excusing herself, she scooped the train of the Dior gown, and headed toward the restroom as her Jimmy Choos tip-tapped on the shiny marble floor. On the ride down, she'd wondered why Colton hadn't brought Alexandra Reed. Was their relationship clandestine? Was she unavailable? Maybe she was Crockett's date. As Mitus Conglomerate's wealth manager, Brigit wouldn't draw suspicion on Colton's arm. Perhaps Alexandra would. And so what if Alexandra was special? The Mitus compound was a safe place to live, Colton was a good time, and she was more connected to Francesco than she'd been in years. But the nagging thought wouldn't go away.

The restroom was empty. After reapplying lip gloss, she checked her beehive updo, ensuring the ten thousand bobby pins were still doing their ten thousand jobs.

Earlier that afternoon, Taylor had fussed over Brigit like a mother hen and had driven Red insane while Red pinned Brigit's hair into an elegant beehive updo. Brigit had selected the couture eggplant purple halter gown, and while this was no ball and she no princess, she'd never attended such a grand event on the arm of a cohost.

Tugging open the door, she startled. A man wearing a baseball cap, baggy jeans and a blue T-shirt loitered in the alcove. As he turned, he lifted something from his pocket. In a moment of panic, she started to bolt, but tripped on the dress and banged into the wall.

"Ouch, that's gotta hurt. You okay?" the man asked.

Brigit tasted the panic. Trembling, she pushed off the wall and faced him. To her relief, the stranger gripped his cell phone, not a gun.

"No coordination." Brigit tucked her evening bag under her arm, lifted her dress and walked with care toward the lobby. *I'm going to lose my mind. Relax. Ray is behind bars and his accomplice long gone.*

In a sea of black tuxes, Colton stood out like a beacon in his white jacket. Confidence, charisma, and a commanding presence followed wherever he went. Though engrossed in a conversation, he looked in her direction. With each step her skin warmed. She couldn't wait to wrap her fingers around his bulging bicep. For support, of course.

"Brigit, this is Crockett Wilde, my cohost," said Colton. "Crockett, this is my Brigit."

Her heart skipped a beat. *Did he call me his?* "Good to meet you, Crockett. I'm Colton's *wealth manager*, Brigit Farnay."

With short brown hair and piercing blue eyes, Crockett stood eye level with Colton and looked more like Colton's cousin than his real one did. "Pleasure, Brigit." Crockett shook her hand.

"Nice lilt. Where are you from?"

Crockett smiled. "The Lone Star State."

"We've got a menu snafu and need to find the event manager," Colton said. "I'll catch up with you in the ballroom." Before waiting for her reply, the two men took off.

The ballroom was comprised of three large salons, their partitions tucked away to accommodate the expected seven-hundred-plus attendees. Bartenders stood at the ready at each of the six bars positioned near the front of the room where two curved staircases met at the landing to the mezzanine level. Too many round tables to count were arranged in the middle of the spacious room, and a small stage had been set up at the far end with a podium and five chairs.

Brigit stood in line for the bar. Though she and Colton had arrived early, the growing crowd indicated it was never too early to start hobnobbing at a D.C. shindig. This networking opportunity was a mecca for Washington's elite, especially with the Mitus name behind it. Though the champagne would settle her nerves, she reluctantly chose sparkling water instead.

With glass in hand, she turned in time to spot Senator George Internado break from his party and beeline toward her.

Oh, great. Smile.

"Brigit, you look lovely." He pecked her cheek.

She gave him a cordial smile. "Good to see you, George."

"This is some event, isn't it?" As he twirled his drink, the ice cubes clanked against the glass. "Mitus sure knows how to get our attention, doesn't he?"

"How have you been?" *I give him less than thirty seconds to bring it up.*

"You know, it must be kismet that we reconnected. We had a misunderstanding that I'd like to resolve."

Zero seconds. "How so?" She glanced around, looking for a getaway route.

"You assumed I wanted us to spend the afternoon together. To be honest, I was offended."

Refusing to comment, she washed down the bullshit with a sip of sparkling water.

"All I wanted was portfolio advice. That should come as no surprise." He tossed back his drink and an ice cube smacked him in the nose. Brigit fought the snicker while George wiped his nose. "I thought it would be smart to discuss that in private. Hell, we were at a restaurant."

Oh, good grief. "How's your new wealth manager working out?"

"Let's move past the hiccup, Brigit. We've worked together for years. What do you say? Kiss and make up?"

Really? "I enjoyed working with you, George, but it's best we leave things as they are."

He stepped so close his whiskey breath stung her eyes. "You know, I can ruin your fucking little career with this much effort." He wiggled his pinky.

"There you are." Colton slipped his arm around Brigit's waist. She greeted him with a relieved smile and he gave her a little squeeze. "George, great to see you." Colton extended his hand.

The senator shook it. "Colton, this event is all the buzz! Your efforts are quite impressive. I could sure use your talents when I run for governor."

A polite smile crossed Colton's face, but his eyes went flat. "Thanks for your confidence, but I haven't raised a penny yet."

George looked at Brigit. "You two look cozy. That explains a lot."

Let it go. "Enjoy your evening, George." Moving away, she turned to Colton.

"Thanks for attending, Senator," Colton said. "Good seeing you."

With her hand wrapping Colton's arm, Brigit found the shortest bar line. The sparkling water wasn't cutting it and her mouth watered for a glass of bubbly. *One glass.*

Colton stepped close. "You couldn't get away fast enough. Not a fan of the good senator?"

"Former client trying to bully me into taking him back." She tilted her face toward his. "He's a nincompoop."

Colton chuckled. "I've heard George called a lot of things, but never that."

She inhaled. Colton's virile scent flooded her nostrils. *Delicious.* Before she could check herself, she tenderly brushed the hair from his eyes.

"Do you have any idea what your touch does to me?" His voice dropped, his lips parted and he looked at her mouth.

He was going to kiss her. And not a friendly peck, either. A full-on mouth-to-mouth smooch. As much as she craved him, she couldn't allow it. This was a business event, an important fundraiser, and he the magnet. Kissing his wealth manager was not only bad publicity, it could thrust her into the spotlight. She jerked back and bumped into someone.

"Oh, my apologies, Mrs. Mitus."

What?

She'd crashed into the photographer.

"Mr. Mitus, a few shots, please?" asked the young man.

Brigit moved away.

"Where do you think you're going?" Colton covered her shoulder with his hand and pulled her close. "You're far too beautiful to leave unescorted."

Gazing up at him, she murmured, "Then don't."

When the photographer finished, the bartender asked for Colton's drink order. "Sparking water with lime."

Damn. She couldn't drink if he wasn't. That man had a knack for thwarting her plans. He collected his drink and they stepped into the mingling fray.

A man sidled over. "Hello, Colton. Wilson Montgomery of

MobiCom." Montgomery's long, hard stare sent goose bumps erupting on Brigit's arms. Standing a head below Colton, his plastic-looking toothy grin was framed by his salt and pepper mustache and goatee.

With an icy expression and narrowed eyes, Colton said, "Cornering me at my gala?"

"It's time we become one big happy family." Wilson raised his glass, toasted the air and sipped.

Colton morphed into a block of granite. "Francesco voted against the merger. Move on."

"Francesco turned down an eight percent premium on the share price. Advise them to revote the merger, *Colton*. And do it Monday. I want this wrapped up before Thanksgiving. Do I make myself clear?"

Her blood pressure jumped. *No, no, no, this can't be happening.*

While staring at Montgomery, he rose to his full height. The air grew electric with anger. "Don't you dare threaten me," Colton said with controlled rage. "You have *no* idea what I'm capable of." With a firm grip on Brigit's arm, he led her away. "Montgomery is the last person I'd ever do business with," he bit out.

Hatred billowed from his jet-black eyes. "I'm right there with you," she said pulling him to a stop. "He's trouble." When he gazed into her eyes, the fury dissolved. "Forget about him. He's nobody." With an assuring smile, she caressed his shoulder. "This is *your* gala. Time to rock this."

Amidst the swirling sea of D.C. power, Colton's shoulders relaxed and he smiled. "Thank you."

Brimming with the confidence Brigit had come to admire, Colton greeted guests until the announcement for dinner. On the way to their table, Brigit heard something that caused her body to stiffen.

"Eve!"

Oh, no! Keep walking.

A woman caught up with her and Colton. "What a great surprise!"

With her heart pounding against her rib cage, Brigit stared blankly at the familiar face of her college friend.

"I'm Heather Peters, from Penn." Her eyebrows shot up. "We froze our bottoms off during football games at Franklin Field."

"I'm sorry, Heather. I think you've confused me with someone else. I'm Brigit Farnay."

Heather's face flushed. "Oh, how embarrassing. You look like my old friend, Eve—"

"*Heather*," blurted Brigit, "this is Colton Mitus, tonight's cohost."

"Hello, Heather," Colton extended his hand. "What brings you to our fundraiser?"

Breathe.

"I'm an attorney at Fitzsimmons and Collier," Heather replied. "Mark Fitzsimmons encouraged all his attorneys to attend. It's a great cause with tons of networking opportunities."

"Well put." He glanced around. "I haven't seen Mark. Is he here?"

"He is. We have a Fitz and Collier table. I'll tell him you asked about him. I swear, Brigit, you look so much like my old friend. They say everyone has a double. Now I believe it!"

"Pleasure meeting you." Brigit hoped she wasn't sporting the zombie look. *Too close.*

To her surprise and delight, Seth and his wife, Barbara, along with clients Frederick and Alyssa Mundy, were already seated at their table.

Seth hugged Brigit, then gave Colton a hardy handshake. "As I'd expect, things going well?"

"Very well." Colton pulled out Brigit's chair. "Brigit's doing a fantastic job."

Brigit pulled her dress train around and sat. "I'm doing my best to manage Colton's portfolio."

"Did I call this one or what?" Seth exclaimed.

"Goodness, honey, a little humility goes a long way," Barbara said. "Business aside, you two look stunning together."

Brigit's face warmed. "Oh, no, we're just—"

"Thank you," Colton said, then facilitated introductions.

Inwardly, she smiled. Rather than draw attention by protesting, Colton was being polite. She snuck a peek at him. Did they look like they belonged together?

During dinner Colton said very little, ensuring all guests had ample time to carry the conversation, but Brigit could tell he was still perturbed by Montgomery's threat. At nine thirty, Colton whispered, "Check my teeth for spinach." His grin sent her heart into a flutter.

"Nice choppers. Are they real?" With a playful smile, she nodded. "You're good."

"But I'm better with you," he murmured.

Her heart bloomed. *What a charmer.*

After excusing himself, he walked onstage and stepped up to the podium. "Good evening." As Colton waited for the chatter to die down, he slipped his hand into his pocket and smiled at the crowd.

He looks like speaking to seven hundred is no big deal.

"For those I haven't had the privilege of meeting, I'm Colton Mitus. Along with cohost Crockett Wilde, I'd like to welcome you to our intimate little gathering."

Brimming with confidence, his charismatic delivery held everyone's attention, including hers.

His message focused on the charity and the value of a donation. After introducing the ten guests of honor—veterans and their families—he cited how the organization provided customized homes or specialized wheelchairs with those funds.

Was his speech memorized or was he speaking extemporaneously? He knew when to pause, when to insert humor, and when to make his earnest plea for those in need, who'd served their country so admirably.

"Tonight, I ask that everyone give *something*." Pausing, he gazed around the ballroom. "Make a positive difference by adding a zero to your pledge."

Brigit pulled her checkbook from her evening bag. She would have donated regardless, but his impassioned speech left her with a newfound respect for the man she'd once believed was motivated solely by his own financial gain.

34

THE HYPNOTIST

Anger clouded Colton's thoughts. If he weren't flush in the spotlight at this multimillion-dollar charity event, he would have decked Montgomery, then had him thrown out. Forcing a smile, he set the stage for the evening's entertainment. "We're in for a treat this evening. Renowned hypnotist Jerry Gardner is joining us."

The guests broke into applause.

"And my cohost, Crockett Wilde, has agreed to be hypnotized. Let's give Crockett a warm welcome."

As Crockett walked onto the stage, several women hollered catcalls. "You've got admirers." Smiling, Colton shook Crockett's hand.

Crockett leaned close to the microphone. "Well, thank you, ladies. Sorry to disappoint, but I'm passing on the hypnosis." Colton was used to Crockett's subtle Texan drawl, but the hooting ladies in the audience seemed to enjoy his southern charm.

"You'll be fine." Colton slapped Crockett on his back.

"Then, you do it."

"I said *you'll* be fine. I'm staying clear of Jerry."

"Remind me how I got myself into this one, Colt."

"You lost a bet." Pausing for emphasis, Colton looked out at the audience. "What do you think? Should Crockett get hypnotized?" More hoots and hollers were heard over the audience's exuberant applause. "They love you, buddy." Colton grinned. "Between you and me, hypnosis probably won't work on you. Your head's full of rocks."

Crockett smiled at the audience. "He's right about that."

The two men had left nothing to chance. Their playful, spontaneous banter had been planned. Months ago, Colton had suggested Crocket participate. To his surprise, Crockett had agreed. The laughter turned into applause as entertainer and hypnotist Jerry Gardner trotted onstage. Colton shook Jerry's hand, patted Crockett on the back, and walked offstage as the spotlights brightened and the house lights dimmed.

"What a good looking and elite D.C. crowd," Jerry said. "Thank you for spending your evening at this worthwhile benefit. I promise you'll be entertained. Right, Crockett?"

"Sure, easy for you to say." Crockett shook Jerry's hand, then a hotel employee helped Crockett mic up.

As Colton weaved through the maze of tables, he slowed to shake several outstretched hands.

"Before we begin, let me explain hypnosis," Jerry said. "It's a state of deep relaxation, not sleep." He looked at Crockett. "You'll be able to hear me and you won't say or do anything against your wishes."

"Whew, that's a relief," Crockett said.

Colton eased into his chair next to Brigit. "Great speech," she whispered and caressed his back.

Staring into her eyes helped ease his tension. "Glad you liked it."

Did she know her tender touch could lift his dark mood? Maybe she knew him better than he realized. And could she perceive how dangerous Montgomery really was? As they shifted their attentions back to the stage, he wondered if he should tell her. *Don't burden her.*

If ever Colton needed to maintain control, it was tonight.

Everything about MobiCom's intention had become crystal clear. Wilson Montgomery was determined to win and he now knew why.

"Not everyone is capable of being hypnotized, but I'm good. I'm *really* good." Jerry stepped offstage and meandered about the room.

Under hypnosis, a woman was instructed to cluck like a chicken whenever Jerry said the word *kiss*. A male guest admitted to being a closet smoker and was hypnotized to meow whenever he felt the urge to smoke. Both agreed to wear a mic. Jerry then asked for female volunteers willing to be hypnotized with Crockett on stage. There was no shortage of excited participants.

"I'm liking this more and more," Crockett said from his seat on stage and the audience cracked up.

Brigit chortled. "Your friend is causing quite a ruckus," she whispered to Colton.

In the darkened room, he laid a possessive hand on her thigh. Had to touch her. She turned, slowly, to look at him. Her intensity struck him like a lightning bolt, the undeniable electricity whirring between them. He needed to kiss her. Hell, lose himself in her, so her sweet soul could assuage his tormented one.

She furrowed her brow. "You okay?"

"All good." Beneath the table, he clenched his free fist. One slug to Wilson's jaw would flatten that motherfucking son of a bitch.

As Jerry escorted four women on stage, he flashed Crockett two thumbs up and the audience laughed. The women sat in chairs next to Crockett and were also wired with portable microphones.

"Please get as comfortable as you can, knowing you're about to be hypnotized in front of a packed room of Washingtonians," Jerry said. "That makes *me* nervous. Ladies, please tell us who you are. Since we're in the political epicenter of the world, first names only." After introductions, Jerry began. "Close your eyes and fill your lungs with a slow, deep breath." He walked them through a visualization of being relaxed, breathing deeply and falling into a restful state.

Colton couldn't pay attention. Too much was at stake. "I have to make a phone call. Be right back," he whispered in Brigit's ear, then headed toward the back of the room.

Two at a time up the stairs, he paused on the landing that overlooked the expansive ballroom. It was chock-full. He hoped his speech, along with the entertainment, garnered a sizable donation for the charity. Feeling like he'd done something that mattered, Colton double-stepped to the mezzanine and pushed open the fire door. After confirming the quiet hallway was deserted, he dialed. Muffled laughter floated through the closed ballroom doors.

"How's the benefit going?" Marjorie asked. "Did you take my advice and bring your crack wealth manager?"

"Brigit is with me. Montgomery showed up and threatened me."

"He's a pit bull." Marjorie inhaled and started hacking.

Colton waited until she stopped. "I can't get into it over the phone, but he's unpredictable and dangerous as hell."

"Hostile takeover?"

"At the very least."

"Then it'll come down to a proxy fight and we'll need sixty percent of the shares to vote it down."

"I'll never let that son of a bitch win. *Never*. And I'll do *whatever* necessary to ensure Crockett Boxes don't get into his hands."

The call ended and he stood in the deserted hallway. The hatred that coursed through his veins used to leave him feeling out of control. But now he was a master at containing his emotion until he could release it in a more *constructive* way. Slipping his free hand into his pocket, he walked back into the ballroom.

The professional fight of his life had officially begun. *Bring it on, old man. Bring it on.*

35

BANG!

B RIGIT FLEW INTO THE ballroom through a side door as Colton returned to his seat. She finger-fluffed her hair and applied lip gloss, making it look like she'd gone to the restroom. Though wrong to eavesdrop on Colton, she had to know. But she couldn't get close enough to hear him without risking his seeing her.

The bars were closed and the booze cleared away. *Damn, I need a drink.* Montgomery's blatant threat had sent shock waves through her. She'd foolishly believed MobiCom would quietly slink away. Whatever Crockett had created must be so revolutionary that Montgomery would stop at nothing to take it.

As Brigit sat down, Colton tenderly cupped the back of her neck with his warm hand, gently squeezed, then removed his hand. This enemy was looking better and better. Colton would have to fight hard to keep Francesco from being absorbed into MobiCom. And she would have to help him. She tasted the bitter frustration.

The show ended and the audience applauded as the women filed offstage. Crockett, sporting a grin, took a bow, shook Jerry's hand, and headed back to his seat. Jerry released the clucking woman and the meowing man, thanked the crowd for their generous donations and wished everyone a safe ride home.

WITH THE BENEFIT OVER, the weighty responsibility lifted from Colton's shoulders. He thanked the guests at his table and pushed out of his chair. Mingling guests swarmed, heaping praise for his outstanding efforts. His viselike grip around Brigit's waist ensured she didn't scurry to her room or hide in the shadows as they baby-stepped toward the exit. If measuring smiles, laughter and applause was any indication, the evening had been a rousing success. But the final determination would be the bottom line. Donations were what counted and Colton had high expectations.

The image of Brigit's body draped over his spurred him through the wall-to-wall crowd of well-wishers toward the door. Sure, he'd reserved Brigit her own suite, but she damn well wasn't going to need it. Not if he had an ounce of control over the outcome.

An hour later, they'd made it as far as the exit doors.

No sooner had they stepped into the packed hallway than they were bombarded by another group of energized guests. Every few minutes, Brigit craned her neck as if searching the crowd. Both he and Tucker agreed she knew who'd vandalized her home. Someone from her mysterious past wanted her dead in the worst way. Colton would do his best to protect her, but he was at a clear disadvantage if she wouldn't confide in him. When he pulled her closer, she caressed his back. Even her simple touch sent blood pounding through his veins.

POP! A deafening sound, like a firecracker exploding in a tiny space, thundered through the hallway.

Fuck—a gunshot!

Brigit screamed, as did several others in the vicinity. On impulse, he pulled her back into the ballroom, forced her to the floor and covered her body with his.

"He's going to kill me!" Brigit trembled beneath him.

My God, she's terrified. Was that bullet meant for Brigit?

"The gun! Grab it!" screamed a woman on the other side of the open door.

"Help me hold him!" called out a man.

"Get hotel security!" shouted another man.

When Colton heard hotel security barking orders, he helped Brigit stand. The handful of guests milling in the ballroom, along with hotel staff busing tables, looked horrified.

"Are you okay?" He scanned her face and body. "Are you hurt?"

"I'm...yes, I'm okay. Are you?"

"Stay here."

"No," she said as he bolted through the ballroom door.

Three men in tuxes held a man facedown on the ground. His hands were pinned behind him. A security officer cuffed him while a second pointed his weapon at the suspect. Two additional guards were cordoning the shaken guests. The man on the ground was not Wilson Montgomery.

Colton breathed and his heart rate slowed back down. "What's going on?"

"Sir, you'll have to step back," said a hotel guard.

"That's the asshole who ruined my life!" The man strained to see Colton.

Colton knelt next to him. *Hell, it's Cranston.*

Years ago, Lance Cranston had been a loose cannon. It would appear nothing had changed for the former CEO and self-made millionaire. His self-destructive behavior had almost collapsed his organization, until Colton had purchased the company and turned things around.

"Sir, we don't know if he's armed with explosives," said a security guard.

"I know this man," Colton said to hotel security. "Please stand him up so I can speak with him."

"We need to wait until the police arrive with the Explosives Unit."

"Lance, are you carrying explosives?" Colton asked.

"No, I'm not," said Lance.

"Let's get some answers. Stand him up," said Colton.

"You'll have to wait," said the guard.

"No, I don't," Colton growled. "Stand him up, *now*."

The security team spoke amongst themselves, then pulled Lance to his feet. After patting him down, the armed guards confirmed he had no additional weapons or explosives. Lance's rumpled clothing and matted hair was nothing when compared to the stench of liquor emanating from him.

Colton placed a firm hand on his shoulder while security stood with their weapons drawn. "Lance, what's going on?"

"You ruined my life," Lance replied.

"Have you been drinking?"

Lance rolled his eyes. "Yeah."

"Drugs, too?"

"Some pills, smoked a little weed."

Colton raked his hand through his hair. "Did you *ever* get clean?"

"No."

"When I bought out your shares, you received millions. What happened to all that money?"

"Long gone, man." Lance glared at him. "You forced me out of my company."

"No. I *bought* you out and saved your organization from bankruptcy. Do you remember our deal?"

Lance's head dropped. "You'd sell me back my shares when I got clean and sober."

"I'm still waiting to do that. Get clean, Lance." Colton slid his business card into Lance's shirt pocket. "The next time you contact me, use the damn phone."

After speaking with security, Colton handed his business card to the one in charge, then addressed the crowd as Lance was hauled away. "Who wrestled him to the ground?"

"I did," replied a middle-aged man sporting a shock of gray hair.

Colton walked over and extended his hand. "Richard, I'm indebted. Thank you."

Richard shook it. "Paybacks will be steep, my friend."

"Call my office after the holidays and we'll set up a meeting." Shifting his attention to the group, he painted on a smile and tried looking relaxed. Somewhat of a challenge after an assassination attempt though.

"That's enough excitement for one evening, don't you agree? Thank you all for attending and safe travels." He scanned the crowd. "Where's my Brigit?" Calling Brigit *his* sounded damn good.

With rosy cheeks, she stepped forward and gave him the cutest smile. Had she liked that or was she relieved to get the hell out of there?

As soon as he clasped her hand, he relaxed. He'd been convinced Montgomery was trying to kill him. When he saw Lance on the ground, he knew he could manage the crisis. Walking briskly through the lobby, they slipped into a waiting elevator. Before the doors fully closed, Colton pulled her into his arms and kissed her. Rising on her tiptoes, Brigit wrapped her arms around his neck and deepened the kiss. The doors slid open. Dammit, they'd reached the tenth floor too quickly. He ended the kiss. She pulled away as they stepped into the hushed hallway.

"This way." She tugged him toward their suites.

She stopped in front of her suite and inserted her key. "Goodnight, Colton. You did a good thing, tonight. Two, actually." Without waiting for his reply, she vanished behind the closed door. Colton smiled. She wasn't getting away so easily.

He entered his suite and draped his jacket on the back of the chair, untied his black bow tie and unfastened the top button of his shirt. Time to unwind. He deserved it. That event was almost a year in the making. At the moment, though, he had more pressing things on his mind.

Brigit.

Dealing with Lance had left him off-kilter. He strode into the bathroom and splashed water on his face. After drying off, he opened the door to the adjoining suite and knocked. *Time for some fun, Ms. Farnay.*

No answer. He knocked again. Nothing. He texted Brigit. *Sleeping?*

Within seconds his phone lit up. *Who wants to know?*

A secret admirer.

She didn't respond. He lifted the cradle and called the front desk. "Brigit Farnay's room. It's under the name Colton Mitus. She's in the suite next to mine."

"Yes, sir. Please hold." After three rings, he hung up and left his room. He knew exactly where Brigit was.

Alone at the bar, she sipped her champagne. He slid onto the stool next to her. "Are you buying?"

"Sure. Put it on my room tab, under the name Mitus."

He smiled. "Drinking alone?"

"Meet my buddy, Mr. Bubbly." She tipped the liquid into her mouth.

"Seriously, I don't want to intrude." If she'd wanted him to join her, she'd have asked.

A coy smile lit up her eyes. "You're resourceful. I knew you'd find me."

"Consider yourself found." He ordered a glass of the hotel's best scotch, neat.

"Congratulations. Tonight was a huge success."

"What an ending, huh?"

"No one got hurt and that's what counts."

They sat in a comfortable silence. The scotch took the edge off, but staring at Brigit brought the heat. When they'd drained their glasses, she ordered a second glass for them both. "You like to drink," he said.

"I like to forget. This helps blur the lines." She took a long draw of champagne.

He moved a tendril from her face, then ran his hand over her bare shoulder. "Who are you running from?"

After setting her glass on the napkin, she tilted her face to peek at him. "Things I can't change, no matter how much I drink. What about you, Colton? What demons haunt you?"

Being a buzzkill would ruin their evening. He shook his head. "Can I buy you another glass?"

Shaking her head, she said, "I'm heading upstairs. Care to join me?"

He couldn't get off that barstool fast enough. They entered the elevator and rode in a sizzling silence. The doors spilled open and they hastened down the quiet hallway. Colton made no assumptions when it came to Brigit, but he had to believe that was an invitation. Wasn't it?

She stopped in front of her suite. "See you." And, again, she vanished behind her door.

Damn that woman. Reading her was impossible. Fine, he'd go to Burke's Playroom. He was too pent-up to sleep and he needed a lot more than his pathetic hand. He wanted the curves of a woman and the warmth of her supple body. And he needed that woman to be Brigit.

She doesn't care what I need.

He slid his key into the slot, opened the door and entered his living room. His suite door banged shut behind him as the adjoining door to Brigit's suite opened.

In three strides, he entered and snaked his arms around her back, pulling her close. Their mouths connected and they deepened the kiss.

This. *This* was exactly where he needed to be.

Their passionate kissing continued until his balls ached. But damn if he couldn't kiss her for days and still not have his fill of her.

Panting, he unzipped her dress and it crumpled to the ground. She started to pull away from him. "No, leave the dress," he growled.

"It's worth a fortune," she whispered between gasps for breath.

"Fuck the dress." He continued kissing her.

She abruptly ended the kiss and gazed into his eyes. "No, fuck *me*. And make it good."

36

THE GOOD STUFF

GOOD? Brigit Farnay was going to get fucking fantastic. With her help, he shed his clothing, whisked her into his arms and laid her on her bed. Still in her heels, she scrambled out and scooted into her bathroom.

"Was it something I said?" he called.

She returned with an unopened box of condoms. "I came prepared." With a smirk, she kicked off her stilettos, pulled back the linens, and tumbled into bed.

"I'm impressed, considering you haven't left the mansion."

"Shut up and kiss me, will ya?" She tore off a packet and ripped open the seal. She lifted it with dainty fingers and waggled her eyebrows. "The fun starts when you let me sliiiiiide this on you."

Her playful mood lifted his spirits. "Happy to oblige, ma'am." She unrolled it over his erection and he planked over her. "You are crazy beautiful, so fucking sexy and too damn fun, you know that?"

"I only know what you tell me and since you won't stop talking, I'm going to have to make you." She wrapped her fingers around his cock and pulled him to her opening. "Now get inside me."

He gazed into her eyes, leaned down to kiss her and slid inside. Her hot, slick core gobbled him up and he didn't stop until he was locked in place.

"Oh, you feel soooo good." She opened her heavy-lidded eyes. She felt fucking amazing. "Tell me what you want me to do."

"I already did." She raised her hands over her head, rested them on the pillows, and spread her legs wider. "Fuck me, Colton."

Somehow this woman could make him forget he was sitting in the eye of the storm in the middle of the Bermuda Triangle. On a long, satisfied moan, Colton withdrew and thrust, pausing to latch onto her erect nipple. Sucking and biting her tender flesh, he met her bucking hips with another thrust and another until her groans shifted to growls and her fingernails scraped his back.

When he kissed her, their tongues met in an explosion of thrusting and sucking as they picked up speed. The harder he thrust, the more she unleashed her inner savage.

"Hell, I'm gonna come already," he growled. "Stop."

"No, no stopping," she panted. "You asked me what I want and this is what I want. I need to lose myself in you."

He slid one hand under her ass and lifted her off the mattress, letting him sink farther on his next thrust. "You. Feel. Incredible."

She wrapped her legs around his back and bit his lip. Groaning, he came so hard, his eyes rolled back in their sockets. Catching his breath, he opened his eyes.

"Make me come, Colton." Her throaty voice was filled with need.

He lay next to her and took her other nipple into his mouth while he found her opening and caressed her folds with his fingers.

When he rubbed her clit, she groaned out, "Yes, harder. Finger-fuck me."

Brigit Farnay wasn't sugar and spice and everything nice. She had a dirty side. Colton slid his fingers inside her dripping sex and found her G-spot.

"Oh, yeah, like that. That feels great."

While gently rubbing, he kissed her and drove his tongue into her mouth. She writhed and moaned. Her free hand trailed his shoulder and down his arm. And then she started bucking and convulsing, her cries of ecstasy making him hard all over again.

When she stopped, she relaxed into the mattress. Through half-opened eyes, she gave him the tiniest smile. "I liked that," she whispered.

He eased his fingers out. "Ditto."

They lay quietly for several moments, lost in their temporary bliss. Then, she rolled toward him. "I want to tell you two things."

"Okay," he murmured.

"Going forward, no matter *what* happens, do *not* let Montgomery win."

Facing her, he asked, "Why do you care so much, Brigit?"

"I'm not sure if I'm the best judge of character, but there's something about that man that's pure evil."

Yes, there is. "You have my word." He kissed her. "What's the second thing?"

"I want to give you a blow job in the absolute worst way."

He shot her a smile. "Now you have my undivided attention."

"It's not your *attention* I want." She gave his thickening penis a playful squeeze.

After cleaning himself in the bathroom, he returned to bed. She crawled on top and kissed him, then gazed into his eyes. As he caressed her beautiful, rounded ass, she ran her fingers through his hair and down his cheek. Something had changed in the way she looked at him. A tender kiss to his shoulder turned ravenous when she bit him. And his groan elicited a saucy smile from her. Her touch aroused him in more ways than the physical. Letting the anticipation build, she inched her way down his torso, either dropping seductive kisses or dragging her tongue along his skin.

With her gaze pinned on his, she placed her lips around his head and twirled her tongue over it. "Oh, Christ, Brigit."

With her hand anchored around his shaft, she opened her mouth and took him inside, closed her lips over his head and tongued his soft flesh. He loved blow jobs. Before Brigit, it had been years since he'd let a woman suck him. Oral sex was intimate. Fucking was impersonal and that was the way he liked his sex. But he could get damn well used to her mouth around his cock.

Her beautiful, sexy mouth.

Her long, throaty moan sent arousal pounding through him. "Mmm, you taste good," she whispered when his juices seeped into her mouth. She took him farther in, then cupped his balls and rubbed them softly in her palm.

"Ah, Brigit, you feel so fucking good."

She sucked him harder and faster, her moans and coos turning into growls and guttural groans. Her head-bobbing frenzy had him racing toward another orgasm.

He squeezed her shoulders. "I'm gonna come."

On a groan, she deep-throated him. With her lips firmly around his cock, he exploded. Euphoria spread over him, replacing loathing with ecstasy. Like a rare delicacy she swallowed him down then slowly crawled up his body, kissing his abdomen and chest, neck and jawline.

Gazing into her eyes, he murmured, "I'm a changed man. You're amazing." He tucked her hair behind her ear and dropped a soft kiss on her lips.

She kissed him back, letting her supple lips linger on his. "You're not so bad yourself," she murmured.

"Let me hold you."

"No sleeping."

"Yes." There was no way he could pull an all-nighter.

"I have nightmares," she whispered.

The fear in her eyes tore at his guts. For the first time, she'd let him in a little. He kissed her forehead. "I'll protect you. All night."

For several long seconds, she stared into his eyes. What was she searching for? Slowly her expression softened and she laid her head on his chest. He wrapped her in his arms and pulled her so close she was almost on top of him. Her nestled body felt right. Within minutes, her breathing changed and she fell asleep. After meeting Montgomery and dealing with Lance's assassination attempt, Brigit had managed to replace his rage with peace.

This woman mattered. So. Fucking. Much.

37

HOSTILE TAKEOVER

"THAT MOTHERFUCKER!" COLTON'S EXPLETIVE broke the late-morning silence as his hands rolled into fists.

Five days had passed since Montgomery's threat. Colton had held out false hope that MobiCom would slither away. No such luck. With his no-interest loan in place, production of Crockett Boxes had begun. The initial shipment was expected in January. MobiCom's aggressive move was their full-tilt attempt to take control.

Brigit flew into his office. "What is it?"

"MobiCom issued a press release and jumped on social media." Colton shoved out of his chair so hard it slammed against the wall. "They've gone directly to Francesco shareholders offering eight percent premium on the current share price."

"Oh, God, no. They're gunning for a hostile takeover."

"And with that kind of incentive, there's no reason why every stockholder won't sell." Colton strode to the window.

"They'll take control with majority shares. We have to stop this, Colton."

"Yes, we most certainly do!" Marjorie McAllister stood in Colton's doorway with Vonn towering behind her.

"Glad you're here," Colton said. "Thank you, Vonn."

As Marjorie shuffled in, Vonn parked her computer bag on a conference chair, then left.

"Yesterday, Dobb began touting reasons why the *acquisition* is the best and most profitable move for both organizations," said Marjorie. "Brainwashed idiot."

"I didn't know you were coming," Brigit said.

"Ready to help us figure this out?" Marjorie bear-hugged her.

"Absolutely," Brigit said.

Colton buzzed Shane for their continental breakfast.

"Vonn whisked me here before I could sneak a nicotine hit." Marjorie lifted a packet of cigarettes from her handbag. "Smoke out front?"

"I have a patio outside my office." Brigit looped her arm through Marjorie's and headed into her office.

While Colton checked email and returned a call, Shane delivered a pot of coffee, a fruit salad and homemade pastries fresh from the oven.

As Colton opened his French door to join them, he heard Marjorie say, "Does he know?" She blew out an audible breath of smoke.

Hidden by the high, thick fire-engine-red hedges separating his stone patio from Brigit's, he listened.

"No," Brigit replied.

"Are you going to tell him?"

"It's only a matter of time before he finds out."

"How do you think he'll take it?" Marjorie asked.

"Under the circumstances, not well. Not well at all."

Colton retreated inside, quietly closed the door then raked his hand through his hair. *What the hell? Is Brigit pregnant?* He'd worn condoms. One of them must have torn. Why hadn't she told him? Why confide in a woman she'd just met? Suddenly, the strangest feeling came over him. He wanted to protect her and their unborn child. He'd make sure she took better care of herself. *No more alcohol for you, young lady.*

The two women bustled past Colton.

"Let's get started." Marjorie poured herself coffee. "What's wrong, Colton? You're ghostly white."

"I'm famished." Brigit selected a warm pastry and sat at Colton's conference table.

Colton flipped his gaze to Brigit's midriff, then back into her eyes. "I'll ask Shane to make you a pot of decaf. Do you need a nap?"

Brigit and Marjorie burst out laughing. "A nap and decaf?" Brigit asked. "At a time like this?"

Marjorie cleared her froggy throat. "If Mitus Conglomerate has nap time, I'm leaving the insanity at Francesco and applying for a position here."

The three worked through lunch, discussing every conceivable strategy for killing MobiCom's hostile takeover attempt.

"Brigit, finish your lobster salad." Colton pointed to the half-eaten food on her plate.

"You're the Clothing Czar *and* the Food Police? That portion was huge. I'm full." Brigit laid her hand across her belly, where his baby was probably the size of a peanut.

My baby. My unborn child.

"You need to keep up your strength." Colton forked fruit salad into his mouth.

"This is all very heartwarming, but could we please stay focused?" Marjorie pushed her plate away. "I'm confident Brigit knows how to manage her food consumption, Colton. So, Brigit, what do you think of Crockett's invention? Pretty damn impressive, right?"

Brigit sighed. "I'm not privy to the details."

Marjorie raised her brows. "Brigit's not a confidante? Don't freeze her out, Colton."

"She shouldn't be overly stressed," Colton said.

"Too late," Brigit said. "My stress levels shot through the roof the day I...um...uh...never mind."

She is pregnant.

At Marjorie's nudging nod, Colton put down his fork. "I've known Crockett since our freshman year at Harvard. Two years ago, he approached me with a project he and his team had been working on. Nicknamed Crockett Boxes, they increase network capacity for both voice and data between cellular towers and mobile devices. Depending on the configuration of the base station's existing equipment, the capacity increase ranges from three to ten times what exists today. That means—"

"Faster throughput and lower cost while serving an ever-increasing population of subscribers," Brigit said.

Damn, she's smart. "You got it. With signed contracts from two of the wireless carriers, the potential is—"

"Hundreds of millions," Brigit said. "And since the product's being assembled at Francesco's factory, the company earns a percentage of every Crockett Box sold."

"Exciting, huh?" Marjorie asked.

Brigit shifted her gaze from one to the other. "This is *huge.*"

Marjorie shot Colton a knowing smile. "*Now* she's onboard."

After more discussion and brainstorming, Brigit rose. "Would either of you like something? Shane's baked goodies?" She patted her stomach. "I'm going to gain some pounds working here."

"Sure, dear," Marjorie said.

The pregnancy is making her hungry. "I'll text Shane," Colton said. "A protein shake is a healthier choice."

Brigit opened the door and glanced back at Colton. "That's fine, but I still need a moment."

NEEDING TO CLEAR HER HEAD, Brigit stepped out front. Now she understood why MobiCom was going full-tilt for Francesco.

Crockett Boxes would take the wireless industry to the next technological level. If only her parents had been around to see this kind of breakthrough. She rubbed her chest, hoping to lessen the pain in her heart.

Colton had personally brought the innovation to Francesco. Through his no-interest loan, Francesco could manufacture more Crockett Boxes, thus controlling output stream and quality. She anticipated the success of the product would catapult Francesco's languishing stock, turning a midsize company into an organizational powerhouse.

With the future of her company at stake, MobiCom had to be stopped. Not because Francesco would be absorbed into MobiCom's operations and cease to exist, but because Wilson Montgomery didn't deserve this win. Colton did. He was the glue holding this entire project together.

She knew so little about the intricacies of corporate takeovers, but Melvin Parsons did. But she'd left her phone on her desk. *Dammit.*

Just then, Vanessa drove up the driveway and parked at the circle. After lifting several designer shopping bags from her trunk, she bustled toward the front door. *What a cushy job.*

"Taking a break?" Vanessa asked.

Shopping during work hours? "Clearing my head."

"Want to go for drinks sometime?" Vanessa stopped on the cobblestone walkway.

Yeah, right. "I'm super busy with work right now." Brigit looked across the manicured property, hoping Vanessa would go inside so she could think.

"I'd go stir-crazy if I were you. You hardly leave the compound. There's a new Tysons restaurant called the Publick House. Happy hours are crazy sick."

"Uh-huh." Brigit whipped her gaze toward Vanessa. "Wait, *what?*"

"Drinks, sometime? Boy, you are working too hard."

"What's the name of that restaurant?"

"Publick House. You've probably heard all the buzz."

"That's it!" Brigit bolted into the house and down the hallway. Flinging open Colton's door, she blurted, "I've got it!"

"Got what?" Marjorie asked.

She closed the door and placed her palms on the conference table. "A possible way to get MobiCom off our backs."

"Go," Colton said.

"Francesco goes public with the innovation. That should drive the stock price up, beyond MobiCom's reach. Everyone will want in. Shareholders won't sell. There won't be enough shares for MobiCom to buy, and without majority, their hostile takeover fizzles. Game over."

Marjorie nodded. "We've been so focused on keeping things under wraps, that might work."

With a nod, Colton strummed his fingers on the table. "That's a solid idea, Brigit."

Marjorie glanced at her watch. "I'll run it by the execs on my way to the airport. We'll circulate our own press release and inundate social media. With any luck Montgomery will choke on the news."

"What about Dobb?" Colton asked.

"I can handle that squirmy worm." Marjorie shoved her laptop into her bag.

Brigit snorted. *Squirmy worm* was one of Marjorie's favorite phrases. Marjorie winked at her.

As Colton stood and buttoned his suit jacket, there was a knock on his door. "Enter."

Red walked in. "Marjorie, Vonn will drive you to Dulles. Colton, tonight's event is confirmed. I need your ear."

"Finally, some good news." Colton stepped aside to speak with her.

Brigit hugged Mrs. Mick. "Thanks for nudging him to confide in me," she whispered.

Marjorie nodded. "I'll keep you posted." Red escorted Marjorie out.

They were alone. When her eyes met his smoldering stare, her body stirred.

"We leave in thirty," he said. "Taylor will assist with what to wear."

Not again. Dread crept into her consciousness, pushing out all those glorious tingles. Leaving the compound felt like tempting fate. Could she refuse? The steadfast look in his eyes was a resounding *no.* "Can you bring another Mitus minion?"

"This is one event you won't want to miss."

His charming grin sent her pulse skyrocketing. That man was too damned hot. In his doorway, she turned back. "I'll be ready."

Secretly she liked spending time with him. With Francesco front and center, it was only a matter of time before Colton learned about her past. Once he knew the truth, he'd want nothing more to do with *his* Brigit. Was it so wrong to follow her heart, just this once?

38

DREAM LAKE

TWO HOURS LATER, COLTON parked the Mercedes near the building in a mostly deserted lot and cut the engine. In the darkened car, Brigit flipped her gaze to him. "Spelunking is definitely an unexpected work event."

He'd never said the word *work*, but she'd figure that out soon enough. With his hand on the door handle, he turned toward her. "No cave crawling." Though Brigit had already stepped out, he walked around to her side, lifted her jacket from the front seat and shut the car door. She'd worn hiking boots, jeans and a brown sweater. "You look great. Why don't you dress like that more often?"

"The Clothing Czar has a lot of rules." She shot him a snarky smile, took her jacket from him and walked toward the entrance.

The soft breeze blew tendrils across her cheek. On impulse he wanted to brush the fly-aways, but tonight was about exercising control.

"I've never been here," she said as they headed toward the entrance.

"Me neither. A first for us both."

Her expression softened. He'd arranged the evening as a show of gratitude. His portfolio was no longer limping along like an injured pup. For the first time in months, he'd seen significant gains. And she'd proven herself a strong ally where Francesco was concerned.

But nothing was ever simple.

Since the break-in, he'd been ignoring Tucker's constant reminders to put the squeeze on her. *She knows the perp,* Tucker had told him. *Get her to talk.* Was this the right venue to encourage her to open up? Truth was, he needed alone time with Brigit. No staff, no work, and no fucking MobiCom breathing down his neck. Like a Neanderthal, he was dragging her ass to a cave.

Best ass I've ever seen.

A young man dressed in Dockers and a black cable-knit sweater trotted into the cool lobby. "Mr. Mitus? I'm Will, your host." The two men shook hands, then Colton introduced Brigit.

Will cleared his throat. "Welcome to Luray Caverns. I'm going to take you back four hundred million years as we explore one of the oldest wonders and beauties of our planet. The temperature throughout the cave is a constant fifty-four degrees."

"Where is everyone?" Brigit asked as they descended into the mouth of the cavern and down the low-lit walkway.

"We close to the public at four o'clock," explained Will. "The caverns are yours this evening."

"Oh, wow." She looked at Colton and grinned. Her beautiful smile was worth the expense.

As Will escorted them through the cavernous rooms, explaining the history behind the cave and how stalagmites and stalactites formed, Colton wanted to hold her hand or stroke her back, but tonight he kept one hand by his side and the other tucked in his pants pocket.

During the tour, they paused to admire Dream Lake cavern. The magnificent stalactites hung down, their reflections captured in the mirrored stillness of the pond. As Brigit turned from the shallow water toward him, she caressed his arm. "Thank you," she whispered.

Every time she left the compound the fear in her eyes tore at his guts. But in the quiet of the cave, her angst melted away. As they stared into each other's eyes, he hungered to pull her into his arms. There was no way in hell he'd be able to keep his distance. No fucking way.

Their last stop was the palatial Stalacpipe Organ room. The backdrop for the majestic instrument was the high ceiling and dramatic stalactites dangling like sand-colored icicles.

"Beautiful," she murmured.

There was a four-person table in the center of the room, covered with a white tablecloth and set for two. A bottle chilled in an ice bucket and a giant bouquet of short-stemmed peach roses with yellow tips filled a vase.

"You're welcome to play the organ," Will said. "Please use these first." Will set down a container of hand wipes and left a walkie-talkie.

Colton handed him an envelope.

"Totally not necessary, but thank you." Will took it and shook his hand. "It plays 'A Mighty Fortress is Our God.'" Will programmed the organ before trotting out.

As the hymn reverberated around them, Brigit stood perfectly still in the middle of the room. "It's breathtaking."

Yes, you are. Needing to be close, he stood beside her.

"Your efforts and the results we've achieved have been outstanding," he said when the music ended. "Thank you for stopping my financial bleeding and for helping ensure Francesco doesn't get absorbed into MobiCom. I thought this would be a memorable way to celebrate and unwind."

She blew out a frustrated breath and faced him. "What's my punishment when I don't fall in line?"

"Losing is never an option."

She wrung her hands. "Sometimes we can't control the outcome and we have to live with the consequences, no matter how difficult."

What was happening? Their fairy tale evening seemed to be unraveling. In an attempt to lighten the mood, he strode to the bucket and lifted the bottle. Her expression fell. "Were you expecting champagne?" He poured a glass of sparkling water. "This is a healthier choice for you and...for...um, for us both."

"Clothing Czar. Food Dictator," she mumbled as she took the glass. He poured another and held it up.

"Cheers." He toasted her. "To a strong and lasting partnership." After taking a sip he said, "May I have this dance?"

Her eyes softened. He hadn't a clue what had upset her, but he'd move on. After setting the organ to replay the song, he slipped his arm around her waist. In silence they swayed to the hymn. Though surrounded by people daily, Colton had been a loner until Brigit had entered his world. From that moment, he'd done whatever necessary to ensure she was by his side.

Reluctantly, she placed her hand on his bicep. But she wouldn't look at him.

The music ended. He stopped moving, but didn't remove his hand from her waist. "Look at me," he murmured.

She refused.

"My strong-willed Brigit." Her gaze drifted to his. The undeniable connection hummed between them. He could hear it as much as he could feel the never-ending magnetic attraction, pulling them closer. Her bottom lip trembled. "Can I get your jacket?"

She shook her head.

"I think your trembling lip is sending a secret message." Unable to resist, he kissed her softly. "Message received."

Her eyes grew misty and she stepped away. The distance left him cold.

"Brigit, there's so much I like about you. I thought destiny and fate were for dreamers and fools, yet here we are. I can't imagine sharing this profound beauty with anyone but you."

Hugging herself, she faced him. "This is magical and I appreciate the accolades. You hired me to do a job and I'll do my best to exceed your expectations."

"Do you know what I like most about you?" He made up the distance between them and moved back into her personal space.

She cocked a brow and hitched her hand on her hip. "I have a pretty good idea."

Relieved the awkward moment had passed and she was her feisty self again, he smiled. "Not even close." He pressed the glass to his lips and tipped the refreshing water into his mouth. "You're the only woman I've ever met who won't back down. You aren't afraid of me. You aren't in awe of me. You may or may not give a shit about me. *I have no idea.*" Clasping her hand, he caressed her silky skin with his thumb. "You're independent and strong-willed to a fault. It's your way or no way. *That* is your sexiest, most appealing quality. It drives me wild. When you flipped me off at Sullivan's, I—"

"Colton, don't."

"Brigit, you're very smart, crazy beautiful, eager for a challenge, sexually insatiable, and different from any woman I've ever met."

"You have *got* to stop talking." She pivoted and yanked the bottle from the ice bucket. With trembling fingers, she topped her flute. He stepped close and their arms brushed. Desire coursed through him. Without glancing at him, she filled his glass.

"What's wrong?"

She shuddered in a breath and pursed her lips. For reasons he couldn't begin to understand she'd become guarded as hell. Time to lighten the mood. He gestured toward the organ. "Why don't you hop up there and try it out?"

"No way." Now visibly shaking, she rubbed her arms.

He picked up her jacket and shrugged it over her, then with two fingers gently hooking her chin, he tipped her face toward him. "Doing what terrifies us makes us stronger when we achieve the impossible. I believe in you."

His encouraging smile wasn't enough to evoke one from her. Her eyes were wide, like a caged animal. "I've never played in front of anyone. Only my mom and dad…a lifetime ago."

"To ensure I can't hear, I'll stick my fingers in my ears." He tossed a nod in the direction of the instrument. "Go on, you can do it."

Walking toward the three-step staircase like she didn't trust her legs, she got as far as the first step. He offered his hand and she placed hers in his. Her fingers were ice cold and her hand trembled. Pain pummeled his chest. He wanted to comfort her, tell her she didn't have to do it. But she'd feel triumphant if she could conquer her fear. And he believed she could. He held her hand until she reached the safety of the platform, then let go. Alone with her demons, she sat on the bench.

"Before you play—" He handed her a wipe, then pulled out a chair and sat.

The player organ housed four rows of keys, too many knobs to count and four pedals. After cleaning her fingers, she placed them on the lowest keyboard and played a few notes.

You can do it.

Her shoulders rose as she inhaled a deep breath. She struck a chord, then tapped out a melody. And then she cut loose. Her emotion, through the music, filled the cavernous room while the echoes danced in the shadows.

Colton sat spellbound. When she finished, an all-encompassing peace surrounded them in a protective cocoon she had spun.

FOR THE FIRST TIME in years, tranquility soothed Brigit's restless soul. Since the death of her parents, she'd always played alone. With Colton's encouragement, she'd overcome a childhood roadblock.

Feeling triumphant, she rose and walked the short distance to the staircase and waited. Two easy strides and he offered his hand. This time, when she touched him she felt his strength and his belief in her. On the last step, they stood eye to eye. "Thank you," she whispered.

Without a second's hesitation, he captured her face in his hands and he kissed her. Soft, tender, and deliciously worshipful.

Did he realize the incredible gift he'd just given her? She did, and she'd never forget it.

With walkie-talkie in hand, Colton requested Will's assistance. After escorting them to the cavern with the small pond, Will left.

Brigit and Colton stood in peaceful silence admiring the still waters of Dream Lake. The glassy surface reflected the long, bony finger-like stalactites hanging from the ceiling, creating an illusion that the water's depth was far greater than a shallow pool. Nature's majestic sculptures had designed a breathtaking sight, a wondrous work of art that filled the room with serenity. The fantasy lured Brigit into seeing something that simply wasn't there. But if she believed it, it must be real. Mustn't it?

Staring into the quiet liquid, she reflected on how her contrived life was as much of an illusion as Dream Lake. Hidden beneath her beguiling surface were secrets, lies, fear, anger, pain, and so much loneliness. And when the harsh light was shone, and the truth revealed, the illusion would be dispelled. Reality would turn everything dark, murky, and ugly.

How she envied Dream Lake.

39

A PAINFUL PAST

A T FIRST, BRIGIT HAD tried ignoring the feelings, and then she'd tried fighting them. In the beauty and stillness of Dream Lake, she silently acknowledged the truth. She was falling in love with Colton. Completely and unconditionally. Instead of feeling joyous, emptiness ripped at her heart. Once he knew her secrets, his rejection would bring unbearable heartache. But how much longer could she withhold the truth?

Will escorted them back to the Stalacpipe organ room and left. Covered dishes had been placed on the white tablecloth—cherry tomato, mozzarella ball and herb skewers, fried chicken bites, roasted potato salad with scallions, and cucumber and sugar snap salad.

"Everything looks great." Brigit pointed to the array of foods. "Did you do this?"

"My specialty is breakfast and grilling," Colton replied. "Picnic prepared by Elliott and Shane." They filled their plates and dug in.

"Tell me about your life prior to Porter, Gabriel and Sethfield," Colton said after they'd sampled everything.

Oh, God, no. She poked at the potatoes. "Nothing much to know. Why do you ask?"

"I'm interested. Where are you from?"

"Earth." She white-knuckled her cloth napkin.

"Well, that's a comfort. Can you narrow it down for me?"

"America."

"How did you find your way to being a wealth manager?" He popped a chicken bite into his mouth.

"I like helping people realize their dreams of having long-term financial peace of mind."

Colton smiled. "You do know that sounds like a commercial, right?"

"No."

"Do you like being a wealth manager?"

"Yes."

"You don't like talking about yourself, do you?"

Though the caverns were cool, she felt like she'd erupt in flames if she didn't change the subject. "I thought we'd discuss a more relevant topic like MobiCom's hostile takeover attempt."

"And just like that, the mysterious princess shuts down the prince who's come to rescue her."

She stared at the strangled cotton in her lap. "I don't believe in fairy tales, and I rescued myself a long time ago." She fidgeted, then blurted, "So, how much did this evening set you back?" Humiliated, she closed her eyes. *Earth swallow me, now.*

On a flutter, she opened them, but was too embarrassed to look at him, so she took several sips of water, hoping to cool her heated cheeks.

"I had just enough pennies in my piggy bank to pull this off. Thanks to you, I'm no longer hemorrhaging cash. Thought I'd splurge." He took a bite of the cucumber salad.

"That was rude. I'm sorry."

He stayed quiet for several seconds, his eyes never leaving hers. "I paid seven thousand to rent the caverns, donated ten to the preservation fund and tipped Will a few hundred."

Brigit's mouth dropped open. "I don't know what to say."

"How 'bout 'thank you' or 'that deserves another blow job.'" He waggled his brows and gave her a playful grin.

She laughed. "In other words, you want a seventeen-thousand-dollar blow job. No pressure there."

He laughed. Her embarrassment was replaced by the lusty thought of doing that to him. Again her body heated, but for a different reason. She needed him in all those ways.

Suddenly his expression turned from playful to somber. "Tucker mentioned he spoke with you about your home. It's disappointing he couldn't lift any prints."

"Ah, so, you brought me here to discuss the break-in."

"I brought you here to show my appreciation, but I am concerned for your safety. And so are you." He set down his fork. "After the gunshot at the benefit, you shouted, 'He's going to kill me.' Who were you talking about?"

"I…um…I was scared and not thinking clearly." She looked away. "I don't want to put you or your staff at risk. I can move out."

"Brigit, I don't want you to leave. I want to help you." He scooted his chair closer and caressed her cheek with the back of his finger. "My brother was murdered in a home invasion when we were ten. I understand the real danger you're in." He pulled her hand from her lap and held it. "Living in fear isn't really living."

Thick silence hung in the air for a long moment. "I'm sorry for your loss," she said and threaded her fingers through his.

He looked down at their entwined hands. "My monster of a father couldn't conduct a legitimate business deal to save his fucking life. He owed some people a lot of money, which he didn't have, so they broke into our home to clean us out. Cain wasn't supposed to be there. They drowned my twin in the tub to prove they weren't messing around." He lifted his face. "I found him, blue and bloated."

In seconds, she was on his lap. She wrapped her arm around his back and hugged him. Though she could never assume to know his pain, she knew her own. "I'm so sorry."

They sat in silence until Colton continued. "The message on your bathroom mirror wasn't a coincidence. Who trashed your home, Brigit? Talk to me."

Was now the right time to come clean? Should she tell him the truth and pledge her support against MobiCom, even if he fired her and kicked her out? "I...uh, I...want you to...um...there's something I need to te—"

Will came jogging into the room. "Sorry to interrupt. I was monitoring the grounds and saw someone in the parking lot. When I checked it out, they were gone, but, well, there's no easy way to tell you this. Mr. Mitus, your tires have been slashed."

AN HOUR AND A HALF LATER, Vonn pulled out of Luray Cavern's parking lot and activated the privacy screen in the Bentley. To Colton's surprise, Brigit curled into his lap, rested her head on his shoulder and nuzzled his neck. He wrapped his arms around her, breathed her beautiful scent and listened to her steady breathing.

He didn't consider himself a romantic, but as the miles blurred by, he thought of how much his life had changed since she'd walked through Seth's door. This woman had an inner strength that rivaled his own. Determined, bold, difficult, sassy. Yet in the darkness, her fear and loneliness spoke volumes.

When Vonn stopped the Bentley at the Mitus gates, Colton dropped a light kiss on her lips. Brigit had barely spoken a word since Will had burst in with the news. She'd looked terrified, so he didn't press her further.

"We're home," he whispered.

The muscles in her back relaxed and she lifted her face to his. "Thank you for a once-in-a-lifetime evening. It meant so much to me." This time she kissed him, then scrambled off his lap.

At the circle, Vonn cut the engine and opened Colton's door.

Exiting the vehicle, Colton said, "Thank you for going the extra mile, Vonn.

"I'm relieved you're both safe," Vonn replied.

In silence, Colton escorted Brigit to her bedroom. When he turned to leave, she placed a soft but firm hand on his arm.

"Stay with me tonight."

40

THE GRAND GIFT

COLTON AWOKE SPOONING BRIGIT, his hard-on pressed against her toned bottom. She didn't stir, so he slipped out of bed, threw on his pants and strode down the hall to his bedroom. When he made up his mind, there was no stopping him. After listening to Brigit play, and watching her come alive at the keyboard, he was determined to complete the project that day.

By late afternoon, he stood admiring the unblemished instrument in his living room.

His thoughts drifted to the previous night. If some asshole hadn't slashed his tires, would Brigit have confided in him? And what would she have told him? Her baby news or something from her past that could help Tucker? Seemed farfetched that the vandalism to his vehicle was related to her home invasion, but he couldn't rule it out, either.

He'd learned nothing about Brigit, but had revealed plenty. Despite being a private person, he couldn't stop talking around her. Going forward, he needed to shut the hell up. Let her spill her guts for a change.

Taylor walked by the living room and stopped short. "I didn't know you played."

"I don't."

She smiled.

With a playful tone, he said, "Wipe the grin, Taylor. Could you bring Brigit out here so she can see her surprise?"

"She'll love it." Taylor vanished around the corner.

Moments later, Taylor led Brigit, with her eyes closed, into the living room, then left.

Colton stood next to the piano, ensuring he could see her expression. "Open your eyes, Brigit."

When she did, her face exploded in a grin. "Whoa, that's beautiful!"

Her happiness tugged at his heart. She lifted the keyboard lid and ran her fingers over the keys. "Who plays?"

"You do."

Her eyes grew wide. "You bought this for me?" He nodded. "Thank you. It's exquisite." She stepped close and whispered, "I can't play in front of others."

"You already have." Relaxing into the oversized burgundy chair, he propped his feet on the ottoman.

She shifted her attention to his bare feet, then let her gaze roam slowly up his body. As their eyes met, she ran her tongue over her lower lip. His thoughts were filled with things he wanted her to do with that sexy mouth and his twitching dick agreed.

"You seem distracted, not that I'm complaining." He tossed a nod toward the instrument. "Go ahead, give it a try."

She eased onto the bench. Brushing her fingers over the keys, she tapped several notes, then spun around. "Fingers in ears."

Feigning frustration, he obliged. She turned, but didn't move.

I believe in you.

As if she'd heard him, she struck the keys. What were the chances? She was playing his favorite piece—"Andare" by Ludovico Einaudi. As the hauntingly moving melody washed over him, she threw herself into the music. When she finished playing, applause shattered the silence. Half the staff had congregated in the foyer, some visibly moved by her performance.

"What the—" As Brigit spun around, her cheeks turned strawberry red. "Thank you." She slid off the bench and edged away from the crowd.

He rose to block her escape and looked at his team. "Guys, what are you waiting for? You've needed a pianist."

"I'll get my guitar." Red headed toward the stairs.

"Chad, help me carry my drums up," said Ryan.

"I won't sing alone." Taylor nibbled her fingernail.

"I'll grab my bass and sing with you," Chad hollered as he jogged after Ryan.

The remaining staff watched from the foyer. Colton sat on the bench and patted it. Reluctantly, she sank down and stared at the keys. What happened to his strong-willed Brigit? "Doing what terrifies us makes us stronger when we achieve the impossible."

She lifted her gaze to his. "You're pushing me into unchartered waters. I don't swim with sharks."

"We both know you can do this, Brigit."

The color had drained from her cheeks, but she swiveled toward the keyboard. Though she had to overcome this and find the gumption, he'd remain seated on the bench, by her side.

Heaving in a breath, she struck the keys. This time she chose "Nuvole Bianche" also by Ludovico Einaudi. The emotion she rarely showed blossomed when she played. When finished, she flashed him a prideful smile. She'd done it again. Last night wasn't a fluke or the magical setting bolstering her courage.

"My brave Brigit." He put his arm around her and pecked her forehead. As she gazed into his eyes, her lips parted. Just as he leaned toward her, Vanessa sidled over.

"You have a never-ending array of talents, Brigit. Colton's hired more than a money manager this time around."

He slid off the bench. *Thank you, Vanessa. You saved me from a major faux pas. C'mon, Mitus.*

From the chair in the corner, Colton watched his team form a makeshift band. They fumbled through several current numbers until they found their rhythm. Even normally reserved Dez joined in on the fun by contributing pitch-perfect harmonies. The remaining staff started dancing and Vanessa sauntered over to Colton. "Time to get those bones a-movin'." Vanessa extended her hand and Colton accepted.

While everyone else danced in the foyer where there was ample room, Vanessa stayed in the living room. That worked to Colton's advantage. While dancing, he had a great shot of Brigit as she made love to the keyboard. And if she wasn't making love to him, the instrument was an acceptable alternative.

An hour later, Shane rolled a cart of iced herbal teas and sparkling waters into the living room.

"No wine, huh?" Brigit stood. "I'll grab a glass."

"I, um…well, I was advised today's event is alcohol and caffeine free." Shane glanced nervously at his boss.

Shaking her head, Brigit continued playing with the group.

No alcohol. You're pregnant with my child.

Their rock band fun ended when Shane announced dinner and the hungry team bustled toward the dining room.

"Glad to see you've still got some 'Saturday Night Fever' moves left in you, Colt," Vanessa said. "I'm going to let Brigit know how much I enjoyed our afternoon."

Vanessa plunked on the bench, wrapped her hand around Brigit's shoulder and glanced back at Colton. He could always count on Vanessa. She was a loyal Mitus employee. Vanessa spoke quietly, but when she removed her hand from Brigit's shoulder, Brigit left the room, head down.

What the hell happened?

Vanessa rushed back to Colton. "That is one strange chick. She might be your best accountant and she plays a mean piano, but she's not all there." Vanessa tapped her skull.

"What happened?"

"I told her how great she played. She told me she didn't need my approval and to stay away from her." Vanessa's eyes glistened and she choked back a sob. "Why doesn't she like me?"

Why would Brigit lash out? That made no sense. If it happened again, he'd speak with her. Draping his arm around Vanessa, he tenderly patted her shoulder. "Thanks for your efforts. You know how much I appreciate you."

Vanessa lifted her tear-streaked face. "I do, Colton, and that means *everything* to me."

41

THE MISSING MASK

A T ONE MINUTE PAST four the following afternoon Brigit hollered, "Woo hoo!" and jetted out of her desk chair. The stock market had just closed for the week and she was ecstatic. Her plan had worked. Francesco's stock price had jumped a whopping twenty-four percent after their technology innovation announcement.

Colton strode into the office, whisked her into his arms and spun her around. "Great work! Your strategy was ingenious. This will shut MobiCom down."

Brigit laughed. Seeing Colton this happy was infectious. *If only.* "Okay, hotshot, you can put me down now."

"Oh, yeah, I don't want you getting nauseous." He set her down as if she were a porcelain doll.

After one twirl? "I'm not that fragile."

He placed both hands on her shoulders and shot her a stern look. "No more secrets. You and I are in this together."

She jumped back. "Wait, what...um...uh...what are you talking about?" Her heart rate skyrocketed. Did Tucker uncover her true identity? Had Marjorie given away their secret? No, she'd never do that. Colton didn't look angry. He looked concerned. Hopeful, even. If he'd found out who she really was, hope wouldn't be springing from his soulful brown eyes. He'd be a spewing volcano of scalding lava.

Colton's phone rang and he sprinted into his office, calling over his shoulder, "Probably Marjorie."

She followed. Colton pressed the speaker button on his desk phone console. "Mitus."

"Colton, Colton, it's Wilson Montgomery. How are we doing today?"

His singsongy voice sent goose bumps careening down Brigit's arms.

"I don't have time—" Colton's tone changed in a nanosecond.

"Make time." Wilson's voice turned staccato.

His eyes narrowed. "The takeover is *never* going to happen." Colton's chillingly cold voice scared her.

"MobiCom is well prepared for anything you or your little underlings might throw our way. Driving up Francesco stock won't stop us. We have a laundry list as long as my——well, let's just say it's *impressive*—of reasons why shareholders should, and will, vote in favor of the acquisition."

Colton grew rigid. "You keep telling yourself that if it makes you feel better."

"I will win, because *I'm* a winner. You will lose, C-C-C-Colton, because you are a l-l-l-loser. And I can pro—"

Colton disconnected the call. He stood motionless for several long and tense seconds. Brigit didn't know what to do or what to say. Should she go to him? Should she give him space? And what was that conversation really about? That was the most bizarre call she'd ever heard. Wilson Montgomery didn't even conduct himself with basic business etiquette.

"I have to leave." Without looking at her, Colton blurted, "I'm losing control." And with that, he strode out of his office.

As Brigit stared at the empty doorway, she shivered from the brusqueness of his frigid voice. Where was he going in that kind of hurry? *The gym!* Should she go after him or respect his privacy? The large wall clock in Colton's office thundered in her ears as she contemplated what to do.

An agonizing minute passed. She needed to know he was okay and bolted. Pushing open the gym door, she glanced around the quiet room. It would be another hour before anyone started working out. Though she didn't expect he'd be swimming, she checked the pool anyway. It was empty, as was the sauna.

Kitchen!

Elliott and Shane were cooking sliders and fries for happy hour. Red and Dez sat hunched over a document at the center island. Brigit stopped short. "Excuse me. Did Colton come in here?"

They looked at her and shook their heads. "No, dear," Elliott replied.

He's changing into gym clothes. She headed upstairs and raced toward Colton's bedroom. The door was closed, so she knocked. No answer. She knocked louder, then peeked inside. "Colton, are you in here?"

He wasn't, but light streamed from his walk-in closet. She ran in and stopped short, gasping for breath. The last and scariest mask—the white one outlined in ornate gold scroll, with the long, white nose and black-rimmed hat—was missing from its hook on the wall.

COLTON HAD DRIVEN ALL of ten minutes when he pulled the Mercedes onto a residential side street and slammed on the brakes.

"Dammit!" He tapped the gearshift into park. Why couldn't he be like other men who took out their frustrations at the gym or drowned them in a bottle of booze? *I'm not like other men.*

Montgomery had gotten under his skin and he had to do

something about it. Masked fucking at Burke's Playroom would relieve his seething frustration.

Brigit had looked stunned. And what about the tiny seed, nestled safely inside her beautiful body? His child. But was it? The baby could be someone else's. He knew nothing beyond what the background check had provided. Maybe she had a nasty habit of getting sloshed and inviting strangers into her home. *No fucking way. That baby is mine.*

Dusk bowed to nightfall. The streetlamp illuminated the mask on the passenger seat. That thing was scary as hell. Alone, under the cloak of darkness, he could admit the truth. "I'm no role model for this child."

Though born of evil, he didn't need to perpetuate it. Time to man the fuck up. Be a better father than his loser of a dad. Now was the time to make that break. Before it was too late. He punched up Ludovico Einaudi on his playlist and drove home.

He cut the engine at the circle, grabbed the mask, and followed the sound of buzzing happy hour chatter into the kitchen. "Excuse me," he called.

All eyes shifted to him. "Where's Brigit?"

"Thought she was with you," Chad said.

"She's not?" Taylor asked.

Had Brigit followed him again? Colton bolted from the room and up the staircase. Maybe she was napping. He knocked on her bedroom door. No answer. When he opened it, her bedside lamp shone on her bed empty. The bathroom light was off. He left her bedroom, closing the door behind him.

At the end of the hallway, his bedroom door was wide open. He'd closed it. He always closed it. As he ran inside, light from his closet spilled into the darkened room. Brigit was curled in a ball on his closet floor.

"Hey," he murmured. "Are you okay?"

Sniffling, she turned toward him. Her eyes and nose were red.

He dropped to his knees in front of her. Panic churned in his gut. Was it the baby? "Are you hurt? Jesus, what's wrong?"

Propping herself onto her elbow, her eyes drifted to the mask in his hand. "Did you?"

He searched her tear-streaked face. "Did I what?"

"Did you fuck some random woman in that mask?"

42

HIS EROTIC NEEDS

WHO DID BRIGIT THINK she was, demanding that kind of information? Colton answered to no one. His chest tightened from his callous thoughts. *Stop being fucking selfish.*

She eyed the mask like it was the bogeyman, and the need to take away her pain pounded through him. "No." Colton gently wiped her tears. "I never went to the party. Couldn't do it."

The sorrow in her eyes faded, replaced by a flicker of hope. She rose on her knees and faced him. "I shouldn't care," she murmured.

"No, you shouldn't."

But now I know you do. And so do I. "I don't deserve it," he bit out.

She lifted the mask, still in his hands. In a millisecond, her expression turned dark, her green eyes bled black with unrelenting passion. "Put this on and fuck me."

He'd seen that look before. Why would she want this? He was damaged goods, but her soul was pure. He would never tarnish her in this way. "No."

She stood and pointed to the black mask he'd worn at the Halloween party. "Then use that one." Her voice sounded husky and breathy. Sexy. Needy even.

His dick grew firm while his heart hammered against his chest.

She turned back toward him. "Is my mask still on the bench?"

It was. He'd assumed she didn't want it or had forgotten it was there. Maybe she'd left it for this moment. Didn't fucking matter the reason. She wasn't going to get her way. Not this time.

"Do you need to watch others screw while you fuck me? Is that how you work through your anger or frustration?" She stepped close and placed her soft hands on either side of his face. "Help me understand."

"I never invited you into my world." Staring into her fiery eyes wasn't helping. He caught her beautiful scent, the sweet aroma luring him closer. "This isn't what you think it is."

Her lips parted. Throwing her arms around his neck, she kissed him, hard. He squeezed her tiny waist and grabbed a handful of her thick mane, pulled her head back, and thrust his tongue into her mouth. Her sexy, throaty moan made his cock throb.

Abruptly, she jerked away. "Take me, Colton. Fuck me. I need this. Do it for me."

Panting, he stared into her eyes. Why would she want this? "I don't kiss them. There's no tender touching. It's not romantic. It's hard fucking and meaningless screwing. Is that what you want?"

"I want you more than my next breath."

He locked his bedroom door and grabbed the condoms from his drawer. Until she told him her baby news, he'd wear the damn rubber. On the way, he scooped up her mask and bolted back into the closet to find her waiting in a black and fuchsia bra, matching thong, and black stilettos.

Fucking nirvana. Hell, he didn't deserve this sexy angel. Her cascading hair rested softly on the swell of her breasts. She gripped her hips, the steamy look in her eyes concealing any fear she might have.

Yes, his needs were extreme and bizarre, but he'd never hurt her. He'd never hurt any woman. Difference was, all the women from his world wanted to be fucked by a masked man. They sought him out. They knew the rules and abided by them.

She took her mask, placed it to her face and turned. Once he'd tied the ribbon, he kissed her shoulder. With her mask in place, she faced him.

His breath came fast. His needs front and center. Seeing her like that made his balls ache. She looked incredible. He gritted his teeth because he wanted to fuck her, hard. Slam into her and take her with everything he had. He lifted the black mask from the hook, placed it over his eyes and tied it. Seconds later he stood naked before her.

She ran her nails down his chest and wrapped a firm hand around his cock. "Mmm, you are so fucking hot."

His balls tightened.

"Do they suck you?" Her breath was coming fast.

"No. I only fuck."

"But blow jobs happen at these sex parties?"

"Yes."

Kneeling, she lapped his head and took him into her mouth. And she sucked, hard. In and out, again and again. Unleashing her own aggression and unrelenting ferocity stole his breath. On a guttural groan, she fondled his balls and pumped his shaft with her other hand. And she sucked him like she wanted him to come ten minutes ago.

She felt so good, too good. He grabbed the clothing rack for support and placed his hand on her head to caress her silky hair. And then he looked down. She was deep-throating him, her head bobbing at a frenetic pace. He bit out a low growl.

So. Fucking. Good.

Her husky groan, paired with the way she rolled her teeth over his head and gobbled him up while massaging his balls, sent him careening over the edge. The orgasm shot out of him. He couldn't even warn her or pull out. Moaning, she slowed down, then pulled off. She lifted her face toward him, her mouth glistening with his juices, her breath coming hard and fast.

He stared at her for several long seconds.

"You taste good."

Fucking hell, she's amazing.

"First, I'm going to finger-fuck you," he rasped. "Then, I'm going to fuck you, hard."

"God, yes." She unhooked her bra and tossed it on the floor.

In one quick tug, he ripped her thong off. Latching onto her erect nipple, he sucked and bit one, then the other—red nibs that plumped from his rough touch.

"Harder." She raised her arms and arched her back, offering him her sublime body.

Kneeling, he placed his hands on her breasts and while fondling them, pressed his mouth to her torso. "Lie down."

She did as he commanded, bent her knees and spread them wide. "Please, I'm going to explode."

He moved between her legs and with his gaze pinned on hers, slipped two fingers inside her dripping core. She threw her head back and whimpered. A charge shot through his body, the energy landing between his legs. His dick stirred. He wanted to drive himself inside her until she couldn't remember her own fucking name.

He withdrew, ran his fingers over her clit and plunged inside. Again and again. Her eyes, framed by the mask, rolled back in her head. Bucking her hips, she whimpered and threw her head from side to side. Her hands tightened into fists.

Watching her, he started hardening. Her movements changed to short, jerky thrusts and she arched off the closet floor and came, crying out his name.

Hearing her say his name, he grew rock hard. Boneless, her tightened muscles relaxed. He withdrew his wet fingers and rubbed them over her nipples.

Slowly, she opened her eyes. "That was so...*fucking* erotic," she said between gasps.

She stroked his erection until it seeped. He needed to be inside her when he came. Tearing open a packet, he sheathed himself.

After rolling onto her hands and knees, she dropped onto her forearms. He caressed her soft ass, then slipped two fingers inside her dripping core. She was more than ready for him, and he couldn't wait to bury himself inside her heat.

She craned her head around. Seeing her masked triggered his dark need. Taking himself in hand, he tunneled inside her. They cried out, the pleasure stealing their thoughts. "Tell me what you want me to do to you," he bit out.

"Take me until I have nothing left to give you."

Pumping faster, he arched over her and fondled her breasts.

"Pinch my nipples." She rocked against his thrusts. "Deeper, harder."

He gritted his teeth as the orgasm took hold. "Ah, so fucking good." Thrusting deep, pounding waves of ecstasy rocketed through him as he came inside her.

After a moment, when his brain had kicked back on, he slowly pulled out and dotted her back with soft kisses. Rising on her knees, she turned and faced him.

He stared into her bright eyes, framed by the mask, for any signs of her sadness that had ripped his insides apart. With her hands hoisted on her hips, *his* Brigit stared back. The fiery gleam in her eyes confirmed he'd done right by her. He took her face in his hands and dropped a kiss on her mouth. She intensified the kiss until they were both breathless again.

"I like your masked world and hard fucking," she murmured. "That's the sexiest thing I've ever done."

He'd never had masked sex with someone he cared about, and when he pulled her into his arms and hugged her, he knew no other woman would ever measure up.

43

FROM BAD TO WORSE

THE MITUS BUSINESS TEAM spent the entire weekend in one long strategy session via video chat with Francesco's team, led by Marjorie.

MobiCom's public offer to buy Francesco stock held at eight percent despite the recent increase in share price. This devious move had forced Francesco to schedule a special stockholder meeting in mid-December. By a simple vote, shareholders would decide the fate of Brigit's company and her possible future with Francesco. If stakeholders didn't understand the ramifications of Crockett's revolutionary invention, or if they wanted to cash in and make the eight percentage points over market share, MobiCom would win. It was that easy for things to go horribly wrong.

Over the weekend, each hostile takeover prevention strategy was white-boarded and analyzed in minute detail. One such shark repellent tactic in particular caught Brigit's attention: White Knight —an investor acquires a publicly traded company to protect it from a hostile takeover.

Could Colton stop MobiCom's hostile takeover by taking Francesco private? By doing so, he'd buy her out of her vested shares and own the Francesco Company...*again*. Her gut had churned for the past three days.

Come late afternoon on Monday, the only thing the group could agree on was to disagree. They'd reached a stalemate. With Thanksgiving three days away, they needed to resolve the problem before the long holiday weekend. Time was running out.

Colton's phone rang and he glanced at the Francesco crew on screen. "Excuse me." He answered. "Hey, I'm in a meeting. Can I call you later?" As he listened, he clenched his cheek muscles. "Don't cry. I'm right here."

Side conversations ceased. Even the Francesco team shifted their attention to Colton.

"I'll pack a bag and be ready. No worries." Colton listened, then hung up.

His eyes were laced with concern. With a tight nod, he acknowledged his employees then shifted his attention to the Francesco team via the large monitor on his conference room table. "Terrible timing, but I have to go. We've got to agree on a strategy and present a united front. If MobiCom gets wind we've reached an impasse, they'll annihilate us. Let's vote tomorrow on which tactic will best stop their hostile takeover. Marjorie, can you handle that?"

"I've got it," she replied.

Colton strode out without even a backward glance at Brigit. He'd abandoned their strategy session for a woman. From the soothing timbre of his voice, who else could it be? Colton wasn't hers, but her aching heart felt otherwise.

"We've been going in circles for hours," Marjorie said. "Before we call it a day, any questions?"

"My brain is mush," Red mumbled.

"Okay team, get some rest and we'll vote tomorrow." Marjorie disconnected and the monitor went black.

"I'm going to work out." Red shut her laptop.

Dez removed his glasses and stood. "Brigit, I need to know if

Colton can swing the White Knight. Do you have a recent overview of Mitus financials I can review?"

"I do." Brigit jogged into her office, retrieved a folder from her desk and handed it to Dez, who'd strolled into her office.

"Knowing Colton, he'll need convincing to make the purchase."

"Why?" she asked.

"If he does this, the lion's share of his finances will be tied up in this one investment. That strategy failed him years ago and he vowed he'd never do it again."

"I don't think he'll have a choice," Brigit said.

"Thanks for this." Dez held up the folder and left.

Alone with her thoughts, Brigit struggled with the reality of her situation. After all these years, she'd come so far only to fail her parents *again*. Losing Francesco was inevitable.

And who was the mysterious damsel in distress responsible for Colton's abrupt departure at such a critical time? Was Brigit fooling herself into believing that what she and Colton had was more than a casual hookup? Maybe she should have heeded Vanessa's warning. Unable to distract herself with work, she shut down. *Time for a drink.* Wine would help blur her reality, if just for a few hours. She ventured toward the kitchen.

As she rounded the corner, a blast of cold air smacked her face. The front door was ajar. Fear punched her gut and she whirled around. The foyer and living room were empty. *Calm down. Vinny Ray is in prison and his accomplice long gone.*

She started to close the door, but froze mid-swing. Colton placed his overnight bag into the trunk of a white sedan parked at the fountain. Alexandra Reed exited the driver's side and hurried into Colton's waiting arms. Nose to nose, the two spoke briefly. He kissed her forehead, escorted her to the passenger door and waited while she folded onto the seat and pulled her long legs inside.

Stabbing pain in Brigit's chest crushed her lungs. She could barely breathe. *Stop watching.* But she couldn't tear herself away from the unfolding scene. Colton got behind the wheel. The car rolled down the driveway and vanished around the bend. Brigit stood there mouth agape, feet cemented in place.

Her cell phone buzzed, snapping her out of her catatonic state. The Pennsylvania District Attorney's number flashed on her screen. *Why are they calling again?* She felt numb, but she had to take the call. Sucking in a monster breath, she answered. "Hello." Brigit stepped outside and closed the front door for privacy.

"Eve, Jim Sausalito. My apologies for not getting back to you sooner. I had an unexpected death in my family."

"I'm sorry for your loss." She hastened toward the fountain. "Someone from your office called me two weeks ago."

"Unfortunately, there was a terrible mix-up and I have bad news."

Adrenaline spiked through her. *Oh, God, please, no. No. No. No.*

"Vinny Ray was paroled."

She swallowed a stream of screams as her heart rate shot into the triple digits. "*What*? I thought he was still in prison."

"I'm sorry. Someone provided you with incorrect information."

She felt like she was going to pass out. "So, Ray was released four years early? When did this happen?"

"Last month."

Rubbing her forehead, she started pacing. "How?"

"State funding crisis paired with an overcrowded prison. Ray was a model prisoner and earned early release. Keep in mind he was found *not* guilty for the vehicular manslaughter charges."

"C'mon, Jim. You and I both know he got off because the police mishandled the case."

"But he *was* convicted after the anonymous caller tipped police to the bags of cocaine in his apartment."

Not so anonymous if you knew what he did to my home. "He's a career criminal, not to mention a murderer. I cannot believe he's free."

"His parole officer confirmed Ray checks in regularly and has already secured a part-time job. He's in Pennsylvania and if I recall, you're from Ohio. He won't risk his freedom by breaking parole."

He already did. She thanked Jim for the call and, with shaky fingers, hung up. Her worst fear had been confirmed. Vinny Ray was free and looking to make good on his threat. He'd broken parole once. What would stop him from doing it again?

THAT EVENING, BRIGIT DRANK more than she ate.

"You okay?" Taylor asked.

"Nevvr beddrrr." She shoved a forkful of roasted golden potatoes into her mouth.

Taylor set down her fork. "Ryan is coming home with me for Thanksgiving. My parents are local, but we're staying the night. If you don't already have plans, please join us."

"You-n-Ryan." Brigit smiled. The grin felt lopsided, like she'd gotten a shot of Novocain. "How sweet. You twos ennyjoy tha hollyday."

After dinner, Brigit staggered downstairs to the home theater room. She selected her favorite Hitchcock movie, "Dial M for Murder," flopped onto the recliner and snuggled beneath the throw. As the movie started, she laid her head on the arm of the cushioned chair.

BRIGIT SILENCED HER ANNOYING phone alarm and winced from the pounding in her head. Vanessa hovered over her. Recoiling in the chair, Brigit gasped. "What the—what are you doing?"

"Going to work out," Vanessa said. "The lights were on. It's almost seven."

Brigit cradled her throbbing head.

"Have a good day." Vanessa took off for the gym.

In search of aspirin, Brigit trudged upstairs before getting ready for work. *Maybe it's time to ease up on the wine.*

During the morning teleconference with the Francesco team, Marjorie asked both teams to email her their vote, which she'd tally and provide to Colton. Brigit typed two words in the body of the email to Mrs. Mick: *White Knight.*

Defeat was a bitter pill to swallow the second time around, too. That afternoon, her phone buzzed with a text from Colton. *No more alcohol. You shouldn't be drinking at all.*

"What the hell?" she said out loud to herself. "You don't get to boss me around." She didn't reply.

On Thanksgiving eve, an eerie silence replaced the normally bustling home. Everyone but Chad and Vanessa had already left for the holiday. For the first time since Brigit had moved in, she'd dressed in sweats. Since the Clothing Czar wasn't there to bark orders, she took advantage of the nonexistent dress code. She joined them for a quiet dinner in the kitchen. While neither were dressed as casually as she, Vanessa's conservative black pants and black turtleneck sweater were the most appropriate attire she'd worn since Brigit had started working there.

"What are your holiday plans, Brigit?" Chad asked.

"I have none," Brigit said. "How about you?"

"Family reunion at my aunt's lake house in Virginia. I'm outta here in ten. It's a two-hour drive and I-95 will be a parking lot. How 'bout you, Vanessa?" Chad asked.

"Big group hug, also known as my crazy family," Vanessa said. "I'm off for eleven days, due back the first Monday in December."

Brigit found this time of year excruciatingly painful. Hearing them talk about their holiday plans reminded her of how alone she was.

"Dude, you never take vacation." Chad forked pasta into his mouth.

"I know, right?" Vanessa finished her iced tea. "Time to shake things up."

"Brigit, every year Elliott cooks a complete Thanksgiving dinner." Vanessa started cleaning up. "It's for staff who stick around and leftovers are scarfed up over the weekend as the crew returns. His stuffing is to die for! And this year Shane baked several pies. Lucky you get to sample everything first."

Not feeling lucky. I'd trade it for my family.

After placing his dish in the dishwasher, Chad said, "Gotta fly." He started to leave, but turned back. "Oh, Brigit, I signed for a package for you this afternoon. It's in my office. And one more thing, ladies, Henninger Security is running their annual maintenance check, so I shut down the system. If I didn't deactivate it, it would signal false alarms all weekend. Pain in my ass." He headed down the hallway. "Happy Turkey Day!"

Anxiety gripped Brigit by her throat. The security system was off and she was going to be alone in a humongous house. Her palms grew clammy. After cleaning her dinner dishes, she hurried to Chad's office.

His spotless and clutter-free workspace looked like a mini-command center. Three poster-sized monitors hung on the wall. Four additional flat-screened monitors consumed his desk, along with two specialized keyboards. All screens were dark. A reminder note on his keyboard read, *Call Henninger before booting up or you'll trigger the alarm.*

He'd left the standard-sized brown box on his desk. It had been forwarded to her from Porter, Gabriel and Sethfield. Her name had been spelled wrong—Bridgette Forney—and the sender hadn't included a name with the illegible D.C. return address.

On her way back to her office, her phone buzzed with a text from Colton. *I'll be home Friday. We need to talk.*

After staring at his cryptic message, she silenced the device and slipped it into her sweatpants pocket. Was he going to tell her about his relationship with Alexandra? Had Tucker pieced together her past? A shudder ran through her. Seeing Colton leave with the leggy brunette had put things in perspective.

Vinny Ray was a tangible threat and Brigit needed to make a

decision. Either take off again or come clean, about everything. By Friday, she'd either be long gone or ready to confess the truth.

Entering her office, she rifled through her desk drawer for scissors. After slicing through the packing tape, she lifted the cardboard flaps. A wave of fear pounded through her and she stumbled backward. Had someone mailed her a dead animal?

She poked the fur with the tip of the scissors. The thing didn't move. On closer examination, she realized it was a black wig. Her heart hammered against her rib cage. She pulled the wig out of the box. No note or receipt. On a hunch, she checked the inside of the wig and let out a strangled cry. It was *the* wig with the snipped orange boutique tag. The one Ray had yanked off her head all those years ago.

Brigit needed to leave. *Now.*

Think, think! She couldn't go home. She'd have to hide. But where? *Think, dammit!* Ray had sent the wig to her office. Maybe he hadn't tracked her to Mitus Mansion. Being in the house alone, with no security system, terrified her. With her thoughts in a jumbled mess, she couldn't formulate a plan. Panicked, she grabbed the wig and bolted upstairs to her bedroom.

With lightning speed, she shoved the wig and some clothes into an overnight bag and ran from her room, slamming the door behind her. The sudden bang sounded like a gunshot and she shrieked. Alone in the darkened hallway, a chill careened down her spine.

She ran through the deserted home to the lower level. As soon as she bolted into the parking garage, she triggered the motion detector. Light flooded the spacious area. Normally filled to capacity, the garage was vacant, save for three cars. The Bentley, the Mercedes-Maybach, and her black Escalade, tucked in the back corner.

Frantic to escape, Brigit fished out her keys as she jumped into the SUV. She threw her handbag and overnight bag onto the passenger seat, shoved the key into the ignition and started the engine.

Go! Go! Go!

Brigit shot a glance in the rearview mirror. Before she could fully grasp what was happening, someone wearing a black leather glove placed a cold damp cloth over her nose and mouth, pinning her to the headrest and muffling her desperate scream.

44

PAIN

BRIGIT WINCED. A SHOOTING pain radiated through her, halting her already shallow breath. Groaning, she gasped for air. *Ow. Ow. Ow.* Cracking open her eyes, darkness greeted her. *Nightmare?* Slowly she regained consciousness. The frigid cold stung her cheeks, her head throbbed, and her blurred vision crippled her ability to see.

Adrenaline shot through her. She was lying on her side, but when she tried to move, she couldn't. Was she paralyzed? Frozen? Bound? Her cheek felt taut. More panic sent her heart into a burst of palpitations. *Vinny Ray.*

She was trapped, unable to move her arms or legs. A thunderous roar, like an earthquake, vibrated her surroundings. Within seconds the rumbles that had interrupted the silence rolled away.

Suddenly, the darkness lifted. Squinting, she looked around. Her cold breath was visible in the air. There were trees nearby, but tall grass and brush blocked her view. *I'm outside.*

Something large and dark sniffed her and she gagged from the vile stench. The involuntary reaction sent waves of unrelenting spasms pounding through her. *Wolf.* The animal licked her cheek and she trembled. The jarring movements nauseating her. This was no nightmare. It was a living hell. More thunderous noise grumbled above, only this time the ground didn't shake.

The pacing predator lay back down, creating a shield from the bitter wind. As the sun broke over the horizon, Brigit had no concept of time, only of pain and of fear. The animal made a few sounds, like whimpers. On occasion it would reposition itself, but stayed close, as if guarding her.

When the sun brought relief from the cold, the beast trotted away. Immobilized, Brigit struggled to remember but fog clouded her memory. Though she floated in and out of consciousness, the pain remained constant. As the giant orange fireball inched toward the red horizon, desolation filled her heart. How could her life end like this? Was this how karma worked in the end?

Every minute felt like a grueling eternity. Nonstop shivering racked her weakened, stiff body. Muffled traffic grew sparse, as did the grumblings in the sky. With nightfall, and the plummeting temperature, she feared she'd die from hypothermia. *Please, not like this.*

Suddenly, car doors slammed shut. "Brigit!" Colton's piercing scream shattered the silence.

"Here." She wanted to shout, but all she mustered was a hoarse whisper.

Maniacal barking got louder. Fear gripped her throat. She tried screaming, but couldn't. Would the animal attack?

"I've got her!" Taylor shouted. Breathing hard, she dropped to her knees. "Hey, buddy, don't bite me." Taylor extended her hand toward the panting animal. It sniffed her, then lay down nearby.

Taylor needed to be warned. "Wolf," Brigit whispered.

"Brigit, you're going to be okay." Taylor tugged off her coat and laid it gently over Brigit. "I'm going to untie you. Are you in pain?"

"Uh-huh." Brigit stammered between chattering.

Colton and Ryan knelt next to her. Tears pricked her eyes. While Taylor and Ryan untied her, Colton gently pulled her matted hair from her cheek. *Relief.* "Thirsty," she rasped.

"I've got water." Ryan dashed away.

Colton removed his coat and laid it over Taylor's, then reached beneath the layers to warm her hands. Worry lines etched his face, the knot between his brows prominent.

"We've got to get her to the hospital." A tear streaked Taylor's cheek.

"My house." Brigit inhaled, sending jolting pain through her torso.

"No. You need emergency medical attention." Colton pulled out his phone.

Returning with the water, Ryan crouched down. As Colton cradled her head, he poured a few sips of water into her mouth. The chilled liquid soothed her scratchy throat.

"Brigit." Colton caressed her cheek. "You need to go to the hospital."

"I'm scared," she whispered. She hadn't set foot in a hospital since the death of her parents. "They died in one."

"I won't leave you."

"Promise?" she whispered.

"I promise." Colton stepped away and made the nine-one-one call.

"How did you get here?" Ryan asked.

"Where am I?" Brigit asked. She was freezing, exhausted and she hurt everywhere.

"You're at Daingerfield Island, in Alexandria," Ryan said. "Near a marina, across the river from Reagan National Airport."

Brigit struggled to stay awake. "I…I don't know."

Colton knelt and stared into her eyes. "The ambulance is on its way." Again, he reached under the coats and held her hands. His large hands did more than warm her frozen ones. She felt safe. Relief washed over her and she choked back a sob. Excruciating pain rocketed through her.

"Wolf?" Brigit asked.

"It looks like a mangy German Shepherd," Taylor said.

"It kept me alive," Brigit whispered. "Please bring it."

The ambulance arrived and paramedics rushed to Brigit's side. After checking her vitals, they placed a brace around her neck. On the count of three they lifted her onto the stretcher. The shooting pain in her torso stole her breath and she gritted her teeth. Just before the ambulance doors closed, Colton climbed in and Brigit tried to relax. He'd kept his promise. The EMT started her on an IV drip and covered her with a blanket.

Unable to fight the exhaustion, she closed her eyes. *I'm safe.*

"You're going to be okay," Colton whispered into her ear.

COLTON STEPPED OUT OF the triage room and called Taylor.

"How's she doing?" Taylor asked.

"The doctor is with her. Do you have the dog?"

"He jumped right in. We stopped for dog stuff and a several bottles of flea shampoo. We'll bathe him in the mudroom. That mutt stinks!"

"I interrupted your Thanksgiving holiday. I'll make it up to you."

"No worries. It kills me to think what would have happened if we hadn't found her."

"Say nothing to the staff. Until we know what happened, I don't want to scare them."

"I understand," Taylor said.

The nurse stepped out of triage and looked around. "I have to go." Colton ended the call and approached the nurse. "Can I go in?"

"Yes, Dr. Hayes wants to update you."

Colton entered the single-unit room. Brigit lay in the hospital bed with her eyes closed. Her hair was matted, her cheek swollen, and her forehead scratched. "Dr. Hayes, Colton Mitus. How is she?" He extended his hand.

"Lucky to be alive," the doctor said shaking it. "In addition to being badly beaten, her ribs are bruised, at best. I'll confirm the degree of damage with X-rays. Looks like she suffered a concussion and appears to have been injected with a substance that probably caused her to lose consciousness. I'll know more once we get the tox report back."

"Can I have a private word?" Colton asked. The doctor stepped out and Colton followed.

"Brigit's pregnant," Colton said.

"Why step out to discuss that?"

"I overheard her talking with a mutual friend and I don't want to spoil the surprise of her telling me."

"How far along might she be?"

"Four weeks."

"I'll add the pregnancy test to the order but hold off imaging her ribs and prescribing a painkiller until the report comes back." The doctor tapped on his tablet. "I do have a piece of good news. We found no evidence Brigit was sexually assaulted. We're admitting her, but it'll be a few hours before she's moved to a room. Things happen slowly around here. I'll let you know the results as soon as I hear."

"Can I go back in?"

"Yes. I'll have the tech draw blood." Dr. Hayes left.

Colton slipped into the triage room and sat in the chair next to Brigit's bed. Her steady, peaceful breathing helped him relax. His concern had escalated Tuesday after Vanessa had told him Brigit had gotten drunk on Monday night. When Brigit hadn't responded to his texts, he'd called Taylor Thanksgiving morning. Brigit wasn't with her. He'd then asked Chad to remote in and locate her phone. Surprised by its whereabouts, Colton asked Taylor and Ryan to help him.

Finding her dumped amongst the bramble bushes on the restricted-access dirt road near the marina in Alexandria had been surreal. Scared the hell out of him. But she'd been alive. And that gave him hope. For a man who needed control, he'd had none.

Absolutely none. He raked his hands over his whiskered face and exhaled an audible breath.

"Colton?" Brigit rasped.

He took her hand.

"I...I need to tell you..."

She was going to tell him about the baby. He leaned close, full of anticipation.

"You don't have to stay," she whispered.

Disappointed, he shook his head. "I'm not going anywhere." He kissed her forehead. His heart broke for her. Someone wanted her dead. But he'd found her. This time, he was able to get help *before* it was too late.

The nurse drew blood and left. After several minutes, Brigit fell asleep. When Dr. Hays returned, Brigit didn't awaken, so the doctor spoke with Colton.

"My suspicions were right. Brigit was chloroformed, then injected with a sedative. That alone could have killed her. Memory loss is always a possibility with a head injury. I've ordered an X-ray of her ribs." The doctor looked up from his tablet. "I'm sorry, but Brigit isn't pregnant." He left.

Pain punched Colton's gut. The loss tore through him like someone had stomped his soul. If he ever got his hands on the motherfucker who did this, he'd rip out his heart and ask questions later.

45

NO MEMORY

D URING BRIGIT'S TWO-DAY HOSPITAL stay, Colton remained by her side. The police questioned her about the attack but she remembered nothing. Her last memory was the weekend marathon meeting with Colton and Marjorie's teams. Though confident Vinny Ray was responsible for the attack, she'd say nothing until her memory returned. By divulging his identity, she'd open the door to her secret past. And that door needed to stay shut until she was strong enough to leave.

As she became more lucid, a recurring image haunted her, like a scene from a horror movie stuck on replay. *Alexandra Reed was nestled in Colton's arms. They drove away and Colton never returned.* She didn't know if it was real or a dream so she said nothing.

On Sunday afternoon, Brigit was discharged. The nurse's aide rolled her outside and she shielded her eyes from the streaming sunlight of the midafternoon sky. The cold temperature, along with her breath's vapor, reminded her of the terrifying attack. *I will get past this.*

Vonn exited the Mercedes and opened the back door. "I'm relieved you're okay, Brigit."

"Thank you."

With Colton's help, she eased into the backseat. Instead of riding up front, he sat next to her. Vonn drove out of the hospital parking lot and the knot between Colton's brows finally relaxed. As the car gained speed on the parkway, the strangest feeling of relief washed over her. If Ray presumed her dead, could she really stop looking over her shoulder?

When Vonn pulled up to the Mitus compound, an armed guard approached the vehicle. Colton rolled down his window. "Good afternoon, Mr. Mitus. Three of your staff have returned. They were cleared to enter."

Her heart dropped. Because of her, precautionary measures were necessary to ensure the staff's safety. She didn't want to put them through this. The gates opened. "I should move out," Brigit said as Vonn drove up the driveway.

"The *only* place you're going is straight to bed," Colton said.

As soon as Vonn parked at the fountain, Colton helped her out of the vehicle and into the house. Taylor and Ryan greeted her with big smiles. "Welcome home!"

A cherry-sized lump lodged in her throat. "Thank you." The dog trotted over, his tail swooshing back and forth. "There's my lifesaver. He's so handsome. German Shepherd?"

"Purebred, according to the vet," Ryan said.

"Thank you for cleaning him up. Did you name him?"

"We have a few ideas," Ryan said.

"King, Lucky, Mojo, and LS for lifesaver." Taylor gently hugged Brigit.

Not even the pain in Brigit's rib cage could stop her from greeting her dog. Moving slowly and holding her injured side, she knelt and patted his thick, shiny coat. The dog licked her cheek. "Hello, Mojo. Thank you."

As she stood, she groaned from the pinching pain.

"That's enough excitement for one day," Colton said. "Let's get you settled." With a tender hand on her arm, he guided her toward the elevator. Mojo heeled at Brigit's side.

"I think the dog owns you." Taylor smiled. "Can I bring you chamomile tea?"

"Yes, please," she said and stepped into the elevator. The doors closed and they rode in silence to the second floor. Brigit couldn't wait to get into bed.

Colton opened her bedroom door and Mojo plunked down in his doggie bed, tucked in the corner.

"Let's dress you in something more comfortable," he said.

"The clothes Taylor brought are fine." She didn't want Colton to see her bruised body. If her nightmarish memory was real, then so was his intimate relationship with Alexandra. She sat on the side of the bed and winced. Even breathing was painful.

"Can I help you get into bed?" he asked.

"Thanks, but I have to do it so I can manage the pain." Moving gingerly, she got into bed and relaxed against the propped pillows.

"Until your memory returns, I don't think we should tell the staff much." He sat on the edge of the bed. But he didn't touch her.

"I agree." Her heart ached for him. She wanted desperately to hold his hand.

"Let's keep the explanation vague. Tell them you were mugged over the holiday weekend and don't remember what happened."

She nodded. "Thank you for staying at the hospital with me. I'm sorry I'm putting you through this. If I could move out, I would."

"No more talking. Rest."

Taylor arrived with tea and settled onto the sofa. "I'll stay with her."

"I'll be back." Colton pecked Brigit's forehead and left. Had she mistaken a convenient sexual relationship for something meaningful? Her heart hurt as much as her broken body.

Throughout the afternoon, returning staff stopped by to express concern and offer support. That evening, there was a knock on Brigit's door. Taylor jumped up and cracked open the door. "She's sleeping."

Brigit opened her eyes. "Pretending."

Tucker and Colton stood in the doorway "Hiya." Tucker's usual laid-back smile was fraught with concern.

"C'mon in." Still wearing a T-shirt and sweats, Brigit was propped against a mountain of pillows and tucked under the bed linens.

Looking like a sentry, Colton stood at the foot of her bed and crossed his arms. She wished he'd hold her, not guard her. As soon as Mojo spied Tucker, he sprang from his doggie bed.

"I heard this fella was your guardian angel." Tucker relaxed onto the sofa. "How are things?"

Mojo shoved a pull toy at Tucker who grabbed the end and the two tug-o-warred while Mojo made playful growly sounds.

"Things were dicey," she said. "I hope to be back to work soon."

"Not likely," Colton said. "The doctor told you to rest."

"I've got some good news." Tucker released the toy and Mojo dropped to the floor and gnawed it. "I found your Escalade."

Brigit held her breath.

"Parked on a side street in Old Town, about two miles from where Colton found you. Spark anything?"

Slowly exhaling, she imagined driving to Alexandria. *No way. I was too scared to leave the mansion.* "I don't know how my vehicle got there, but I didn't drive it."

"It was locked. No damage," Tucker said. "My guys are dusting for prints. I checked with the City of Alexandria P.D., but there were no incidents around Thanksgiving. Helps that I'm a former Fairfax County police detective."

Shifting in bed, Brigit winced. *Great, a former cop.*

Tucker glanced at Colton and Taylor. "Could I speak privately with Brigit?"

Taylor headed toward the door. "Shane baked you something *chocolaty*. I'll be back with dessert." Colton left with her and shut the door.

Brigit started overheating and slowly tossed off the bed linens.

When she reached toward the water bottle on her nightstand, she reared back in pain and grabbed her ribs.

"Here you go, darlin'." Tucker handed her the bottle, then sat on the sofa arm and chatted about his ski weekend in Vermont. His attempt to put her at ease didn't, but she was grateful for the distraction.

Once finished, Tucker rested his forearms on his thighs. "Now, sweet cakes, I've a good hunch the person who vandalized your home is the same one who tried to kill you. Time to make this easy on both of us and tell me who you're running from."

Brigit swallowed hard. Was now the time to come clean? What if her assailant wasn't Vinny Ray? *Of course, it's Ray.* Telling Tucker would open Pandora's box. Afraid of the repercussions, she shook her head. "I'll tell you as soon as I remember."

Tucker waited. And waited. And waited. Their stare-down continued until Mojo rolled on his back and started snorting, the pull toy still in his mouth. "Okie Dokie." Tucker slapped his thighs. "When you're ready, I'll listen."

Colton returned. As he set the tray of goodies down, he looked at his cousin. But Tucker just shook his head.

Colton hugged his cousin. "Thanks for everything."

"Colt, I'll call you tomorrow." Tucker patted Mojo. "Sorry about your holiday. Wish I'd been here for you."

I interrupted his Thanksgiving with Alexandra.

"Be well, Brigit," Tucker said from the doorway. "Call me if you remember *anything*." He left, pulling the door shut.

Colton placed the tray on the bed then eased down next to her.

"How was your Thanksgiving?" she asked, though she didn't have the emotional strength to hear about Alexandra.

A rueful smile touched his eyes, but he didn't respond. Instead he scooped chocolate truffle pie onto the fork and held it in front of her. "Shane insists chocolate is the cure-all."

"You don't have to play nursemaid." She opened her mouth and he gently placed the utensil inside. Tiny tingles scurried through her. Even in her broken state, she missed him.

"If you want to talk about what happened...with the...well, you know. I think talking would be good for us both." Colton forked a large piece of pie into his mouth, then washed it down with coffee.

Talk about what? The attack? How could that be good for them both? She wasn't sure what he meant, but she got confused easily.

"You scared the hell out of us. You were banged up."

She broke eye contact. Gazing into his beautiful brown eyes was killing her. Of course he didn't want to lose her. She was his wealth manager and a convenient sex partner. He offered her another bite of dessert. "Colton, you really don't need—" A knock on the door interrupted her. "Come in."

Alexandra Reed glided into the room. Brigit's stomach dropped. *Oh, no. The girlfriend.*

"Hey," Colton hugged her. "I didn't know you were coming."

Brigit looked away.

"Hitched a ride with Tucker. Been outside on the phone." Dressed in leggings, boots and a sweater, Alexandra looked like the girl next door. She was makeup free and her long dark hair was tucked behind her ears. Alexandra eyed the pie. "That looks good."

"You want a piece?" Colton asked.

"A big one."

Oh, God, no sex talk.

"Be right back." Colton headed toward the door.

"Why don't you take Alexandra with you?" She did not want to make chitchat with the girlfriend. She'd endured enough torture.

"I came to see you, Brigit." Alexandra sat on the edge of the bed.

Mojo sat up, yawned, and moseyed over to greet her. While petting Mojo, Alexandra expressed concern over what had happened. "I worry about Colton. Your being here has made a difference."

Brigit's head throbbed. "Having financial peace of mind is a big deal."

"No, he likes having *you* here." Alexandra gave her a sweet smile. "Colton has always been somewhat of a loner."

"Oh, I...um...I'm just doing my job. I don't want to interfere or anything." Brigit fisted the bed sheet.

"I want to get to know you better."

What? A threesome? A shiver ran through her. "I'm not into that sort of thing, but good for you if you are." Brigit forced a smile and gave Alexandra two thumbs up. *This is so awkward.*

"Into *what*?" Alexandra scrunched up her nose. "You've lost me."

Colton returned. "Brigit, would you like to give this to Mojo?" He handed her a doggie treat.

Ohmygod, he's throwing me a bone, literally.

Colton sat on the loveseat and Alexandra moved next to him. *Please don't feed each other.* Taking the dessert from Colton, Alexandra took a bite. "I heard he saved your life. He's well trained."

Of course, he told his girlfriend the real story. "Are you talking about the dog or Colton?"

Alexandra and Colton laughed. "Did you tell her?" Colton asked Alexandra.

"I'm about to." Alexandra forked a piece of pie into her mouth.

"Please...really...I don't...I'm not up for—" Brigit said.

Tucker popped his head in. "Goth Girl, I have to go."

"Tucker! Why do you still call me that?" Alexandra glared at him.

After he stopped chuckling, he added, "Honeykins, what else would I call you?"

With plate in hand, Alexandra gave Brigit a tender hug. "Feel better. Colton, thanks for getting me through the holiday." Alexandra kissed his cheek. "I love you. Will you tell Brigit for me?"

"Will do," Colton said. "Love you both."

Tucker and Alexandra left.

They love each other. My head is killing me, but I heard that. Brigit pulled the bed linens up around her neck. "I should probably get some sleep."

"Brigit, do you have family I can contact? They're welcome to visit you. Stay here, too."

"No, no one."

He sat on the side of the bed and cupped her hand. "Where are your mom and dad?"

"Killed by a drunk driver," she blurted. Pain, along with the concussion, clouded her ability to think straight. She needed to be quiet.

"Is that why you were afraid to go to the hospital?" He caressed her fingers one at a time. God, his compassion was tearing her apart.

"Yes, but not because the hospital did anything wrong. My mom died of her injuries the next day. My dad woke from his coma a week later, but only survived long enough to tell me how much he and my mom loved me. His dying words were that I make the family business my own." Brigit shuddered in a breath. She'd never shared that with anyone, yet somehow telling Colton helped ease her pain, a little.

He kissed her hand and her cheek. "I'm sorry. That's a big hurdle to get over."

She desperately missed his touch. But he had a girlfriend, so she tugged away her hand. "Their deaths are a heavy burden."

His eyes grew wide. "You were the drunk driver?"

"Good God, no. I hardly drank back then and I'd *never* drink and drive."

"I'm not following. Why blame yourself?"

"My mom and dad had been angry because I'd decided to go to grad school, rather than work at their company. They were overprotective and overbearing. I was making a stand." She shrugged. "You know, exerting my independence. We hadn't spoken for a month. They were on their way to visit me when they were hit head-on. If I'd listened to them, they'd still be alive and my life would have gone in a totally different direction."

"Did you return to work at the company?"

She started trembling. "The company was bought by an entrepreneur investor. I lost it, too." A lone tear trickled down her cheek. Before she could swipe it away, Colton tenderly brushed the tear with his thumb.

"You've endured so much alone." He caressed her hand, then held it.

She'd divulged way too much. *Must be the pain meds. Stop talking!* Clearing her throat, she asked, "How about you? Besides Tucker, do you have family?"

"My mom and Alexandra."

She forced a smile to hide her pain. "That's nice. You think of your girlfriend as family."

Colton screwed up his face. "Alexandra isn't my girlfriend. Where'd you get that idea?"

"You two are close."

He grimaced. "Not that close! Alexandra Reed is my baby sister."

46

GETTING CLOSER

COLTON COULDN'T WAIT ANOTHER second. Gently cupping her cheeks, he murmured, "I need to kiss you."

"Okay," she whispered.

He pressed his lips to hers and the bad disappeared. Everything felt fucking perfect. Hell, he'd missed her so damn much. She had no family to lean on and no one to help shoulder the pain and loss. He couldn't imagine life without his family.

Brigit's shoulders relaxed and a tiny whimper filled his ears with her sweet sound. And now he understood why she was private, walled-off and guarded with her feelings. She'd learned to be strong for herself and by herself. He kissed her again.

She smiled. Her beauty and strength shone through her pain. She'd get through this. He'd make sure of it. And this time she wouldn't be alone. He'd be by her side every step of the way. Especially if she didn't yet know she'd lost their child.

There was a knock on the door. "I'll send whoever it is away," he said.

"It's probably Taylor. She's been so good to me."

"Enter," Colton said.

Taylor looked from one to the other. A tiny smile flitted across her face. "According to the discharge instructions, Brigit needs to walk for leg circulation."

"Thanks, Taylor," Colton said.

"Like I said, she's the best," Brigit said.

Taylor beamed. The dog trotted to the door, stopped and turned. He wagged his tail and barked once.

"Taylor, how about I help Brigit, if you don't mind running Mojo out back?" Colton asked.

"Of course not. Come on, boy." Taylor and Mojo left.

Colton rose. Moving slowly, Brigit got out of bed and stood still for a few seconds. He extended his arm. "Hold onto me."

"Alexandra Reed is your *sister*?" She took a few small steps, then gripped his bicep. "I'm wobbly."

Her tender touch sent energy and warmth coursing through his veins. "I've got you."

She ambled out of the bedroom and they strolled in silence to the end of the hallway, turned and headed toward Colton's bedroom. After one lap, he broke the silence. "Reed is our mom's maiden name. Alexandra has a public career and likes to keep a low profile but she wanted to confide in you. The staff doesn't know she's my sister."

Brigit stopped and looked at him. "She must think I've lost my mind." She laughed, but immediately grabbed her side and made several small jerky motions. "Ow, that's painful."

"Go easy. Why would she think that?"

"I thought she was your girlfriend and interested in a threesome. No wonder she looked confused."

Colton burst out laughing. When his belly laughs subsided, they started walking again. "If she brings it up, I'll tell her it was your concussion talking."

"So you spent the holiday with your sister?"

"And our mom. She recently underwent brain surgery to remove a tumor. Unfortunately, it turned out to be malignant. Though she'd hired full-time nursing care, I've been spending as much time with her as I can. My mom told Alexandra about her health issue on the day you met her. She was devastated."

Brigit stopped and looked at him. "I'm sorry about your mom."

"Monday of Thanksgiving week, Kimberly had a setback. Alexandra called me from the hospital. That's why I left our strategy meeting. It was a tough holiday. My mom's been through so much."

"So have you." Brigit caressed his arm and his body stirred from her soothing touch. She furrowed her brow. "How'd you find me?"

"When Chad connected your phone to the network he activated a locator app. You might think it's invasive but I use it for emergencies. Since Cain's death I'm overly protective of people I care about. Your phone saved you."

"No, Colton, *you* saved me." Brigit wrapped her arms around his back and rested her cheek against his chest. "I'm so grateful."

Relief surged through him. Folding her in his arms, he kissed the top of her head. Her strangled sobs shredded his heart. After several seconds, she pulled away and ambled into her bedroom. Using the furniture for balance, she walked slowly to the bathroom and closed the door.

While waiting in her bedroom, he rubbed his hands down his scruffy whiskers. Why was she still so guarded? Couldn't she see how much he cared?

Mojo bounded in and plopped in his bed with Taylor following close behind. "Colton, how are you holding up?" she asked.

"I'm relieved," he replied. "Thank you for taking such good care of Brigit. I'll stay with her tonight. Get some rest. She's all yours in the morning, although I can hire a day nurse."

"You know I took care of my mom for all those months. I'm happy to help Brigit." Taylor scooted out and closed the door behind her.

Brigit emerged and knelt to rub the dog's head. "Good night, sweet Mojo." His tail wagged and he licked her hand. She struggled to get up.

In a flash, Colton knelt next to her. "Lean on me." She wrapped her fingers around his outstretched arm. "You ready?"

"Yeah." Slowly, he stood and she rose alongside him. Wincing, she grabbed her side. "God, that hurts."

They stood, inches away from each other. "I'd take your pain if I could." Again, he couldn't resist and he damn well didn't want to. His kiss was soft, gentle, and filled with hope. He kissed her again. Kissing her felt fantastic.

She lifted her face to his and gazed into his eyes. "I've tried to fight this…us…but I have no strength left."

"Then don't." He kissed her. "Do you know how fucking important you are to me?"

Color blossomed on her cheeks. "Yeah, sure, everyone likes their wealth advisor."

"Not like this, they don't." He cupped her face in his hands and kissed her as if she were a priceless porcelain doll. Then he ran his tongue along her lower lip but even that wasn't enough. Her lips parted and he eagerly stroked her tongue. And he hardened from her soft, sweet moan. Once she regained her health, he'd make love to her. Reluctantly, he ended their kiss. She needed sleep. "Let me tuck you in."

"Where's Taylor?" Brigit asked.

"I'm staying."

Her lips lifted. "I can't sleep in sweats."

"I'll help you take them off."

Her brow furrowed and she broke eye contact. "I don't want you to see me like this."

"Let me help you, Brigit." She stared into his eyes for a long moment then gave him a little nod.

He found a cotton nightshirt in her closet and helped her undress. She'd been through one hell of an ordeal. Her shoulder, torso and thighs were blotched in shades of purple. Seeing her like this reminded him of Cain and he bit back the emotion.

Before covering her in the nightshirt, he dotted her bruises with tender kisses. "You are so beautiful."

She looked sleepy, but there was a tiny spark in her eyes. After tucking her in, he went into the bathroom. When he exited, he removed his phone and set it on her bureau.

"Will you lie with me?" she asked.

He stood by her bedside. "I don't want to hurt you."

"You'd hurt me more if you didn't."

He removed his pants and shirt, but kept his boxers on. His stiff penis didn't care about her broken body. In spite of her injuries, she was still the most beautiful sight he'd ever seen. When he pulled back the linens and crawled in next to her, she smiled. While at the hospital, she'd had nightmares, so tonight he left the bathroom light on and the door cracked. He didn't want her waking in total darkness.

"Can I hold your hand?" he murmured. She found his hand beneath the sheet. This felt so right. *She* felt so right.

After a few moments of silence, she spoke quietly. "I need to know something."

"Uh-huh."

"Why does the Francesco Company mean so much to you? You've invested in many businesses over the years, but this one seems special. Why?"

Her fingers had tightened. Did she realize she was squeezing his hand? "You want the short or long answer?"

"Long."

"From as far back as I can remember, my dad scared the living hell out of me and I couldn't get two words out without tripping all over myself. I developed a stammering problem. A group of kids at school bullied me, but I had Cain. He was fearless and he had my back. When he died, I kind of died with him. One night, about a month after his death, I overheard my dad tell my mom that the wrong son had been taken from him."

Brigit gasped. "Oh, my God."

"She kicked the son of a bitch out. Between speech therapy and Alexandra making me read her bedtime stories every night, I stopped stammering. Going to Harvard boosted my confidence, in part because I could start over." They'd both been staring at the ceiling. He looked at her. "After getting my MBA from Harvard I started Mitus Consulting. Two years later, I closed it."

She craned her neck to look at him. "Why?"

"It failed and I needed to step away. I took a year and retooled. When I started Mitus Conglomerate, the Francesco Company was my first big win. It changed the tide of my career. It was defining proof that I wasn't the loser my jackass of a father told me I was." They stared into each other's eyes and the air between them grew electric.

"Francesco set you on your path to success," she murmured.

"Investing in that company changed my life." He rolled toward her. "And now, with everything at stake, I could lose it, and with that, Crockett Boxes. Too many people are counting on me to get this right. I cannot fail."

"You won't."

Beneath the blanket, he stroked her arm, then gently lifted her hand out to examine it. "Hmm."

"What is it?"

"Where's that silver bracelet you always wear?"

She stared at her arm. "Oh no, it's gone! My parents gave me that bracelet." She broke down and sobbed.

She was too injured for him to pull her into his arms, so he did the next best thing. He got her a box of tissues, wiped her tears, whispered words of encouragement and waited. When she finished crying, he dotted her face with doting kisses until she smiled. Then he said something that made his guts churn as soon as he uttered the damn words. He promised her that everything would turn out okay. Now he really was carrying the weight on his shoulders because he had no fucking idea if that would be the case.

Would she even make a full recovery? Had she miscarried before the brutal attack, or would he have to be the one to break the devastating news about the baby? And how in the hell was he going to keep Francesco out of MobiCom's hands without doing the one thing he vowed he'd *never* do again?

47

BAD NEWS

E IGHT DAYS FOLLOWING THE attack, Brigit still remembered nothing. Had she been lured away? Or had Vinny Ray slipped onto the property and abducted her?

She tried not to let the missing bracelet affect her, especially in light of her traumatic injuries, but the meaningful gift couldn't be replaced. The Yurman Collection offered bracelets so similar it would require a discerning eye to note the subtle differences. But the last physical connection to her mom and dad had been permanently severed.

That evening, Brigit held the stair rail and plodded downstairs. Taylor had convinced her to have dinner with the staff. Flanked by Taylor and Mojo, Brigit paused in the foyer to admire the elaborate Christmas decorations and beautifully trimmed tree in the living room, then continued into the dining room. Only Vanessa's chair remained empty. When the staff saw her, they clapped. Her spirits brightened from their warm welcome.

As desserts were devoured and after-dinner liqueurs relished, Colton tapped his water goblet. The chatter ceased. "We have a Christmas tradition. The newest Mitus employee places the Santa hat on Michelangelo."

"Brigit," Taylor said.

"And Shane," Brigit said. "Anyone else?" Colton shook his head. "Shane, let's do it together," Brigit suggested.

Shane flushed. "Um, okay."

With phones at the ready, staff congregated around the statue. Colton held out a red velvet apron skirt and the red Santa hat.

Shane snatched the hat. "I'm staying clear of David's junk."

As the staff snapped pictures and shot videos, Shane hatted David and Brigit tied the red velvet skirt around the statue's waist.

"Brigit, I'm glad you joined us," Colton said. "The more you do, the more you'll remember."

The following morning Brigit trudged back downstairs wearing black pants, a burgundy sweater, and her cushy slipper boots. After promising Colton she'd limit her computer time and would rest if she tired, he'd agreed. Booting up her computer, she silently rejoiced in the normal routine.

Seeing Mrs. Mick later that morning would further boost her spirits. Unfortunately, her visit wasn't social. Since Marjorie refused to discuss anything by phone, Brigit anticipated bad news.

Midmorning Brigit pussyfooted toward the French doors, leaned against the doorframe and stared out back. Something had been niggling at her. The more she tried forcing the memory, the farther it receded into her mind.

"Hey," said Colton. "You okay?"

Staring at this man could make her forget every crappy thing that had happened. He had that kind of an effect on her. "There's something I need to remember."

"You think?"

Her lips lifted. "No, something *else*. Something important. I can't remember what I was doing before I--" She pursed her lips.

"Before you what?"

Tell him. She sighed. "Before I saw you leave with Alexandra."

He cocked a brow. "I heard you got drunk the night I left. Was that the reason?"

"Oh, don't flatter yourself." She smirked. "The entire afternoon is hazy. Whatever I'm supposed to remember is important."

"There you two are!" Marjorie's booming voice broke Brigit's concentration. Mojo trotted over to Marjorie. "Hi, doggie. He's big. Should I be worried?"

Brigit smiled. "Mojo's a sweetheart."

With her sights set on Brigit, Marjorie bustled toward them. "You look—" She shook her head, draped her arm tenderly around Brigit and kissed her cheek. "I'm relieved you're okay."

Me too, Mrs. Mick.

"I like the security detail posted outside the gates." Marjorie hugged Colton. "You've been taking good care of our girl?"

"No, no, I haven't." Colton fought a smile. "Any particular reason why I should be?"

As Marjorie swatted his arm, her throaty laughter lifted Brigit's spirits.

"Today's the first day I'm back in my office." Brigit walked slowly toward Colton's office. "I need a head start."

While they sat around Colton's conference table, Brigit rubbed Mojo's head and thick, furry neck. Though having Mojo nearby soothed her, her heart pounded like a jackhammer. From the look in her eyes, Mrs. Mick was about to drop a bomb.

Perched on the chair's edge, Marjorie rested her clasped hands on the table. "You've both endured a lot. I wish I could candy-coat what I have to tell you, but that's not my style."

Out of habit, Brigit went to fiddle with her bracelet, but the familiar keepsake was gone.

"I called a handful of Francesco shareholders with whom I have history," Marjorie said. "They seek me out at annual shareholder meetings and I have a friendly rapport with each of them. The feedback wasn't good. They think merging with MobiCom is the way to go."

Shaking his head, Colton pushed out of his chair. "Montgomery?"

"He and Dobb are putting the fear of God into them." Marjorie lifted a cigarette pack from her bag. "They're misleading shareholders."

"How?" Brigit asked.

"By telling them Crocket's innovation is risky and has, at best, a fifty-fifty chance at success. And they're touting MobiCom's inflated purchase offer. You know, *cash is king.*"

"Do you have that shareholder list?" Brigit asked. Marjorie fished the papers from her computer bag. Brigit glanced at the list. "Let's divide this up. Shareholders need to know the truth."

"Two minutes." Marjorie tapped out a cigarette. "Vonn got to me before I could grab a smoke. I'm going outside." She stood. "Dobb is a damn traitor. We need a knight in shining armor."

Brigit whipped her head around. "What did you say?"

"I'm going to smoke," Marjorie replied.

"No, the other part."

"Dobb is a traitor."

Brigit jumped out of her chair and immediately grabbed her side. "Ow! I remember! Mitus Conglomerate has to take Francesco private. Colton, you have to be Francesco's White Knight."

Colton shook his head. "I ruled that out. Too risky."

Marjorie rolled her eyes. "Wait, didn't we vote?" Brigit asked and Marjorie nodded.

"You don't get to choose, Colton," said Brigit.

"I damn well do," he replied. "It's my money we'd use to purchase Francesco."

On a huff, Brigit looked at Marjorie. "What was the outcome?"

"The majority chose White Knight." Marjorie checked her email. "One vote for each of the following: Killer Bees, Pac-Man and Poison Pill."

Brigit snorted. "Those aren't the best strategies to stop this hostile takeover. Marjorie, why don't you have that smoke, then we'll call the shareholders?" Brigit ambled toward her office. "Colton, this situation is screaming for a White Knight."

"Listen to your crack wealth manager." Marjorie followed.

Brigit opened the French doors and the two women stepped onto the patio. Marjorie lit up and they stood in silence.

"That's me," Brigit whispered, holding up the report. "I'm Spider Holdings."

Marjorie's eyes grew wide. "Coming home, after all." She inhaled, turned away and blew out the smoke.

Brigit's shoulders drooped. "That had been the plan, but I'm about to lose Francesco all over again."

"No, honey, you're saving the company. MobiCom *cannot* win. They'll make tens of millions on Crockett Boxes and Francesco will become a postscript. Sammy and Nick would be proud of you." Marjorie finished her cigarette, stomped it out and threw it away.

The women worked at Brigit's conference table. After dividing the list, they started calling Francesco shareholders. While some pledged their support, others only agreed to attend the upcoming shareholder meeting. Brigit expected Colton would join them, but he remained in his office. Something was definitely wrong.

Late afternoon, Vonn poked his head into Brigit's office. "Ten minutes to departure, Marjorie."

"If anyone can get through to him, it's you." Marjorie packed up and gently hugged Brigit. "Full recovery. That's an order." Marjorie traipsed into Colton's office, said goodbye, and left.

Brigit stood in his doorway. "Can I have a word?"

He shot her a stern look over his shoulder. "Don't try to convince me."

Hands on hips, she stood in front of his desk. "I know my limitations. One of them is swaying the most stubborn, most controlling man I've ever met." She parked herself in the guest chair. "I do have one good piece of news."

He perked up. "Montgomery slithered into his hole."

"Unfortunately, no. But we do have a solid commitment from a group of investors."

"Who and how much?"

Brigit heaved in a breath. "Spider Holdings has the single biggest chunk of Francesco stock with twenty-two percent. The investors pledged in favor of taking Francesco private. They're dead set against a hostile takeover." Her fate was sealed. She'd thrown her full support to Colton.

He tapped his fingers on his desk. "Significant, but not enough."

"Colton, look. You have to be Francesco's White Knight. That's our best chance at stopping MobiCom."

As he leaned back, he clenched his jaw muscles. "My first business venture failed because I invested too heavily in a company that went belly-up. I vowed never again."

"This is different. You believe in Francesco and in Crockett Boxes." She stared into his troubled eyes. "And I believe in you."

After holding her gaze for several seconds, he strode to his picture window. With his back to her, he continued. "I'll do it, but only to keep that son of a bitch Montgomery from winning." He turned. His eyes were brimming with so much hatred she trembled.

"I thought this was about Francesco's success and Crockett's innovation. When did things become personal?"

"The moment Wilson Montgomery stepped into the picture." He walked over and smiled. But she didn't believe his plastic expression. He offered his hands.

The second she clasped them, a chill shot down her spine. They were ice cold.

He escorted her into her office. "Run a report of my holdings and we'll see what damage we can do before the market closes for the week. Sell whatever is necessary." Without a smile or his signature nod, he headed back toward his office.

"Wait." She walked over and looked him firmly in the eyes. "Something isn't right. In good conscience, I can't complete *any* trades if you're not behind this decision."

They stared at each other for a long minute. When she ran her hand down his chest the tight lines around his eyes softened. "Wilson Montgomery is coming after *me*," he bit out.

"I don't understand."

His jaw muscles clenched as he shifted his attention past her and out the window. She waited and waited. Finally, she broke the silence. "Please, Colton." Again, she touched him, this time caressing his shoulder.

Slowly, his gaze met hers. After a long pause, his eyes softened, his jaw relaxed, and color flooded his cheeks. The man she'd come to admire and respect stood strong.

She breathed.

"I didn't know who Montgomery was until I met him at the gala," Colton said. "He was a complete stranger, but the threatening tone in his voice gave him away."

Perplexed, she furrowed her brow. "Who is he?"

"After twenty-three years, my good-for-nothing father has returned with a motherfucking chip on his shoulder."

"Oh, God, no."

"Wilson Montgomery is Wilson Mitus."

48

INTIMATE

D RESSED IN HIS ROBE, Colton opened his bedroom door to a dimly lit hallway. It was Monday, after midnight, but he couldn't sleep. In several hours, he and Brigit would fly to Ohio for Francesco's special shareholders meeting, scheduled for Tuesday. By a simple vote, the shareholders would decide his future. Either the Francesco Company and Crockett Boxes would be his, or they'd be MobiCom's. The thought of Wilson Montgomery winning soured his stomach.

"You'll never amount to anything, you stupid, useless child." Those words haunted Colton's dreams, but, by day, they'd turned him into an indestructible powerhouse. Pushing past the bitter memories, he set off down the hallway.

With the exception of Francesco stock and his real estate holdings, Brigit had sold every position in his portfolio. But even with the millions on hand, Colton didn't have enough to match MobiCom's inflated offer.

After spending the weekend analyzing possible scenarios, the Mitus team and Francesco executives agreed on a strategy. Mitus Conglomerate would pay shareholders a three percent premium over the current stock price. That offer was five percentage points lower than MobiCom's, so to sweeten the deal, shareholders would be given options to repurchase up to twenty-five percent of their current shares after one year at the Mitus purchase price.

Everything hinged on convincing shareholders that the impending success of Crockett Boxes made their options of greater value than MobiCom's quick cash. Colton's chances of winning were slim. He'd risked his entire career on believing that somehow, some way, those shareholders would see the value of long-term financial gain in lieu of making a quick buck.

Light spilled into the hallway from the bottom of Brigit's closed bedroom door. There was never a moment he wasn't drawn to her, but he wasn't looking for a late-night booty call, so he padded downstairs.

As he approached the kitchen, the air grew chilly. The French door leading to the screened porch was ajar. Someone had forgotten to close up. He started to shut the door when he noticed a lone figure curled up on the couch.

Brigit sat alone in the dark, her face bathed in the moonlight's soft glow. Pausing to appreciate her beauty, he realized she was crying. His shoulders dropped. It hadn't even been two weeks since the brutal attack and he hadn't asked her once, all weekend, how she felt. She'd worked diligently alongside him without letting on if she was in pain.

"Hey," he murmured. As she turned, she quickly wiped her cheeks. He stepped outside. "Where's your shadow?"

She cracked a smile. Her smile did it for him every single time. "The cold isn't Mojo's thing. He's conked out in his bed."

He draped the throw over her lap and sat close. She looked adorable in her cozy white bathrobe and big slipper boots. "Whatcha doing up so late?" He gently thumbed a runaway tendril from her face.

"Same as you." She angled toward him on the sofa.

They gazed into each other's eyes. The undeniable attraction whirled around them. He wanted to lift her onto his lap, wrap his arms around her and kiss her until they were breathless and hungry for more. Did she feel the energy humming between them? "Thank you for going the extra mile this weekend," he said. "Are you in pain?"

She rubbed her chest. "Nothing I can't handle."

"How's your memory treating you?"

"What's a memory?"

His lips lifted. "It'll come back."

"I worry that it won't, but I'm too focused on Francesco to think about who did this to me."

"You care about that company as much as I do."

Breaking eye contact, she stared straight ahead. "Francesco should remain its own organization. MobiCom doesn't get to claim Crockett Boxes." She shivered beneath the lightweight throw.

Draping his arm around her, he scooted close and kissed the top of her head. "I'll warm you."

They sat in silence for a few moments.

"It's time you knew," Brigit murmured.

Finally. She was going to tell him about the baby, their baby. Maybe even come clean about her mysterious past.

"Colton, is that you?" Vanessa called from the kitchen. Brigit's body stiffened beneath the blanket. Dancing onto the porch, she said, "It's your lucky night cuz I had one helluva vacation and I'm ready to whoop it up!"

Dammit. Colton pushed off the sofa to greet her. "Welcome back, Vanessa."

She threw her arms around him. "Oh, I didn't realize you—" With wide eyes, she stepped back and tugged out her earbuds. "*Brigit.* Isn't it kinda late to be number crunching?"

"We have a big meeting tomorrow and couldn't sleep," Colton said. "Good trip?"

"Um, yeah, great. Feels like I've been gone *forever*. What did I miss?" Vanessa couldn't stop staring at Brigit.

"It's late. I'm going to bed." Brigit removed the blanket and rose.

"Vanessa, when did you leave?" Colton asked.

"Night before Thanksgiving, on the heels of Chad. Why?"

"Did you see anyone outside the compound?"

"Nope, but I wasn't looking." Vanessa furrowed her brow. "Should I have been?"

Brigit took a few steps toward the French door. "Goodnight."

"Brigit, wait," Colton said. "Vanessa, are you staying out here?"

"Alone in the cold? Uh, *no*." Vanessa spun around and strutted into the house.

Before Brigit stepped inside, Colton placed his hands on the back of her shoulders. When she turned toward him, he asked, "You want to finish what you were about to tell me?" Her expression fell and she shook her head.

Dammit, Vanessa.

Her beauty drew him in and he brushed his lips against hers. "Exercising control has grounded me and defined me as a man. When we're together, I can't control myself." He kissed her again.

"You're exhibiting plenty of control now." Her breathy voice was whisper quiet. She gently finger-combed his hair out of his eyes. "Ask Santa for a brush."

Heat flamed his body. As she lowered her hand, he dropped a lingering kiss on her palm, then let go. "I'm on Santa's naughty list," he murmured. "A lump of coal for me."

Her smile sent a bolt of electricity shooting through him. He missed her so damn much. But he wouldn't lay a hand on her until she was ready. Hell, he didn't even know if she wanted him anymore.

"Don't forget to lock up." She shuffled out of the kitchen.

He threw the bolt and fell in line with her. In silence, they walked upstairs.

She stopped at her doorway. "Goodnight, Colton."

"Sleep well, Brigit." He looked into her eyes. Normally bright and fiery, they looked troubled. If Vanessa hadn't barged in, would she have finally opened up? Second-guessing that woman was pointless.

He couldn't resist touching her, so he slipped his hand around the nape of her neck. Desire pulsed through him and his body came alive. Caressing her soft skin reminded him of how their bodies molded together. He inhaled her sweet scent, wanting to get lost in her. Instead of telling her how much he missed and needed her, he kissed her forehead and walked away.

After closing his bedroom door, he tossed his robe on the foot of the bed and lay down. Naked beneath the linens, he closed his eyes but he was too revved up to sleep. The Francesco Company and Crockett Boxes would be his or he'd be forced out of the single biggest undertaking of his career. He clenched his hands into fists. Wilson Montgomery made his blood boil. Who returned after two decades, hell-bent on ruining their son? *My asshole of a father, that's who.*

There was a light tap on his door and then it opened. An angel appeared in his doorway, backlit by the amber hallway light. Brigit crossed into his bedroom. "I can't sleep."

His body responded to her sultry voice. Tossing back the covers, he got out of bed. With each step his heart pumped faster. As he closed his bedroom door, her coconut fragrance smelled like the best vacation he'd never taken.

Moonlight streamed through his bedroom windows, bathing her in an ivory glow. She untied the silky sash, pulled the robe from her shoulders and let it slip onto the floor. Her naked form turned him hard in seconds. Beautiful breasts. Pert nipples. Creamy skin. But it was her inner strength that stilled him. Gazing into her eyes confirmed his feelings.

"I need you, Colton." Her husky voice was filled with everything he'd waited to hear. Determination. Hunger. Desire. *His* Brigit stood before him.

As he pulled her into his arms, he whispered, "I've missed you."

Standing on her tiptoes, she smiled. "Me too."

He smiled back. Nothing mattered but that moment. *Their* moment.

With a tender touch, she cradled his face in her hands, then pressed her lips to his. A burst of desire flooded his veins. She deepened the kiss and their soft moans filled the silence.

His world had been filled with masked screwing and hard fucking. Surrounded by fetishes and dark desires, he'd found a sexual world where he fit in and was welcomed with open arms and legs.

But this woman was different.

When the kiss ended, she led him to the bed, but paused to pull a condom from his night table drawer. That told him a lot. She was physically *and* emotionally ready. "Would you like me masked?" she asked.

Her words hung heavy. *She really is an angel.*

Sitting on the edge of his bed, he held her hands. She was the light to his dark and she had the ability to do what no one had ever been able to do. Free his tormented soul. "Tonight, I need to see your beauty when I make love to you."

Her satisfied expression made him smile. He wrapped his arms around her waist and as he kissed her, he fell back onto the bed. They lay together, her on him, staring into each other's eyes.

She stroked his hair away from his eyes. "Promise me something."

"What?" He laid a tender kiss on her lips.

"No matter what happens at Francesco's shareholder meeting, or what you might find out, remember how special this night was and how much it meant to us both."

BRIGIT AWOKE WITH A START. The bed linens were soaked. Dread crept into her consciousness. Someone watched from the shadows. Colton slept, peacefully. No, wait, something was wrong. His cream-colored pillowcase was crimson. Bolting upright, she winced in pain. His pillowcase was drenched in blood.

She screamed. He didn't move. She shook him, but nothing. Vinny Ray emerged from the shadows. He threw back his head and howled, his raucous laughter piercing her ears.

"No, no, no, no!" Brigit's arms flailed. Although she scrambled to get out of the bed, she couldn't move.

"I was drunk the first time, Eve Francesco, but not tonight," spat Ray. "This time, I'll get the job done."

"Help!" she screamed. "Help meeeeeee!!!"

"Shhhh, it's okay," said a soothing voice in the distance. Someone touched her arm and she jerked awake, gasping for air.

"It was just a dream." Colton kissed her forehead. "I'll get a cool washcloth."

Sweat trickled down her temple. Her heart pounded so hard she couldn't catch her breath. *Ohmygod, that was terrifying.* She examined the sheets. They were blood-free. She slipped out of bed and checked the door. It was ajar.

"The door is open." She scurried back to bed. "Someone has been in here."

Colton looked down the hallway. "It's quiet." He closed the door.

"Please lock it." Shaking, she pulled the linens around her neck.

Immobilized by fear, her eyes darted about the room, checking and double-checking. Vinny Ray hadn't been in there. Or had he? Did she have a nightmare? Or had someone been lurking in the darkness, watching them sleep?

49

HELLO, EVE

"MELVIN, ARE YOU STILL there?" Brigit had stunned her attorney into silence. Phone to ear, she sat on the edge of her bed and waited.

"Let's confirm, shall we?" Melvin Parsons' normally booming voice was quiet. "You're voting all twenty-two percent of your shares in *favor* of Mitus Conglomerate taking Francesco private. *Everything* in your Spider Holdings positions."

"Yes, that's correct. *All of it.* I'm flying to Columbus for tomorrow's shareholder meeting. If you can't delegate your voting privileges in time, please vote on my behalf. MobiCom is attempting a hostile takeover and I've advised Colton that the White Knight is his best defense."

"You advised Colton Mitus? I must've entered an alternate universe. I knew I shouldn't have taken that sleeping pill."

"I have to run. I'll explain when I return."

"I'll add you to the accounts and text the confirmation. The only thing left to say is good luck and safe travels."

With bags in hand, Brigit hurried downstairs to reconfirm with Ryan that he'd take care of Mojo while she was gone. After hugging her dog and giving him a treat, she headed out front.

Cold afternoon air smacked her face and she slipped on her leather gloves. Disturbing nightmare aside, she was ready to stop MobiCom.

Vonn stood next to the Bentley talking on his cell phone. "Thanks," he said and hung up. "Brigit let me get those." He placed her bags into the trunk.

"Did Colton charter a plane?" she asked.

"You're flying commercial. Columbus is expecting snow."

Colton stepped outside looking energized and full of swagger. "Ready to do this?" His confident smile was a direct result of their late-night fireworks.

"Forgot my wallet." Vonn bolted past Colton. "Courier is delivering a package," he called over his shoulder as he ran inside.

An unmarked white van rambled into sight. Brigit craned to see the driver, but the sun's reflection bounced off the windshield. The vehicle stopped at the top of the driveway and, to Brigit's relief, a woman exited.

The courier's long, black hair trailed down her chest, a black knit cap covered her head and dark sunglasses shielded her eyes. She opened the back of the van, pulled out a package and headed up the cobblestone walkway.

"I'll sign for that," Colton said.

The courier stopped. "How you been?" Her strained voice gave Brigit the chills. "Does my hair remind you of something?" She dropped the box, whipped off her hat, and with it, the long black wig, revealing a man with a buzz cut.

Fear pounded through Brigit. "Oh, God, no," she choked out.

"Uncle Vinny has come to make good on his promise." He swayed, then whipped off his sunglasses. "Remember me now? I'm your goddamn worst nightmare and I've got a motherfuckin' score to settle."

The reason she'd changed her identity and her looks, then moved hundreds of miles away to pick up the pieces of her shattered life and start over, stood a mere forty feet away.

"Who are you?" Colton pulled out his phone.

"No calls, rich boy," Vinny Ray said. "This ain't your business."

"Like hell it isn't," Colton bit out. "You're on my property."

"Leave him out of this, Ray," Brigit said. "This is between you and me."

Ray pulled a small handgun from his jacket pocket and waved it around. "I'm calling the shots now, aren't I, Eve?"

Cringing, she blurted, "Put the gun down. We can talk."

"Talk?" Ray sneered. "Sure, I'll start. You owe me five years, bitch."

Her fingers tightened into balls of fury. "Go to hell. You killed my parents! Fuck your five years!"

Ray staggered forward. "Feel better you got that shit out? 'Cause now it's my turn." He raised his gun and fired, twice.

Something whizzed by her ear, then pain ripped through her arm. Shrieking, she fell to her knees.

Three more shots rang out and Ray crumpled to the ground. Brigit whipped her head around. Vonn stood on the cobblestone entryway, his gun jutting from his clasped hands. Worried staff peered through the living room windows while Mojo barked and growled from inside the house.

"There's been a shooting on my property," Colton said. "I need two ambulances."

Chad rushed outside, slamming the door behind him. "How can I help?"

Colton shoved his phone into his hand. "Give the emergency operator our address."

Taylor cracked open the front door. "Is Brigit okay?"

"Stay inside!" Colton knelt by Brigit. "Were you hit?"

"Yes." Feeling lightheaded, she swayed forward.

Cradling her in his arms, he opened her coat and unbuttoned her suit jacket. "I don't see a chest wound. Let's check your arm."

Vonn knelt beside Ray as the dark pool of blood expanded on

the cobblestone walkway beneath him. With two fingers pressed to Ray's neck, he shook his head.

"Paramedics and police are on their way," Chad said, then squatted next to Colton.

"I've got her." Colton tossed a nod in Vonn's direction. "Make sure Vonn's okay."

As Chad bolted over, Colton flipped his focus back to Brigit. His eyes were coal black and a shadow fell across his face. A shudder ran through her. His jaw ticked and he looked away.

Even though she'd tried to tell him, more than once, Vinny Ray had done it for her. Brigit's contrived life was unraveling. The burn in her arm was nothing compared to the frenetic pounding in her chest. Her secret past had collided with her convoluted present at the worst possible time. She needed Colton to look at her. "Can you help me sit up?"

"The bullet tore through your sleeve," he said, refusing to make eye contact. "Let's get this coat off, so I can see where it lodged." Carefully he helped her remove her coat.

"Ow, ow, ow." The arm of her charcoal suit was blood-soaked. *Payback is painful.*

"I've got to stop the bleeding. This will hurt," he said, then applied pressure.

She winced. With her other hand, she squeezed his arm. Of course it would hurt. Her past had been exposed, along with a five-and-a-half-year-old sin. When she'd sought vengeance, she'd not given thought to future consequences. A man lay dead, but not before exposing her true identity.

And the man she'd once despised now appeared to despise her. Colton had morphed into a block of stone. Though he attended to her wound, the warmth in his eyes had faded. His energy mirrored rolling thunder during a blinding rainstorm.

The wailing sirens cut off as whirling lights of two ambulances, two police cruisers, and a fire engine loomed into view. The caravan filed up the driveway and parked.

While the first responding police officer spoke with Vonn, two paramedics assessed Vinny Ray. Then, Ray was covered with a sheet and hoisted onto a stretcher. Though she blamed him for the deaths of her parents, she'd never wanted him to pay for his crime with his life.

"It's only a flesh wound, but you'll need sutures," said the paramedic, kneeling next to her. Accepting her fate, Brigit was placed on the stretcher.

When Colton finally looked at her, his flat stare reminded her of his warning. *Don't ever deceive me.* "I have to leave you." The weight of his harsh words stung.

"I'll stay with her," Chad said. "Brigit, I'll meet you at the hospital."

"We're going to need statements from everyone," said the police officer.

Colton checked his watch. "I have a flight to catch."

"Then we'll take yours first," said the officer.

In the ambulance, tears pricked Brigit's eyes. She'd never make it to the airport in time. But crying wouldn't make anything better. Crying never solved a damn thing. Somehow, someway, she'd get to that meeting. Stopping Montgomery hinged on her being there.

As the siren wailed, and the vehicle moved down the driveway, she closed her eyes. *Will you walk into my parlour? said the Spider to the Fly. 'Tis the prettiest little parlour that ever you did spy.*

She had become the fly, snagged in the very web she'd weaved.

COLTON CHECKED IN AND boarded with first class. Once seated, he stared out the window. Now, he could think.

After the gunshots, his first priority had been determining whether Brigit's wound was life-threatening. Then everything about his enigmatic Brigit Farnay fell into place.

Brigit Farnay, *his* Brigit, was Eve Francesco. The realization stunned him. Initially he'd dismissed it. But the blatant truth was impossible to ignore.

Brigit had deceived him by keeping her identity a secret from him. They'd grown close, or so he'd thought. Hell, he'd confided things he'd never told *anyone*. Yet she'd said nothing. Had she been playing him this entire time? And if so, why? What did she stand to gain by not telling him the truth? They were on the same side, fighting against a hostile takeover threat. The Francesco Company meant *everything* to them both.

He was perplexed as to why she'd not contacted him after her parents had died. In light of her father's dying wish, he would have found a place for her at Francesco. There was always room for someone as smart, hardworking, and dedicated as Brigit Farnay.

No, dammit, that's not who she is. She's Eve Francesco.

He had questions. Fortunately, he was about to spend the rest of the day with someone who probably had answers.

The flight attendant took his beverage order and that of the elderly woman sitting next to him, then promptly returned with their drinks. Colton drained his sparkling water.

"You got a love note," said the elderly woman.

"Excuse me?"

"Turn your napkin over," the woman whispered.

Sure enough, there was a phone number on the other side. Colton flipped the napkin, number down, back onto the tray.

"Not interested?"

"No, ma'am. Would you like her number?"

The woman laughed. "Oh no, honey. I wasn't sure if you saw it." Colton smiled.

"Does that happen to you a lot?"

He shrugged. "From time to time."

"You're a handsome fella. Girls like that. In my day, I liked the wild ones, but my Stanley swept me off my feet and I never looked back."

"Where is Stanley now?"

"He passed last year after sixty-three years of marriage. Four children, a ton of grandbabies, and now I'm a great-grandma."

"I'm sorry for your loss."

"Thank you, honey." She sipped her coffee. "So, you got yourself a sweetie?"

"I thought I'd found *the one.*"

"You know how you know for sure?"

He shook his head.

"Here's something I tell my young-uns when they come to their Grandmama for advice." She gave him a little smile. "Can you imagine living your life without her? If you can, move on. If you can't, well, then never, ever let her go. But that means you gotta stick by her, even when things get tough. You got to weather the storms *together* so you can bask in the sunny days." The elderly lady winked, pulled out her knitting and got busy.

"Thank you," Colton murmured, then looked out the window as the plane went wheels-up.

When they landed, Colton took the woman's roller bag from the overhead compartment and placed it on the aisle for her.

"Good luck, honey."

He tossed her a nod and exited the craft.

After checking into his Hilton suite, Colton headed downstairs. Midweek guests moseyed in and around the busy lounge. He scanned the room for Wilson Montgomery. Good thing the slimeball wasn't there or he'd kill the son of a bitch. Marjorie sat at a lounge table, too focused on her phone to notice him roll out the chair and ease into it. "I made it."

She looked up. Her pleasant expression fell away upon seeing him. "Where's your crack wealth manager?"

Colton was done answering everyone's fucking questions. Time for some damn answers. "My crack wealth manager's been delayed. Her past has caught up with her."

Marjorie furrowed her brow. "What does that mean?"

"She was shot, though nothing life-threatening. Chad booked them on the last flight tonight."

"We're expecting a big snow. Let's hope they land before the runways ice over." Then her eyes grew huge. "Did you say she was *shot?*"

"Some nut job posing as a courier ranted about their past, called her *Eve*, then shot her. Bullet grazed her arm. She was carted to the ER for stitches."

As the color drained from Marjorie's face, she inhaled her beverage.

That's what I thought. "Hope that wasn't vodka or you'll be no good to me tomorrow."

"Club soda. I'm going to swim in the good stuff tomorrow. I don't care what time the shareholder meeting ends. Even if it's eleven in the effing morning, I'm having a shot of something good and strong."

"Brigit Farnay never added up until today." Colton shot Marjorie a stern look.

The server appeared. "What can I start you off with? Would you like to see our menu?"

"Your best whiskey, neat." He looked at Marjorie, "Would you like a refill and something to eat?"

"Another club soda," Marjorie said to the waiter, then looked at Colton. "I can't eat. Shattered nerves."

The server left.

"Brigit hasn't been Brigit her entire life, has she?"

"How would I know? I just met her—"

"Cut the bullshit, Marjorie." He arched a brow. "*Everything* hinges on teamwork."

Marjorie looked away. The silence hung heavy for a long moment. "Since you think you know, why ask me?"

"To get you to tell me I'm wrong. To fill in the missing pieces. To confirm what I've deduced. Hell, I need some damn answers. Is she Eve Francesco?"

She cast her gaze squarely on him. "Yes, she is."

"Why'd she change her identity?"

"That I don't know. After Brigit—*Eve's*—parents were killed, she dropped out of grad school to attend the trial. Somehow the drunk driver got off, scot-free. During the trial, I tried to reach her about your interest in Francesco, but she never returned my calls or emails. She just vanished." Marjorie swiveled to face him. "That photo on my desk—"

"Brigit. Her artwork is plastered all over your wall. Clearly, you two were close."

She nodded. "I loved her like she was my own. Still do. I almost had a stroke when she waltzed into Francesco as your wealth manager. She never told me why she'd changed her identity and her looks. The past is the past for a reason, right? She was an adorable child and a pretty young woman, but she's a raving beauty now."

"I'm quite aware of how attractive she is." He shot her a hard stare. "Can we stay on track?"

Marjorie lifted a pack of cigarettes from her handbag, removed one, and tapped it on her palm. "Ever since you took Francesco public, she's been hoarding that stock. She's Spider Holdings."

Colton's eyes widened.

"Uh-huh," Marjorie said. "Our girl has the lion's share with twenty-two percent." Marjorie leaned close and he got a whiff of tobacco breath. "You might want to redirect that raging inferno rolling off you. She told me—and I quote—'Wilson Montgomery cannot get his grubby hands on my company.'" Marjorie stood. "I need a smoke."

"Not yet. We're not finished."

Her eyebrows shot up.

He patted her chair. "Sit down."

She leaned her backside against the table and looked over her shoulder at him. "The Francesco Company was all that child knew. Her parents were obsessed about grooming her to run it. They taught her to analyze spreadsheets in the first grade. She was smart, but they pushed her, hard. They wanted her to excel, in everything. I loved them dearly, but they bordered on insane when it came to their daughter. They limited her playtime with her dolls. They kept playdates short and focused. She didn't take regular piano lessons. She studied with a master and was required to practice two hours daily. Reading poetry wasn't enough. She was expected to write it." Marjorie shook her head. "Eve was the sweetest little girl. I felt sorry there wasn't a sibling or even a dog to relieve some of the pressure."

"The man who shot her sounded like he was getting revenge." Colton shrugged. "You think you know someone and then this shit happens."

"You do know her. She encouraged—no, she *insisted* you take the company private. She's losing Francesco all over again. That's gotta be killing her."

"Why didn't you tell me?"

Marjorie's jaw ticked. "Tell you what? And how would betraying her help any of us? I lost her once. Wasn't about to push her away. You're both fighting for the same thing. Who she was and who she is—I'm not sure that matters in light of what we're up against."

His phone buzzed with an incoming text and he lifted it from his pocket.

She grabbed her purse. "Back in five. Going to smoke myself to death, which at the moment is tempting."

"Are you staying here?" he asked.

"Absolutely. With snow in the forecast, I checked in hours ago." She took off toward the lobby.

The text was from Chad. *Brigit released from hospital. Stitched and ready to fly. Headed to Dulles.* Sprouting the rumblings of a major fucking headache, Colton's temples throbbed.

The server delivered their drinks and Colton took a long pull of whiskey. He had enough information to get him through the meeting. There was only one person who could fill in the blanks, but first, little Miss Francesco needed to get her ass to Columbus.

. . .

FIVE O'CLOCK IN THE MORNING. Colton rang the front desk, again.

"Yes, Mr. Mitus."

"Have Brigit Farnay or Chad Wright checked in?"

"No, sir. As soon as they arrive we'll pass along your urgent message."

He hung up and rolled back onto the pillow, then stared out the window at the chunky white snowflakes rapidly drifting into view. Earlier, both Brigit and Chad's phones went straight to voicemail. Their flight had landed hours ago. *Where in the godforsaken hell are they?*

He'd contacted his staff. No one had seen or heard from them since the ambulance carted Brigit away and Chad had followed after speaking with the officer.

Colton threw back the linens and sat on the edge of the bed. His throbbing hard-on ached. Screwing just any woman—masked or unmasked—had lost its appeal. Brigit, or Eve, or whoever the hell she was, was all he thought about. She was all he wanted and she spurred his desire to be a better man. He felt different when they were together. *Good* different, like shit mattered.

But right now he was pissed. He'd bared his fucking soul. Told her things he'd never shared with anyone. She'd played the caring part well. He clenched his jaw.

That'll teach me. Last time I relinquish any damn control.

He steamrolled into the bathroom. Today's goal was simple. Save Francesco from that asshole Montgomery. For starters, Brigit needed to vote her shares his way. Now that he knew who she really was, he fully expected she would.

He turned on the shower and brushed his teeth while the water heated up. A plan started formulating. He spit into the sink, raised his head and smiled in the mirror. Eve Francesco was going to do a hell of a lot more than just vote her shares.

50

DEFENDING FRANCESCO

C HAD HEAVED OPEN THE ballroom door and Brigit stepped into the shareholder meeting, already in progress. Because of the impending snowstorm, the last flight to Columbus had been oversold. Refusing to give up, they'd driven to Columbus. What should have been a seven-hour trip had turned into an eleven-hour ordeal. The blinding snowstorm had slowed traffic to a crawl.

With her arm secured in a sling, and still wearing her bloodied and ripped charcoal suit, she surveyed the large crowd. Was this a sign investors cared about the future of Francesco, or were they ready to throw their support to MobiCom? Though her arm ached, she'd made it this far and would see this through to its end, no matter what the outcome.

Montgomery stood at the podium, listing reason after reason why the shareholders should vote for the merger. *Monster.*

Lining the stage behind him were two long tables with Francesco executives seated on the left and MobiCom's team to the right.

Game faces on.

Colton sat tall in the first seat. With his jaw set in a hard line, he was the epitome of power, confidence and determination. Pride filled her heart. It was a privilege to be part of the Mitus Team.

She'd caught glimpses of a magical life with Colton at the gala and at Luray Caverns. Working with Colton exhilarated her. He was the most riveting man she'd ever known. Their partnership was powerful and provocative and intense. Each time they shared a bed, their explosive passion confirmed her feelings. She loved him so much her heart hurt.

After today, she'd never see him again. Colton Mitus was too sharp to ignore the ugly truth behind her shrouded past. Had she betrayed him? He would see it that way.

Colton peered out at the audience and she snapped back to reality. She'd known this day would come. What she wasn't prepared for was the emptiness. When it was time for goodbye, her heart would break.

"Francesco's lackluster stock continues to tell the tale," Wilson said. "Their so-called revolutionary wireless innovation—Crockett Boxes—is a pipe dream, at best." Wilson pulled a Plexiglas box from beneath the podium and held it up. "Hey folks, it's their wireless contraption!"

A few in the audience chuckled and someone in the back of the room booed.

Not funny, you idiot. She loathed Montgomery, not because he wanted a company he didn't deserve, but because he'd inflicted a world of hurt on his son. What parent did that?

An evil one.

"All kidding aside, friends, MobiCom gets results. We've already done great things with better products, faster turnaround delivery times and stronger relationships with vendors and manufacturers. If you don't believe me, look at the stock. Vote your shares and reap the financial rewards *today*. No one has a guarantee on tomorrow. Thank you." The audience applauded as Montgomery returned to the first seat at MobiCom's table.

Next, Marjorie introduced Colton. He rose, buttoned his suit and shook her hand. Then, he adjusted the microphone and smiled at the crowd. "Good morning and thank you for being here."

After voting her shares, Brigit would head home and resume her life at Porter, Gabriel and Sethfield, as if Colton Mitus had never existed. *I'll never get over him. Never.*

"Today is a defining day for Francesco employees and shareholders."

Brigit scanned the audience. No heads buried in phones. That was good.

"The industry stands on the brink of a major turning point in wireless technology. In the past decade we've made tremendous strides to improve communication, streamline efficiencies and get the job done for less. Those are sound qualities of an industry leader and the ones you'd expect me to tout. But there's something the Francesco Company and Mitus Conglomerate have that MobiCom does not. You won't find it in any of the quarterly reports. It's not discussed at executive meetings or amongst the board of directors. It can't be bought and not even MobiCom can steal it, like they're trying to do with Crockett Boxes." He paused. "That all-important quality is heart."

As the room became pin-drop quiet, Brigit caressed her sling, trying to soothe the throbbing pain in her arm. Her heart filled with pride. That man was the real deal. Her parents would have adored him. Her eyes stung, and she swallowed down the emotion.

"In a landscape where market trends rule, churning out better-than-expected earnings reports is the difference between corporate life and death, and being second equates to losing. *Heart* is not a quality organizations brag about having because it's not tough."

Colton scanned the audience as if searching for someone and her heart picked up speed.

"Many believe a company oozing heart can't possibly be competitive." A knowing smile spread across Colton's face. "But that's where organizations like MobiCom fail. It's their Achilles heel. While Francesco and Mitus conduct business with heart, we aren't going to roll over and allow a bully like MobiCom to waltz in at the eleventh hour and take our innovation away from us." Colton's eyes narrowed. "We're too damned smart to let them dictate our future."

Several in the audience clapped.

"Six years ago, I took an avid interest in the success of the Francesco Company. Over the years I've remained anchored to this organization. Why would a corporate investor like myself choose one company over the tens of dozens I do business with annually? At their core, Francesco employees and shareholders have heart. Even today, Nicholas and Samantha's only child, Eve Francesco, is the embodiment of that winning quality."

Oh, God, he must hate me. Brigit's heart ached.

Again, he scanned the crowd. This time he found her. Even across that large room his intensity and strength stilled her. *He's the love of my life and I've lost him.*

"And now, I'm honored to introduce you to the true face of Francesco. After too many years, Nick and Sammy's daughter has finally come home. Please help me welcome Eve Francesco." With his signature smile, he flipped his gaze to the back of the room. "Eve, please join me."

Brigit swayed as the room went all wobbly, then her heart took off like a locomotive speeding down the tracks.

Chad grabbed her elbow and steadied her. "You okay?"

"I will be. Excuse me. I have to join Colton on stage." Chad gaped as she set off down the center aisle.

Halfway down, a hand shot out. "Good to see you, Eve." Jimmy from accounting pumped her hand. "Make us proud."

I can do this.

Mrs. Mick stood like a beacon as Brigit stepped onstage. Marjorie hugged her and whispered, "Bury Montgomery."

"Over the years, her commitment to Francesco never waned, even when life threw her unexpected curveballs," Colton said.

"Doing what's best for Francesco has kept her moving forward. Welcome back, Eve."

As Brigit walked to the podium, Colton turned and extended his hand. Everything was happening fast, yet things were moving in slow motion. Their hands connected and a bolt of energy surged up her arm, straight to her heart. She gazed into his eyes. Doing right by this man took center stage.

He pulled her close. "Shut MobiCom down."

The intensity in his eyes and the determination in his voice snapped her out of her daze. He needed this. Mrs. Mick expected this. The employees of Francesco deserved this. She'd been working toward *this* moment for six long years.

Time to rock this.

She took the podium. "Thank you, Colton." Pausing, she smiled at the audience. "Hello, Francesco. Being home feels *great.*"

Sparse applause filled the room.

"Colton is right. Francesco has heart, but what's a heart without a soul? Having a conscience and doing the right thing can be tricky in today's business climate. Outperforming last quarter's bottom line, exceeding shareholders' expectations and driving business forward is stressful and demanding. I'm not saying those qualities are inherently wrong. They're not. But what MobiCom is doing is deceitful and underhanded. If MobiCom wins, we're applauding their efforts, handing over a lifetime of effort and telling the wireless community, along with the business world at large, that working without a heart or a soul is acceptable. Never mind having a moral compass. Let's bully our way in, throw a little money around and make room for the new sheriff."

Her jitters settled down and she took a calming breath.

"After my parents' tragic deaths, Colton Mitus took the reins and continued pushing the limits. Not only did he carry out their ambitious goals, he exceeded them. They dreamed of taking the company public. He accomplished that in three short years. Nick and Sammy had discussed factory enhancements and improved health benefits for employees. Mitus Conglomerate worked with the Francesco leadership team and made that happen. Francesco has the lowest attrition rate in the wireless industry. Why do you think that is? Francesco employees are valued. They know their contribution makes a difference. And now their time has come to help launch an innovative product that will make them the rock stars of the telecom world."

A round of cheers rang out and confidence filled her heart. For the first time since she'd lost Francesco she wasn't worried about failing her parents or even failing Colton. She believed in herself and she'd be damned if she'd fail herself. Her six-year journey would not end in defeat.

"I'm confident Nick and Sammy would have been thrilled that someone as intelligent, passionate and ethically sound as Colton Mitus has made so many strides and had such a positive impact on their organization. While capitalism thrives on competitiveness, what MobiCom is attempting to do goes against everything Francesco stands for. From the inception of Crockett Boxes, Colton chose Francesco as his wireless partner. He believes in Francesco employees and their abilities. Francesco's factory is poised to manage the increased workload as demand for the product increases. And Francesco stakeholders are ready to manage to the next level of success. MobiCom is counting on us to sell out. I believe in Colton Mitus, in Mitus Conglomerate, and in the long-term partnership between the two companies. Join me. Vote to take Francesco private."

The audience erupted in applause, some jumping to their feet and cheering.

Marjorie stepped up to the podium. "Thank you, Eve, and thank you, Colton. We now move to the voting portion of today's meeting. I'd like to invite Francesco's first daughter to cast her ballot."

Brigit did what needed to be done. As she walked off the stage, Colton appeared by her side. With his large hand on the small of her back, he guided her toward the voting stations.

His touch sparked a myriad of responses. Her skin heated where his hand pressed against her clothing. She felt empowered by his side. No other man would ever evoke such raw emotion. Of this she was certain.

"Great speech," he whispered. "Thanks for pushing to get here."

Business. Her chest tightened. That's why he'd hired her, after all. She'd done her professional best and if he harbored resentment because she'd concealed her true identity, he was smart enough to know that airing his personal grievances would only hurt their chances of winning. They had to act as a united front. But that's all it was. An act.

She had to keep it together so she wouldn't shatter into a million pieces.

Several voting stations equipped with laptops had been set up on pedestals flush against the wall, allowing shareholders to cast their ballots electronically.

"Together, as a show of solidarity." The huskiness in his voice surprised her.

As soon as they cast their electronic votes, shareholders closed in, forming lines and chatting amongst themselves. Though their eyes met in the thickening crowd, several Francesco executives ambushed Colton and gobbled him up.

After six long years, her journey had ended where she'd begun. The loneliness that had plagued her then had returned, only this time her heart was broken for a very different reason. She needed some air and a good cry. So, she escaped through a side door and stepped into the quiet hotel atrium.

"Not so fast," said a voice behind her. "Where do you think you're going?"

51

ALL IN

"YOU CAN'T KEEP RUNNING," Marjorie said.

Brigit shuddered in a shaky breath. "I have no reason to stay. I had a job to do. It's done. I'm no longer needed."

"I know you. You're not thinking clearly. You're hurting. If you were a child, I'd take you for ice cream."

Brigit smiled. "We'd sneak out of that building like prisoners on the lam."

Marjorie laughed. "You saved Francesco, honey. Your speech was the right balance of facts and emotion. I'm so damn proud. Mom and Dad would have been, too."

Brigit's eyes grew damp. "I gotta get out of here. And think."

Marjorie's gaze floated over her face. "My car is with valet. Room five-thirty-one. Why don't you take a little drive? Make sure your route has been plowed."

She swiped a lone tear. "Thank you."

"I'll be here until a winner is announced and then I'll root my ass on a barstool. Celebrating with the good stuff or drowning in cheap booze." Marjorie took a backward step toward the ballroom. "Go. You'll feel better. I promise."

COLTON GLANCED AROUND, BUT Brigit was nowhere in sight. The area surrounding the voting pedestals was packed, so he headed toward the back of the room and ran into Marjorie.

"She gave a powerful speech, don't you think?" Colton asked.

"You need to head out."

His eyebrows shot up. "Excuse me?"

"Where's Sherlock Holmes?" she asked.

"What's going on?"

"She left and you need to go after her. I'll text you the address." Marjorie pulled her phone from her pantsuit pocket. "Bring her back, Colton."

Twenty minutes later, Chad pulled up to the entrance. "Aw, crap. You know I don't do well at these places."

"Drop me off and I'll drive Marjorie's car back," Colton said.

Fluffy snow blanketed the cemetery grounds. The place was deserted, save for a lone car parked by a weeping willow. Brigit stood alone in the freezing cold. As Chad pulled up behind Marjorie's silver Lexus, Colton grabbed Brigit's wool coat from the backseat.

"You did one hell of a job," Colton said. "Thank you for getting her here."

Chad smiled. "You betcha. See you back at the hotel."

With her coat in hand, Colton stepped outside. As he shut the door, a wind gust blew the snow in drifts around his feet. He set off through the snow. *She must be freezing.*

He draped her coat over her shoulders and stared at the snow-covered headstones. In silence, he put his arm around her and paid his respects.

Any anger he'd harbored after he'd pieced together her identity melted the second he saw her standing in the back of the ballroom. She'd made it through a nasty snowstorm and in the same clothing that sported a bloodstained and torn suit jacket sleeve. Though her beauty shone through her pain, she'd risked a lot to make it to that meeting and throw her support his way. And she'd given up her dream for his. Her dedication and loyalty said it all.

Even more than any of that, he loved her. Completely and unconditionally. The elderly lady's words of wisdom confirmed his feelings. They'd weather the storm *together* so they could bask in the sunny days.

Now all he wanted to do was comfort and protect her. Then he wanted to take her to his hotel suite and make love to her, for hours.

He knelt down and, with his gloved hand, brushed the windswept snow off the headstones. "Samantha Brigit Francesco. Nicholas Farnay Francesco," Colton read. "That answers that question."

"Why are you here?" She crossed her arms and her coat fell to the ground.

Pain shone from her emerald eyes. Strong-willed Brigit was trying to push him away. He picked up the coat, brushed off the snow and helped her put it on. "Because you are. And to learn about your life."

"Hmm, so you're here for information." A tear slid down her cheek. "Ask away."

He slid off his glove and with a soft thumb, wiped away her sadness. "I'm here because the woman I'm crazy in love with ran out when I needed her by my side. Come back so we can celebrate or accept defeat. *Together.*"

She turned to him and a sliver of a smile softened her lips.

He folded her into his arms. "I love you, Brigit, and I can't live without you. I'm sorry for the hell you went through, in part, because of me. Had I known—"

Her heartfelt smile touched his soul. "You had me with *I'm crazy in love.*"

Holding her, he kissed her reverently.

When the kiss ended, she murmured, "I love you too, Colton. So much."

The joy he felt would be short-lived. He would lose her. *His* Brigit would be offered an executive position at Francesco. Marjorie would see to that. Brigit Farnay would resume her life in Ohio. And begin again as Eve Francesco. His gut ached, but that would be his secret. What was one more?

His phone rang and he lifted it from his pocket. "It's Chad." He tapped the speaker button. "What's happening?"

"The lines are thinning," said Chad. "Get back here for the announcement." He hung up.

With Brigit cradled in his arms, Colton trudged back to the car. "You are a dynamo." He flashed her a smile. "The bigger the challenge, the more determined I am to win. And I'm all in with you, Brigit Farnay." He placed her in Marjorie's vehicle, then settled into the driver's seat.

"You're all in, huh?" She clicked the seat belt into place.

"All in." He started the engine and headed out of the cemetery.

Colton had poured millions into a revolutionary product with Crockett and signed a long-term manufacturing agreement with Francesco. If they lost, he'd have to start over again. But he'd made a bold career choice and stood behind this risky business decision.

Time to find out if the shareholders agreed.

52

AND THE WINNER IS...

T HE SPINDLY MAN STOOD at the podium, cleared his throat and tapped the mic. "Can you hear me?" Peering at the nodding faces, he continued. "Okay good. We have the preliminary results to announce. The absentee ballot deadline is this evening at midnight. Final confirmation will take several days and an email will be sent, along with a written copy—"

"For crying out loud, spit it out." Wilson Montgomery hollered from the back of the room.

Brigit's mouth went dry.

Marjorie clasped her hand. "Ready?"

Swallowing hard, Brigit nodded.

"The vote is seventy-nine percent to twenty-one percent," said the spindly man.

Brigit and Colton exchanged nervous glances.

The man's lips curved into a crooked smile. "The proposed sale to MobiCom has been rejected. Congratulations, Mr. Mitus. The Francesco Company is yours."

The room erupted in applause and gleeful shouts. They'd defeated Wilson Montgomery.

"Yes!" Brigit hugged Marjorie with her good arm. "We did it!"

Colton hugged Chad, then threaded his arm gently around Brigit's waist. "You made this happen."

Smiling from ear to ear, she said, "*We* made this happen." A plum-size lump formed in her throat. Colton deserved the company and all the success that would follow once Crockett Boxes rolled out.

"Victory!" Marjorie threw her arms up and Chad bear-hugged her. "Whew, am I relieved. Drinks are on me."

Reaching up, Brigit kissed Chad's cheek. "You're the real hero, you know that? I wouldn't have made it here without you."

"Name your reward." Colton slapped Chad on the back. "A raise? An extra week of vacation? You're all about more security equipment, right?"

Grinning, Chad shifted his attention to Brigit. "What I'd really like is an introduction to the hot brunette with you at Sullivan's." He glanced at Colton. "Kathryn, right?"

Brigit laughed. "Consider it done, but take the raise, the extra week of paid vacation, *and* the new gadgets. You deserve it all."

As shareholders migrated toward the exit doors, they expressed their congratulations. When the room had emptied out, Wilson Montgomery sauntered over. "I underestimated you, Colton."

Colton's smile dropped and his eyes grew ice cold. "That was always your downfall."

"You've assembled quite a team here." Wilson winked at Brigit. "I'm impressed you cozied up to Francesco's heir. You're more like your dear ol' dad than I gave you credit for."

Brigit wanted to smack his face. *What a pig.*

Colton placed a possessive hand around her shoulder. "Wrong again. I'm nothing like you. Nothing at all."

Dobb sidled closer as Wilson extended his hand to Colton.

"Ah, save it," Marjorie said. "And take your lackey with you. Dobb's office has already been cleaned out and fumigated."

Glaring at Marjorie, Wilson slid his hand into his pocket. "You're a first-class—"

Marjorie shoved her index finger up to his face. "You so much as *glance* in the direction of the Francesco Company and I'll have the Securities and Exchange Commission breathing down your back."

On a grunt, Wilson did an about-face and marched out of the ballroom with Dobb close on his heels.

"There go two of the slimiest men I have ever met," Brigit said.

"Boy, was he trying to get a reaction out of you." Marjorie patted Colton's shoulder. "But you're too smart to take the bait."

"Marjorie, that CEO position is yours. What do you say?" Colton asked.

As Marjorie tapped a cigarette on her palm, she shifted her attention to Brigit. "Isn't it time our crack wealth manager took the reins?"

Brigit had dreamed of nothing but returning to her past. Her parents' expectation had set her on the unwavering path to *this* moment. Her father's dying wish was that she make Francesco her own. So, why didn't she feel the exhilaration she'd imagined? She was finally free to reclaim her birthright and resume her life. Was their vision what *she* truly wanted?

As she stared into Colton's eyes, gratitude washed over her and her heart filled with love. Though she'd always miss her mom and dad, they'd want her to live a happy life. The guilt, the anger and the grief that had propelled her forward lifted a little.

Eve Francesco had finally found some peace.

"Mrs. Mick, I agree with Colton. *You* are the absolute best person to run Francesco."

"Thank you," Marjorie said. "I'd be honored. Would you consider taking Dobb's board seat?"

Brigit beamed. "Now, *that* I'd love."

"Should I expect you'll be redoing your office at Mitus?" Colton asked.

"No, I wouldn't change a thing."

"Not even the location?"

"*Especially* not that." Colton's smile made her heart flip. She had absolutely made the right decision.

"You two make a damn terrific team, you know that?" Marjorie said.

"We sure as hell do," Colton replied, his eyes never leaving Brigit's.

"So, Brigit, what should we call you?" Chad asked.

"My name..." She flipped her gaze back to Colton. "My name is Brigit Farnay."

"So, *Brigit*, something's been bugging me for weeks." Chad ran a hand over his unshaven chin. "When you met Marjorie, she asked if you were a soccer fan. What the hell was that?"

Brigit and Marjorie laughed. "As a child, I'd spend Fridays after school with Marjorie," Brigit explained. "She was *supposed* to be teaching me about the Francesco Company. Instead, we'd paint or draw, read stories and do anagrams. I loved our Fridays." Pausing, she smiled at Mrs. Mick. "Soccer fan is an anagram for Francesco."

"Speaking in code. I'm impressed," Chad said. "Marjorie, I'll walk with you to the lounge. I could use something strong right about now." Together Marjorie and Chad left the ballroom.

Alone in the ballroom, Colton clasped Brigit's hands. "We did it."

Brigit could stare into this man's eyes forever. "Thank you for being Francesco's White Knight."

"I saved your company and you saved me," he murmured. For the second time that day, she melted. "You know, I have my father to thank for something."

"*What?* That man almost took down your business."

"Because of him we forged a partnership."

"Are you saying Montgomery thrust us together?"

"No. We managed to do that on our own." He softly kissed her and her heart flooded with love.

With a smile, she kissed him back. "Ready to celebrate?"

"In every way imaginable," he replied pulling her gently into his arms.

53

AN INTIMATE AFFAIR

FOLLOWING A CELEBRATORY DINNER at a downtown Columbus restaurant, Colton, Brigit and Chad said their goodbyes to Marjorie before returning to the hotel. It was too late to drive back to Virginia, plus Colton had a more pressing need to stay the night.

His Brigit.

Though she'd put on a good show, Colton could see her pain. Not only had she sacrificed her dream, she'd entrusted him with her legacy. Now it was his turn to take care of her. Once alone in their suite, he snaked his arms around her. "How 'bout a backrub, my love?"

Her eyes sparkled. "I like the sound of that," she said, but her expression quickly turned somber. "I owe you an explanation."

"And I owe you a debt of gratitude. We can talk, but not now. Tonight is about pampering *my* Brigit."

Her relieved smile brought him peace. "Thank you," she murmured. "I could use a shower, but I can't get my stitches wet."

"I'll run a bath and *personally* make sure your arm stays dry."

"Will you join me?"

"I'll be the guy washing your back." He pecked her cheek, walked into the spacious bathroom, and turned on the water in the Jacuzzi. When he exited, he found her struggling to remove her blouse.

"Getting you naked is my specialty." After helping her take off the sling and shed her blouse, he gently kissed her arm over the gauze. "Are you in pain?"

"Like crazy, but you make it all go away."

He unzipped her skirt and knelt to peel off her black stockings. Seeing her in her lingerie reminded him of their first night together. He'd found her breathtaking then, but that was nothing to how much he adored her now. After sliding off her panties, he rose, then unhooked her bra and pulled the satin fabric from her breasts. Her beauty stilled him and he paused to appreciate her perfect feminine form. God, he wanted her.

In his arms. In his bed. In his life.

"You have way too many clothes on." As best she could, she helped him undress until he stood naked before her. With a sultry smile, she wrapped her hand around his erection. "Let's go play."

He tied her hair in a bun, supported her into the tub and eased in behind her. She relaxed against his chest and he laid his hands on her tummy. Feeling complete with her nestled in his arms, he murmured, "I could stay here with you forever."

"Me, too, but shriveled isn't my best look."

"I love all your looks." Colton kissed her shoulder.

Craning around, she kissed his scruffy chin. "Today was huge, for us both. I'm so relieved and happy we won."

"Game changer." He drizzled warm water over her chest and watched it trickle down her breasts. "Why didn't you contact me after your parents died?"

As she spun around to face him, water splashed against the sides of the tub. "You don't remember?"

"No, I don't. Go easy. You'll get your stitches wet."

"I left messages and sent emails. I even made a special trip to see you, but got turned away at the mansion gates." She blew out a frustrated sigh.

Her news stunned him. "You know me, Brig. I've never ignored a potential business opportunity and I wouldn't have blown you off."

She shrugged. "Well you did, but let's not dredge up the past."

"From the day we met in Seth's office, I've thought about you and only you."

Her expression softened. "That's sweet, but why are we talking about this now?" She lathered the soap and covered his chest with bubbles.

"You're right. Talking can wait." He kissed her, savoring how her mouth molded so perfectly to his.

"Much better," she murmured, her eyes sparkling.

"Now that you've met Montgomery, you can understand why having integrity is so important to me," he said caressing her cheek. "And you're so damn beautiful. I would have remembered you."

"Fine, let's do this now. We never met. We never spoke by phone. The woman who screened your calls told me you weren't interested. You responded to one of my many emails and echoed what the gatekeeper had said."

What the hell! "When was this?"

"Five and a half years ago."

His blood pressure rose. *I'll deal with this tomorrow.* "Please accept my apology. I'm sorry you were treated so rudely." He kissed her forehead. "Let me rub you."

After several seconds, the tension in her eyes faded. "Apology accepted." Moving slower, she turned back around. While massaging her shoulders, he forced himself to refocus his thoughts and his energies on Brigit. Everything else could wait until they returned home.

"Thank you," she said snuggling into him. "I feel better." He rested his hands on her tummy and she moved them to her breasts. "I want you, so badly."

With sensuous strokes, they washed each other, then left the water for the warmth of the bed.

He planked over her and she smiled. One soft kiss turned

ravenous, but as soon as she guided him to her opening, he aborted the kiss. "I don't have a condom."

"It's okay. I don't want anything separating us."

Colton lay next to her. "I don't either, but this is more of a risk than I'm ready to take. And besides...you just...lost...the baby."

Her eyes grew wide. "*Baby?* What baby?"

"I overheard you talking to Marjorie. She asked if I knew. You said it was just a matter of time before I found out." Awareness lit up his eyes. "Oh, hell, you were talking about your former identity, weren't you?"

"I was."

"I thought you'd miscarried or lost the baby during the attack."

"Wow," she said caressing his shoulder. "That's a big deal. How did you feel about that?"

Placing a possessive hand over her tummy, he said, "I wanted to protect you both. It killed me when the ER doc told me you weren't pregnant."

With a gentle touch, she blanketed his hand with hers. "I'm sorry you had to go through that." After several seconds, her eyes flashed with recognition. "Ah, so that's why you told me to stop drinking. I would *never* drink if I were pregnant." She planted a huge kiss on his mouth. "Thank you for caring about our baby."

"Always," he said. Though he'd ached for their loss, relief washed over him for what they *hadn't* lost.

"I'm on the pill for medical reasons," she explained. "Tonight, I want us to make love without a condom."

Unable to remember the last time he'd had unprotected sex, he promised himself he wouldn't come until she did. Rising over her, again, he said, "I don't want to hurt you."

"We'll go slowly." She guided him to her. "I need you, Colton."

Pleasure shot through him as he tunneled inside. Then, with their connection complete, they shared knowing little smiles between two lovers.

A surge of emotion filled him as their bodies ebbed and flowed like gentle waves kissing the shoreline. In a protected cocoon of love, they bared their unmasked and vulnerable souls. And then, they let go. As she contracted around his unsheathed penis, her erotic cries and quivering body sent waves of ecstasy surging through him.

He loved this woman with every fiber of his being. She'd freed his tortured soul and he'd spend the rest of his life showing her how much he adored her. In the afterglow of their lovemaking, they snuggled close.

"Do you want a family?" She peeked at him through her lashes.

"I'd never considered it until I thought we'd already started one."

"And now?"

He kissed her forehead. "I'm all in."

A little smile flitted across her lips. "I'd love to be a mom someday."

"You'll be an awesome one. But before we start trying, I want you all to myself for a good, long while."

"How 'bout we practice making one again?"

"You're the boss."

On a laugh, she kissed him.

54

YOU'RE FIRED

T HE FOLLOWING AFTERNOON COLTON sat at Chad's desk while
they scrolled through archived email. "Open the *Completed
Deals* folder," Colton said.

Inside that folder was one titled *Deep Six*. Chad clicked on that
and dozens of emails populated the page. Together they read a few.

"After Brigit told me how she'd been treated, I knew I'd find
something," Colton said. "This is reprehensible."

"You've never seen these emails?" Chad swiveled to face Colton.

"No."

"How did this happen? You have a guiding hand in every aspect
of the business."

"When Mitus Consulting failed, Vanessa stayed, even though I
couldn't pay her a salary. I never suspected her loyalty came with
such a high price." Colton's hands tightened into fists.

Vanessa had dismissed a potential opportunity with a successful
Northern Virginia commercial real estate company. And she'd
rejected a meeting request with a start-up cosmetics company that
had become an industry giant.

"SGV Cosmetics had one of the biggest IPOs in the past five

years." Colton's pulse kicked up. "Not only did she sabotage my business, she negatively impacted my reputation as a businessman."

"Hmm," Chad said after reading several more emails. "I see a pattern. She only rejected the women. I think she wanted to keep them away from you."

"She cost me millions," Colton bit out. "Send those emails to my printer. Three years ago, I promoted Vanessa to staff manager and hired Red to backfill her position. Check Red's archived email."

Chad clicked over. "Looks like Red was burning the midnight oil and engaging *everyone* who contacted you."

"My business surged around that time," Colton said. "I could barely keep up. Find the emails from Eve Francesco." Colton strummed his fingers on Chad's desk.

"Got 'em," Chad said after searching. "There's one response. Did you send this reply to her?"

Ms. Francesco,

Thank you for your interest in Mitus Conglomerate. My future plans with the Francesco Company do not include you. In light of that, I'm not comfortable reviewing your plan, whatever its perceived value and merit. And please, no more drop-ins.

Best wishes,
Colton Mitus

"Hell, I never even knew she'd reached out to me." Colton pushed out of the chair and headed for the door. "No wonder Brigit despised me."

"Are you speaking with Vanessa?"

"I'm way past talking."

"I doubt she'll go quietly. I'm here if you need me."

On his way back to his office Colton texted Vanessa. *Meet me in my office.* Blood pounded in his temples as he grabbed the printed emails and waited at his conference table.

A moment later Vanessa stood in his doorway. "You need me?"

Once a model employee, she looked like a tramp. Her low-cut sweater and miniskirt were better suited for a nightclub than the workplace. When he'd instituted casual Fridays, he still expected his employees to dress like professionals. By tomorrow, her attire and her crafty ways would be history.

"Vanessa, have a seat." Firing employees was his least favorite task, but in this case, she deserved to go.

She pushed his office door closed with such force, it slammed shut. "Oops, don't know my own strength." She perched on the edge of the chair and arched her back.

She looks like she's posing for a centerfold. "You know I'm not one for small talk, so I'll get right to the point." He slid over the two emails. "Tell me about these."

After reading them, she pushed out of her chair and walked to the window. "Ancient history."

"Why did you dismiss these opportunities?"

"You don't expect me to remember every incidental thing that happened over the years, do you?"

"Your job did not include making executive decisions about what organizations I did or did not do business with, yet you rejected these two inquiries outright. Explain yourself."

"I made choices with your best intentions in mind." Turning, she crossed her arms and her breasts spilled from her sweater.

Your tits are of no interest to me. "I lost millions over these two potential deals. There were dozens of emails like these."

Vanessa sighed. "You're doing better than ever. Maybe I thinned the herd for you. But honestly, I don't remember."

You don't have an honest fucking bone in your body. "Your unprofessional, deceptive behavior is unacceptable."

Her mouth dropped open. "What?" She smirked. "Oh, I get it. You're messing with me."

"Please have your bags packed by the end of the day."

Her eyes grew beady. "This was Brigit's idea, wasn't it? That woman has been a thorn in my side from the moment she entered *our* house."

Colton's lip curled into a snarl. "What's Brigit got to do with this?" As he stood and faced her, his lips slashed into thin lines.

With her hands rooted on her hips, Vanessa glared at him. "After more years than I care to count, I'm getting the boot."

"Deceptive actions have consequences. Leave me a forwarding address for your final paycheck."

Vanessa strutted to the door and flung it open. "Keep it. I'm gone." She stormed out.

He'd anticipated a different scenario, filled with drama. *I got off easy.* He lifted his desk phone receiver and dialed Chad's extension. "It's done."

"That fast? How long did you give her?"

"She's leaving today."

"Hmm, no pushback. Thanks for telling me." Chad hung up.

Colton strolled into Brigit's office. She sat at her conference table, clicking away on her laptop. Sneaking behind her, he put his arms around her neck and kissed her cheek.

"Oh!" Brigit flew out of the chair. "You scared the hell out of me."

Colton looked surprised. "I'm sorry. Why are you still so jumpy?"

With her hand on her chest, Brigit shuddered in a breath. "Even though Vinny Ray is gone, I still feel unsettled. I can't remember the attack." Pausing, she gave him the once-over. "So, Mr. Mitus, what can I do for you?"

Though she was being playful, her edgy and breathy voice made his cock move. "I'm here to ask you out to dinner tomorrow night."

"No Mitus event or last-minute demand?"

With a sly smile, he shook his head.

"Like a date?"

He grinned. "Yeah, like a date."

She lifted her face to his. "There is one place I'm curious about."

God, he wanted her. But when didn't he? He inhaled her irresistible scent. "Name your spot."

"I'd like to attend a masked sex party."

55

SEALING THE DEAL

FROM THEIR PRE-SHOW DINNER at the elegant Marcel's in D.C., to the Kennedy Center benefactor cocktail reception and opera, Colton made sure Brigit's evening had gone off without a hitch. He wanted their night to be unforgettable.

After stepping inside the Mitus guesthouse, she leaned up and kissed him. "Thank you for a wonderful evening. Why didn't we go straight to the party?"

"I want to talk to you." Colton closed the front door, grasped her hand and led her into the living room.

"Sounds serious." She tapped the fireplace remote on the coffee table. As canary yellow and cerulean blue flames erupted behind the glass plate, she sat ramrod stiff on the edge of the sofa cushion.

Though he'd made her uncomfortable, she'd soon understand. He removed his suit jacket and laid it over the back of the recliner. "I've no intention of returning to the sex parties, so I tossed every mask except the one I used with you."

Her eyebrows shot up. "I thought you'd relocated them because I moved into your bedroom."

It was time for her to know how deeply he loved her. "*You* are all I want. All I need."

She furrowed her brow. "I see."

Easing onto the cushion beside her, he lifted her hand and kissed her finger. "Why don't you look elated?"

"I'm surprised."

"How 'bout I paint a picture and if you still want to go, we'll go."

"Fair enough." Leaning back, she crossed her legs. The vintage gold and cream gown fell away, exposing her shapely legs.

"Wow." He ran his hand along her shapely thigh. "You look amazing in that dress. I'm a very lucky man."

"Yes, you are." As she smiled, her nose crinkled.

Too cute. He pressed a lingering kiss on her mouth and his body warmed. "The show is located in a private home with a setup similar to the one you saw here."

"I survived that."

"You flew upstairs before it ended."

A pink hue covered her cheeks. "Well, there was that."

Colton wanted to be completely forthright. "Afterward everyone heads to the Playroom. It's a large, candlelit space filled with nothing but beds and sofas. Bowls of condoms everywhere."

Her eyes widened. "Orgy?"

"Mostly twosomes, although threesomes happen. Occasionally, there are small groups."

"Good God." Brigit fiddled with the diamond pendant resting on her chest.

"It's extreme, especially since everyone is masked." He took her hand. "Some masks are damn intense, like the ones you saw in my closet."

Staring into his eyes, she paused for a few seconds. "Good call on the sex parties, but our masked sex was hot. Any chance you're available to do that tonight?"

He dropped a lingering kiss just below her earlobe. "That can be arranged." Her breathy moan ignited his need and he started to harden.

"I'd like for us to return to Uninhibited," she said. "How does that sound?"

"Very sexy. But I just watch."

With a smirk, she added, "Good thing your rules don't apply to me."

He laughed. "Like hell they don't."

As she squeezed his hand, her smile fell away. "Since we're putting it all out there, I'm sorry I kept my identity a secret. I tried telling you, more than once…in spite of the fact that the truth could have ruined *everything*.

"But it didn't, Brigit," he said and kissed her hand.

"No, it didn't." After running her fingers through his hair, she caressed his cheek. "My love found a home when you came into my life."

He felt the same way. *This is it.*

"I knew you were special from the moment I saw you," he said. "When we met, your defiance struck a chord. I was intrigued. I love how smart and strong-willed you are. And every day you're more beautiful than the day before. You've helped me let go of my painful past and the demons that haunted me. You make me want to be a better man."

"Thank you." She smiled sweetly. "Though I tried fighting it, I sensed our strong connection from the beginning."

"A connection that will never end." He got down on one knee.

"Oh," she gasped.

Surprisingly, her shocked expression calmed him. This *was* a big deal. The most important decision either of them would ever make. Would she think it too soon? Would she even say *yes*? "I adore you. Being together feels right."

She swallowed. "Uh-huh."

He pulled the small, black, Harry Winston box from beneath the sofa cushion. Slowly, he opened it. The five-carat, emerald-cut diamond was surrounded by a halo of round diamonds. Pink diamond baguettes flanked either side of the platinum setting.

"Marry me, Brigit."

***

SHE THREW HER ARMS around his neck and kissed him, again and again. The kisses turned passionate and she pressed herself so close she almost knocked him over.

Laughing, he ended the kiss. "Is that a *yes*?"

"Yes, a million yesses." She extended her shaky hand and he slid the ring onto her finger. "I wasn't expecting this."

"Lemme see that rock, if you can lift your hand."

She proudly displayed the ring. "It's *magnificent*. You have great taste."

"It's *you*. Brilliant, beautiful, sparkly, flawless."

She laughed. "I love that! But I have a lot of flaws, Colton."

"Not a one." He stood, pulled her into his arms and kissed her. "I want you."

Standing on her tiptoes, she murmured, "I'm all yours."

Suddenly, a flash of light caught her eye over his shoulder. Vanessa charged down the hallway, holding a large kitchen knife over her head. She looked crazed, her eyes bulging as she raced toward them.

56

ATTACKED!

"Noooo!" Brigit yanked Colton out of the way as the knife sliced through the air, narrowly missing his shoulder.

Vanessa stumbled forward, spun around and extended the blade toward him. Her blonde hair was oily, her sweater was stained, and the stench of stale booze hung in the air. "I gave you the best years of my life and you propose to *her*? I can't fucking believe it! I made you who you are! And this, *this*, is how you repay me? I'm gonna kill you, you ungrateful son of a bitch!"

During Vanessa's rant, Brigit flew to the security panel on the wall near the front door, punched all the emergency buttons, then bolted back to the living room. "Get away from him!"

With a rabid look in her eyes, Vanessa redirected her wrath and the knife toward Brigit. "And you, you money-grubbing slut! I had things under control until you got here!"

Charging, Colton kicked Vanessa in the solar plexus. She buckled forward, mouth agape, desperately trying to breathe. He gripped her wrist, spun her into a choke hold and squeezed. "Drop the knife or I'll fucking kill you," he growled.

Gasping for air, Vanessa released the weapon. Colton grabbed her forearms, slammed her to the ground, and buried his knee into the small of her back. Brigit quickly kicked the knife out of Vanessa's reach.

"You're hurting me!" Vanessa shouted.

"Shut the fuck up," Colton said through gritted teeth.

Though trembling, Brigit dropped to her knees beside Colton, undid his holiday tie, and began binding Vanessa's wrists.

Vanessa turned her head and spat. "Get away from me, bitch."

Brigit froze. A silver corded Yurman bracelet clung to Vanessa's wrist.

"See something familiar, *little* Brigit?" Vanessa hissed.

"Oh my God, that's my bracelet." Still shaking, Brigit unhooked the jewelry.

Suddenly, she couldn't breathe. Beads of sweat formed along her brow as terrifying images flashed through her mind. Being hoisted into the passenger seat of her Escalade. Dumped onto the cold, hard ground. Kicked and kicked again. Then tied up and left to die. Alone in the cold, scary darkness.

Clutching her chest, Brigit cried out. "Oh, my God! You! *You* tried to kill me." The room started spinning and she choked back another wail.

The front door banged against the wall. Vonn burst into the living room, gun drawn.

"Get over here," Colton shouted, "and tie her up!"

Dropping to his knees, Vonn holstered his Glock, then quickly secured Vanessa's wrists. "Chad told me she'd left without a scene. I knew that wasn't the end."

"Make sure she doesn't move," Colton said. "She's been drinking, but she's strong."

"I should clear the house," Vonn said.

"No, the police will do it," Colton replied. "I need to help Brigit."

"Fuck Brigit," Vanessa rasped.

Vonn took Colton's place, pressing his massive weight on Vanessa.

"I can't breathe, you idiot," Vanessa hissed.

"Silence," Vonn bit out.

Colton pulled Brigit into his arms. "My God, I'm so sorry."

"Oh, Brigit, oh, Brigit!" screeched Vanessa. "Colton, you're a pussy-whipped fool!"

"*Enough.*" Vonn pushed Vanessa's face into the carpet and held it there.

Unable to catch her breath, Brigit could not stop shaking. Vanessa Ellison had tried to murder her.

"Let's get you some water." With a firm grip on her waist, Colton led her into the kitchen, then poured her a glass. "She won't get away with this."

Feeling numb, Brigit drained the glass.

"Don't let her see you like this," he whispered.

Nodding, Brigit said, "I'm okay." But, she wasn't. Hand in hand they returned to the living room.

Brigit fixed a hard stare on Vanessa. "I had you pegged for a first-class bitch from day one, but you're crazy."

"You fucked up my long-term plans. I needed you gone." Vanessa's chilling voice sent a shiver through Brigit. "You got one swift kick because Colton rented those damned caverns for you. I *loved* ruining your storybook evening by slashing his tires."

"I could fucking kill you," Colton growled. "You're insane."

A maniacal grin spread across Vanessa's reddened face. "He wanted *you* by his side at the gala. Your punishment? Another kick." Hatred poured from her eyes. "That fucking piano earned you a third strike. But I unleashed my wrath when he took you into *his* bed. That last blow should have finished you off. My only regret is not dumping you in the Potomac."

Oh, my God! Feeling nauseated, Brigit clutched Colton for support. *Lunatic.*

Vonn dug his knee into Vanessa's back. "Prison is too good for you. You're a monster."

"You're an asshole, Vonn. I don't deserve this cruel treatment. I'm Colton's most *loyal* employee." As Vanessa craned her neck around, her expression softened. "Colt, I stood by you from the beginning. I believed in you, did whatever necessary to ensure your success. I kept all the pretty ladies away. But *she* ruined everything! Let me go and I won't press charges. We can work this out, like two rational adults in love."

Brigit whipped her gaze to Colton. "What's she talking about?"

His lips were slashed into thin lines, his cheek muscles clenched. "I'd planned on telling you. Just not tonight."

The tightness in Brigit's chest returned.

"Vanessa sabotaged my business," Colton said. "I never knew you contacted me until a few days ago."

Brigit's rubbery legs gave out and she clutched the sofa to keep from crumpling.

Just then, Taylor ran into the room with police and paramedics close on her heels. Her hand flew to her mouth. "Oh, no."

"I'm Officer Henson," said the taller man. "This is my partner, Officer Smith. What's going on?"

"I'm Colton Mitus. We were attacked by a former employee."

"Stand her up," Henson said.

As if she weighed nothing, Vonn lifted Vanessa to her feet.

"Ma'am, is that true?" Henson asked.

Vanessa lunged toward Brigit, but Vonn yanked her back. Even so, Brigit recoiled.

Henson stepped between the two women. "What's your name?"

"That bitch got me fired!" Vanessa glared at Brigit.

"Ma'am, I smell alcohol on your breath. Have you been drinking?" Henson asked.

"Fuck you."

"That type of language won't be tolerated," Henson said, then addressed Colton and Brigit. "Why don't you tell us what happened?"

Brigit explained how she'd been attacked over Thanksgiving.

"Is that what happened?" Henson asked Vanessa.

Vanessa rolled her eyes. "That man is mine. Case closed."

Eyeing Vonn's weapon, Officer Smith inquired, "Sir, do you have a permit to carry?"

"Vonn Savage, Mitus security. It's in my wallet in the main house."

Smith nodded. "We'll need to see that. Have you cleared the premises?"

"No."

"I'll take care of that." With his weapon drawn, Smith headed down the hallway. A few moments later, he returned. "I found an empty whiskey bottle, duct tape, rope, another kitchen knife and a keyless remote to a Cadillac."

Brigit gripped Colton's arm. "After I was attacked, my Escalade was found two miles from where I was dumped."

"Good to know," said the officer. "Mr. Mitus, you and your staff won't be able to return here until forensics has completed its investigation."

"Understood," said Colton.

Officer Henson arrested Vanessa, read her her rights, and cuffed her. As he led Vanessa out, she turned. "Colton, I'll never give up on us." Then she shot Brigit a death stare. "He's mine. Don't ever forget that."

57

HOLIDAY PARTY

B RIGIT TUCKED HER TOES into her Christian Louboutin stilettos and looked at the wall hooks that once housed Colton's mask collection. His black mask from Halloween and the one he'd bought her were all that remained. Even though Christmas was two days away, she'd decided to give him one of his presents later that evening.

"I love when you wear your hair up," Colton said as he buttoned his brown silk Armani sport coat.

She flashed him a smile. "I love when you don't shave." Turning away, she revealed the unzipped back of her black Versace cocktail dress.

Stepping close, he trailed his fingers down her back then kissed the nape of her neck. Slowly, he zipped the dress. "Something's not right."

When he finished, she gazed into his eyes. "What's wrong?"

"I'm zipping. Shouldn't I be removing your dress?"

Leaning up, she whispered into his ear, "You'll get to do that plus a whole lot more before the night is over."

"How can we arrange for *that* party to start now?" He kissed her.

"No can do. I've been looking forward to meeting your mom all week."

His eyes softened. "She can't wait, either."

His black dress pants and cable brown sweater hung perfectly on his sculpted frame and she ran her hand down his chest, over the soft knit. "Let's rock this party." They left their bedroom closet and walked hand in hand down the hallway.

"I'm disappointed Shaniqua and Monica already left for New York," she said.

"Tucker left this morning, too. We'll have a dinner party after the holidays when they're available."

"I love that idea."

Unclasping his hand, he caressed her bottom. "I have a lot of ideas you'd love."

Her body warmed from his frisky touch and she gave his butt cheek a little squeeze. "Me, too." As they walked down the stairs, she said, "It's so quiet. Where is everyone?"

The normally bright foyer was illuminated only by the flickering candlelight spilling from the living room. When they got to the bottom of the stairs, a chorus of "Congratulations!" streamed from the living room. To their surprise, the staff had congregated around the baby grand.

With his tail wagging, Mojo trotted over and Brigit rubbed his head. "Hello, my sweet boy."

Elliott, Shane, Ryan and Taylor walked in, each carrying a tray of champagne flutes. "Thank you, Taylor," Colton said as he lifted two glasses. "For *everything*."

Chad belted out a whistle. "Okay, a toast, so...quiet down!" He raised his glass and waited until all eyes were on him. "Colton, Brigit. We wish you the best and we love you. Congratulations and bottoms up."

After lots of clinking glasses, the group sipped the chilled bubbly.

"I'd like to add something." Taylor cleared her throat. "In many ways, we're family. Our living arrangement is impossible to explain, so I don't try to anymore. Even though I love my job and all of you, something was missing. It's whatever makes a house a home. Turns out it was never a something, but a *someone*. Here's to Brigit." She raised her glass.

Brigit's eyes misted. "Thank you, Taylor. You guys are my family and I'm grateful for all of you." She rubbed Mojo's head.

Elliott and Shane, clothed in their black chef's uniforms, pivoted toward the kitchen.

"Wait," Red said. "I heard you two refused to surrender your kitchen to caterers, but you're joining us after dinner for the *live entertainment*, right?"

"As long as the entertainment remains clothed." Elliott tipped his toque.

The staff burst into laughter.

"Oh, God, I'll drink to that." Taylor raised her glass.

"Did no one like my wild parties?" Colton asked.

The room quieted.

"I thought they were...um...*exciting*." Shane's cheeks turned scarlet.

The group cracked up again.

"Tonight's entertainment involves your fiancée," Ryan said.

Colton shot Brigit a puzzled look.

"I've agreed to play a few Christmas carols." Brigit squeezed his hand and he squeezed back.

Colton raised his glass to the staff. "Thank you for your efforts this year. It's teamwork that makes us successful. Pick up your bonus checks tomorrow before you head home for the holidays."

The doorbell chimed and Vonn threw open the front door. While Brigit was excited to meet Colton's mom, butterflies tumbled in her belly. In walked Alexandra Reed holding Colton's mom by the arm. Though somewhat frail, Kimberly Mitus was an elegant woman. Her dark hair was cut blunt at her neckline with side-swept bangs. Even with the aid of a cane and a doting daughter, Kimberly carried herself with grace.

"Come meet my mom," Colton said to Brigit.

"Merry Christmas, dear," Kimberly kissed her son's cheeks.

Colton threw his massive arms around her but hugged her gently. "You look great, Mom. I'm glad you're here."

The sweet embrace between mother and son tugged on Brigit's heartstrings. She admired the woman who'd endured the loss of a child and carried on without a spouse when Wilson had failed his family so miserably. Kimberly Mitus had been both the backbone and the heart of the Mitus family.

"Mom, this is Brigit Farnay. Brigit, this my mom, Kimberly Mitus."

Kimberly's eyes softened. "I've heard a lot of wonderful things about you."

Brigit hugged her. "I'm so happy to meet you, Mrs. Mitus."

"Call me Kimberly." Her gaze floated between Brigit and Colton. "I'm relieved my son has found his copilot."

"Congratulations!" Alexandra hugged Brigit. "I've always wanted a sister."

"Me, too," Brigit said.

"Hello, Kimberly." Dez gave her a soft hug. "I have the paperwork you requested. Should we take care of things before dinner?"

"What paperwork?" Colton asked.

"My will, son. I'm feeling energized and I'm awake." Kimberly looked at Dez. "Two things I used to take for granted. Lead the way, my friend."

Alexandra's eyes filled with tears. "I'm sorry...I can't do this." She set off toward the kitchen.

Kimberly sighed. "Alexandra is all emotion, whereas Colton contains his."

Brigit darted on her tiptoes and pecked Colton's cheek. "I'll go to her."

COLTON HELPED HIS MOM remove her coat. Then, with a rueful smile, Kimberly wrapped her long fingers around Dez's arm and ambled down the hallway toward his office. Though Colton's eyes stung, he cleared his throat and turned away. *Stay strong.*

The doorbell rang and Crockett squeezed into the foyer, thick with people. "Merry Christmas!"

Colton slapped him on the back. "Glad you could make it." With a smile, he added, "You look good, bro. Showering helps."

Chuckling, Crockett extended the bottle of Dom Perignon. "For toasting or to share with the fiancée. Congratulations on the big news."

"Thanks. Great vintage." Colton grasped the champagne. "I never thought about marriage until I met Brigit. It's all about finding the *right* woman. You next?"

"Hell no."

Colton pointed to the bouquet. "For me?"

"You're a smart ass, you know that? Where's Brigit?"

"Consoling my sister."

The knot between Crockett's brows deepened. "Did something happen with your mom?"

"All things considered, she's doing well." Colton paused, then cleared his throat. "She's reviewing her will. That upset Alexandra."

"Totally understandable. I'm sorry."

"Thanks." Colton threw an arm around Crockett and the two men headed toward the kitchen. "So, how often do you talk to my mom?"

"Every week."

"No wonder she calls you her favorite."

"Not me." Crockett glanced around. "That baby sister of yours has always been her golden child."

After setting the champagne on the kitchen island, Colton asked, "Elliott, did Brigit come through here?"

"Porch," Elliott called as he opened the oven door.

Just then, Brigit and Alexandra rose from the sofa and hugged.

"How long has it been since you've seen Alexandra?" Colton asked.

"Eleven years. Goth girl had just graduated high school."

The two women scooted inside bringing a blast of chilly air with them. "Too cold." Brigit's teeth chattered as Colton pulled her close.

Alexandra stopped short and her eyes grew wide. "Crockett."

After several seconds, Crockett murmured, "Hello, Goth Girl."

The corners of Alexandra's lips lifted. "Thanks for talking, Brigit," she said though her gaze remained locked on Crockett. "Excuse me, I'm going to check on Mom." As she exited the room, she glanced over her shoulder before vanishing around the corner.

Like a locomotive, Chad barreled into the kitchen, escorting a blushing Kat whose white-knuckled grip choked the neck of a wine bottle.

"Kat!" Brigit exclaimed.

Kat bear-hugged her. "Hey bestie!"

"Merry Christmas, Kathryn." Colton kissed her cheek.

Kat offered the bottle to Colton. "Your home is beautiful."

After introductions, Brigit hugged Crockett. "Good to see you."

"Congratulations." Crockett handed her the bouquet. "I heard you said yes."

"I did, and I couldn't be happier." Brigit cradled the giant bouquet in her arms. "Thank you. These are lovely."

Elliott shooed them. "Please, out of my kitchen. Shane, uncork the champagne, then put the flowers in a crystal vase."

Smiling, Colton shook his head. "I'm being ordered around in my own home."

"Your home. *My* kitchen!" Elliott winked.

Shane collected the items and the group scooted into the living room, but not before Chad collected five flutes filled with chilled bubbly.

"Friends make the best family," Crockett said and raised his glass.

"Hear, hear," Kat said.

"Merry Christmas," Chad said and looked at Kat. "Here's to a damn good New Year." Her cheeks flushed.

Colton gazed lovingly into Brigit's eyes and tapped her flute. "Better together."

Brigit beamed. "To the man with the Mitus touch."

WHEN THE LAST GUEST had left, the couple retreated into their bedroom. Brigit needed alone time with her man.

Colton pulled her into an embrace and gazed into her eyes. "Hello, fiancée," he murmured.

Feeling deeply loved and totally adored, she smiled. "I have something for you. Santa came early."

"Lucky Santa." Through their smiles he kissed her. "I have a surprise for you too."

She caressed his crotch.

Colton ended the string of doting kisses, took her hand and strolled into the sitting room. "No, a real surprise." He sat on the sofa and patted his leg.

After she got comfortable in his lap, he slowly ran his hand up her thigh until his fingers vanished beneath the dress. Her breath caught. Delicious tingles had her blood pumping as the air sizzled between them. With one possessive hand on her bare skin, he reached down with his other hand and plucked a wrapped box from the side of the sofa. "A 'too big for the stocking', stocking stuffer."

Brigit lifted the lid. Resting on a bed of tissue paper was a framed picture from the gala. "I love this, Colton." The two were gazing lovingly into each other's eyes.

"I thought you might. That photo says it all."

She kissed his cheek. "Thank you for this special gift. Be right back." With frame in hand, she disappeared into their bedroom.

After setting the photo on the bureau, she collected a gift from their closet and sat beside him.

"For you." She set the gift box on his lap.

"First, I have a confession," he said.

Her stomach dropped. *A confession?*

"There's something I haven't told you about the Francesco transaction."

Oh, no. Her chest tightened.

He placed the box on the coffee table and enveloped her hands in his. "Melvin and I converted your Francesco shares back to private equity. You still own twenty-two percent of the Francesco Company. I want us to be true partners in every sense."

She stared at him for several seconds, absorbing the weight of his words. "Oh, Colton." Beaming, she flung her arms around him. "Thank you! You are the most wonderful man I have ever known."

"How wonderful?" he murmured, then brushed his lips against hers.

Placing the box on his lap, she gave him a flirty grin. "You're about to find out. Go to the guesthouse and open this. I'll be there shortly."

COLTON UNWRAPPED BRIGIT'S GIFT and swelled with anticipation. As he donned the black silk pajamas and ornate black and silver baroque eye mask, his imagination went to dark, erotic places.

Five minutes later, there was a knock on the guesthouse door. Colton swung it open. His breath caught and he hardened. Brigit stood on the doorstep, covered in a full-length red hooded cape, her fiery green eyes framed in a white and gold Venetian mask. She was his best fantasy come to life.

A low, raspy groan shot from the back of his throat. "You are so fucking sexy."

"Good evening, Wolf." She ran her tongue over her lower lip.

"Miss Riding Hood."

She opened her cape and revealed a black lace push-up bra and thong, a garter belt with thigh-highs and open-toed stilettos.

His gaze roamed freely over her beautiful body, then back into her eyes. "You look good enough to eat," he growled.

With a beckoning smile, she extended her hand. "I guess you'd better invite me in, then."

A NOTE FROM STONI

Thanks so much for reading my *debut* novel, THE MITUS TOUCH! Writing this book was a labor of love and a journey that changed my life. Penning a novel was a dream of mine that finally took root, then grew legs. I didn't know what I was doing, or what I was getting myself into…I just knew it was something I *had* to do. Never did I imagine that I would learn so much, have so much fun, meet so many amazing people, and actually complete a novel. But I did!

I hope you enjoyed my love story…and yes, I'm aware that the scene in Colton's basement is a little unusual. Sometimes life imitates fiction. Sometimes fiction imitates life. In this particular case, I'll never tell.

I'm very grateful you read my story. Thank you!

Dying to know what's going on between Crockett Wilde and Alexandra Reed? Read Book Two of The Touch Series and find out...

It's always fun to hear from readers. You can drop me a note at Contact@StoniAlexander.com.

To learn about my upcoming releases, be the first to see a cover reveal, or participate in a giveaway, sign up for my Inner Circle newsletter at StoniAlexander.com. When you do, I'll send you my steamy short story, MetroMan.

All of my books are available exclusively on Amazon and you can read them FREE with Kindle Unlimited.

Cheers to Romance!
Stoni

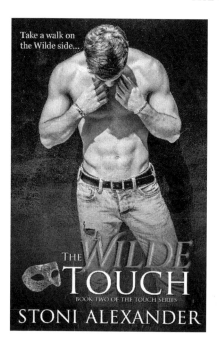

Looks can be deceiving...

Emmy-winning journalist Alexandra Reed returns to the DC area with two goals in mind--care for her ailing mom and steer clear of devastatingly handsome Crockett Wilde. But the man who stole her heart, then broke it, is impossible to avoid. As her life spins out of control, she finds pleasure in her secret escape...*and that's where things really heat up.*

Tech CEO Crockett Wilde is at the top of his game, but beneath his calm surface lies a raging volcano. When he finds the monster who abducted his sister, he'll unleash a decade of pain. The one person who can subdue his demons—beautiful, headstrong Alexandra—wants nothing to do with him. Yet he's determined to set the record straight and not let the love of his life get away.

As Alexandra follows a trail of suspicious incidents, Crockett seizes the opportunity to prove he's not the bad guy she believes him to be. Together they unmask an underworld of evil. But their lives change in unimaginable ways the moment she goes missing.

Grab THE WILDE TOUCH or Read FREE on Kindle Unlimited!

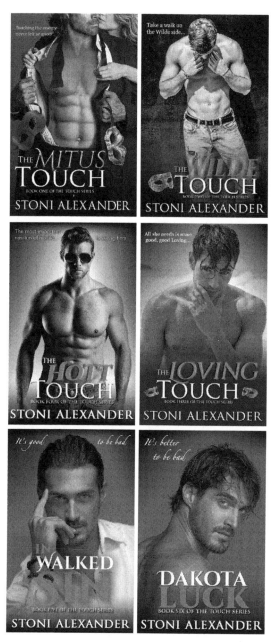

The Touch Series - Romantic Suspense

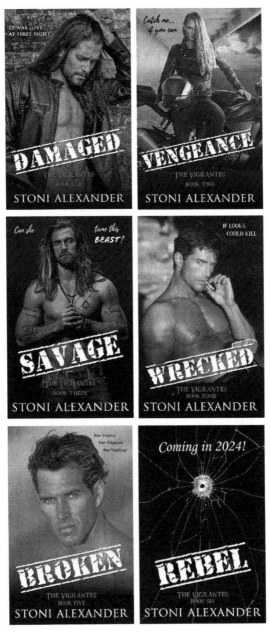

The Vigilantes Series - Romantic Suspense

LOOKING FOR A SEXY STANDALONE?

 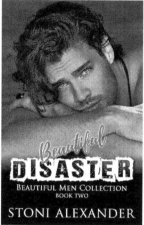

Beautiful Men Collection - Contemporary Romance

Grab them or Read FREE with Kindle Unlimited!

ACKNOWLEDGMENTS

Embarking on a lifelong dream takes courage and a swift kick in the pants. I owe an eternity of gratitude to my husband, Johnny, who knew the *exact* words to motivate me to take that first step.

Along the way I've been fortunate to receive the guidance and tutelage of many talented and generous people.

Thank you to my family for encouraging me and supporting me as I ventured into uncharted waters.

Thank you to my beta readers Amy, Dianne and Cheryl for reading an early and not-ready-for-prime-time version. Your constructive feedback helped a million-fold.

My critique group *rocks*! Many thanks to authors Magda Alexander, M.C. Vaughan and Andy Palmer.

My heartfelt gratitude to author Laura Kaye for making such a positive difference.

My appreciation to John Clark for his law enforcement insight.

A special shout-out to pilot A.P. for navigating the air traffic control lingo.

I had a zillion questions for wealth manager Daniel Fischler. Thank you for sharing your knowledge and for cheering me on.

Thank you to my proofreader, Carole, for catching things no one saw and for your unbridled enthusiasm.

To Merriam-Webster: I would be lost without you.

Thank you to authors Angela Ackerman and Becca Puglisi for *The Emotion Thesaurus*. An invaluable resource.

And to my lovely muse: Thanks for working overtime, especially while I sleep. About all that dark chocolate I consume, that's for you, babe.

ABOUT THE AUTHOR

Stoni Alexander writes sexy romantic suspense and contemporary romance about tortured alpha males and independent, strong-willed females. Her passion is creating love stories where the hero and heroine help each other through a crisis so that, in the end, they're equal partners in more ways than love alone. The heat level is high, the romance is forever, and the suspense keeps readers guessing until the very end.

Visit Stoni's website:
StoniAlexander.com

Sign up for Stoni's newsletter on her website and she'll gift you a free steamy short story, only available to her Inner Circle.

Here's where you can follow Stoni online. She looks forward to connecting with you!

- amazon.com/author/stonialexander
- bookbub.com/authors/stoni-alexander
- facebook.com/StoniBooks
- goodreads.com/stonialexander
- instagram.com/stonialexander

Printed in Great Britain
by Amazon

51432138R00223